THE DARK SYNTHS
SONG OF THE ELLYDIAN
BOOK IV

C.K. RIEKE

Books by C.K. Rieke

Song of the Ellydian I: The Scarred
Song of the Ellydian II: The Last Whistlewillow
Song of the Ellydian III: The Fallen Apprentice
Song of the Ellydian IV: The Dark Synths
Song of the Ellydian V: Master of Daggers

Riders of Dark Dragons I: Mystics on the Mountain
Riders of Dark Dragons II: The Majestic Wilds
Riders of Dark Dragons III: Mages of the Arcane
Riders of Dark Dragons IV: The Fallen and the Flames
Riders of Dark Dragons V: War of the Mystics

The Dragon Sands I: Assassin Born
The Dragon Sands II: Revenge Song
The Dragon Sands III: Serpentine Risen
The Dragon Sands IV: War Dragons
The Dragon Sands V: War's End

The Path of Zaan I: The Road to Light
The Path of Zaan II: The Crooked Knight
The Path of Zaan III: The Devil King

Copyright

This novel was published by Crimson Cro Publishing
Copyright © 2025 Hierarchy LLC

All Rights Reserved.

Edited by Tiffany Shand
And Zach Ritz.
David Woolf - Beta Reader
Cover by the author and Heather Brantman

All characters and events in this book are fictitious.
Printed in the United States of America. No part of this book may be used or reproduced in any manner whatsoever without written permission except in the case of brief quotations embodied in critical articles or reviews.
This book is a work of fiction. Names, characters, businesses, organizations, places, events and incidents either are the product of the author's imagination or are used fictitiously. Any resemblance to actual persons, living or dead, events, or locales is entirely coincidental.

Get the Free Prequel Short, *Three Songs*
CKRieke.com

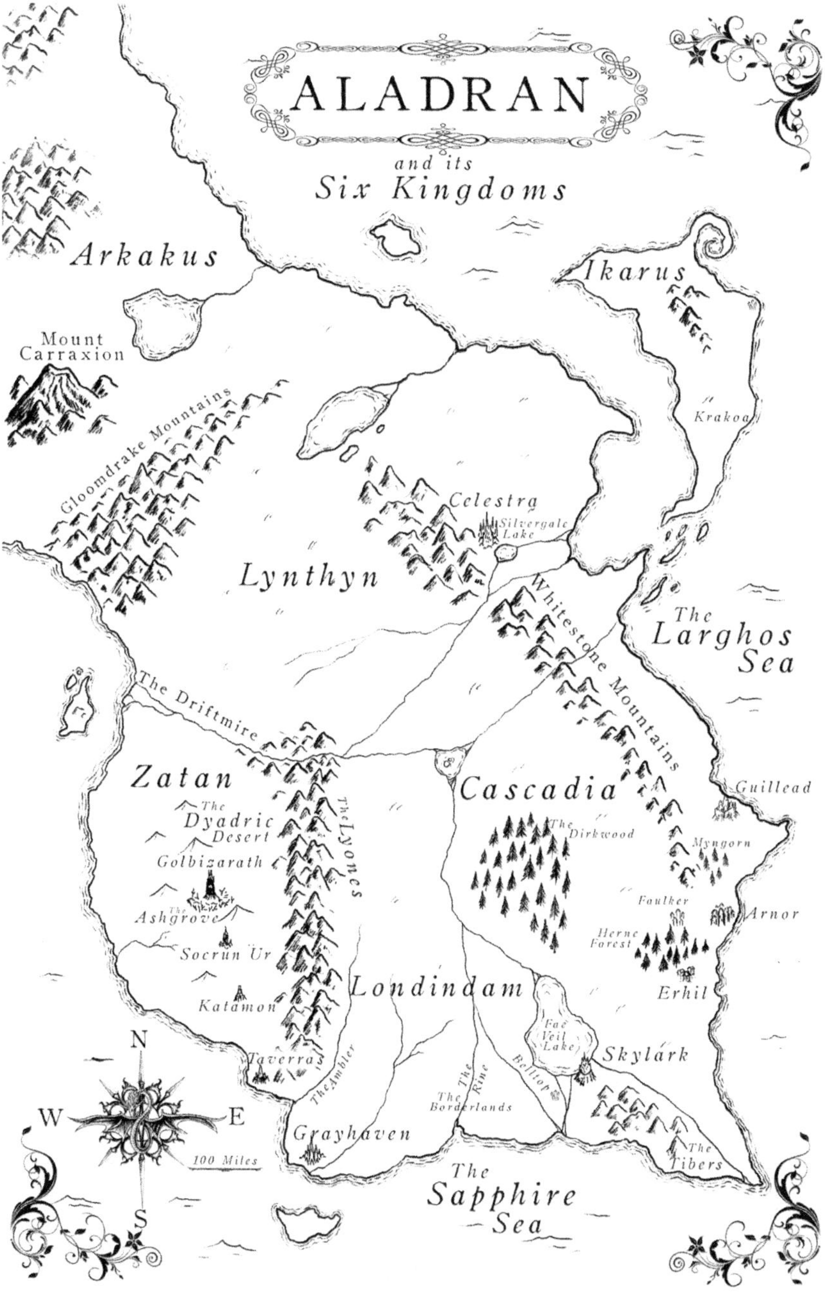

ALADRAN
and its
Six Kingdoms
Arkakus
Mount Carraxion
Gloomdrake Mountains
Ikarus
Krakoa
Celestra
Silvergale Lake
Lynthyn
Whitestone Mountains
The Larghos Sea
The Driftmire
Zatan
Cascadia
The Dyadric Desert
Golbizarath
The Ashgrove
Socrun Ur
Katamon
Taverras
The Lyones
The Dirkwood
Guillead
Myngorn
Faulker
Arnor
Herne Forest
Erhil
Londindam
Fae Veil Lake
Skylark
Belltop
The Rine
The Borderlands
The Ambler
Grayhaven
The Tibers
The Sapphire Sea
N
W
E
S
100 Miles

PART I
THE FALLEN ARCHMAGE

Chapter One

The Ellydian, the connection of all things, triumphs in all aspects of this world. When wielded by its strongest, through the ages, it has brought mountains crumbling down to the earth. It has sent its wielders soaring through the skies, flying to places faster than the beat of a hummingbird's heart. It has inspired stories of love that have lasted throughout all the ages of man.

However, there are things the Ellydian cannot overpower. The condition of the human form and spirit still cast long shadows. Even the most powerful and wise Lyrians of the ages cannot overcome these things.

For all its abilities, even at its most potent, the Ellydian still cannot overcome the most basic of human certainties.

Fear, loss, aging, and death.

Four certainties.

Four curses.

But they are four things that define humanity.

Fear may be overcome, but it is possibly the most primal instinct in man. Overcome by some; most succumb to it.

Loss is the curse by which age surpasses those who perhaps, and more often than not, should have been given the torch of life—rather than those that live longer, giving in to the urges of greed, lust, and power.

Aging is met with the gift of long life, slowly clawing away at your muscles, sucking away the sturdiness of your bones, and cracking the once unmarred skin. Hair thins, teeth break, and eyesight diminishes, all making way for our later, wiser years.

And death. Many who have wielded the Ellydian were driven mad by the pursuit of life eternal. Which serves as a guide to all who do. Spend your hours and years in the pursuit of that which is attainable, that which will serve humanity and make the pain of others less.

For with what time we are given, our greatest gift from all the gods, beseech that which drives you, that which makes our world a better place, and gives you strength for tomorrow.

-TRANSLATED *from the language of the Sundar. The Scriptures of the Ancients, Book I, Chapter XX.*

JANUAR 6, 1293.
Dyadric Desert, Zatan

SOREN, sure as shit, didn't sleep a wink that night.

HE BROODED.

HE CURSED THE GODS. All the gods.
And he cursed himself.
After all that happened that night, as the earliest rays of the warm morning sun lit the leftover carnage on the desert landscape, Soren's core burned hot. His thirst for revenge was left burning like a cauldron smoldering; a roaring fire beneath it. It

was doubly intensified as he trudged along the sand, blackened to near ash by wicked dragonfire.

As he walked the sands, alone, the broken, toppled tower of Golbizarath lay like ancient ruins behind. Thin wisps of smoke still rose from where the great old Lyrian Syncron Mihelik broke the top of the tower from its roots. Then the top of the tower lay to waste beside the old archmage's broken body.

Soren knelt, driving his fingers into the sands of the dune he perched upon, like a hawk surveying the far-reaching, seemingly never-ending sands. He brought the black sand up to his nose, small granules filtering through his gloved fingers, aching and blood-stained. He sniffed the sand. The acrid smell of brimstone from the dragonfire stung his nostrils.

He knew all the dirt of Aladran. Throughout all his years, he smelled the dirt to deepen his connection to his world, to show respect, and to heighten his senses.

But he'd never smelled this. He'd never smelled anything like this...

A fucking dragon… What are we going to do now… with a dragon in Aladran?

He knew it saved them. The massive, ancient dragon that felt the size of the sky itself—burned the horde of Shades that was going to kill them all—turning them into the devilish black monsters themselves. But the dragonfire somehow killed the nearly invincible Shades.

Now there are two things that can kill those things…

He stood back up, letting the sand fall from the side of his palm. In his other hand, he slid Firelight halfway free of her sheath with a metallic ring. She glistened in the sun like seawater at dawn, the waves of light shimmering like layered veins of fine ore.

To the south, Soren peered into the thick Ash Grove, and the distant lands beyond, from which they came. The Ash Grove was a maze of long dead trees, once a great oasis, sucked dry by the desert, and left to rot over time. But in the expanse of those dead trees, Soren had a wonderful, yet saddening, memory.

Cirella.

He got his last goodbye with his lost love. He'd cherish that for the rest of his days, he knew.

He got his goodbye...

He turned, facing the broken desert tower and the great Dyadric Desert.

Far, far beyond the golden desert, though, Seph was being taken through the sky to the place Soren had been trying to keep her from almost her entire life.

Another failure. Perhaps his greatest yet.

He clenched his teeth to keep his lip from quivering. His dark hair flowed out from under his hood, dancing on his chest in the early morning breeze. A breeze that brought with it a bitter realization—Seph was far away. Alcarond and Kaile had taken her to the capital. Alcarond, the current archmage, and sole Lyre Synth in Aladran, was taking Seph to the king.

This failure was almost too much to bear. His eyes felt heavy, almost full enough to burst. The blood in his arms and chest felt molten hot and thick, like glue. His dagger hand was ready to fight, ready to fight the whole king's army single-handedly. Soren would've fought every single Drakoon, the king's personal guards, with his bare hands.

But there was no killing to alleviate his despair.

He was left to let that regret fester in him like the Chimaera plague.

He was ready to die. But yet he wasn't.

There was too much to do. He was in too deep. Seph was out there all alone. And now the world knew who she truly was—the last of the Whistlewillow bloodline. And she was going to the devil's nest.

So much didn't matter then.

The war, Alcarond's power, Kaile's betrayal.

All that mattered was getting her back.

Soren trudged back down the dune, leaving long rips in the black sand, revealing the golden sands beneath. Below, at the base of the broken tower, were his comrades.

Davin Mosser, with his thick arms folded over his sturdy barrel belly. The handle of his double-sided ax rested on his hip as his beard blew on his chest. His pale violet eyes looking up at Soren with a sort of terrible dismay.

Blaje Severaas, the infamous Desert Shadow, loomed beside the dwarf. Her turquoise eyes sparkled like ravishing seawater. Her thick midnight dreads fell over her chest and back. Her shamshir blade tucked away in its sheath at her hip, ready and eager to cut into any who stood in her way. And Soren felt quite lucky that she was on his side. They'd only known each other for a short while, but she'd already proven her aptitude at killing, and Soren's stomach fluttered occasionally just at the sight of her.

Sable, Seph's cat, did circle eights between Blaje's boots. Sable had an instinctual way of knowing who had the least favor of cats, and sticking to them like a fly to honey.

The newest arrivals to their party, though, were the most striking, even for their motley group. The two bears with thick silver hides Soren had first met all the way in the Myngorn Forest. Two bears, huge and terrifying, with eyes like liquid molten gold. Both stood behind the foreign dwarf and the Desert Shadow. The bears had come with Mihelik through the portal to combat Alcarond. But Mihelik's body couldn't withstand the fall from the top of the tower, and Alcarond flew away once he got what he wanted.

"We should bury 'im." Davin glanced over at the old Syncron's body, covered in a tan tarp. The old Syncron's frail hand stuck out from the tarp, its bony fingers still grasping his staff—the Staff of the Stars—carved of a fine dark wood with white jewels encrusted into it. Soren sighed at the sight.

"Then what?" Blaje scratched her cheek.

"Dunno. But digging gives the mind plenty of time for thinking." Davin went to the tower, disappearing into a new crack in its side. Both bears moaned at the sight of their fallen friend.

Blaje walked up to Soren, still lost in his anger, but as she looked into his eyes and placed her hand gently on his chest, he soothed. It wasn't enough to calm his fury, but his rage was replaced by something else, something he didn't want, but came flooding through him like he was the broken tower, torn and fallen asunder.

Soren felt his eyes well with tears. He tried hard not to blink. He didn't want them falling in front of her. But he felt like a part of him was gone. The only family he had was stolen, ripped away like his heart was torn from his chest. All the other failures of his life paled to that.

Blaje didn't say a word, but then pressed her forehead to his, knowing that finally sent the tears streaming down his cheeks. He may have lost Seph, but he knew he wasn't completely alone anymore. She pulled away, wiping away his tears as her finger skidded across the scars on his face.

He hoped she would say something. He hoped she'd say it's going to be all right. He hoped she'd say, "we're going to get her back." But Soren knew the truth. Seph was gone. Seph was long gone. And Kaile had betrayed them all. Kaile not only betrayed Soren's trust, but even worse—Seph's.

Soren didn't even say thank you. He and Blaje both exchanged silent understandings, and with a nod, she turned and walked away. Davin approached from the tower, three shovels in hand. Blaje took one and walked toward the fallen Syncron's body.

"Here." Davin handed Soren one. "Diggin' helps work through stuff. At least it always has with me."

"How many have you dug?" Soren muttered, grabbing the shovel's wooden handle.

"Too many, my friend, far too many…"

"Me too." Soren followed the others. All around, he gazed up at the broken piles of dead Shade bodies. Blackened burnt bone frames crumbled together. The occasional obsidian eyes were left sparkling in the early morning sunlight. Soren remembered the enormous dragon as it flew in, destroying the horde of Shades that were about to consume them. And he wondered… *How did that dragon come right then? Right when we needed it most? It didn't burn the tower or us… just the Shades. Just the Demons of Dusk.*

He assumed he'd never get an answer to that question, but it still lingered. Through his pain, he thought there was more at play than just their world being slowly consumed by the awful monsters that plagued the plains when no sunlight shone. The world was starting to fight back.

There was hope. There was still hope…

They walked over to Mihelik's body. Lord Belzaar's was near, behind Soren, draped in cloth as well. The two silver bears stood on the other side of the fallen archmage. Their once menacing gazes faded as they whimpered at the loss of their friend. One, the male, nuzzled Mihelik's hand, still holding his legendary staff. The female moaned up to the sky, her huge nose pointing up to the blue, starless sky.

Davin went to the side of the tower, sending the tip of his shovel into the hard ground. Soren and Blaje helped. None talked as they dug the hole. This could be no shallow grave. This was Mihelik Starshadow. The most renowned Lyrian Syncron in all the world. Soren and his friends would allow no scavengers to pick at his bones from a shallow grave. They dug deep. The full six feet beneath the ground. And when they'd finished, Blaje and Soren threw their shovels aside and delicately laid Mihelik's body within. His staff fell from his fingers as they lifted him.

It was dark in the deep ground. No sunlight crept in.

"The staff?" Blaje was atop the grave, glaring at the staff. "Don't want that falling into the wrong hands."

"Aye," Davin groaned with his arms folded over his brawny chest. "Don't want Alcarond, Zertaan, or any of the other king's Synths getting their mitts on that."

"We should bury it." Blaje pointed off far into the desert. "Bury it where they'll never find it."

"No." Soren pulled himself out of the grave, dusting his hands off. "The staff will go to Persephone."

"Soren…" Davin scratched his thigh.

"It's going to her…" There was no uncertainty in Soren's words, and there was no response from the others.

I'm going to get you back Seph, and together we're going to kill the ones who've ruined our lives. Just stay alive, Seph, just stay alive long enough for me to find you…

Chapter Two

After the old archmage's body was tucked away under six feet of earth, the realization finally set in. With the legendary Syncron's staff firmly in Soren's grasp, and his wish of giving it to his niece Seph, the weight of everything felt fixed upon his shoulders. It was enough weight to cripple any man.

But Soren wasn't just any man.

He had failures. More than he could count. But he was ready to cut the world in half if it meant quenching his thirst for revenge upon those who harmed his family.

A delicate wind washed over the vast desert, and the loud moans of the two silver bears met it with a melancholy tune. It made the desert sound as if it were playing a series of sad minor notes of the fallen archmage.

"Anyone want to say anything?" Blaje asked. "We shouldn't linger here much longer. Nightfall will be upon us, and the Shades were defeated once, but their numbers are staggering now."

Soren snorted, glancing over at the body of Lord Belzaar,

the reason they were all the way out in this desert. They didn't have the strength, or time, to dig all the graves needed for all those corpses in the tower. So beasts and time would take them, Soren thought.

Soren cleared his throat, striking the Staff of the Star's tip into the sand.

"Mihelik Starshadow returns to the great infinity, beyond our realm. With him, he takes a soul grander than any who walk the earth. His compassion, his courage, his wisdom, and his sheer unimaginable power will be missed. He was the greatest of the Syncrons, and one of the bravest men I ever knew. He faced great adversity, even being labeled an enemy of the people, and the crown. All the while, everything he did was to help Aladran, and all that live in it. In our short time together since I discovered his isolation in the Myngorn, he quickly became an ally, saving all our lives from King Malera Amón at the burning of Erhil."

Davin and Blaje both hung their heads, hearing the words with deep intent. Sable ran up Davin's back, sitting upon his shoulder like an onyx statue. Her dark green eyes glared down at the grave, also eyeing the two bears who lay near.

"I will miss him, as I'm sure we all will. No other will ever be quite like him, inspiring humanity to keep dreaming hopeful dreams of what this world can become again. He was a light in the darkness, like a torch breaking the shadows. I even met him when I was just a boy. My parents were there, and the way they talked about him after, it was as if he were part god. They told me how lucky I was to meet such a master of the Ellydian. They told me how much such as him were as rare as two-headed owls, and as powerful as the tides. I wasn't sure how to take their words about him as a kid, but now I do. Now I understand what a man like him was—and is.

"Mihelik Starshadow is a flame of hope in this dark, dark

world. The Chimaera, the Demons of Dusk, the king and his madness... It all makes us feel hopeless, desperate, and scared. But a man like the archmage, he could cut through the endless despair with a wave of his staff. His knowledge of all things could raise spirits soaring through the dark clouds." Soren sighed, twisting the staff's bottom tip in the sand. He swallowed, keeping his voice firm.

"One glimpse at his majesty would make one feel like there was a god looking down on us. We aren't completely alone in our misery. There was only one Mihelik Starshadow, and another... there will never be. So rest easy, friend. Know that you left this world a better place, and that we will fight for what you believed in until the very end. Whether that be a victorious one, or a defeat, our swords will swing and stab true, and those that wield the Ellydian will forever remember you as a bastion of light in our Aladran."

"Well said." Davin nodded in approval, still with his head down.

"Yes," Blaje added. "Even in his exile, many in Zatan always believed the archmage did what he did for a reason. There were too many years of good to overshadow them with what the king had labeled as treachery. Word will quickly spread of his true deeds to save this world. For word is spreading like wildfire of the king's true evil."

"He'd like that." Soren knelt and patted the sand that buried his friend. "Farewell, my archmage..."

The air shifted from the warm afternoon sunlight to a frigid chill as clouds swept under the golden sun. Both bears rose, their howls filling the air with their deep, melancholy tones. It was a sound that echoed for miles—full of remorse and loss. Their howls made Soren's ribs vibrate, and the deep sadness hit him like a shovel in the chest.

Once their howls faded, drifting off like a vague, foggy

dream, Blaje tied her thick dreadlocks behind her head with a strip of tan leather.

"We should be off," she said, her keen gaze scanning all around them. "The camels should be well rested now after the battle. The question is, where to?"

Soren didn't hesitate. "Seph. We're going after her."

Davin sighed, stroking his beard. He and Blaje exchanged glances, showing expressions that soured Soren.

"We're going after Seph. There will be no debate."

"Soren." Davin's voice had a soft intent to it. He stroked his beard as if searching for his words carefully. "They're taking Seph to the king. They're taking her to Celestra, deep in Lynthyn."

Soren nodded. "And?"

"Soren." Davin took a short step forward with his hands out at his sides. "That's a thousand miles from here…"

"More like seven hundred," Blaje added softly.

Soren gritted his teeth.

"Soren." Davin's eye twitched slightly. "They may be there already. It would take weeks to get there. I'm truly sorry to say this, as we have no more Syncrons on our side, let alone one powerful enough to teleport or fly like Alcarond did. But… Seph is on her own…"

Soren lunged forward, eager to grab Davin by the collar and shake sense into him. Yet, he stopped short, fists clenched at his sides.

She's my only family! He wanted to shout. *She's your friend too! She trusted you. She trusted us to protect her!* He wanted to scream, but he kept the words inside. Davin dug his heels in, expecting Soren's reaction to his statement, but Soren restrained himself, stopping short of grabbing the dwarf.

"This may have been Alcarond's plan all along," Davin added, bravely in the face of Soren's anger. Soren's chest heaved and his knuckles whitened. "Send Kaile into our ranks, learn about us, gain our trust, and Seph's, and when the time came, Kaile would flip and help his master. We were taken for fools, outsmarted. Even he was…" He pointed at the fresh grave.

"Breathe…" Blaje placed her hand delicately on Soren's chest. He felt her calming energy cool his rapid heartbeat.

He shut his eyes and inhaled deeply through his nostrils, smelling the burnt skeletons all around.

"We can't let her die," Soren groaned, with his eyes closed.

"We aren't," Blaje said. "But Davin's correct. She's on her own. She's going to have to figure out how to survive long enough for us to get there. And…"

"And what?" Soren opened his eyes and gazed deep into hers.

"Your old master… The reason we came all the way into the middle of the old desert. What about him? We can't just ignore the sequence of events that led you to getting that dagger from Vellice. And by such obscure means, with so much emphasis on keeping its origin secret. Even Garland didn't know how it came into his possession. If your old master is alive, and if he knew Firelight could defeat the Demons of Dusk, then what else does he know?"

"He died," Soren muttered. "I said my goodbyes many years ago. How is it possible? Why would he hide that—from me?"

"We need to find out," Davin said in a low voice. "If he's still alive, then we have to find out what else he knows."

One of the bears growled. Sable meowed at its side.

"I have no idea where he could be." Soren rubbed his brow. "And the only one who might've known where he was is lying under that cloth." He pointed at Lord Belzaar's motionless body.

"If he's here," Blaje said, insinuating the desert, "the Calica may know where to look. Even Lady Sargonenth at the Brink may lead us in the right direction."

"Aye," Davin added. "And Lady Drake in Skylark would be the other to ask. With Mihelik gone, our number of powerful allies is shrinking." He sighed. "Lady Sargonenth is a Doren Syncron. If we wish to get someone in our crew that can defend against the Synths we're sure to run into, then we may ask her to join us. Zatan is now in open rebellion against the king. It might be worth asking."

"That's south." Soren cracked his knuckles, not liking the idea of traveling in the opposite direction of Lynthyn, and Seph.

"It is true if we were to run into one of the king's Synths," Blaje said, playing with the tips of her dark dreads at her navel, "we will be at a serious disadvantage... a Syncron ally will be needed in our quest to save her."

"Lady Drake," Soren murmured, deep in thought. "She's our best hope at finding a wielder of the Ellydian from the Silver Sparrows. But she's all the way in fucking Cascadia! Fuck!" He slammed his fist into his thigh. "How the fuck did I let Kaile fool me like that? I *knew* he came from the capital. How could I be so foolish? And now Persephone is up there all alone." All strength left his legs, and he dropped to his knees—his soul crumbling. He stared down at his hands, turned upward with the deep folds in his palms stained with faded blood. "She's in chains, going into the depths of the king's dungeons. They're going to send her into their 'Re-Enlightenment,' but fucking torture is all it is... how did I let this happen?"

"They fooled us all, brother." Davin's words were filled with bitter defeat. "I should've cut Kaile's head off as soon as I found out he was Alcarond's apprentice."

"Mihelik trusted him," Blaje said. "That's what you told

me. He convinced you to trust Kaile. Perhaps it's worth trusting in the old man. Perhaps he knew more than…"

"He's dead, Blaje. He's fucking dead…" Soren shouted up at her.

"Don't fucking take it out on me." Blaje pointed a stern finger of warning at Soren. "You can self loathe and throw your tantrum all you want, but that won't change the past."

Soren knew she was right. There was nothing that his self-hate would do to change what happened.

"Now get on your fucking feet and let's come up with a plan."

"You're right," Soren said. "Somehow Seph wrangled Firelight back to me." He stood, gripping the dagger's hilt and its lightless black pommel. "She didn't give up, and neither will we."

"So where to?" Davin asked. "We're gonna stand out like black tar on white silk with these two giant bears, though. Something to keep in mind…"

"The stones and your disguise spell?" Soren asked, already knowing the answer.

"Doubt it would work on animals that big," the dwarf said. "And I don't have any more to use. Seph and Kaile still have two of the Drixen pendants. I don't even have one for Blaje. There's still that one million torren reward on your head—might even be more now…"

"One million torrens…" Blaje shook her head. "And with the lies the king is surely spreading about you… there's going to be half of Aladran after us."

"Well, we'll have to start spreading our own truths out into the world." Soren scratched his chin. "Who do we know that has that ability?"

"I will spread word to the Calica," Blaje said with pride. "My people will do whatever it takes to back us in this fight…"

"Something tells me you won't have to spread word far…"

Davin's face lit with a smile and renewed vigor as his gaze hit the far horizon to the west.

Soren and Blaje spun to look west. Both bears rose on their hind legs, getting a good view of the far desert dunes.

Soren couldn't believe what he saw.

"The Calica," Blaje muttered in awe. "My people have come…"

Chapter Three

Upon the dunes that surrounded the broken tower of Golbizarath, in the middle of the old desert, and at the tail-end of the ancient Ash Grove, dozens of shadowy figures on camelback looked down upon them. Soren readied to draw Firelight, but Blaje nonchalantly put her palm on the back of his hand, preventing him from freeing the Vellice dagger.

"My people," she said with a ring of pure hope in her voice, "they've come!"

"Sure is a lot of them." The apprehension was thick in Davin's words as he scratched his beard and the bears grumbled, unsure.

"Come," Blaje said. "They will give us guidance. The Dune Matron will give us answers, and I have much to tell my people of what transpired."

The caravan of the Calica shifted on their camels at the sight of their small pack at the bottom of the dunes, and a lone rider at their middle rode down the long dune, weaving between the broken, burnt bodies of the Shades. The others followed her.

As the Calica approached, their leader was quite the intimidating sight. She wore a large headdress of tan furs. The furs flowed behind her, rising a foot above the tip of her brow and falling all the way down her back. At her shoulders were sharp red feathers from a bird Soren didn't recognize. Golden bracelets went all the way down her arms, glistening in the sun's rays. And beside her, two riders carried banners that whipped hard in the winds as they rode. Both banners were a sandy brown with a red paw over a golden sun.

Both bears growled, their thick hides straightening on their backs.

"Easy," Blaje insisted with a wave behind her. "These are my people. You have nothing to fear with them. They are the protectors of the desert. They do far more for the people of the desert than the governments that say they do."

"I look forward to hearing what they have to say," Soren said. "Is there a Syncron in their ranks?"

Blaje nodded. "There should be one, yes. A Dor."

Soren cracked his knuckles. Syncrons and Synths always worried him, even if they were on his side. Soren loved a fight, and enjoyed being the underdog, but when it came to the Ellydian—magic always won against the sword. Always...

The Calica came down the hill and stopped in rows of ranks before them. Blaje, Soren, and Davin stood side by side, eager to hear what the tall woman with dark skin, long black dreads, and headdress had to say. There were many more than the dozens he had originally seen on the hill. Apparently, when the Calica moved, they moved with over a hundred soldiers, much unlike what Soren knew about Blaje, who seemed to hunt the desert alone.

The Calica blended into the desert like cinnamon melting into butter. The shade of their armor camouflaged against the sand as smoothly as thinly stretched gray clouds across the night sky. Their tan hoods and cloaks melded perfectly with their world, and Soren tried to pick up tricks from their garb that he may use to his advantage.

Soren still had the Twilight Veil, giving him the ability to hide in shadow, but the bright, relentless desert sun provided no shade. Landran taught him the best mentors were always those that were masters of their craft. And the Calica were certainly that.

As the Calica stood before them in rows, Blaje dropped to a knee. Soren and Davin exchanged glances, but followed Blaje's lead.

"Dune Matron," Blaje said, glaring down at the sands.

"Desert Shadow," the tall woman replied from the camel's back. "I know the man who kneels behind you by the scars on his face. Soren Stormrose of Tourmielle. Went by the alias Soren Smythe for the years after the burning of Tourmielle. It's a rare honor to meet such a legendary swordsman, and the only man to combat the Demons of Dusk, and live to tell the tale. I do not know the half-height man that fights by your side."

Blaje rose, and others did the same, wiping off their knees. "This is Davin Mosser of Mythren. A hardened warrior and loyal companion. He has my blessing to walk our sands."

"Those two creatures do not belong here," the matron said with a raised, slender, black eyebrow.

At first Soren thought she was talking about him and Davin, but he quickly realized the entire Calica were glaring at the two bears. Sable approached the matron's camel and began weaving between its feet.

The bears gazed back at the Calica, but the male suddenly had an itch behind its ear that required more attention than the over hundred soldiers before them.

"They came with Archmage Mihelik Starshadow from a portal spell." Blaje turned and pointed to the top of the crippled tower.

"The bears are from Myngorn Forest," Soren added. "They were meant to depart with their friend back to the forest after helping us. But... things didn't go how they were supposed to."

The matron stroked her chin. "Things go the way they go. Like the winds, man cannot control his fate, but he can try to guide his course with sails. Whatever Mihelik planned, that man rarely made mistakes. I would suppose the bears were meant to be here, to remain with you. Or at least that's what Shirava had planned."

Soren nodded.

"Tell me," the Dune Matron snapped. "What transpired here? And is that Mihelik under the ground?"

Blaje lifted her chin. "Yes. He died a warrior's death, and we should begin planting seeds of his sacrifice so that it may spread far and wide. He was never a traitor. He betrayed the king because the archmage knew of his evil, and in the end, died saving our lives."

"Go on," the Dune Matron pressed.

It was then that Soren noticed a pair of men on camelback to the queen's side who were madly scribing upon sheets of papyrus.

They're recording history. They're writing everything while it's all fresh so that time will remember what happened here. Clever...

They told her about the journey to get to the tower, fighting the Shade with Firelight and the word it spoke before Soren killed it. They told her about going up into the tower, Kaile flipping sides and betraying them. Mihelik's arrival in the portal to save their lives was certainly the pinnacle of their tale as the scribes' wrists flicked fast. Finally, they told her about the dragon that surely saved their lives, and that Seph was gone.

Soren decided not to tell her about his vision of his lost love, Cirella. He would keep that close to his heart. It was the final goodbye he'd prayed for—begged for—many sleepless nights.

"Dune Matron Scarletta," one of the Calica said after searching the tower. "All within are deceased. We counted two hundred and seventy-eight Shades dead." Again, the scribes didn't miss a word of their conversation.

The Dune Matron nodded, with little expression on her face.

"These are dire tidings," she finally said, looking up at the broken tower and the northern sunlit sky. "These small victories we make inch us closer to a free world, but we are still facing overwhelming odds. You kill a Shade, surely a dozen more spawn under moonlight. You kill a Synth; they capture the last Whistlewillow to turn her into their new weapon."

"She won't turn." Soren's voice was mean, bitter. "Never."

"Regardless of what you believe." The Dune Matron held an icy gaze at Soren, showing an inner strength and wisdom he didn't expect from the leader of a wandering gang. He suddenly harbored a renewed respect for what he always assumed was a ragtag bunch of scoundrels that tried to rule the desert from the shadows. But knowing Blaje then, and meeting with her wise leader, changed his views. "They took your Persephone because they believed they could control her, so they will try. I know you know King Amón and his madness more than most, but that man's sickness grows, and his lust for power knows no bounds. He will flip her to his side, or she will die, at no lack of agony, I'm afraid."

"Can you help us get to her?" Soren stepped forward, his arms out at his sides. "Blaje said you have a Syncron in your ranks. Can you help us? Lynthyn is far, and their defenses great."

A flash of something sparked on the Dune Matron's stoic face. She blinked hard and turned her head so her chin touched her shoulder. She let out a delicate sigh.

Is that... sadness?

"Dune Matron?" Blaje stepped forward, both eyebrows raised and her fingers splayed. "What has happened since I've been away?"

The Dune Matron lifted her chin high and cleared her throat. "We *had* a Syncron, yes."

"Sive? Sive is... dead? Oh, no..." Blaje's head sank, and her shoulders slumped. Davin placed his hand on her arm. "What happened?"

"He leapt," the Dune Matron said. "Once the Calica and Lady Sargonenth declared war on the capital and the king, Sive... decided to end things before the war began."

"Your Syncron killed himself?" Davin grumbled with a cocked eyebrow. "Why would he do such a thing? Didn't he know how much his Ellydian would be needed?"

"I think that's why he did what he did." Soren crossed his arms. "One Dor to go against the king's Synths. That's a battle that could cause even the strongest wielders to have nightmares."

"But you're leaving your people helpless," Davin said, his words cutting through the grief that hung heavy in the desert air.

"He did what he did," the Dune Matron said. "Sive had his demons, and he is at peace now. We are searching for another. But presently all Zatan has is Lady Sargonenth and her Dorens of Taverras. We have no way of aiding you on your journey to free your niece, I'm afraid."

Soren hung his head, thinking of the distance between him and Seph. She was stranded with that traitor Kaile and Alcarond. His fists squeezed, feeling the sweat in the creases of his palms.

"However," the Dune Matron said. "All is not lost. There is still time, and we rally more to our cause every day. More are enlightened to the truth. Our army is growing. And a dragon roams the skies, capable of destroying the night army of Shades and Black Fog. Hope, although it may not feel like it, spreads like the Chimaera over the lands of Aladran. The Silver Sparrows, my Calica Clan and the empire of Zatan stand against the evil that has corrupted the capital. You, Soren Stormrose, are the beacon of this fight. The guiding light that inspires all in our world. You, who first killed three Shades, fought off a Black Fog with nothing but your wits and your dagger, you who are Scarred, yet fight back past your grief, will show the king and his minions fear, where there was none before."

Soren took a deep breath, his chest swelling. "I will do what I must to kill the king. Whatever it takes. Even if it means my own life."

"Soren." The Dune Mother leaned forward on her camel, waving him to approach.

He walked to her side, smelling the camel's hide and her rich perfume, which reminded him of a field of fresh lilacs with sweet notes of honey.

The Dune Matron looked deep into his eyes, and he was pulled into the deep browns of her irises as if magic drew him in. But she had no magic. It was only the strength and wisdom that resided in her. He was completely entranced, but what came from her lips was so bitter, Soren felt the sourness at the back of his tongue.

"Soren," she said. "What I say now is painful, but absolutely true in every regard. So heed my words carefully, and with great strength. You will have time to contemplate them on your journey. I take no pleasure in saying this, but it must be said, and it must be said now." She took a deep breath, the kind of deep breath a queen takes before telling her people of great tragedy. "Soren, your niece has been taken. It was by design. She is now in the enemy's hands. And whatever befalls her, you must press on."

Soren took a quick step backward, feeling a twitch in his eye and the bitterness in his mouth.

"Even if your Persephone dies, Shirava protect her and her innocence, you must persevere in this great war. Millions of lives are at stake. The king, the Demons of Dusk, all of it… our world will crumble if we don't win this war. And it's a war that you, Soren Stormrose, are the figurehead of. You are the general that will lead these armies, and you need to rise to that. The Knight Wolf, the archpriest, the Drakoons, and every Synth that follows the king must find death, and in dealing those blows, you will finally wreak your revenge, and when that time comes, I hope you finally find your peace."

"Seph isn't going to die." Soren's words were laced with poison. "She won't. She'll find a way. She's going to live until I reach her, and then I'll bring the Nine Hells to Aladran itself, if that's what it takes."

The Dune Matron leaned over and pressed her hand on the spot between his neck and shoulder. "I know you will. You will do us proud. For you know defeat, Soren. You know it more than most, but inside you is a strength that the ages will remember. Songs will be sung of your victories and your retribution. You have allies in this world, and you're going to need them. Trust them. Let them help guide you, for more heartbreak will come, but you must overcome your regret. Don't let it fester, poisoning your soul. You are destined to be the greatest warrior of our generation. Fulfill your destiny. Kill the king, and take your place as the savior this world has prayed for. Even if Persephone falls, you must fight on. Aladran needs you."

The words rang in Soren's head like an echo in a deep, wet cave. *Even if Persephone falls… If Persephone falls…*

She won't. I'm not going to let her die… Hang on, Seph… I'm coming…

PART II
CELESTRA AND THE PALE SYNTH

Chapter Four

I n this world, teeming with every wonder of life, the decisions one makes will influence how life responds. If one chooses rightly, riches may be incurred, or life may end. There is no true guide in life, but trust instinct, and choose your righteous path. More often than not, what one thinks is most true to thyself will prove the best way forward.

However, for those that wield the Ellydian, those decisions are of utmost importance. Not just for thyself, but for the realm.

For those that harness the connection of all things, with the potential to move mountains, change the tides, and kill thousands with a flick of a wrist and the humming of a tune, the fork between good and evil is not always clear.

Many that have fought to make the future brighter became remembered through the ages as tyrants, madmen and unimaginably powerful evil. Others, who were bright stars of hope and change, perished far too early for their wings to spread and their gorgeous light to shine.

For those that wield the power of the Ellydian—let not fear and despair corrupt thy soul. Chart your course true, aim for your guiding light, whatever that may be, and let not temptation pull you from your path. For that path is your anchor to enrichment, salvation, and good. Define yourself early and fight, tooth and nail, to your end.

For evil lurks. Sometimes where you expect it, and sometimes with a smile and a warm cup of tea.

-TRANSLATED *from the language of the Sundar. The connection of all things, Book 1, Chapter XIII.*

700 MILES AWAY.

Celestra, capital city of the Kingdom of Lynthyn and the Realm of Aladran.

A SINGLE CANDLE flickered in the room's corner. It danced with a relaxing exuberance, casting a bouncing shadow on the back wall of the square room with a whimsical sort of playfulness.

Seph stared at the candle's light and the flickering shadow. It was her whole world. However, where often fire inspires hope, gives warmth and peace, that candle did neither...

The bindings on her wrist behind her chafed and cut into her skin. Every time she twisted the tight, coarse rope, it sent a surge of pain scuttling up her arms, tingling her brain.

Her mouth was dry as sand as the cloth that gagged her tasted harshly of rust and old iron. Her dry tongue scraped against it, causing her to nearly wretch every time she tasted the metallic cloth. She lay on her side, her feet bound too, with the other end of that rope tied to the wooden bed frame which she laid upon.

There was no mattress, no sheets, no pillows. There was only the scratchy wooden bed frame in the dark room. All that she had were her thoughts, the candle, and the pain.

Seph remembered being flown through the air by Alcarond, with Kaile beside her, apologizing meaninglessly repeatedly. She remembered fighting the dagger away from

Alcarond, and with all her power, hurtling the Vellice dagger back to Soren. That was her only saving grace, she thought. In every other respect, she'd lost. She'd lost everything.

I've got to get out of here... but how? This has got to be the deep dungeon of Celestra. How the fuck would I ever get out of here? I've never been to the capital, and I'm scared something terrible is about to happen to me...

Just as she thought that, she heard soft footsteps on the other side of the door. No words though, only the shuffling of feet, as a key slid into the door from the other side. The latch popped as she swallowed hard, completely helpless on her side, and without a staff, a tuning fork, or even her mouth to hum a tune.

The door hinges squealed as the door swung open slowly.

She expected to see Alcarond, or Kaile, or the king. She most certainly knew the king would want to see her. She'd never felt special in her life, except when she finally found a purpose with Soren. That gave her life meaning. But she *knew* her name carried great meaning.

Seph knew they were going to try to turn her. But even bound and gagged, she knew she'd never give in. But even with the power of the Ellydian, she was in the devil's den, and fear was potent in her. She would try to be brave, but she deeply screamed for Soren to come help her. She prayed to Shirava to protect her.

When the door was finally open, a hooded figure entered the room. She squinted in the dim light. The man carried a lantern, blinding her even more to his identity. She could tell it was a man by the shoulders under the cloak, but his face was hidden by the blinding light.

"Persephone Whistlewillow," the man's voice said. He sounded too young to be the king, but she recognized it from somewhere. He was at Erhil, she knew, but couldn't remember from which man. "You were thought dead long ago. But here you are... Marvelous... Truly marvelous, you've lived this long. An honor really... The last living Whistlewillow..."

Seph was gagged, or she would've shouted a string of curse words that would hopefully make the man scuttle back off into the shadows.

But as he walked into the room, shutting and locking the door behind him, she caught a glimpse of the profile of his face. He was much younger than the king and his normal cronies. He was handsome even. Clean shaven with a sharp chin and a perfect nose. Long waves of auburn hair fell from his hood. He set the lantern down on the table, and standing up straight, pulled his hood all the way back, revealing his face to her.

She recognized him, sending a shiver of fear down her spine and what felt like a vice clamping her chest. Seph knew then that she truly was at the mercy of all the evil she had been fighting against. Standing before her was the king's right-hand man in all things.

Archpriest Solemn Roane VII. Why is he here? What does he want from me? Soren... where are you?

The archpriest approached, standing at the bedside, so that his hip was only inches from her face. She bit at the gag, trying to bite it in half, but it sent an explosion of rusty iron into her mouth.

Solemn then sat; the wooden frame creaked under the weight. He sent the backs of his fingers gliding down her cheek, sending the vice squeezing her chest tighter. Beads of sweat dropped from her brow, and her hands fought her bindings viciously behind her.

Her face angled up at the man, appearing only in his late twenties, early thirties perhaps, but his gray, granite eyes held a deeper light to them. No, not light. A darkness. His stony eyes held a deep darkness, like staring down into a well at night. Like staring into the abyss.

"I've longed a great deal to finally meet you. Meet you properly, I should say." The archpriest sat beside her, twisted at the waist to glare down at her. She shrugged her gaze away, instead glaring at the lantern on the table in the room's corner. "The Ellydian, the most powerful source of magic in our world, isn't usually hereditary, but in your case, it is, and seems to get stronger with each generation. It's a shame your parents didn't swear fealty to his grace. They both could have been powerful Lyres, but instead... well... you know how things went..."

Seph bit her gag, her rage overtaking the awful taste in her mouth.

"I'm most curious to see where *your* fealty lies within the coming weeks..." He caressed her bare arm. Goose pimples like pinpricks shot up her arm, and she squirmed against his soft touch. "I certainly hope you choose right, and the righteous path. Shirava has plans for you, young Whistlewillow. If you choose the right path, you will be rewarded beyond measure. Archmage Alcarond will shower you with knowledge far beyond what you could imagine, and King Amón will grant you land, title, and treasure far beyond your wildest dreams. You will have offspring that will inherit your magic, and you will show them the path. It's a beautiful gift you're being given now. Far more than you would ever get out there, sleeping in the mud, walking the bitter sands, learning the ways of the heretic."

Seph growled, shrieking to break free of her binds.

Archpriest Solemn bent over and whispered into her ear. The feeling of his breath in her ear made her whole body shiver.

"You see," the air from his breath sent an icy chill into her ear, "even if you swore allegiance to the king right now, that would not be enough. What you're going to experience here in the depths of the kingdom is unimaginable pain. You see,

Persephone, there's a thing about pain. There's something spiritual in it. It cleanses, it purifies the mind, body, and spirit. It's a truly beautiful thing when done correctly."

You sound like the king and his obsession with fire... I wish I could turn my head and spit in his fucking face...

He pulled his head back, and she desperately avoiding looking up at him.

"I see your fear. I smell it." His voice took a sinister turn. She could almost hear the smirk creeping up on his face. "Fear and pain will break you down, bend your will to ours, and when you're finally broken, then you will truly be ready."

He bent again, and she heard his mouth open. His wet tongue touched the bottom of her cheek, and he licked all the way up her face. It slid up her cheek like a snake slithering along her sweaty skin. Once at her brow, he pulled his head back, moaning in ecstasy. "So sweet. So young. So much potential. And your fear is ripe. You will prove to be one of Malera Amón's greatest assets in the war, and if you don't, then he will have the victory of extinguishing the light of the Whistlewillows forever. That would be a victory in itself, but not one that I wish for. I wish for you to grow and blossom into your true potential. Together, we can recreate this world into a beautiful, peaceful land rife with order and subservience. Shirava will bless our war and lead us to the promised land."

Seph wiped her cheek on her shoulder, sending up a menacing glare at the archpriest.

"Spite, hatred, resilience. Good..." He smirked. "Good..."

He stood. His back was to her, and he stood there, still, unflinching, as if deep in thought.

"I will remember this day. I will cherish it. I believe that you and I have a destiny to fulfill in Aladran. We have a mission. It's a mission with a higher purpose; one few would understand. These lands will be purged of their wickedness. They will be cleansed of non-believers and false zealots. We will tear down the corruption and lead with order. That is the true path. That is what Shirava wishes, and that is what we will see to the end."

Seph groaned, fighting at her bindings. The wooden bed frame scraped her arm and leg.

"You've got spirit, child," he hissed. "I like that. You're going to need it for what's to come. How I'd love to remove your gag so that we make speak, but there will be time for that later after your Re-Enlightenment. No reason risking you singing a note and crushing me from the inside out. We know all things about the Ellydian here, so what you expect to surprise us with won't work, while you'll be in for all manner of surprises. Can't cast without your mouth open..." Two of his fingers pressed against his temple.

Seph crooned a tune behind her gag, but felt no connection of all things. She fought at her bindings again, but they were tight and cut into her skin.

Archpriest Roane glared down at her, deep in thought as she thrashed. He cocked an eyebrow. "I heard you sent that dagger of Vellice back to your uncle... Wise. Foolish, but wise... Archmage Alcarond would surely have gone back for it, to retrieve such a splendid, magical weapon... but... the dragon..." There was a seething tone of anger and frustration in the back of his throat. "A dragon has returned to Aladran. The first of its kind in centuries. Sarrannax..."

He knows the dragon's name? Oh, yes... I heard the archpriest came from Eldra during the same time Silvergale Lake of Celestra flooded. Seven years ago, maybe eight now... He knows of the dragon... and by the sound of it, he and Alcarond know the danger it presents... Interesting...

"No matter. The dragon is old, far older than most. Its strength has waned in its years in its gold-filled horde. Nothing changes. We move forward to save this world. The dragon will return to Eldra, or it will die. As for you... Persephone Whistlewillow, stay strong. Eat when they feed you and drink when you can. Many have died at the hands of your new master. Endure young Ayl. For only through this pain will you ascend to your true calling… The Black Sacrament awaits. It is your future. It is your destiny."

The archpriest grabbed his lantern and left the room, draping it back into near darkness. Only the flicking light of the candle remained. And Seph again was alone, and so very far away from the only people that cared for her.

Soren, Davin, Blaje, Mihelik… I need you. Please help me… Please…

Chapter Five

There was a click of the door latch. Seph startled awake. She couldn't tell if it was morning, night, or somewhere in between. Past the gag in her mouth that numbed her tongue, she smelled the damp air through her nostrils. It smelled of deep earth, and old, old stone.

Her focus narrowed on the door as it swung inward. Two men entered; both soldiers, both wearing the gold and white of Lynthyn. Upon their crests at the center of their armor was the symbol of the snake and the lion, also symbolizing the capital city. Neither spoke, but both grunted as they forcibly grabbed her by the arms. They lifted her from the bed, untying her binds from the bed frame.

There was little use fighting them. They easily overpowered her, lifting her and carrying her by the arms through the door and out of the single candlelit room.

Her feet and toes dragged along the dark stone corridor. The soldiers carried no torch or lantern, but there was light up ahead. Its light danced vibrantly, and Seph guessed there was a torch around the corner. The two men carried her down a series of pathways, all underground, with no hint of sunlight through any cracks. There were no decorations on the walls; no paintings, tapestries, or statues. Instead, there were many rooms with gates, bars, and she saw a handful of head-height cages with chains within.

A fear lurched in her, and she fought hard to suppress it, to swallow it down. But the archpriest's words lingered in her mind. *Pain... Unimaginable pain...*

Fear was no stranger to her. She'd been woken up by problematic boys more than her fair share at Mormand Orphanage in Guillead. It was the shrill kind of terror that felt like fire blazing in her veins, causing her limbs to fight, even when lack of light prevented her from seeing her attackers. She'd always seemed to find a way out of those situations. Usually clawing, biting, and screaming until she could run and escape to the rooftops where she'd feel safe. She might've been bruised and sore, but she always somehow seemed to get away.

But this was different.

She was bound and gagged. These soldiers weren't mischievous, gross boys from the orphanage. And there was nowhere to run to. There were no alleys to duck into, no known escape route through Guillead to the rooftops.

As they dragged her through the cells, another thought hit her like a boot into the soft spot of her stomach.

Kaile.

That was the hardest blow of all.

I've never trusted anyone like I trusted him. Soren was the only one I'd ever trusted since Tourmielle burned. And Soren abandoned me. I understand now why he did it. But now the only other person in this world who I gave my trust to, betrayed me in the worst way.

Did Alcarond come for me? Or was I just another grab while he recollected his fallen apprentice?

During that fight at the top of the tower of Golbizarath,

Seph had a vague memory of a shimmer of light on the side of Kaile's neck. It was when he was defending the archmage. It wasn't much, but there was something there. What was it? She'd never seen it before. But she knew if she ever saw Kaile again, she'd kill him. There'd be no time for questions.

Eventually, after a long descent deeper into the prison, the two soldiers led her to a door at the end of a long hallway.

Her eyes blinked hard at the sight of the door. It was unlike anything she'd ever seen. All the other doors underground had been wooden or steel, with iron bars. This door, however, made her heels dig in hard, pushing with all her strength away from it, but the strength of the guards was too much for her.

It was massive, looking more like a mural of steel with ribbons of different shades of metal streaming throughout. The ribbons were like wafting clouds or flowing currents. They sparkled with hues of gold, silver, and blue. Its mouth was the iron door, but the decorations that sprawled out from its mouth reached out six feet on both sides.

More like a gateway to the Nine Hells, Seph fought with all her might. She tried to force a tune from her throat through the gag, but no Ellydian came. A soldier grabbed the huge black latch, unlocking it with a series of pops and clicks from inside the immense door.

After opening the door, it opened in a wide arc from its huge hinges. They threw her in. She landed on her side, the dusty stone floor scraping her arm and cheek. Seph quickly shimmied onto her back, gazing up at the two, who showed little expression. They hardly acknowledged her before closing the door behind them, but not locking it before they left down the hall.

The wide room was dim, and Seph could barely make out the walls, as only a single torch burned by the door. She struggled to look all around, her hands still tied behind her back, and her ankles tied so tightly together the blood in her feet pulsed. She spun to look behind her into the gloom, and as her eyes adjusted, she made out the forms of dark structures in the room. A long table, which was a piece of iron or wood that looked like a coffin, and many things hanging from the walls. Some looked like weapons, but she definitely recognized a coiled whip hanging on the wall.

I don't like this place. I don't like it at all. It smells like old blood, and death.

As she looked into the darkness, a reflection of torchlight beamed back. It was a pair of red eyes, like fiery rubies glaring at her. They were unflinching, unblinking, and Seph suddenly felt the urge to be anywhere but there.

As the pair of eyes grew, slinking toward her like an asp's slithering forward, the figure's silhouette emerged, and Seph quickly recognized it as another she saw when Erhil burned.

I truly am in the devil's nest. Soren… help me Soren… please…

Zertaan of Arkakus, one of the king's chief Synths, and the one who helped the Knight Wolf curse Soren, strode around the table and into full view of the torchlight.

"Finally," Zertaan hissed, standing over Seph, glaring down at her with her demon red eyes, and pale pearly skin glowing like cotton in the flickering light. "I've waited long for this, young Aeol."

Seph bit at her gag and fought again to free her hands, but Zertaan simply smirked down at her.

"Do you know where you are? And why you're here?" Zertaan knelt. Her thin blond hair draped over her shoulders and nearly hit the floor. Her black robes creased as she knelt, and the albino Synth's fingers reached out, her sharp nails gliding through the air toward Seph's face.

Seph's body tightened. Sheer terror erupted from her core to the tips of her fingers and toes, causing her to freeze. She squinted her eyes hard, expecting the worst from the Synth.

But instead of the nails sinking into her skin, the Synth's arm slid past her cheek, fiddling with the gag's knot at the back of her head. The Synth untied the gag, and she pulled it free from Seph's mouth.

Now! I've got to cast now! As powerful a spell as you can muster! Use an A note. Keep it simple. Nothing too fancy. Fierce and effective! Zertaan is powerful, so make it count!

Seph opened her mouth to hum the A, but with her lips wide and round, another ping of terror and confusion ripped through her—as nothing escaped her lips, not even a speck of a sound.

Her arms still tied behind her back, she tried again, and again, but nothing left her throat. No voice sounded.

"Amazing, isn't it?" Zertaan said, standing back up, her thin pale arms swaying at her side. Her angular face resembled an asp, her predatory eyes never leaving Seph. "Whoever created this room made it for the purpose that no Ellydian can be summoned. No pitches, no tunes, even ringing metal makes no sound. It's old magic that still rests deep in the stone of the walls. A spell erected ages ago that still persists, and is just as strong as the day it was cast. Magic lost to time, but potent enough to keep this process… efficient…"

"What magic?" Seph said, suddenly shocked to hear her own voice.

So I can't hum to cast, but I can speak? This truly is some old dark magic…

"Even Archmage Mihelik Starshadow, the greatest of us all, before his treason, couldn't figure out the spell that binds this room." Zertaan turned and walked away, her long black robes skirting the stone floor. "For if another could wield this magic, then that person may nullify the strongest of us. But this, here, is truly perfect for our purposes."

With her back to Seph, staring up at the far corner of the bleak room, Zertaan had an unmistakable darkness to her.

Seph knew she was the Synth that helped the Knight Wolf curse Soren with his scars. She cast the spell that bound their fates as William Wolf carved the three scars down Soren's face, marking him as his forever prey. The hunt that would continue, tormenting Soren, until the day the Knight Wolf finally decided to take Soren's life, when he finally decided that Soren had been tortured with his failures enough.

Zertaan moved as if no steps carried her, she spoke as if a demon serpent was implanted in her throat, and her gaze was terrifying enough to make most men soil themselves, forgetting to run, freezing in place, fearing they were staring into the gaze of death itself.

King Amón's albino Synth of the volcanic Arkakus in the western realm of Aladran. This is one of the last people in the world I'd ever want to be stuck with. I don't think I've ever been so afraid in all my life. But I've got to stay strong. I've got to resist whatever comes. Stay strong Seph, think of your family. Think of mom and dad. Do it for them. You can't turn into a Synth. You can't become one of them. Resist! Resist!

Seph realized she'd been staring at the floor while deep in thought, building up her mental toughness. She heard clothes hit the stone ground, and her gaze darted up to Zertaan. Where dark robes had been, was an exposed pale bare back and arms. Her robes were collapsed with deep folds at her ankles. On the dark Synth's back were tattooed markings of black and red characters in a language Seph didn't recognize, and a deep panic clasped Seph's windpipe. She realized she truly was in an evil place, with an evil woman, and all the sudden, Seph didn't feel so resistant. Her breath caught, her eyes widened at the terrible woman standing over her, and her heart beat so hard in her chest, she thought it may explode at any second.

"This room is called the Abiron. It's as old as the first walls of Celestra and this Tower of the Judicature. This is where you will go through your Re-Enlightenment." Zertaan spread her thin arms out wide, with her chin rising and facing the ceiling. Her long thin blond hair fell down her back, partly covering thousands of tattooed characters on her skin. "Here, I have the honor of showing you the true path, and ridding your mind of all disease that the Silver Sparrows have implanted in you. I will show you the way to peace, justice, and order."

Zertaan's head dropped and cocked to the side over her shoulder. Her crimson eyes pierced deeply into Seph. "And it will be my honor to guide you, through immense pain, to the path of the righteous…"

"You're not righteous." Seph forced the words through her terror. "You're fucking rotten. Rotten to your core. You ruined Soren's life. You were there in Tourmielle. They needed Synths to kill my parents. No fire could have done what you did to them. You ambushed innocent families and burned them alive. I know it. I know it with all my heart that you not only cursed Soren, but that you helped kill my parents. Mihelik wouldn't have done that. Alcarond perhaps… but you… you enjoyed what you did, didn't you? You're a murdering devil, and one day, I'm going to kill you for what you did to my parents!"

Zertaan spun slowly, facing Seph. Covering her breasts and stomach were the same tattoos as her back. Seph swallowed hard, watching the sorceress glare down at her. A toothy smile lit her face, and the sharp points of her teeth seemed to cut into her lip. "Synth… What a useless word. Created by Mihelik Starshadow to try to discern who is 'good' and who is 'evil.' Such a simplistic view of the world. Black and white. Just and unjust. Shades of gray surround us in this world. I am no Synth. I am no Syncron. I am Zertaan Barindunne of the House of the White Asp of Arkakus. I was there when your house burned. I watched the light of your parents' eyes diminish and fade off into oblivion. Yes. I helped kill your parents. And now, I'm going to turn you into my apprentice. I'm going to cause you pain unlike anything you've ever felt.

And in the end, when you belong to me, you will thank me for what I've done. For when you are finally reborn, and I show you the greatest answers of the universe, you will become the greatest Lyrian the world has ever known... and you will belong... to me..."

Chapter Six

Within the cell, which the Synth Zertaan called the Abiron, Seph felt as helpless as she ever had in all her life. The room spun into spiraling fear. It clung thick with the dew of despair and the whole world seemed to break and crumble. Hope had fled far away, and no light of optimism shone into the deep, overwhelming darkness.

Zertaan glared, nude, her pale skin covered with the markings of red and black ancient letters and words, unreadable to Seph. She stalked the room, going to the room's far corner, and Seph heard metal instruments scraping along the tabletop as the Synth grabbed each one, inspecting them in the faint torchlight before setting them back down.

"A knife," Zertaan hissed, her back to Seph. "Simple, archaic, extremely versatile."

Seph wanted to scream, wanted to yell for help, but fear caught her throat, and no words came out.

"Too much too early." Zertaan placed it on the table, picking up another tool. "A hammer, fine for smithing, great for smashing, but too much as well. Hard to savor the pain."

Finally, a tear dropped from Seph's eye with a hard blink,

and she wished she was far, far away from this evil place. She prayed to Shirava for help, and she prayed that Soren would burst into the room, cutting this terrifying woman down, and he'd wrap Seph up in his powerful arms and tell her it was all going to be okay.

But Seph knew the truth.

She was in a worse situation than she could imagine. She was in the king's grasp now, and Soren and her friends were so very, very far away...

Davin, with his ax and his dwarfish humor, Blaje and her seemingly lifting hatred for Seph were both desperately missed. She fantasized about Davin storming in with his ax, and Blaje flying through the air in a masterful spin with her shamshir blade, ready to cut the Synth down. Seph even missed Sable and her mean hiss when the time came.

"Here we go," Zertaan said, picking up another tool and a length of rope from the dark table. She turned and walked toward Seph, but before she reached her, she set down the unseen tool, knelt, still fully nude, grabbed Seph by the arms and picked her up with a strength such a thin woman shouldn't possess.

Even if Seph fought, she knew she couldn't fight such a woman. Her hands were like tight squeezing, constricting snakes. Seph could feel the pressure on the thick bones in her arms. Zertaan lifted her and made her sit in the chair beside her.

"Crying?" Zertaan hissed. "Good..."

Zertaan untied Seph's hands, but quickly tied her wrists to the chair with fresh rope. Seph's ankles were still bound, and Zertaan's knots were skintight and caused the last bit of breath to escape Seph's mouth.

Zertaan turned after satisfied with the knots.

"I'm not going to join you," Seph muttered with a strong a voice as she could gather. "I'll never be one of you. And I'll never help you with anything. You helped kill my parents. I hate you. I'll never help you!"

Zertaan spun again quickly with a mad smile. She grabbed the tops of Seph's arms and suddenly threaded her legs under the armrests of the chair, sitting fully on Seph's lap. The intoxicating scent of honey and something stronger—an odor Seph didn't recognize—filled Seph's nostrils with a sort of overwhelming smokiness. Seph choked like she was inhaling campfire smoke.

The Synth's nose nearly touched Seph's. The odor from the Synth was fogging Seph's thoughts. She felt dizzy; she felt helpless, and she was very much terrified. Zertaan's bare legs sat on Seph's thighs, and her breasts hung just below Seph's gaze. Her breath reeked of gin and a harsh, foul odor, as if she'd just eaten a bunch of rotten, maggot-filled meat.

"I'm glad to hear you say that." Seph had to close her mouth to avoid inhaling the Synth's awful breath. Seph's stomach tightened and rolled over. "I don't want this to be easy or quick. I want both of us to savor this experience. In many ways, it's like birth. Or rebirth, I should say. For new life to be created, something must die. The energy of one will return to the earth to spawn anew. Do you hear me, Persephone Whistlewillow? This change you're going to experience is something we will share for all of time. I want it to be as memorable as anything. I've waited my whole life for an apprentice like you. And here you are. Magnificent. The youth you carry exudes from you. I can almost taste it..."

Zertaan cocked her head slowly to the side, smelling Seph's breath exhale from her nostrils. Seph turned away, her chin forcibly touching her shoulder.

But Zertaan grabbed her chin and pulled her gaze toward her. They were left staring deeply into each other's eyes.

"You're going to learn to respect me. You're going to learn to follow me, and you're going to learn to love me."

The dark Synth moved her mouth forward, her lips puckered. Seph tried desperately to pull away, but Zertaan clasped the back of her neck, squeezing with the raw power of her fingers. Seph wanted to fight. She wanted to pull away, but Zertaan forced her lips against Seph's. They were scratchy, and the Synth's tongue slid out of her mouth and forcibly separated Seph's lips. The Synth licked Seph's teeth, which she refused to open. Zertaan grew frustrated and licked up the side of Seph's face, all the way from her cheek to the side of her eye.

Zertaan stood, a dark, empty shell of an expression on her sinister face. Her red eyes glowed in the torchlight like cursed rubies. It felt as if she were possessed by a demon at that moment. Devoid of life, seeking only torment—she appeared more like a Shade than a human—and she lifted a tool from the table.

Seph's stomach tightened and curdled.

In Zertaan's hand was a small knife. But it was sharp. Sharp tipped, and with razor edges, the Synth held the knife between the two.

An inescapable terror surged through Seph. She knew there was no help coming, and that made her situation that much more terrifying. She'd been face to face with Shades, the Black Fog, and Glasse, the most powerful Synth in all of Londindam, but tied to the chair, and with no magic, Seph felt that raw sort of fear that made every second feel like an hour.

Zertaan slid the knife down to Seph's navel, and Zertaan pulled up her shirt with her other hand. The cold steel of the knife's tip touched her belly button, and the expression on Zertaan's face was emotionless as a viper's. Her red eyes darkened, glaring down at the knife's tip, intoxicated by it, entranced by it, and Seph screamed for help.

But no help came.

Soren was miles away, and Seph was stuck in the most secure fortress in all of Lynthyn.

Zertaan moved the knife to the side, away from her belly button, and to Seph's left hand. Seph cried and fought to pull her hand away, but Zertaan grabbed it like a python, squeezing her arm, pinning it to the armrest.

Seph kicked and screamed and fought as Zertaan slid the knife tip under Seph's fingernail. It cut into her index finger as Seph's entire body shook from the pain. Seph squeezed her eyes closed as tears streamed down her cheeks. She prayed that Shirava take her away. She prayed for Mihelik to arrive in a portal and murder the Knight Wolf's Synth in cold blood.

But again, no help came.

Every twist of the knife cutting into her finger sent Seph reeling in pain. She screamed until her voice was raspy, harsh, and weak. Zertaan's stony gaze was fixed upon her work, twisting the knife deeper and deeper into Seph's finger.

The pain was more than Seph could take. She sobbed. The sharp, cutting pain quickly subsided, albeit briefly. The feeling of the cold steel left her finger, and Seph looked down to see her fingernail perched upon the blade's edge. Sticky blood bound the two together. Air hit the fresh wound and Seph gasped.

The Synth held the blade between the two of them, showing Seph her work. Thick blood dropped from the blade's tip, landing on the stone floor with a dull plop. Seph's chest heaved from deep breaths, as she felt lightheaded and her vision clouded.

"Do you repent your past transgressions? Do you vow to uphold the king's law with your sacred Ellydian, and swear unyielding fealty to your one true king?"

Zertaan stared into Seph's eyes, with her red pupils being the center of Seph's foggy vision. The dark Synth waited eagerly for an answer; her mouth, thin lips slightly agape, a slight twitch in her eye, and the unmistakable lust for power on her breath.

"Do you repent, Persephone Whistlewillow? Do you repent your sins?"

Seph, panting, lifted her chin, sighed, and as Zertaan leaned in to hear her next words, Seph spat directly into the Synth's eye. Zertaan hissed and pulled away, wiping it from her eye.

"Little bitch. You little fucking bratty whore!"

"Fuck you, and fuck the king!" Seph snarled, trying to free her arms from their bindings to the chair.

"Fuck the king, eh?" Zertaan wiped the spit from her eye, and cocked her head at Seph, grinning wildly. "I didn't expect you to break easily, and you certainly didn't disappoint. I am definitely going to enjoy this…"

The blade flashed between them, torchlight reflecting off the parts of the sharp blade unspattered with blood.

Seph recoiled as the blade shot down, stabbing into Seph's hand, its tip digging into the wood beneath. A shrill scream left Seph's throat as the pain erupted up through her arm, digging like hot iron nails into her brain. With the blade cut through the middle of her hand, Zertaan leaned in so closely that Seph could smell her rotten breath. She twisted the blade violently back and forth, reveling in Seph's agony.

The Synth leaned in to whisper into Seph's ear. "This is just the beginning. You and I are going to spend a lot of time getting to know each other. I want to learn the capacity for your pain. I want to know you better than your friends know you. I want to know you better than you know yourself, and when you finally crumble and break, you're going to pray to me. You're going to beg me to be your master. When you're finally, completely, utterly broken, then I will help to put you back together. You'll love me like a sister, like a mother, like a god."

"I'll never follow you. I'll never turn against my friends. Someday you'll get yours. Soren's going to come and cut your fucking head off, and I'll spit into the hole where your head used to belong."

Zertaan swung her free hand, striking Seph in the cheek and temple. Her power was incredible, and terrifying for such a small woman. Seph's vision fogged further, and the gloomy world swirled and spun. Zertaan grabbed Seph by the chin, forcing her to focus on her red eyes, only inches from Seph's. The smell of the Synth's breath was harsh with sulfur and spit.

"No passing out yet. We've got to have some fun first." Zertaan smiled a wide toothy smile with the sharp points of her teeth showing. "We've got more exploring to do. Now... where should we go next? The feet maybe? The stomach? Your tits? No... How about..."

Zertaan trailed the blade's tip up Seph's arm, finding a point in the middle of the underside of her forearm. She jabbed its sharp point into the soft skin there, causing Seph to groan through clenched teeth. Beads of sweat poured down her brow, dripping off her eyebrows. They streamed down her cheeks, plopping onto her shirt as Zertaan cut into her skin.

Seph couldn't watch as the Synth cut into her arm. Glaring up at the ceiling, glowing and flickering in torchlight, she tried to picture herself in a far off place, far away from the capital, and far away from the evil woman she was bound and at the complete mercy of.

She chose to imagine herself with Soren. It was a peaceful, serene night, with trickling snowflakes weaving through the wintery, leafless tree limbs above. She imagined a warm fire, and her arm tightly pressed up against her uncle's. Soren was her safe place. He was her protector. He was coming for her; she knew. But he was also up against impossible odds, and he was so very, very far away...

Cling to this, thought Seph. *Focus your attention on there. Think about him. Think about him being able to defeat any man, any monster, any Synth. He's coming. You're going to get through this...*

Stay strong…

Survive…

"No taking your mind off the fun…" Zertaan hissed, and Seph felt an excruciating pain in her arm.

She looked down to see Zertaan with a pair of pliers gripping a section of her skin, and the Synth was pulling hard up, tearing the flesh away from her muscle.

Seph screamed in pain and agony, and there was no imagining the pain away.

"Soren!" Seph yelled up into the room, with his name echoing back. "Soren, help me, please…"

"That's it…" Zertaan's voice was full of pleasure, lapping up every scream, every groan, every cry for help. "Call to him. Bring that traitor here. Let me do far worse to him than this."

Seph shot an angry glare at Zertaan. Seph gathered every morsel of hatred in her body. "I'm going to fucking kill you for this. Nobody's going to save you from me. When the time comes, you're going to get yours. I'm going to get out of here, and I'm going to fry you down to your bones. Your disgusting eyeballs are going to boil out of your fucking head, and you're going to beg for mercy!"

"I like this side of you." Zertaan pulled up on the pliers, peeling more skin back, and Seph screamed a hearty, gut-wrenching shrill pitch into the desolate room. "We're going to have a long, long time to play together before you finally become… mine…"

"Shirava, please… protect me from this evil. Please, help me…" Her vision fogged and thick tears fell from her wet eyes.

But none of Seph's prayers or cries for help were answered in the dark room called the Abiron that day or night.

Seph endured pain she indeed could never have dreamed of, as the Archpriest Solemn Roane VII of Eldra told her she would.

Seph, many times, thought she would die from the pain,

even wishing it. But she never once succumbed to the dark Synth's call to repent and swear allegiance to the king. She knew that wouldn't stop the torture, even if she lied.

Eventually, after hours of Zertaan having her way with Seph's mind and body, she placed all her tools on the table, washed her hands of the blood, and left without a word, only a smile that reminded Seph of the demon she was.

Seph fell into darkness, spiraling through infinity, plummeting into what she thought may be death.

Chapter Seven

Echoes of a booming sound rang in Seph's ears, causing a quake in her brain that woke her violently. Her eyes shot open, letting in the candle's light on the table. She squinted hard through the throbbing in her head, her focus slowly regaining.

Immediately, the rust and iron taste in her mouth gripped her, causing her to gag through her throat that felt as dry as sand. Her hands were bound tightly behind her back as she lay on her side. She squirmed, unable to break the bindings at her ankles that tied her to the bed frame. The gag in her mouth drowned her attempts to cast, but her Ellydian was dormant, with the blasted gag filling her mouth.

Again, the door swung open on heavy hinges, and she quickly realized she was back in the original room she woke from. These two soldiers that entered were different, but both wearing armor with the sigil of Lynthyn—gold and white, with the crest of the lion and the snake intertwined—and she knew she was helpless to resist them. But she tried anyway.

They picked her up, not saying a word. One unbound her ankles and they quickly dragged her out of the room, and back into the dungeons beneath Celestra. They took her the same path as before, as she struggled to break free, but their grips were unrelenting.

She was soon back at the elaborate door to the Abiron; ornate iron and steel with streams of dazzling, ancient colors. They opened the door, and what Seph expected to see, a waiting Zertaan, was only half correct.

Within the room, filled with brimming light from torches and lanterns, were six figures, all of which Seph recognized when Erhil burned, and all those innocent people died.

Zertaan was there, draped in black robes, looking impeccably proud of herself, and gave Seph a seductive wink. Also, there stood the Archpriest Roane, with no expression on his youthful face. He wore long, white silk robes with golden trim. On his head was a tall, five-peaked biretta, and in his hand was a golden crosier with diamonds of black and silver rippling up it in waves. Between Zertaan and Solemn Roane was the least recognizable face in the room, but Seph knew she was the Synth Sophia. Long wavy hair down to her navel, flowing down her red and black dress. Her dress went up to the top of her neck, cupping her tan face. She was stunning, even in Seph's terror. She looked the sort of woman Seph would want to become, if she lived past all this. Sophia's tan arms were adorned with dozens of gold and silver bracelets, and her fingers were covered with sparkling rings. Within her grasp was a staff of dark, auburn wood pocketed with rough ore patches of gold and green gemstones Seph didn't recognize.

The last three in the room were so recognizable that sheer, primal rage welled deep in Seph's chest at the sight of them. Two of the legendary warrior Drakoons; their entire bodies were covered in sleek, slender dark armor. Their eyes were the only part of their body that showed through. Reddened, veiny and menacing, their gazes were glued to Seph. Both had their curved swords sheathed at their sides, and both their helmets had that unique webbing pattern on their sides. Seph vividly remembered them from the fight at Erhil, when Soren, out of full desperation, launched Firelight at the king, past the Drakoons. The Vellice dagger would have killed him, if it were not for the archpriest's intervening, leaving a gash on the side of the king's face.

And there he was—between his royal soldier Drakoons—King Malera Amón. His piercing, deep blue eyes like seawater took Seph all the way back to Erhil, watching the Knight Wolf and his men torch every foot of the town, and she remembered the screams, the shrill terror, and the utter, unworldly horror.

She remembered his eyes, and his thick black beard, but the rest of him was far different from before. At Erhil, he wore the rarest armor in all of Aladran; crafted in Vellice, glittering like no other metal, in waves of gold and silver. Within the Abiron, he wore no armor. He wore a fine white shirt with the sleeves rolled up to his elbows. The black hair on his forearms dotted his tan skin and veiny muscles. He wore black pants tucked into fine, intricately sewn leather boots. His golden crown sat on his wavy black hair, six jeweled spikes rising up, each representing a kingdom of his realm. At his hip, the most legendary sword in all of Aladran rested—Storm Dragon. Its hilt and pommel were of unmatched design and craftsmanship. Hundreds of micro jewels were inlaid in its metal, causing it to shimmer like no light Seph had ever seen. It resembled something between a rainbow's light, and the deep black of Soren's Firelight.

And finally, on his cheek, was the scar Soren left on his thick skin. A single scarred gash left by Firelight. It was long, slim, and straight. Soren hurling his dagger at the king nearly killed him. But Archpriest Solemn's deflection saved the king's life, leaving the scar as a reminder of the king's near fate, and leaving a lasting reminder of Soren and King Amón's hate for one another.

"Hello, child," the king said. His voice was deep, with a tinge of curiosity and a taste of disdain. "I've waited long to finally see you again."

The two soldiers that carried Seph into the room left, closing the door behind them, leaving only a narrow slit. Zertaan walked over, her dress sliding on the stone floor behind her. She took the gag out of Seph's mouth, letting it fall to the crest of her collarbone. Zertaan reached over and poured a glass of water from a pitcher beside it. As much as Seph wanted to hate Zertaan, still feeling the burning in her arm and the throbbing in her finger, the sound of the fresh water made her dry throat *crave* it.

Zertaan brought the glass up to Seph's lips and poured in, which Seph tasted quickly, and then gulped it down hard, letting it spill over her mouth and onto her cheeks and lap.

"Welcome to my capital city," King Amón said. "You have never been here, but your parents, Calvin and Violetta Whistlewillow, spent many years here before you were born. They were legends, learning, teaching, growing in strength."

"Until you murdered them..." Seph growled. Her fists balled, and she felt her knuckles eager to crack him in the jaw.

"An unfortunate occurrence," the king said, turning to the side. Both the Drakoons sidestepped to be an exact distance from him, never taking their maddening gazes off Seph. "But a necessary one..."

The archpriest shifted under his robes, nodding at the king's words, and adding his own. "Those that oppose the will of his grace, the law of our land, and the word of our creator, Shirava, must be punished. The Ellydian is far too great a force. It cannot be used by those who do not conform, and promise to use that power for the greater good. Your parents swore allegiance against the crown, to the Silver Sparrows, a plague upon our divine lands."

"They did not! They fought for good! They were just and

kind people!" Seph wanted to tear the walls of the Abiron from the foundation of the dungeon, crushing everyone in the room with her boiling rage. "You call these Synths just? Look at them. Look at the evil they are. They burn villages with innocent people? Women and children?"

Zertaan's hand raked Seph's face, and Seph instantly felt the cool air hit the fresh lines that the Synth's fingernails cut into her face.

"I'll never be like them," Seph spat between her and the king.

"You may very well not become a servant of this kingdom." The king raised an eyebrow, inspecting the small young woman before him. "But I would much rather prefer you to join my flock. There is a greater purpose to cleansing these lands of the filth and decay wrought within my shores. The last century has brought with it misery, pain, and suffering. But I will restore these lands. There will be peace and unity again." He folded his arms over his muscular chest. "I need the Ellydian to accomplish such a realm. And you, young Whistlewillow, have the strongest attachment to the connection of all things. Through your blood, you will make offspring that will change the dark path of this world, helping create a new, bright future, free of burden, free of sickness, and free of the evil that plagues these lands at night."

"The way you view us is... askew," the Synth Sophia said. Her voice was firm, yet her words delicate, deliberate, and poignant. "The terms Synths and Syncrons hold no meaning here. Archmage Mihelik Starshadow created those terms to divide us. We are all children of the Ellydian, studying it constantly, practicing the tones, notes, pitches, and rhythms that ripple through this world. Good or bad doesn't pertain to the Ellydian. Those are human devices. The Ellydian is pure, ancient, primal, and beautiful."

Seph was somehow entranced by the way Sophia spoke

about the Ellydian. It reminded her of how Soren spoke about it, but he was much more fearful of its power. Kaile had an eerie obsession when speaking about it, as if it were a god in its own right. But Sophia, she revered it in a way Mihelik talked about it.

"To grow as powerful as you could become," Sophia said, "you must join us. That is the only way to gain true knowledge and power. The world out there is feral, and your knowledge will be severely stunted. Here, Persephone Whistlewillow, in the coming decades, you would become the archmage. You would become the most powerful Lyre in all existence. That is your destiny. You can help shape this world in your image." Sophia strode forward and raised her chin, took a deep breath, and then relaxed her shoulders with a soft gaze. "But you cannot accomplish those things, and reach your full potential, unless you swear allegiance to our king."

"Like you?" Seph said in a low voice. "Like her?" Seph shot a menacing glare at Zertaan, whose face twisted in anger back at her.

"We would become your sisters," Sophia whispered. "And the pain would stop. You'd have a new future here. Please, Seph, join us. It's the only way."

"Become a slave, or die? Those are my only choices?"

"Not quite," Archpriest Solemn Roane added, lowering his chin to his chest. A darkness seemed to creep through the room, sucking all hope out through the crack in the door. "Zertaan is an expert when it comes to pain. Emotional and physical. You won't die, but you will live in excruciating agony as long as your soul can bear it. This can go on for years without death, or without you agreeing to do what is right. What is just... a cleansing of the soul. That is your third option."

"Then I pick death!" Seph's words filled the room, echoing back at her.

"Nonsense!" the king said, replacing the lingering echo

with his own. "You're too powerful and promising to simply die. That would be too great a waste. You are the last of your line. You are the last Whistlewillow, a lineage as old as recorded history. You *will* join me. Death is not an option. You *will* become a Lyre. You *will* become my greatest weapon in this war. You *will* revere me, and I will reward you with the gifts of the universe."

"You're insane..." Seph's mind raced with all the tragedy wrought in her life because of the man standing before her. She vividly remembered the flames that incinerated her town growing up. The screams, the panic, the smell of burning flesh returned to her nostrils.

Both Drakoons shifted, their armor clacking as their powerful hands gripped their swords.

With a delicate wave of his hand, the king motioned for them to stop. Their hands released their swords.

"I have never seen the world so clearly," the king said, raising his head so only his black beard was visible to her. He inhaled deeply through his nostrils. "I see everything. Archpriest Roane has helped me see the truth through unclouded eyes. The Demons of Dusk, the terrible Chimaera, the Silver Sparrows—they are all part of the same sickness that spreads like an evil shadow across Aladran—and soon it will spread to all corners of this world. There is a hidden war being fought, and the Ellydian is how we will save our world. It is how *I* will save this world."

"You're the plague," Seph muttered. "When Soren comes. He's going to find a way to kill every last one of you. I've seen what he's capable of. You act like your dreams are filled with worry for your people, for the Black Fog and Shades, but I know what you're *truly* afraid of... him. I've seen him kill deserving, evil men like you with his bare fists. He won't hold back when he comes. He's going to lead an army so powerful that the walls of your city will crumble, your halls will burn with his wicked fire, and your crown will fall from your miserable head."

"I must admit…" Sophia said with an eyebrow raised, and a curious scan of Seph, still hot with rage, "…I like this one. It will take much to break her spirit, but when it does, she will become a powerful wielder of the Ellydian, and become a great servant in your war, my king."

The king's gaze was heavy upon Seph, tied to the chair, a third his size, and shaking with fury. "Perhaps. Or perhaps her spirit will not break. In which case, there are other ways to persuade her…"

Other ways? Persuade me? What does he mean? I can't help but think about the glowing light on the side of Kaile's neck that was never there before…

Seph squinted at Zertaan, knowing she was the one who put the curse on Soren when the Knight Wolf cut the three scars down the side of his face.

They know some magic we don't.

I've got to find out more about what they're doing. What they did to Kaile and Soren… and I've got to find a way to reverse it…

"The great Whistlewillow." Zertaan rubbed her hands as her eyes dimmed. "You're going to be my greatest project…"

Seph wanted to stay strong, but her finger was throbbing. Where the fingernail used to be was an open wound, half-scabbed. And the wound in her arm seared in pain as the cool air hit it. She wanted to stay resilient, but she knew the dark look in the Synth's eyes well. Seph was in a for a long night, and helpless to stop what was coming.

"We will speak again soon." The king's words were chilling, icy to the core. "I'd wager that your tone will be much different the next time. And eventually, you'll be on your knees, begging… *begging* to allow you into my flock. For the sooner you repent, and love me, the sooner you will have access to the knowledge of the stars themselves, you will grow into one of the most powerful sorceresses of the modern age. You may even surpass the prowess of Zertaan Barindunne of the House of the White Asp of Arkakus, and Sophia Allathine, Shadow Sorceress of Lynthyn."

The king turned to exit, and Seph searched for parting words to spit at him, but anger and worry clouded her mind, freezing her lips.

The Drakoons followed him as if welded to his sides, permanently fixed to him. But the king suddenly froze and spun. The side of his face glowed in the burning torchlight by the door. One eye glared at her, and a rare smile curved up.

"You may even become stronger than Archmage Alcarond Riberia over the years. His obsession with the Demons of Dusk will either prove to be a great asset, or a distraction. But one thing is for certain, now that his apprentice has returned to his side, the Black Sacrament is on Kaile Thorne's horizon, and should he pass the ultimate test, you and he—together—will be unstoppable…"

Seph wanted to scream as the king turned and exited the Abiron. She wanted to bite her binds free. She wanted to kill them. She wanted to kill everyone in the room, everyone in that miserable dungeon. But she didn't. She was gripped by hatred, frozen by betrayal, and completely and totally afraid.

Archpriest Roane exited without a glance or a word, and Sophia Allathine followed. Sophia closed the door behind her, and all that was left were Seph and Zertaan.

Zertaan said nothing, and went to the rear of the room, back to her dozens of terrible tools on the tabletop.

"Now… Seph… where were we?"

Chapter Eight

Kaile's feet slogged beneath him as he fought as hard as he could to run. It was black, as black as a moonless winter night. A deep chill gripped him, freezing his heart as he clasped his chest.

Something unseen chased him. But as hard as he fought to move his feet, they felt weighted like boots full of icy seawater.

He panted, struggling, gasping for breath.

Terror filled him.

Whatever chased him was nearly upon him.

Kaile could feel its breath on the back of his neck, causing the hairs to straighten and freeze.

He thought it was death for a moment. That eternity had finally come to claim his soul for his sins.

The terror enveloped him, causing him to fall to his knees in futility.

He lost.

He'd lost everything he'd cared about.

And as the darkness consumed him, he gave into the thought that he'd failed his idol, and his closest friend.

"I'm sorry, Soren. I'm sorry, Seph. I'm so, so sorry…"

KAILE JOLTED AWAKE.

Cold sweat covered his brow.

He heaved heavy breaths, sitting up quickly, wide-eyed and full of a mix of panic and relief.

His slick palms clasped the silken sheets of the bed. His gaze darted around the dark room, only a moonless sky lighting the dim room from the window beside him.

His legs swung to the side of the bed, and he cleared his brow of sweat with his sleeve. The long, deep wounds on his back from the silver bear's claws stuck to the bandage there. He winced as the fresh scabs tore as he moved. It was a biting, shooting pain and a bitter reminder of his betrayal.

His long reddish-brown hair fell before his eyes as he glared down at his feet. Beads of sweat fell from its tips onto his pant legs and onto the floorboards. He took a deep inhale through his nostrils, exhaling deeply. He stood and unlatched the window, letting the brisk winter air rush into his face.

The relief of being alive, and death not taking him, hit him like more of a kick in the testicles than a sense of relief.

He knew he deserved to die for his betrayal.

His treachery for those who trusted him most would take more than forgiveness.

He needed to be punished. He needed to atone for his greatest sin.

And the worst part…

Seph… She's down there all alone. She's at the complete mercy of Zertaan, a wicked woman by all standards.

"Shirava, please watch over her. Please protect her… Give her the strength to survive whatever pain she's going through. Take me if you must, to save her. She and my brother are all that matter to me…"

Kaile leaned out of the window, putting both hands

together and praying. "Soren will never forgive me. I know him too well now. He'll kill me for what I did, and rightfully so. But Seph... oh Seph... what have I done?"

Kaile glared out the window at the vast empire of Celestra, capital of all the free world. Sparkling like mountains covered in glowing diamonds, the city reached out for miles. The Lūminine Grand Cathedral resided at the city center, towering over the people of Celestra like a beacon of light and hope. Centuries-old, and as majestic as any structure in all of Aladran, that's where Archpriest Roane worked tirelessly to preach the gospel of the great goddess Shirava.

From the cathedral, the city sprawled outwards like an interconnected series of spiderwebs, each shooting its silk out in all directions, forming new webs. The city spires and glowing towers reached the surrounding mountains, creating a network of military outposts and communication towers, with a constant flow of ravens coming and going from the capital, spreading the word of the king to all surrounding kingdoms and their cities.

Kaile knew this was the center of all the wars: the civil war, the war against the spreading Chimaera plague, and the war against the Demons of Dusk. Kaile was back where he started, forced back with his master, and he felt lower than ever.

All his aspirations, all his pride, were gone like a pile of ashes blown away by a powerful gust of wind. He'd wanted to grow into a powerful Syncron, helping fight off evil, help to defeat and drive away the Black Fog and Shades, and he wanted more than anything to gain all the knowledge of the Scriptures of the Ancients and ascend to one day become the archmage.

But that was all gone now.

He collapsed into his bed, staring up at the ceiling, remembering every awful moment atop the tower of Golbizarath in the desert of Zatan.

Alcarond came, and Kaile turned on his friends.

His stomach lurched and tightened as he remembered the look on Seph's face as she begged him to stop. Kaile remembered Davin's confused and lost expression. He remembered Blaje with a complete look of devastation stricken on her face, and he vividly remembered Soren's scowling, seething rage.

The Archmage Mihelik is dead because of me... Seph is in terrible danger because of me... and it's all because I wasn't good enough to stop him...

Alcarond...

Fucking Alcarond...

He played me.

He played me like the fool I am...

And now I'm here.

Helpless.

Alone.

Cursed.

This was his plan all along.

And I did exactly what he knew I would do...

Why? Why didn't I see it?

Am I stupid enough to be used like a pawn in this game they play?

Kaile spent hours that night staring blankly out the window, letting the wintry air fill the room.

But he didn't feel the chill.

He needed it.

He needed to feel something, anything, except that pain that threatened to consume him.

<hr />

THE MORNING RAYS broke through Kaile's window, like beams from the Halls of Everice itself. A warmth filled the room, washing away the chill that hung in the air. The light blinded Kaile, pouring onto his face. He pulled the soft covers back over his face and flipped to his other side, letting the warmth hit his back.

He'd slept, but the thought of Seph in the Tower of the Judicature made him feel physically ill. The thought of Zertaan and those terrible men down there doing unspeakable things to her made his stomach turn, his skin crawl, and streams of tears wet his pillow.

A loud knock came at the door.

Kaile pulled the covers in tighter.

Moments later, the knock returned; this time harder.

Kaile knew he couldn't hide from the world forever, and he knew he needed to face his fears. He couldn't free Seph. The halls of the Judicature were impenetrable and sealed with old magic. If he was to save Seph, the girl who meant the most to him in this world… then he'd have to do it with words, not the Ellydian. He stood and walked to the door, opening it inward.

One of the tower's maids was at the door. Her eyes shot wide as she looked at Kaile, and she bit her lip. She shook it off and averted her eyes.

"Master Kaile, the archmage wishes to see you in his chambers." She bowed and walked off down the stone stairwell quickly.

He returned back to his room and went to the mirror, hanging on the wall above his desk. With his sleeve, he wiped the fine layer of dust from the mirror. Kaile looked at himself with shock, as if looking at a different person. His skin was tougher, with tiny wrinkles at the corners of his eyes. His face was far darker than normal, from all the sun exposure in the Dyadric Desert. He was unwashed, and streaks of tears gave the look of spiderwebs down his cheeks. His hair was wild, strewn across the side of his head like branches in a tumbleweed.

Going to the water basin next, he hand pumped water

through the faucet and washed his face in the icy cold water. It made him gasp, but a deep breath of air returned to his lungs.

"You can do this," he muttered to himself, closing his eyes, and thinking of how to stand up to Alcarond with confidence and composure. "You've got this."

He threw on a fresh robe of dark seawater blue with white floral decorations sewn down it. Next he grabbed his staff, the short one Davin had given him, and apparently the king and Alcarond had let him keep. He glanced at the dark wood staff with embedded emeralds and the moonstone at its tip.

Kaile left the room and climbed their tower, the Illuvitrus Sanctum. As old as the city itself, beside the cathedral, and far, far older. It had been a beacon of hope for all humankind throughout the ages, but in recent years, there had been a shadow that had fallen over the tower of the study of the Ellydian. There was a new power in their world. The Demons of Dusk had revealed their new danger, leaving the once most powerful beings in the world, the wielders of the Ellydian, powerless to defeat.

Two floors up were the archmage's chambers, once the quarters and study of Mihelik Starshadow for many years before Alcarond succeeded his title. It was the home of nearly every other archmage prior for thousands of years.

Standing before the door, with morning sunlight trickling in through the small glass windows of the enormous round tower, Kaile took a deep breath, gripped the old iron knob, and entered Alcarond's chambers.

Chapter Nine

The archmage's chambers were a transformative place for Kaile Thorne. He'd learned unimaginable things about their world he never, ever would have dreamed of in his hometown of Krakoa, on the island kingdom of Ikarus. He'd been a terrified little boy when he'd first been brought to the tower, and learned from the two brightest archmages. He felt special, full of inspiration and aspirations, but now he simply tried to restrain his pain and anger.

The room was wide and round, broken up by massive pillars that shot all the way up to the top of the tower. Circular wooden staircases led up to shelves upon shelves of books that held the oldest knowledge in all of Aladran. It was all at Kaile's fingertips, and he'd read every single word. But the words he wanted to read most of all were gone, burned forever by Mihelik, now just scattered ash—the Scriptures of the Ancients.

"Come, my apprentice." Alcarond's voice carried through the hall, from a far corner, hidden behind one of the stone walls that broke up the chamber. The aroma of candlelight and a low burning fire in the hearth filled the room. Tables were covered with scattered papers with impeccable calligraphy.

Kaile walked toward the voice. The floorboards creaked beneath him as he approached. Something was off, though. Something about the room was different. Kaile had been in there hundreds of times, thousands even, and he'd been there enough to tell that something wasn't right. The air hung thicker than normal, carrying a weight he didn't recognize. It was almost as though the room was—afraid—scared stiff, paralyzed in terror. But Kaile brushed it off and proceeded further into the study.

As he walked around a stone wall, he saw Alcarond laying on his couch behind his desk. He was staring up at the high cone ceiling, and all its lattices and woodwork. At his side lay his staff, Diamond Dust. Kaile only glanced at it, instinctually thinking if he'd have enough time to cast a spell powerful enough to kill the man before he could reach for his great staff, defend, and attack. The archmage's arms were wrapped in thick white bandages with splotches of pink seeping through. Kaile remembered the burns on his master's arms during the battle with Mihelik Starshadow—his former master.

I still can't believe Alcarond defeated Mihelik. The pupil truly did replace the master... Oh, poor Mihelik... he fought so hard to save us... and at the end, it cost him his life, and here we are... separated and broken.

"How do you feel?" Alcarond said with a groan, sitting up and putting his bare feet on the floor. Kaile still couldn't tell what was different about the room, and brushed the thought away.

"Not great," Kaile said, folding his arms, looking his master straight in the eyes.

"That's to be expected." Alcarond picked up his dragon-head staff, and walked straight over to Kaile, arcing around the desk.

He stood nearly Kaile's height, his dark skin gleaming from the sunlight that poured from the massive windows behind. His long black hair sparkled with streaks of white and gray, and his wise eyes showed a deep power at the edge of divinity. Kaile could feel the immense power within his master, as the Ellydian lived in every inch of the sole Lyrian sorcerer in the world. "I am sorry for the way things went, and for the way they must proceed forward."

"You deceived me," Kaile said, holding the spite and anger in his stomach, and not contaminating his words with them. He knew Alcarond wouldn't kill him. Kaile was too valuable, and the archmage had spent too much effort on him to simply destroy his investment. But Kaile knew the capacity for his master's destruction when poked. "I understand why you let me go with Archmage Mihelik and Soren now. Your plan worked perfectly. But my trust in you is tarnished, and will never be returned. You betrayed me and made me betray my friends. How did you do that? How did you control me the way you did? I've spent years in your service, and even though I fled, and I'm well aware of my treasonous acts, I feel I deserve an answer."

Alcarond gripped Kaile by the arms, squeezing his biceps, inspecting his apprentice up and down. "You've grown. You're not the same boy I brought here from your broken home. You're not the same boy who set the sea ablaze. I see you're war-hardened. You've seen proper battle, and won. You've indeed made new alliances, and I'm proud of the man you're becoming."

"Enough with the compliments. I need an answer, Alcarond. Am I cursed to obey you forever? When and how is such a magic cast?"

Alcarond gave a clever smile. "Please sit, let us talk."

"I'll stand where I am."

Alcarond nodded and returned to his desk, taking a seat.

What is different about this room? It's really starting to get under my skin... Keep your staff ready, and your tuning forks in hand...

"You have been branded with an Alluvi Omnipitus—or the Godkeeper Rune. I placed it upon you the first day you arrived here in Celestra. You may feel betrayed, but it's quite a common practice with the archmage's apprentice."

"Why did you tell me? If it's so common practice, why did you keep it secret?" Kaile noticed his fist was balled and his voice was raised, causing his words to echo in the chamber. He loosened the grip on his staff and relaxed his free hand.

Alcarond didn't respond immediately, instead opening a side drawer in the mahogany desk and pulling out a bottle, two short glasses, a curved pipe and a pouch of tobacco. He poured the two glasses half-full with the amber-colored liquor, which Kaile recognized as brandy from the semi-sweet, thick aroma.

"No thanks. I don't want any. I just want answers," Kaile said with a wave of his hand.

Alcarond took a deep sip, smacking his lips after, and leaned back in his high-backed leather chair, stuffing the tobacco into the pipe. His wide shoulders were silhouetted in sunshine, and his silver robes shone in silky waves and creases.

"I couldn't and didn't tell you because I needed to keep it secret for its use back there in the desert. You understand this, I'm certain. You know me, Kaile Thorne, and I know you..." He sparked the pipe and puffed, exhaling it before him, causing the desk before them to appear as though a rolling fog hovered over it.

Kaile knew that was true, and little rebuttal for it. And even worse, he knew Alcarond was right to do it, because in the end, it worked exactly as the archmage had planned.

"And Seph?" Kaile's voice let a croak slip out, as hard as he tried to push the words out without showing emotion.

"You know the answer to that question." Alcarond had a

deep, strong resonance in his voice, as if disappointed in his long-trained apprentice.

Kaile had no logical response, and only emotion came shining through. "You can't let them do that to her down there!" He slammed his fist onto the desk, but Alcarond didn't stir, he... he even seemed to enjoy it. "You hear me? If you care about me at all, even a tiny speck in your dark heart, please, please! Don't let her go through Re-Enlightenment! I can't let her get hurt like that. I can't let her suffer, all because of me..."

Kaile slumped back from the desk, feeling absolutely powerless and defeated. His stomach was in knots, his heart pounded in his chest, and his legs felt wobbly, as if he may collapse.

"Do you want me to explain what you already know?" Alcarond finally said after another sip and a long puff. "We could talk in circles about this, even though you know what must be done. But we could also skip the needless nonsense, wasting our time, and you could just admit what I already know..."

Kaile wanted to rebuke what he knew Alcarond was referring to, but he couldn't find the words, and deep down, Kaile knew it to be true... at least partially. As he'd contemplated his feeling for Seph many, many times.

"...You love the young Whistlewillow."

Kaile's head sunk. His hair fell before his eyes and his chin tucked to his chest as he exhaled deeply.

"Love is what holds the world together, my apprentice. I'm proud of you. I'm happy for you that you get to feel such immense passion. But I also warn you, the pain you feel deep inside is but a taste of the pain love creates in all of us. It's a terrible price to pay for the brief warmth and overwhelming power. Love is everything, and it is a curse. I warn you to keep your emotions locked away. Keep them, but keep them deep, buried within your soul. But there are more important things in this world. You know this. You are destined to take my seat as the Archmage of Aladran. Your feelings will guide you to places you don't need to go." Alcarond suddenly stood, feeling much larger than Kaile, causing him to stagger back. "There are more important things that need your attention, not the distraction of a little girl from an orphanage in that shithole, Guillead! You need to be strong for what's to come. You need to focus on your work. These revelations of the Demons of Dusk and Soren's successes in defeating them has changed everything. What happens in the Abiron is necessary, and in the grander view of these new discoveries, is of no concern to you."

Kaile's legs finally gave out, and he sat in the chair behind him, slumping over and staring at the floor.

"Persephone Whistlewillow will come out of her Re-Enlightment, a new woman. A devout woman. She will have the power to shift the winds, change the tides, and even fly through the clouds like a magnificent bird. We need to build her to be what she was destined to be, what her parents refused to be, and she too, one day, goddess willing, will become a great Lyre that will be spoken about for centuries."

"You're wrong." With those words, it felt all the air in the chambers was sucked out and only a dark, omnipotent, foreboding shadow crept in. The sunlight faded as clouds filled the sky above Celestra. Kaile stood, rising with all the courage he could muster. He glared straight into Alcarond's furious eyes. "You're on the wrong side of this fight, master! You can't see because you're blind in your books. The Silver Sparrows are going to win this war. And they need your help!"

"Enough!" Alcarond swung Diamond Dust between them, the dragon's head, black staff hanging heavy with the weight of the Ellydian. Kaile backed off and held his staff up. No tune rang out, and neither hummed a note, but the room felt like lightning was about to strike. "I let you play your games, apprentice, but you are home where you belong now. You have every right to feel the emotions that blind your vision, but you will not speak in such treasonous terms."

Kaile chose his next words carefully. He knew he couldn't defeat the archmage. Kaile was only an Ayl, and Diamond Dust was the second most powerful staff in existence, save for Mihelik's staff. He cleared his throat. "You may not see the truth now, but you will. I just hope it's not too late before you open your blind eyes."

"Sit," Alcarond demanded. Kaile lowered his staff, and Alcarond did the same. They both sat, glaring at each other, analyzing the other. Kaile knew he'd ignited something in Alcarond, whether that was a chip in his hardened devotion to the king, or cracked their relationship further, he didn't know.

"We will have many talks about these issues," Alcarond finally said, leaning back and puffing his pipe with his arms folded over his chest. "But I wish to continue your training promptly. So we must work to resolve these discrepancies and repair our allegiance. The Demons of Dusk are growing in numbers, and the emergence of Sarrannax of Eldra has shifted the tide of this war. After we left the battlefield in the desert, a great dragon flew in and decimated a massive horde of Shades with its dragonfire, saving Soren and your friends from certain death."

A pounding rush of adrenaline shot through Kaile, causing his fingers to stiffen and his heart to pump hot blood throughout his body. "What? A dragon? Here? In Aladran? And it killed Shades?" Kaile fell back to the backrest of his chair and glared out the windows at the overcast sky. "A dragon?" His eyes narrowed, and he smirked. "A dragon!"

Alcarond held a deep sense of pride at the word. The wrinkles at the corners of his eyes darkened and he stroked his chin in contemplation. "Yes. We may have a great ally in our true battle."

"Soren and the others are still alive?" Kaile didn't expect a happy answer from his master, but he was met with a nod. Kaile's legs bobbed in excitement.

At least there's that. Soren, Davin, and Blaje are still out there, and they're going to come for me... they're going to come for Seph.

Kaile felt a shadow fall over him, as if his soul was sucked dry by a spider in his chest. A huge hand clasped Kaile's shoulder from behind. It felt like a bear's paw, clutching him, about to sink its tremendous claws into him.

He immediately knew what the terrible feeling was that he felt when he entered the room. Kaile turned his head to the side. He saw the muscly hand with thick veins squeezing his shoulder with the restrained power of a mountain. A man towered over him from behind, emerged from the shadows behind him, as silent as a mouse. With golden hair flowing down, contrasting starkly against his ebony armor, the man's unnatural blue eyes lit like turquoise gems. The man was enormous, the biggest man Kaile knew, and the most terrifying.

"Sir..." Kaile muttered. "Sir William Wolf? What... what are you doing here?"

The Knight Wolf leaned down, his long silky hair brushing against Kaile's neck, sending terrible shivers down his skin. The enormous man sniffed Kaile; his hair, his neck, and the crown of his head.

Kaile froze. He felt the Knight Wolf's hand might crush his shoulder completely if he said the wrong thing, or moved the wrong way. He felt as vulnerable as an ant under a looming, shadowy boot heel.

"Tell me, apprentice..." the Knight Wolf said in a voice that could seemingly crack stone. "Soren... how does he fight?"

"W—What...?" Kaile stammered.

"Answer his question," the archmage said, with the tiniest sliver of what Kaile recognized as rare fear.

"He... he fights well," Kaile said. "He's the strongest I've ever seen him. He fights even harder and ruthlessly, as the old tales say."

The Knight Wolf stood up tall again, and a single word left his mouth. "Excellent."

Kaile swallowed hard, still paralyzed from the power emanating from the knight. The Knight Wolf's grip released him, and Kaile's breath returned to him. By the time Kaile turned, all he saw was the Knight Wolf's cape of lavish red and gold scraping the ground behind him as he left. He also saw the enormous, world-famous Vellice blade the Ember Edge fastened on his hip. The tip of the long, broad sheath skirted just above the ground, sending a shiver throughout Kaile's body. The Knight Wolf left the room, leaving a stark, lingering silence. It was as if the room itself trembled, hiding through emptiness.

"I'll take a glass of that now," Kaile said, and Alcarond poured it with an ever-so-slight tremble in his hand.

PART III
THE DUNE MATRON

Chapter Ten

There are but two constants in this world.
    Death. That which we all must suffer, our return to earthen dust, transforming into new life.
    And change. Nothing lingers infinitely. Time rallies on, despite dreams and victories, or fear and loss. The moon continuously curves. The seas unrepentantly move, never remaining the same. Some won't see tomorrow, while some are born never taking even a first breath.
    Pain can be paralyzing, yet temporary. This world makes no promise of fairness, and in the end, everything dies.
    But, there is hope in change.
    From great loss and pain, new hope can flourish.
    Hold not to your defeat. For we all must overcome or delve into darkness, succumbing to our dark woes.
    Winter warms to spring, spring bleeds to summer, summer relents to fall, and fall withers and dies to winter.
    Even the brightest tune of the Ellydian cannot save us from the ultimate call of infinity.
    So, take each day as a new chance, a new spring, and a new pledge to speak your truth, wield your sword against oppressors, and show this world what you are capable of.

For if every man and woman alive lived with courage, and not fear, in their hearts, this would be a beautiful, inspiring world.

-TRANSLATED *from the language of the Sundar. The Scriptures of the Ancients, Book III, Chapter XI.*

THE DYADRIC DESERT, Zatan

THE DESERT WINDS WHIPPED HARD, biting into Soren's face as grains of sand flew into the growing stubble on his face. The camel beneath him groaned as they rode through the sandstorm, inching their way slowly to their destination for the night, a place the Dune Matron said would protect them through the night from the Demons of Dusk, and provide them with springs to replenish their water.

"Hope she knows where this fortress is..." Davin shouted through the storm, his beard whipping harshly to the side. "Even the bears are starting to get nervous. You can tell by the way they keep looking back."

"She will lead us there." Soren held his hood down, enough to break the winds, but not low enough to not be able to see his immediate surroundings. "One night of rest, and then forward to Lynthyn, and then to Celestra."

Davin didn't respond, only recoiling into himself. Sable hid herself in his lap beneath a linen blanket.

Soren knew Davin didn't agree with his decision to press on to save Seph. Davin didn't have to say the words, but Soren knew he thought it was suicide. Soren knew he thought that—because it was—there was absolutely no way to slash their weapons and win the war.

The Synths that dwelled in the king's realm ranged in all

THE DARK SYNTHS

levels of magic, but there were many. Soren knew he had no chance of getting Seph out of there alive. That was why he planned to do it *himself*.

It would take some convincing, but Soren couldn't save his only remaining family. Then he didn't know if he could be their general. Revenge only went so far, and besides, he moved better alone.

"Look!" Blaje held her arm up, pointing straight ahead to the north.

Soren raised his hood and peered northward. It was a speck on the horizon, but it was there, a building of white on an endless sea of tan sand.

"We're almost there," Blaje said. "Sortistra. The fortress beneath the sands." She sighed deeply, full of relief.

Davin gazed up, only seeing a foggy glow of a hazy sun beyond the storm. "None too soon, either. We're losing daylight."

The camels trudged through the blinding sandstorm; a maelstrom of hard sand that bit like beestings, and winds that blew like invisible sea waves.

They pressed on further and further, and Soren caught glimpses of the lead of the caravan of Scarletta, the Dune Matron. The red feathers at her shoulders whipped hard in the storm, but he respected she was the one to lead her people through the madness.

The glimpses of the Dune Matron caused Soren to think again of their lack of Syncrons, and the fate of the one Syncron who casts themself to their peril at the news of open war. She'd told Soren that the Syncron's name was Sive, and that they chose an early end instead of entering into war with the king's Synths. Soren thought it was cowardly. For all the pain and loss he'd felt in his years, and at times even prayed for the silence and relief of the afterlife —Soren was a soldier. Death in battle was the only way to go, he knew, or the long wait for death's embrace from a long-lived life.

They approached Sortistra, and the men and women of the Calica caravan shouted, leading all toward the fortress of white.

Sortistra was round and not as tall as one might think of a desert fortress. Fifteen-foot walls with short towers along the outer walls. The towers stood only another fifteen feet, with many arrow slits and the battlements between had pyramidal stones like teeth rising up from the bleak desert. The fortress would be underground—an ancient structure created long ago, hiding the city from the desert.

Sortistra's gate was a great gate of iron painted white, with streaks of brown and tan, making the latticed iron camouflage into the desert immaculately. Only the white stone of the fortress shone like a huge pearl half-pressed into the earth from Shirava.

The soldiers of Calica rushed to open the wide gate, letting sand cascade down its layers of iron. Sable poked her head out from under the blanket on Davin's lap and meowed, leaping down from the camel and running inside with her tail cocked up like a question mark. The Calica soldiers fumbled backward as the two silver bears strode into the gate, both barely fitting under the raised gate, their massive bodies entering the darkness beyond.

Torches sparked within, their glow lighting the stone interior of the fortress. Soren, Blaje, and Davin rode in as soldiers took the reins of their camels. The three dropped down, a full inch of sand falling to the ground from Soren's tunic as he landed.

He looked behind them and out the huge gateway. The storm raged on fiercely.

"Shirava is either trying to keep us from leaving the

desert," Davin said, brushing the sand from his beard, "or she's helping to cover our tracks."

"I don't believe she does either. She simply is." Blaje pulled down her hood, shaking her dreads, and shaking her arms as the ringed jewelry on them clattered.

A Calica soldier approached from the far end of the vast room filled with camels and the dozens of men and women. The silver bears inspected the outer walls of the room, sniffing and growling. Sable walked delicately beneath them. Torches sparked all around, preparing for the night within the dark stone fortress. "Dune Matron Scarletta wishes to speak with you in one hour's time. Two floors down in a mess hall on the south wing."

Soren nodded, and the soldier scampered back off toward the head of the caravan and their leader.

"Have ya been in this place before?" Davin asked. "I'd love to get this blasted sand off me before getting some shuteye, hopefully in something softer than a bed of scratchy hay, poking into my sides all night."

"Once, I believe." She pulled her long hair back behind her, wrapping and tying it with a strand of twine. "When I was a young girl. My family brought me here with the Calica. I don't remember it well. But I remember below. Being in the dark. No moon, no sun, and no sound."

A friendly soldier to their side, who seemed curiously interested in their conversation, said, "There's wash basins one floor down, and four floors down. I suggest the one four floors down —gets less busy."

"Thank you," Soren said, looking at his friends. "Shall we? C'mon, Sable."

The cat stopped and looked over her shoulder at him. Her wide forest-green eyes sparkled before she ran after him. Soren, Davin, Blaje, and the black cat took a torch and headed down a stone stairwell, walking down into the gloom. Soren had a hand gripping Firelight. Never could be too cautious…

They went the four floors down, only peeking into the dark floors, but skipping each until they reached the fourth. The torchlight illuminated a wooden door to their right with a placard with a drawing of three drops of water, and they entered.

Davin and Soren quickly went to pumping water from the well, eventually catching, and cool water poured into the wooden basins. The water was cold.

Each of them undressed. Davin got into the cold water immediately, letting out a deep sigh and lathering his dusty blond hair and brown beard with soap.

Blaje hung her clothes and removed the rings from her forearms. Davin averted his gaze, but Soren could feel his wandering glances upon him.

Soren removed his tunic, leather armor beneath, and felt the cool air hit his bare chest. Blaje glanced his way. She was fully naked, staring straight into Soren's eyes. Her arm covered her breasts as she lifted her long legs into the water basin. Soren was enamored. The curves of her body and the kindness in her fixed gaze reminded him of the kiss they shared before their battle at Golbizarath.

He was torn by his feelings. It seemed every time he felt a connection to a woman, it always ended in disaster. In recent years, Alicen was the most gut-wrenching of all. Betraying him, and everyone in Erhil, to the king and his Synths.

But this felt different. Soren *trusted* Blaje.

Really trusted her.

He felt a burning desire to explore that trust, and the way she made him feel when she was near. The way his stomach tightened around her. The intoxicating smell of the floral oils in her hair, and the deep pull of her wise, powerful eyes, and the warm feeling he got in his chest from a rare smile cast his way.

She got into the water up to her neck, letting out a deep sigh and a shiver.

Soren removed his boots and pants and got into the basin beside her. The cold water caused the air in his lungs to escape, and an icy shiver went all the way up from his toes to the back of his neck. He grabbed the soap and lathered his hair quickly.

The cold water turned from icy and biting to soothing; calming his shivering body and rejuvenating his weary muscles and bones.

"What do you think?" Blaje asked, with her head back over the basin's wooden rim.

"About what?" Soren's head was back as well, but he cocked his head to look at her, and Davin beyond her.

"Everything…"

"I feel…" he began, trying to put his jumbled thoughts into clear words. "This is another calm before the storm. I'm grateful your people found us and brought us here. But we need to prepare for the upcoming war. We are greatly underpowered now that Seph and Kaile are gone." A hard pit in his stomach formed at the mention of her name. Like a sledgehammer barreling into his stomach. "That's a betrayal I don't know if I'll ever be able to get over, let alone forgive."

"Forgive?" Davin's voice echoed in the dark hall, lit by only the single burning, flickering torch. "Ain't no fucking forgiveness. No way. I'll squeeze that twerp's head from his neck like popping an infected pimple."

"That's quite the visual," Soren said with a brief laugh. Blaje smirked, but didn't respond.

"If I ever see that boy, or Alcarond again, ain't no way I'm letting them speak a sound. My ax will give them a new hole in their head before they get the chance."

Soren pulled his head under the water, feeling the crisp water flood all over his face. He ran his fingers through his soapy hair, then broke the water's edge, letting out a deep moan from his chest.

"I don't know what I'll do if I see Kaile again," Soren said, knowing his words were true. "I don't know."

"What do you mean, you don't know?" Davin said in a deep, resentful tone, glaring hard at Soren. "He took Seph. He played us for fools, and now we're stuck miles and miles away from her."

"I feel that something else is at play here." Soren rubbed his cheeks, scratched his chin, and thought hard. "This war is getting more and more complicated. The dragon, Landran alive—sending me the dagger—Kaile betraying us out of nowhere and choosing his master after all the terrible things he's done."

"Remember, Soren," Blaje said softly, "Kaile is a student of the Ellydian and has lived for years in the capital. He's being trained to become the future archmage. The boy who set the sea ablaze... he has an ambition that few would know. He's dangerous, and now... he's our enemy..."

"I agree," Soren said. "He's chosen his path."

But what Soren didn't say was... he knew the feeling of not being in control. He knew the feeling of losing yourself and making mistakes in times of chaos. The curse that plagued Soren from Zertaan's magic, and the Knight Wolf's blade that cut the scars into his face... the world had grown complicated. There was no black and white, only shades of gray.

"So..." Davin groaned, scratching soap into his beard with his short, muscly fingers. "Where do we go from here?"

"Dune Matron Scarletta will share with us her knowledge," Blaje lifted a long leg from the dark water, lathering it with soap. "She knows more about the desert than any, even more than Lady Sargonenth. She will help guide us on a path. We walk into the unknown now. We have enemies in every corner of the world now. The bears may become great allies, but they will make us anything but invisible as we make our way closer to the capital."

"Soren... you?" Davin nodded in agreement with Blaje.

"We cannot take the capital without a great army, and a siege that may last for weeks." Soren folded his arms at the thought. "The capital has many Synths capable of casting all manner of horrific spells upon those that attempt to take the gates to the great city. Celestra has never fallen to an army. Silvergale Lake and the Whitestone Mountains help to protect the city. But..."

The last word filled the air in the long room, causing a curiosity to linger.

"But...?" Blaje squinted.

"I could get in. I could sack the city from within. Alone."

Davin had to bite his lip to not shout in anger, and Blaje sighed deeply, pinching the top of her nose.

"Listen to me carefully, Soren..." she finally said, reaching over and grabbing him by the hand as cold water splattered to the floor from her elbow. "You need to let those thoughts go. We'll win this war, but we've got to be thoughtful, resourceful, meticulous, and trust each other. You can't win by yourself. You've got to let go of the vagabond that took over when you lost your family. You aren't roaming Aladran from city to city aimlessly anymore. You have purpose, you have courage, you have a destiny to fulfill."

"You may not understand," Soren squeezed her hand gently, appreciating the touch. "With the Twilight Veil and Firelight. I could get in and kill enough to weaken them, and you could lead the army after taking the city when I cut down their legion of Synths from the inside."

"So, what? You die killing half their Synths?" Blaje shot back. "You die a martyr, and you leave us with the other half an army of Synths, the Drakoons, and the remaining king's army? Thanks, but no thanks. And you're leaving out one very important detail… the unkillable, The Knight Wolf."

Soren slid his hand back into the basin, and Blaje withdrew hers.

The lock Soren had no key for. The puzzle that had no solution. His curse was too great. The spell was too strong, carved deep into his soul. He remembered William Wolf killing his friend Bael before his eyes, helpless to save him. Soren gritted his teeth and all the torment the Wolf had caused him.

"Get that thought out of your head," Davin said in a deep voice, resting his head back. "We're in this together. Hopefully Scarletta can give us some information that will guide us. We cannot hope to sack the city on our own. We need to be conniving, and we're going to need a hell of a lot of luck."

Chapter Eleven

✥

After they were washed up, and each of them wore fresh linens while servants washed their armor, a Calica soldier led them to the room above, and they awaited the Dune Matron. Each of them sat in chairs before a great chair of dark-stained wood with rich grains. Smaller chairs spread out on both its sides like wings spread wide.

Soren tried to sit up straight, but slumped down, his eyelids pulling down as if weighted by hooks and iron bars. He couldn't remember the last time he'd slept. He felt as if life was one long, waking dream.

But the sudden scuffle of boots in the room stirred him awake. His eyes shot open, and he saw both Davin and Blaje were watching him. Blaje stood, and the other two did the same. Sable walked around Soren's bare legs, purring loudly.

The Dune Matron entered from a side door. The wide room was lit with four torches—two framing each of the room's two doors. A dozen candles flickered on the long table that separated Soren and his friends from the great chair on its other side. The room glowed with a soft amber radiance.

The tall woman with ebony skin wore none of the elaborate outfit she wore back out in the desert. No headdress of feathers, and no long, sharp red feathers at her shoulders. Even the golden bracelets that decorated her arms were gone. Her long black dreads were pulled back and wrapped in a huge bun behind her. She wore an elegant gown of pearly ivory with a black floral pattern sewn on its chest and sides. Her oak eyes looked devoid of light, as if the candlelight could reach their depths.

She sat, with a couple of attendants sitting in the chairs beside her. Both had tablets, quill and ink laid on the table before them. They dipped the tips of the quills immediately and began scribing instantly.

"Well, here we are," Dune Matron Scarletta said, her head completely still as she gazed at Soren.

"Here we are..." Soren said, sitting up straight, forcing himself awake.

"What is your plan?" Scarletta folded one long, slender leg over the other, letting the soft fabric glide down both sides elegantly.

"Straight to the important question," Davin said. "And a good one at that. Soren?"

All eyes in the room fell upon him.

"You want me to lead your armies," Soren said as an attendant from behind placed glasses on the table before them and poured a deep red wine into each. Blaje and Davin both sipped, while Soren thought about his next words carefully.

I want to lead their armies. I want to kill King Amón. But I also want to go out on my own. I need to decide, and now...

"But..." he said, causing a stir in the room. "We also need to rid this world of the Demons of Dusk. We fight a war on two fronts, and the war with the king, we must fight from the shadows... for now..."

"Continue," the Dune Matron pressed.

"We cannot take Celestra. We don't have the forces, and

are completely overpowered by the Synths in the capital. The Silver Sparrows still fight in secret, and we have no idea of the number of Syncrons in their ranks. Zatan is openly at war with Lynthyn and the king, but that is the only kingdom, as far as I'm aware. The king will strike here—and hard."

"Let him," the Dune Mother grumbled while the two scribes wrote swiftly, their quills scratching the papers like fingernails on sheets.

Blaje took a deep gulp of wine and folded her arms in pride. Davin nearly leaped out of his chair at her words.

"To win in open war against the king, we would need to scatter his forces, take them out slowly. It would take years, and we would need to have a vast network of spies." Soren thought, scratching his chin as he drank the cool wine, warming his chest. "Or... I go in and kill the king, cutting the head from the serpent."

"Even you couldn't reach him," Scarletta said, leaning forward. "Your reputation proves very true, Soren Stormrose; fearless, cunning, and a loner. You are not a rogue in this war, you are meant to be a knight. Remember who you were before your loved ones were slain and your face scarred. There will be battles fought in the shadow, but his war is coming to light. More kingdoms will join us. This will be the war to end all wars. We win, or our world falls deeper into ruin and chaos."

Davin set his glass down hard on the table. "It's only a matter of time before the Shades and Black Fog begin attacking the cities. And there's nothing to stop 'em."

"The dragon Sarrannax can defeat them," the Dune Matron said. "But it is a dragon; wild, divine in its might, and unpredictable."

"Which raises an important question." Blaje cracked her knuckles. "How did Sarrannax come to the desert the moment we needed it, and scorched the sands, killing all those Shades that were about to overrun us, turning us into them? Either

Shirava truly is watching over us, or the dragon knows something we don't."

"I fear the great old dragon of Eldra will fight its own battles," Scarletta said, unfolding her legs, and switching them so the other was on top. "We cannot count on the dragon's aid, as well as we cannot forget its might. It will do what a dragon does."

"A dragon..." Davin muttered, rubbing his temples. "A dragon in Aladran..." He laughed to himself.

"So, what will you do?" The Dune Matron asked with her chin up.

"Why don't you tell me what you would have me do?" Soren asked. "There's no one right answer, and you have many thoughts on this issue, I'm certain."

Dune Matron Scarletta moved to speak, but a side door suddenly burst open, causing all in the room to stir. Some soldiers nearly drew their swords all the way from their scabbards. But in rushed another attendant, shuffling quickly across the hall. She stopped at the Dune Matron, apologized for interrupting, but held out something small in her hands. The Dune Matron lifted an eyebrow, gazing with her dark eyes down at the attendant's open hands. She reached in and plucked out a tiny scroll.

"A raven," Blaje muttered.

Soren scooted up on his seat, watching intently as the Dune Matron unrolled the scroll and read it in the candlelight. She read for a few minutes, and then let it coil back up, springing up into her hand before resting both hands delicately on her lap.

"What is it?" Soren asked, scratching his thighs.

"It just arrived by raven. It's from Lady Drake of Skylark."

Lady Drake? How could she know we're here? And send a raven so quickly to this exact spot. Well, she is the leader of the Silver Sparrows, so she's got to have some powerful secrets...

"What's it say?" Davin blurted.

"Lady Drake gives her condolences for the passing of the old, great archmage. She and he were friends for decades, and she is grieving his loss."

Soren wanted to ask how she could know of Mihelik's passing, and so quickly after his death. But he knew the network of spies belonging to all sides was vast in Aladran.

"Will you read it in its entirety?" Soren asked softly, showing as much respect as he could command. "We are all on the same side of this war, after all."

The Dune Matron glanced around the room, deep in thought, before pulling the scroll back out, holding it taut, and read.

"Great Dune Matron Scarletta Empressal, may this raven find you well and true. In light of recent events in your lands of Zatan, and the loss of great allies, I reach out not only to share insights into tidings in the rest of the world, but to express my condolences for the passing of Archmage Mihelik Starshadow. He will not only be missed by this woman, but by all of Aladran. He will not be forgotten, and when this war is behind us, I'll make sure he's remembered for who he truly was—the greatest of our age. Now, with the unfortunate taking of Persephone Whistlewillow and Kaile Thorne re-aligning with the king and his master Alcarond, we must hasten in our fight. The Silver Sparrows grow in their ranks. More Syncrons join our cause with each passing week, and with all of Soren's advancements showing cracks and vulnerabilities in not only the crown, but the Demons of Dusk, hope shines once again over Aladran."

Dune Matron Scarletta took a deep breath and sighed, but continued reading.

"However, King Amón has sent his men south. Soldiers now occupy Grayhaven in the aftermath of Edward Glasse's slaying, or rather failed attempt at the Black Sacrament. His men have commandeered ships, and sent them off for the lands of Garrehad, and for Vellice."

"Vellice?" Soren shouted. "He's going after more Vellice steel."

Davin grunted. "They won't make it across the Sapphire Sea and back. Even with those ships."

"The waters are treacherous," Scarletta said with a slight twitch in her eye. "But they are not impassable. They may bring more weapons from Vellice for the war against the Demons of Dusk." A wry smile lit her lips with a thought Soren instantly knew he could read.

She wants to steal the weapons once they get here… Brilliant.

"They won't get many," Davin said. "Weapons of Vellice are far rarer than diamonds, and only the masters can craft such perfect blades. They won't part with whatever they have easily."

"Continue reading, please," Soren urged.

She cleared her throat and continued, "Soldiers have come to Skylark as well. Our alliance remains secret, but I know not for how much longer. The arrival of the dragon Sarrannax has stirred great worry in the king and Archpriest Solemn Roane VII, who hails from Eldra, and knows the wrath of dragons well. This may cause the king's grasp of his kingdoms to tighten. With Zatan in open rebellion against the crown, he will send forces against you, and against Soren, Davin Mosser and Blaje Severaas. His hatred grows, and I fear his devastating fire will spread. But while all may seem bleak, my spy within the capital sends good tidings too. There is disarray and fracturing of the echelon of power within Celestra. Kaile, returning into their fold, has created factions. Seph, however, in Re-Enlightment, I fail to find optimism in. She will either turn to the king's will, or she will fall into a terrible demise…"

The Dune Matron paused, and all gazes in the room fell upon Soren.

He closed his eyes and took a deep, deep breath.

Calm your rage. It does nothing for you here. Save it. Bury it. Use it when you need it most. Focus on her. You'll unleash that rage when the time comes. Hold on Seph... I'm coming...

Scarletta read on. "I do not know the way forward. I cannot see past these tidings that cast a great fog over our land and our path. Soren must do what he deems best and truest. But tell Soren this—it was something my mentor told me when I was young and full of youthful determination—be true to yourself, and keep those you trust close—they will not only aid you, but help guide you. None of us can truly enact change alone. Let the wings of justice carry you forward through harsh winds, and when the storm's chaos makes all feel lost, fight on. Fight with everything you have. For in the end, our fight, and our friends, is truly all we have in this world. Soren will lead us to victory, I know it. I believe it. I only wish he will believe it himself. The past is gone. All losses are gifts, whether or not we realize it. All that matters is now. All that matters is the war ahead, and a brighter future for tomorrow."

Soren steepled his fingers and gazed down at his lap. He knew she was right. However haunting his past and his failures were, there was hope. As long as Seph drew breath, there was still time...

"There's one last thing here," Scarletta said. "As for the passing of Mihelik Starshadow. He left no heirs. In his will, he proclaimed..." The Dune Matron sighed, itching her cheek. "He left all his worldly possessions to whom he deemed the future of the power of the Ellydian—Persephone Whistlewillow, and Kaile Thorne."

"Kaile?" Davin shouted, rising to his feet. "No way he's getting anything! Mihelik's dead because of him!"

"A most unfortunate circumstance," the Dune Matron said, closing the scroll and letting it roll back up into her fingers. She handed it back to the attendant, who quickly took it and held it up to the flames of a candle. It quickly scorched and fully caught aflame. She dropped it into the candelabra as Soren watched the parchment burn to ash. It made him think of the Scriptures of the Ancients, and Mihelik watching them burn—all the knowledge of the old world burned away—because of the mention of an old, dark magic he wanted to hide for eternity.

"In the morning you will leave this place," Scarletta said. "There's a hidden tunnel that leads to Lynthyn. It's been sealed for decades, and will hide your progress toward the capital, if that is your path forward."

"Yes," Soren said. "Celestra is our destination. But I must find my old master, Landran Dranne, as well. There are questions I need answers to."

"Landran Dranne... alive?" Scarletta asked with both eyebrows raised. "After all these years? The legend is still alive? Yes. We need to make contact with him. He could be a significant force in this war. His prowess with a sword is world renowned. His swordplay rivals yours, the king's, and the Knight Wolf's. I will send word to all corners of Aladran in search of him."

"Don't," Soren interjected. "I think I know where he may be, actually."

"You do?" Davin and Blaje both said at the same exact moment.

"There's only one place I can picture him hiding out all these years, as well as he did. And I plan to make way for there first... Arkakus."

Chapter Twelve

"How could you know that?" Blaje asked Soren, with her brow furrowed. Half-annoyed he'd been keeping the information from him. "How could you know where Landran is? And why didn't you tell us before?"

"It occurred to me just now, while thinking about traveling to Lynthyn," he said. "Landran Dranne is world famous, and his face is easily recognizable from his portrait in so many books about combat. There aren't many corners he could go to without word spreading. For if he was found by one, and word spread, then many would come wishing to be his pupils. The king would surely seek to enlist him in his service, should he find Landran is alive after all these years. He may even enslave him for insight into me."

"Arkakus, then?" Blaje muttered, playing with the tip of a long dreadlock that lay over her chest. "That would be an excellent place to hide if one wished to not be found."

"While your Dune Matron read about the king sending ships for Garrehad for more Vellice-crafted weapons, it made me think of something Landran once told me." All in the room listened, for even the soldiers of the Calica surely revered Landran's legacy. After all, Soren was one of the best swordsmen in all over Aladran, even defeating a Black Fog with just a dagger and his wits. "He said his goal in life was to share the knowledge his master taught him, and then spend his later years away from everyone. I was only a teenager when he talked about it. He said he'd have no wife and sire no children. He told me he'd go to the end of the world—where he could live in peace—but where the hunt was good, and fire grew from the earth."

"Sound like Arkakus all right," Davin said, sipping the dark wine. "Desolate, grim, and with rumbling, angry volcanoes at its heart."

The Dune Martron leaned forward in her chair. "Do you know where your old master would be, exactly? Arkakus may be a bleak kingdom, but it is the largest of all, and difficult to traverse."

"I don't." Soren took his glass from the table and swirled the wine within. "I'd say head for Mount Carraxion. He's a man of extremes. I'd think he'd pick the roughest terrain to inhabit and nest."

"That will take us further away from Celestra." Blaje crossed her legs and leaned back in her chair, folding her arms.

"I know..." Soren said, doubting his own plan.

Davin growled from deep in his throat. "We'd be fools to attack Celestra head-on without Syncrons. This may buy us, Dune Matron Scarletta, and Lady Drake time to gather more."

"But Seph..." Soren muttered to himself.

"She's tough." Blaje placed her hand on Soren's thigh. "I've seen it in her. I don't believe the king will kill her. He knows he needs her. She's a Whistlewillow, of the greatest lineage of Syncrons in our world. King Amón may have many lower Synths under his control, but there's only one of her, and only one of Kaile. She'll survive until we reach her. My heart says so."

"I hope you're right." Soren pinched the top of his nose, gazing down at the ground beneath the table. "I can't lose her. It's my fault she left Guillead in the first place."

"She left on her own," Davin said. "She left of her own choosing. We all chose this fight, and who knows if we're gonna make it out alive after all this. She chose her destiny, like we all did. The time will come to save her. But we need Syncrons, Soren. You can't sneak into the capital city and fight every last person within. Even with the Twilight Veil and Firelight, you'd fall, and they take those weapons and use them against us. We find Landran and find out what his plans were. He might have ideas about how to win this war. I heard of Landran Dranne even all the way in Mythren. We could use another strong swordsman in this war. I say we head for Arkakus, but we'll need horses."

"Horses I will give you," the Dune Matron said. "As well as other gifts to aid in your quests."

Soren, Blaje, and Davin didn't respond, but each was eager to hear about what Scarletta Empressal was alluding to.

"You have your magical stones of disguise," she said with an all-knowing, clever tone in her voice. "A rare gift of Mythren, which many would love to get their hands on in this continent. You carry the ancient relic, the Twilight Veil, for hunting in the shadow, and you, Soren, carry what you named Firelight, the most powerful dagger in our world. But where you go, into the darkness of the old secret tunnel that leads to Lynthyn, you could use the gift of sight where only darkness dwells…"

The Dune Matron nodded to the corner of the room, behind Soren. Soren turned and looked over his shoulder to see a female soldier reach behind her, grabbing something tucked behind her belt. The soldier approached Soren, pulling something draped in silk from her back to her front. She stood before Soren, and then knelt with her head bowed and the silken item held up for him.

"Soren Stormrose of Tourmielle," the Dune Matron hailed in a firm voice that echoed off the walls of the underground room. "I gift to you a great treasure of the Calica Clan. It's something that has been in our employ for thousands of years. A rare artifact of the old world, before the Great Divine Flood."

The soldier unwrapped the silk from the top of the item, as Soren hovered over it, eagerly watching the soldier delicately reveal the artifact. After the last corner of silk was removed and flopped down to the sides of the soldier's hand, Soren gazed hard in amazement at what he saw.

"I give to you, Soren, the Nocturn Infier Piedran Coraza. It's old Sarin language for… Shadowflame Heartstone."

Within the silk's center, Soren inspected the Shadowflame Heartstone.

Deep black like a moonless night, encased in a silvery lattice of fine metal Soren didn't recognize, but with a slight glimmer within of sparkling stars, the Shadowflame Heartstone seemed as rare a treasure as a wish-gifting pixie, or a magical, fabled unicorn.

Soren lifted the jewel. It was warm to the touch, as a human heart would be, and a chain of gold fell from its crest. As the rough skin of his fingers touched the jewel, a quarter the size of his fist, the specks of white like stars within, stirred. They swirled like a squall, flowed like a divine stream, and glowed like fireflies.

He took the necklace and put it over his head, letting the deep black stone dangle on his chest. It felt as if it weighed nothing, but its warmth soothed his chest, brushing away all weariness like dead leaves blown clean off the spring ground.

"May it lead you to find your path in absolute darkness." Scarletta bowed her head to him.

"This is a high honor, Soren," Blaje said in awe. "I've seen the Shadowflame Heartstone but once, and it was locked away deep underground in our safest treasure house. It's one of a kind, shrouded in mystery, but undeniable in its ability."

"Thank you, Dune Matron." Soren bowed. "You honor me, and I will use it to fight this war from the shadows. King Amón and his army will feel the vengeance of Firelight."

"Where you go, Soren Stormrose," the Dune Matron said in a grave tone. "Danger will surely follow. Trust your instincts, and fight. Fight hard. For this war will be long and painful, with many missteps along the way. Use the Heartstone to guide you, when even light has abandoned you."

"We're going underground," Davin said, stroking his beard. "Dwarves are not known for any fear in the safety of caverns and caves, but here… in Aladran… the Demons of Dusk lurk. We'll need to be cautious, and quiet, if we go through that old tunnel of yours."

"There are no Black Fog or Shades in the tunnel," the Dune Matron said with a wave of her hand, attempting to brush his worry aside. "The entirety of the tunnel is lined with thick stone walls and has remained sealed since the arrival of the Demons of Dusk eighty-five years ago, when the first Black Fog was seen lurking on the plains under a moonless night."

"Dune Matron…" Something occurred to Soren he hadn't told her. Something important, and the scribes looked up from their scribbling, dipping their quills into fresh ink. One licked their lips. "There's something I've forgotten to tell you… something of immense importance… The Shades… they speak."

Gasps filled the room.

"I know not how much… but I heard one utter the word 'no.' I'm certain of it. The Shades were men once. I believe the Black Fog transform them into night creatures. They are more than monsters that lurk at night and kill. They turn men's hearts black and turn their bodies and minds into pure, evil killers and devourers. If they win, there will be nothing left in this world except… them…"

The Dune Matron sat back in her chair, rubbing her chin. "This is indeed troubling." She glanced at Blaje, who nodded quickly back.

"It is true," Blaje said. "The Shades are coming for all of us, to turn us…"

"We're going to need more Vellice steel," the queen muttered, leaning forward so her elbows rested on her thighs, unregal, and showing the troubling thoughts that rolled through the leader of the Calica's mind.

"I believe the archmage knows this now," Soren said, fiddling with the Shadowflame Heartstone around his neck, letting the dark stone lay on his chest. He cracked his knuckles. "Kaile has surely shared with his master this tiding. Alcarond is obsessed with the Demons of Dusk, and the king and the archpriest will certainly know this."

"We're all on the same side against 'em," Davin said with a snort. "Fighting two fuckin' wars at once. What have ya gotten us into Soren?" Davin sent a sly wink at Soren, while putting his huge hand on the hilt of his ax, nudging it playfully.

"To win this war," Soren said, twirling the Heartstone hanging from his neck. "We're going to have to win on both fronts. Only then can we rest and give this world to someone worthy to guide it toward peace."

The Dune Matron Scarletta glared up at the ceiling, scratching her neck. "It has been many years since peace was a luxury shared in Aladran. But we can bring it back. The dragon Sarrannax may swing the scales back in our favor, or at least lessen the overwhelming odds."

"Your gift may prove to swing the scales even more," Blaje said, eyeing the stone Soren spun in his fingers.

"Soren," the Dune Matron said. "You wield the Vellice dagger Firelight, given to you by your master, Landran Dranne. You carry the Twilight Veil, crafted by the Sundar of the old world. And now you carry the Shadowflame Heartstone, one of our people's greatest treasures. With these weapons, you will become the deadliest killer in all the world. The shadow and darkness is your new home. Let it lend great strength to your already hardened hand. The coming war will send everything the king and the Demons of Dusk have at you. You scarred the king's face, and you killed Shades. The world is coming for you, and you need to be ready."

"I will be," Soren said, releasing the Heartstone as it fell back to his chest. A fresh vigor filled him. He knew he spoke true. He was ready. He was ready to take on the world. He knew how to kill the Demons of Dusk, and he knew the king wasn't immortal now. "Everything dies."

The Dune Matron nodded in approval. "Everything dies…"

Chapter Thirteen

❧✦❧

Celestra, Lynthyn

THE COLD STEEL chains clacked together, sending a metallic echo throughout the dark room of the Abiron. Torchlight flickered from two torches that rested on both sides of the one door to the room where no Ellydian could be conjured. Candles burned dimly on the tabletop in the far corner of the room.

Seph, dazed and overwhelmed with pain, gazed at the foggy shadow that loomed large on the wall behind her. The shadow was of herself, hanging from tightly tied chains that suspended her. Her body swayed from the chains that hung from the ceiling.

Her knees and elbows burned like hot iron spikes prodded into the bones there. The chains around her wrists and ankles slowed the blood flow to her hands and feet, causing them to throb excruciatingly. A thin chain wrapped around her neck,

THE DARK SYNTHS

the other end of which was held by the nude tattooed woman who stood before her.

Zertaan's breath reeked of hard liquor and smoke. The Synth's blood-red eyes were glazed over with a wet sheen, while she giggled to herself as she tugged the chain. It squeezed Seph's throat as she hung helplessly.

A drop of Seph's blood ran down from her brow to her chin, falling to the cold stone floor, and plopping to a pool of wet blood. Seph gasped from the choke chain as Zertaan sneered with sharp-looking yellow teeth. The Synth's golden hair fell down both sides of her face—frazzled and frayed—as she grinned widely. Her woozy gaze was angled down at the pool of blood.

Seph had lost track of how long ago Zertaan had hung her from the chains and began guzzling from the green bottle on the back table. It had been hours, but Seph knew not how many. Seph's head throbbed and ached like cold needles rattling around in her brain. She longed for, prayed for, the dark Synth's game to end, so that she could be freed of the binding, squeezing chains. The pain was so crippling, Seph knew she might succumb to unconsciousness at any moment. The human body and mind could only withstand so much...

"Isn't this fun?" Zertaan slurred, foggy eyed. "Getting to know each other after all this time?"

Seph didn't respond. She feared speaking might make the pain in her head even worse, which was hard to imagine.

Zertaan lunged forward, pulling herself toward Seph with a tug of the neck chain. Staggering before Seph, attempting to glare angrily at her, Zertaan seemed like the most terrifying thing in all of Aladran. Seph wished to be stuck before a pack of Shades, wished to be anywhere else in the world, rather than stuck in the bowels of the capital city with the monstrous Synth.

"Pain purges treasonous thoughts," Zertaan said, stroking

Seph's chin with her sharp fingernails. The overwhelming stench of the amber booze on her breath made Seph's stomach lurch into her throat. "You know what… let's play a game…"

The idea made Seph want to scream. She wanted to scream Soren's name. She wanted to scream so loudly that hopefully someone in the kingdom would come down to save her, to rescue her, to give her some relief from the unrelenting torment and pain.

"I have a fabulous idea." Zertaan released the neck chain and spun, nearly falling to the floor. A wicked cackle left her lips. The tattoos on her pale nude body seemed to come to life through Seph's wet eyes. The hundreds of lines of text in a mysterious language appeared to move along her skin. "I think it's an idea the king would approve of greatly!" Zertaan grabbed a wooden stool from a dark corner. She stumbled over and threw it onto its side beneath Seph.

Seph struggled to free herself from her prison. With her arms and legs tied behind her, the struggle only made the pain surge hard through her body, sending ripples of unrelenting anguish in her already burning limbs and joints. A growl rumbled through her clenched teeth.

"Good," Zertaan hissed in an alarmingly sober tone and with a deathly gaze unwavering upon Seph. "I like that."

Zertaan grabbed a small, corked bottle from the cluttered table, strewn with instruments to cause great bodily harm. She uncorked it, and Seph's nostrils smelled a faint trace of what smelled like lantern fuel. Zertaan upturned the bottle onto the chair, emptying its alcohol-smelling contents onto the chair and mixed into the cool blood that puddled on the floor.

"No," Seph muttered, wide-eyed, pausing in her fight to break free of her bonds, and absolutely terrified.

"Nothing like fire to purify a tainted soul!" Zertaan turned and grabbed a candle from the table, holding its delicate flame between the two of them, both gazing at the dancing flame. Zertaan watched it with an acute fascination, and Seph with an overwhelming fear.

"I dedicate this dance to the powerful, magnificent, and all-knowing King Malera Amón! May his rule last a thousand years, and may he quash all that rebel against his divine right! May the flames purge you of your evil and wickedness!"

The Synth cast the candle onto the toppled stool. Instantly it engulfed in flames and Seph felt the heat. The flames licked at her shins, and she felt the warmth burn onto her inner thighs and the heat began roaring up her stomach. Seph finally screamed, a gut-wrenching, twisted, throat-cracking scream. She thought it must have reached the city streets above. She fought to break free of the chains as beads of sweat poured down her brow, dribbling off her eyebrows and lashes.

The flames rose.

They tempted igniting her clothes, but Seph fought, sending her knees flailing. The heat was unbearable on her kneecaps and shins, and the metal chains on her bare skin grew in terrible temperature.

"Stop! Stop! Please stop!" Seph cried. She tried to fight the words from coming from her lips, but the pain was unbearable, and she thought she might die. She thought she wouldn't beg ever, wouldn't grovel for mercy, but one look in the Synth's wicked glare showed there was no mercy to give in those serpentine, devilish red eyes of the albino from Arkakus.

"Do you repent?" Zertaan stared into Seph's eyes as the flames grew from the ground beneath Seph. "Do you repent your wicked ways?"

Seph choked down any words that would give Zertaan any more pleasure.

"Do you repent? Daughter of the fallen Whistlewillows, Calvin and Violetta? Do you repent, so that not only your soul may be saved, but theirs' that surely burn down in the Nine Hells?"

Seph fought the raging flames beneath her, clenching her teeth and trying to think of anything that would abate the pain.

Zertaan jerked the neck chain forward, pulling Seph toward her with an incredible strength from the Synth's hand. "Repent, you little bitch! Repent or your miserable parents' souls will burn forever from the shame you bring them!"

Seph unclenched her teeth, and Zertaan grinned, eagerly waiting for the words.

Spit flew from Seph's lips into Zertaan's eye. A thick ball of mucus that sent Zertaan reeling back in disgust. She released the chain and Seph went swinging helplessly from the ceiling, giving her a brief respite from the immense heat.

"You little…" Zertaan grabbed her shirt from the chair beside her and wiped the spit from her eye. "You know what? I like this. I like this side of you. You're going to force this Re-Enlightment to go on and on. I'm going to lavish every second, every minute, every day and week that this takes, until there's nothing left of you but a limbless body and head with no eyes or tongue. I'm going to cut you to pieces until all that's left of you is an empty, broken, sad shell of a once powerful Syncron with so much potential."

Seph didn't say a word, but her swinging halted, and she once again was forced to fight off the flames that threatened to catch her clothing, and her…

"That's enough for now," came a voice from the crack in the door.

They were both so engulfed in the moment, both were shocked by the man entering the room. The door to the Abiron opened outward with a squeal of the old metal hinges, and a man in lavish blue robes strode in.

"Archmage Alcarond," Zertaan said, clearing her voice and attempting to sober herself.

Alcarond kicked the stool beneath Seph into the wall behind her, exploding into a ball of searing flames. "Get her down."

Zertaan glowered, but went over to her clothing on the chair, and fumbled for the keys within her pockets. She put a shirt over herself before going over and unlocking the chains one by one. Seph was so relieved, and overwhelmed by exhaustion and pain, she almost thanked Zertaan instinctually.

Alcarond helped catch Seph and helped her to the chair she was normally tied to. Seph flopped into the chair, and Zertaan bound her wrists and ankles to it with rope. Seph's skin was sensitive from the heat of the chains, and the tight rope irritated it further. But that pain she could handle. Seph was at the brink of passing out, but fought to stay awake, mostly curious why the archmage had made Zertaan stop her game, and Seph had her own questions for him…

"You're not to kill her," Alcarond said, a mean glare lighting his face, gleaming in torchlight. "Is that understood? This is Re-Enlightenment, not a death sentence."

Zertaan nodded before turning her back to the archmage, but Seph caught the frown of disgust on her face as she spun.

The archmage towered over Seph as she slumped in her chair, hanging on the edge of hallucinations. She felt his power, his raw power over the Ellydian as he loomed over her, not speaking. Her chin fell to her chest, but she felt strong, calloused fingers touching the tip of her chin, lifting it up. Before her was Alcarond's face, inches from hers.

He knelt, staring into her deeply. His dim gray eyes were like ancient stones, clear as day, while the rest of him fogged in Seph's delirious haze. The pain coursed through her body like lava gushing in her veins, nearly erupting them as her heart pounded in her chest.

Looking at the archmage, and his angular, strong face with flowing black hair with streaks of silver, his face shifted. Its dark shades lightened, the silver streaks of hair faded to black, and three scars cut down his eye.

"S—Soren..." Seph muttered. "I need help... please come... please..."

Alcarond sighed, releasing her chin and standing. He turned to face Zertaan, who was half-smug, half-faking worry. "You need to be careful in your practices. If you press too much pain upon her, then she'll be permanently scarred, and may become useless to me... and the king."

"Yes, archmage," she said in a soft tone, and with a delicate bow.

He turned back to Seph. "Persephone, do you hear me?"

Seph nodded. "I know... I know shouldn't have brought the cat with us... but Sable is so cute, and I needed a friend..." Her voice trailed off into unrecognizable words and mutterings.

"That's enough for tonight," Alcarond said firmly, not looking back at Zertaan.

"But... archmage..." she began.

He whipped around hard, facing her and squaring his broad shoulders. "What more do you expect from her this night? She's done. She could go into shock from more torment. She's nearly unconscious. Whatever pain you put her through would be for your own pleasure, and not for the service of binding her allegiance to the king." He pointed a stern finger between her eyes. "We want her as one of our finest, not buried six feet into the ground. Do you understand? My will is the will of the king. Now, send her back to her cell to rest. You may return to your work tomorrow, but remember my words."

He left the room like a stormy sea wind, leaving a heavy weight in the Abiron. Seph mumbled nothings to herself, and

Zertaan was left with sharp, clenched teeth and her pale fists in balls.

"Someday I'll be archmage," Zertaan hissed through her teeth. "And you'll be the one abiding by my commands."

The Synth glowered with wicked hate at Seph, with a twitch in her eye.

Seph heard Alcarond's words, and desperately wanted to be taken to her cell, even gagged, so that she may lie and succumb to the sleep that called out to her, screaming from every joint in her body.

Zertaan went again to the table, grabbing something unseen, but as she turned to Seph a flash of metal glittered in the torchlight, before Zertaan lunged and Seph felt the sharp, excruciating pain of the metal piercing her side. Seph jolted, screaming in anguish. Zertaan pulled back, smirking in glee as Seph looked down at the grip of a dagger protruding from her side, just next to her stomach. Blood poured from the fresh wound onto the chair's seat, down the leg and onto the cold stone floor.

"Don't die, now," Zertaan said with a high-pitched squeal. "Don't want to upset the archmage now, do we? We wouldn't want the last little Whistlewillow to die off, now would we?" She took the bottle from the table and upturned it into her mouth, guzzling the liquor as it dribbled down the sides of her mouth and onto her chest. "We'll continue our fun tomorrow." She went to leave the room, but stopped just short, glaring at Seph and the dagger still in her. "Now don't go and die on me, you hear? Don't want all the fun to end just yet…"

As she left, Seph succumbed to her pain and fell into a deep, dark, dreadful sleep she thought may be the icy grasp of death.

DARKNESS SHROUDED HER VISION.

Seph opened her eyes as best she could.

Dim candlelight dotted the dark room, casting swaying, flickering light upon the dark walls of the room.

Pain returned to her. Unrelenting anguish that ran throughout her whole body like an ocean battering rocks and shores with its crashing waves.

"S—Soren... Kaile... Davin..." she cried, tears streaming down her cheeks and with quivering lips. "I—I don't want to be here anymore. I—I want to go—go home..."

Her head was so filled with scattered thoughts and her vision so blurred, she knew she was dreaming. The room swayed, the air was thick with what felt like morning dew, and looking down, the dagger still sticking out from her side would surely have killed her.

"This is a dream," she muttered in her daze, but then began to sob. "I need help. Somebody please help me... I'm so scared... so scared..."

The minutes and seconds of the dream passed like sand slowly filtering down a broken, shattered hourglass; sand pouring in spurts and suddenly stopping and bursting down again.

Through the silence of the room, a murmur of something caught her ear. It was faint, like a mouse scuttling across a pitch-black room. She heard something; a humming from within the walls of the room. The sound was faint, but it was... beautiful.

As angelic as the scent of a newborn babe, and as true as the ringing of Soren's Vellice-steel dagger as it slid from its scabbard, the noise made the room feel like a warm glow had taken over the darkness.

What is that? It's so soothing it's pulling me in... it's pulling me back into darkness... or... maybe it's light?

Seph struggled to stay with the sound, to bask in its

warmth, even cutting through pain, and sending waves of relief through her. But the pull of fatigue was too strong. Even as she drifted helplessly back into the void, the sound of the dagger clanging to the floor beneath her wasn't enough to keep her focus upon the warm, true sound, and she fell back into darkness.

Chapter Fourteen

Kaile drew a deep breath in, filling his lungs, settling his nerves and sent a great shake down his arms and cracking his neck; finally letting out a great exhale. The Drakoons that stood at both sides of the throne room door didn't pay him any mind, at least not with their eyes. Each wore sleek black armor with sharp points darting out from corner plates like spindles. Theirs eyes were lifeless; reddened pupils surrounded by veiny skin and deep wrinkles. Their thin curved swords were fastened in their scabbards, and their shining black helmets full of toothy mouths and fanning spindles at the back, didn't move one inch.

Kaile knocked on the thick throne room door of hardened mahogany. Riveted iron plates striped down the door, reinforcing such a seemingly impenetrable door. The door cracked open outward, letting out a breath that sent Kaile staggering backward clumsily, one foot catching the other.

An attendant in fine white linens ushered him in. She bowed and motioned for him to follow the long red carpet into the Grand Hall throne room, filled with a warm glow of sunlight from the hundreds of windows, rising high up into the enormous room. At the room's rear rested an empty throne, at the top of ten carpeted stairs. The throne was immense, wrought of black iron, but with elaborately decorated pieces of dark-stained wood, enhanced with an inlay of ivory and gold. A single gem was inlaid at its crest, a gleaming white jewel that cast a dazzling glow of all shades of color, as the sunlight from the windows danced upon it.

Kaile walked down the carpet, glancing up at the streaming banners that flowed down the columns that rose fifty feet to the high ceiling. The banners flashed the sigil and colors of the kingdom of Lynthyn—a warring lion and serpent, entangled in battle in lavish gold and brilliant white.

The attendant tailed him, eventually telling him to wait twelve paces before where the stairs started up to the throne. He stopped, and she walked back to the room's entrance behind.

Kaile's hands went to his back, where he nervously fidgeted with his fingers. There was much on his mind, and after receiving the king's command to see him less than an hour prior, even more thoughts rushed in.

I've got to get Seph out of there. Somehow. I've got to convince him that she's good and can serve him without more pain than she's already endured. I'll beg if I have to. But I know that won't work. The king only recognizes strength, and despises weakness.

Whatever it takes, though...

Whatever it takes...

A door opened behind the throne. Kaile couldn't see it, but certainly heard it as the heavy door creaked open, and many armored footsteps poured out of whatever room lay beyond.

"Kneel," came a commanding voice, dropping Kaile instantly to a knee, bowing his head so that his reddish-brown hair fell before his face, nearly to his chin.

"All hail King Malera Amón, King of the six kingdoms, and Lord of Aladran," a man in violet and burgundy robes proclaimed. He shuffled into the room, with six Drakoons trailing behind in two rows. Kaile marveled at their expert precision—the way their strides were completely in unison, the angles of the sheaths at their hips were exact, and the sound from their armor was muted, but in precise rhythm.

After the Drakoons and the man in burgundy robes entered, taking their spots before the stairs, all attention upon Kaile, the king entered.

Knots tightened in Kaile's stomach as the king walked in. The king wasn't wearing his Vellice armor. Kaile knew that was for battle and regal ceremonies. Instead, he wore a long black robe with flowing gold trim. He may have worn no armor, but he surely had something beneath the robes, Kaile thought. And Storm Dragon was fixed on his hip. His golden crown with six jeweled spikes rested on his wavy, black hair as he strode up the stairs without casting a glance at Kaile.

The king sat, sturdy, with his broad shoulders fitting into the throne as if it were erected for him.

"Stand." The king's voice was low and strong. The Drakoons didn't flinch. The attendant in burgundy bowed and left the staircase, meandering to the far wall behind a column.

Kaile stood, bowing his head. "Your Grace..."

"You look... older, stronger." The king's glacial blue eyes beamed down upon Kaile. "Alcarond has been a fine master to you."

Kaile bowed, not saying a word, choking down his resentment at Alcarond for forcing him to betray the one he cared about most in this world.

"I sense anger in you." The king leaned forward, one powerful mitt on his thigh, the other waving slowly toward him, as if sensing the hatred Kaile fought to bury deep down inside. "Good. Let it drive you and focus it on your studies, young man. It will fuel you, but do not let it consume you. Too many have fallen to their lust for hatred and revenge. Soren Stormrose is a perfect example of such lost grace."

Kaile clenched his eager teeth, wishing to flash and unleash a barrage of damning words at the king. The exact same king who burned innocent people alive under the guise of a plague.

The king sat back, stroking his bushy black beard. "Nothing to say?"

"Why did you summon me, sire?" Kaile fought to keep his voice from croaking or cracking.

"I wanted to see you with my own eyes. I wanted to have a conversation, and congratulate you for a job well done. And Kaile Thorne, to welcome you back home."

The fucking bastard. Congratulate me for betraying Seph? Home? This isn't my home. My home is out there, with them!

The king waited a few seconds and then scoffed with a snort. "Still, nothing?"

"I plead with you, your Grace. Take mercy on Persephone Whistlewillow. I know she has wronged you. But she is young, impressionable, and hard-headed. Show her mercy. I ask you, please... I will continue my training, and I will become a powerful Syncron for you. But keep her alive, and have Zertaan show restraint..."

"Wine!" the king shouted, and the attendant rushed up to the king with a bottle and glasses. "For me and the apprentice." The man in burgundy poured the king a glass, urgently yet delicately—not spilling a drop, then poured another and brought it down for Kaile. "Alcarond told me you had feelings for the Whistlewillow child, and now I see that for myself."

Kaile took the wine from the attendant, who rushed back off to the wall.

Two seconds ago, he would've politely refused the offer, but after the king's statement about Seph, and Alcarond, and Kaile's inability to hide his feelings outwardly toward her... he drank.

"Love is blinding, apprentice to the archmage. Especially in youth. Beware its pull. Its clouds clear vision, and it robs us of conviction. Lust will dull the sword hand, and dim wits when the Ellydian is needed."

Kaile nodded. He didn't know what else to do. "I have no feelings for the girl, other than companionship. She has showed exceptional merit with the Ellydian, sire. She has become an Aeol without any training, other than by book. Persephone has the potential to become a Lyrian one day. But she needs training. Real training. And I fear Re-Enlightment through spite may scar her too deeply, wounding her connection to all things."

The king nodded, swirling his wine, deep in thought. The Drakoons were as motionless as stalking panthers. "You may be right, apprentice."

Kaile nearly staggered back, but caught himself. *I am?*

"But do not believe me a fool. I know your true intentions, perhaps even better than you do. Zertaan of the House of the White Asp is a renowned specialist in turning Synths back to Syncrons. And I need Syncrons for the coming war."

You're no Syncrons. You're the Synths. He's got it all backwards. He still thinks he's good. Even after all the people who've died because of his lust for power and fire.

"Zertaan will not permanently damage the girl," the king said. "She will be marred, and have bruises that last longer than those that blemish the skin. But it is a necessary cost." The king set his wine down on the table beside the throne and rose. His voice boomed as he spoke, echoing throughout the hall as if a great god had arrived down on earth from the Halls of Everice. "Persephone Whistlewillow, the last descendant of her legendary line, has broken many laws, killed my men, and fought alongside the murderous, savage Silver Sparrows!"

"But... but my king..." Kaile said, taking a step forward with his palms held out and open.

The Drakoons angled immediately toward him, each grabbing the grips of their curved swords.

Kaile withdrew his step quickly.

"I—I was only going to say that should you show her mercy, it will show your conviction to hold her up, once enlightened back to sanity. It will show you are a just, strong, and wise king."

"Zertaan will continue her Re-Enlightment how she sees fit." The king's face twisted, snarling with a lip raised, showing a slight white of a canine tooth. "That will be the end of our talk about the girl. I have other matters I wish to speak with you about."

Kaile sighed. "You want to know about the Silver Sparrows…"

"I do…" The king sat. "I do greatly."

Kaile knew he was in danger then. If he lied and the king found out, then Kaile would face worse punishment than Seph, but if he told all the truth, then those that trusted him would all be in grave danger. That would be a second betrayal to Soren and the others. He knew he needed to figure something out, and quickly. The king's gaze was heavy on him, and wanting answers quickly.

"Who leads the Silver Sparrows?" the king demanded, gripping the throne's armrests tightly.

Kaile decided the only way to get out of the situation was to give a believable mix of truth and fiction.

"Mihelik Starshadow was the leader of the Silver Sparrows." Kaile concentrated a great effort into meeting the intense king's gaze. "Soren has inherited that role, and leads the rebellion against you now."

The king thought about that, stroking his beard and subtly tapping his boot.

"There are others. Many others. Tell me about them."

"I don't know many names. They are secretive. They used

code names. The ones in Grayhaven differed from the ones in Zatan. They looked like normal people. I could describe their appearances if that would help."

King Amón took an angry gulp and wiped his lips with his sleeve. "You're hiding things from me. I don't like it when my Syncrons *hide* things from me."

"I'll tell you all I know." Kaile put his hands behind his back and puffed out his chest. "I fear it will be inadequate for what you would wish of me, though. I was kept in the dark much of the time. Soren didn't trust me fully, and rightfully so…"

"Yes, you will give me full descriptions to our artists, and you'll give a full account of your journey to our historians. You will leave nothing out. So you say Soren is the leader of the Silver Sparrows, do you?"

Kaile nodded. "I believe he is now."

"He'll be hard-pressed to fight a war with only a dagger and a scattering of uneducated Synths against my legion of Syncrons. They will be quashed shortly. And then we can focus on more important ventures."

"Sire? Ventures? Such as?" Kaile asked, his fingers tapping at each other nervously behind his back.

"Why, to destroy the Demons of Dusk, now that we know how. We will suffocate the awful Chimaera. And we will build an army of Syncrons that will restore balance to Aladran. I have dreams of a realm that is unstained with blood. Justice will be wrought in every kingdom. And there will be only order!"

To his side, as the king shouted his proclamation, Kaile saw a candle flicker out of the corner of his eye. The flame danced backward from the king, as if the king's breath stirred it.

Unusual. There's no breeze in here. That was something else.

"I will destroy the Silver Sparrows. The Knight Wolf will

have his fun, and I'll take Soren's head and dagger as my trophies."

"Yes, my king."

"How does that make you feel, Kaile Thorne of Ikarus? How does it feel to tell you that I'm going to kill Soren? What emotions does that stir in you?"

"Soren means nothing to me, sire. I used him to get insight into the enemy. He's a skilled swordsman and soldier. There's no denying that. But his death means nothing to me." Kaile focused every morsel of strength in him to lie as much as he did without showing an inkling of deceit.

"We shall see." The king took a long gulp, finishing his glass and waving the attendant over for another. "This war will rage on, and we shall see where your heart truly lies, apprentice. You jumped into that portal Mihelik cast of your own free will. You left my servitude and became an outcast and a traitor in one single leap. You are only here again because of Alcarond's grand plan that brought the last Whistlewillow here. We will see your true colors, and I sincerely hope you play the game the right way. I'd hate to see your bright future get tarnished by… lies…"

Chapter Fifteen

Again, even after finding the fortress, protecting them from the world, Soren had a dreamless night.

Even after receiving such a mysterious, prized gift from the Dune Matron and the Calica, Soren spent most of the night staring up at the ceiling to his room. To his left was Blaje on a cot, and to his right snored Davin; Sable curled up on his stomach and chest, purring blissfully. The two bears rested above with the camels.

There was just too much to think about, and even with the overwhelming exhaustion that consumed his body and mind, he found no sleep.

I'll sleep when I'm dead, he told himself.

At the forefront of his mind was always Seph. He hoped there was some relief for her all by herself at the capital. Lady Drake had spoken of her single spy up there, within the king's nest. Kaile was there, but he was being groomed back into their flock, Soren knew. He was far too prized an asset to waste. He may be an Ayl, but Alcarond and the king were hopeful he would pass the Black Sacrament someday, revealing a whole new world of power to him.

Another thing that kept him restless—but should have had the opposite reaction—was Cirella.

My love. Saying goodbye to you helped heal old wounds. But seeing you, hearing your voice, whether real or just a vivid dream—makes my heart miss you dearly. You were my one. You were my chosen. You were supposed to be my future. Not this.

He turned to his side, facing Blaje as she slept soundly. A ping of guilt pinched his stomach deep within. Soren had relations since Cirella's death; those that were attracted to the danger he represented from the scars that were cut deep into his face. Alicen was a standout. When they laid together, most of his troubles seemed to wash away with the tide, always returning back to shore. But the moments of bliss, distraction, and passion always dulled the pain—at least temporarily.

But Blaje…

She was something different all together.

Soren gazed at her as she slumbered peacefully.

Her head rested on her arm as she slept soundly. She was as striking as any woman he'd ever laid eyes on. The curves of her body under the blanket were womanly, yet showed her strength. She was a warrior—a beautiful, ruthless, and cunning warrior. Yet, her lips were plump and curved just the right way. Her skin, aside from a couple of small scars from battle, was youthful and vibrant. Her hair smelled of spring.

When she was around him, he felt a sense of peace, of companionship, and he struggled with the fact that his feelings for her were only intensifying.

Focus on the war.
Focus on the upcoming battles.
Focus on saving Seph!

The thoughts helped him briefly.

But he'd catch a glimpse of her on her camel, riding the sand dunes like a warrior of old tales. She may be the most fearsome being in all the sands: the Desert Shadow, the first blade of the Calica, and now… his ally.

The kiss they shared, it meant something to him.

It was more than a last chance kiss before battle.

It was more than a, this may be our last night in this world, kiss.

There was something there. He felt it, and he hoped she did as well.

❦

THE MORNING CAME with no hint of sunlight. Underground in the fortress of Sortistra, torchlight and commotion down the hall was the only indicator of daybreak. The darkness gave him a dire reminder of the sunless journey they had ahead, through the old tunnel, and into Lynthyn.

Going underground was never something anyone thought about anymore. The Demons of Dusk retreated from the light of the sun, nestling underground into their hideaways. No humans went there. None that wished to live, at least. The Black Fog and Shades had killed most animals that roamed the night. Even deer were but a fleeting memory. Those that lived in the woods were protected, or at least was the case until recently—until the Synth Glasse called a Black Fog into the capital of Grayhaven—when the creature and Soren fought. Soren eventually drove the monster off, revealing what was a shining, liquid substance beneath the fog's flesh.

That thought made Soren wish that the one person most obsessed with ridding the world of the Demons of Dusk— Archmage Alcarond—was on his side. Together, they could work jointly with the new revelations about the creatures that roamed and hunted the night plains, and maybe find a way to defeat them.

But that wasn't the only war anymore.

The king had to be dealt with.

The Knight Wolf had to pay for his evil deeds.

The world had to be saved from these madmen.

And Soren seemed the only one who could lead such a quest.

It's my time.

This is my last chance at revenge.

It's my last chance at redemption.

Save Seph. Kill the king.

Then you can die.

Then you can rest in peace and be with your love.

But the battle comes first.

There is war to win, and then… you can die.

"What are you looking at?" Blaje yawned as she stirred away. Her eyes were narrow slits, and Soren didn't know she was looking back at him, but he didn't shy away.

"You."

She laughed. "You didn't sleep, did you? Stubborn as the Nine Hells."

He smiled. "That's the truth."

"Maybe you should try clubbing yourself on the head at bedtime. Might work better." Blaje swung her legs to the side of the cot and rubbed her eyes with another great yawn. Sable circled her ankles.

"Maybe tomorrow night," Soren said, thinking of the darkness they surely were in, and thinking maybe he should have knocked himself out. There'd be no safer place to rest than the fortress they were in, and he'd probably kick himself for his lack of sleep later.

Blaje stretched her arms out high over her head, with her dread coming undone and flopping onto her chest. "Maybe you'll sleep after the war is done."

He laughed. "I have the feeling when this war is done, I'm going to sleep for a very, very long time…"

"Let's get up," Blaje said. "It's going to be a long day, and the quicker we get on our way, the quicker we get into Lynthyn." She grabbed her pillow and tossed it over Soren at the snoring dwarf on his other side. It crashed into him, and he stirred awake with a deep snort and smacking of his lips.

"Another hour," Davin groaned. "Who knows the next time we'll get a bed like this…"

Soren and Blaje left Davin to snooze a bit longer, both getting dressed and heading out into the mess hall just outside of their room. There were rows and rows of tables with soldiers already sitting, spooning up some sort of earthy smelling porridge with a slight hint of vanilla.

They ate together, with Blaje speaking in the local language of Sarin to many of the Calica men who gathered around. They had many questions for their first blade, and she seemed to have answers. Soren caught bits and pieces of the conversation, as Landran had taught him some of the desert language.

Davin emerged from the room an hour later, and Sable ran and jumped up onto the table Soren and the others sat at.

"That was a slumber worth telling tales of. Dreamless, refreshing and waking with a stiff pecker."

"Davin…" Blaje groaned, pushing her porridge away.

Soren laughed. "That's the soldier I know. Are you enjoying getting to know him, too?"

Blaje took a roll from the table and flicked it his way. He caught it in his muscly fingers. "You best stop throwing things at me today. I'll turn around and gladly go home, and you can go into the miserable tunnel on your own!"

"I'm so sorry," Blaje said with a rare smirk. "Didn't know you were such a sensitive dwarf. You want me to scratch your beard like you're a dog? Will that make you feel better?"

"You know what?" Davin said, walking over to her, the tip of his head level with hers as she sat. He lifted his chin. "Give 'er a scratch. Been too long since me beard felt the touch of a woman."

She went to scratch with her nails, but Soren gently pushed her hand back.

"Oh," Davin said. "Getting jealous? The Desert Shadow has taken a likin' to me, and all the sudden the great Soren gets a bout of jealousy?"

"Not jealous," Soren said, leaning over his porridge and eating a sloppy bite. "Just don't know what parasites are living in that mangy forest you got living on your face."

Davin sent his huge mitt flying, swatting the side of Soren's head playfully. "Insult my beard, you insult me... and you may have hell to pay for it. Lack of sleep ain't gonna be an excuse to save you from my fury!"

"Fair enough, friend." Soren laughed. "But maybe don't go asking every woman you run into for a stroke. Good recipe to get slapped yourself."

Davin sat, and a soldier slid a bowl of the porridge in front of him. "I don't... I don't ask every woman... I have quite high standards, if you must know!"

"Well." Blaje swirled her spoon in the thick porridge. "I'm flattered then."

Soren noticed a slight rosy flush hit Davin's cheeks.

The soldiers around laughed.

A half an hour later, they were suited with their armor and ready for the journey ahead. They walked up to the top floor, tiny windows flooding the room with warm desert sun. The two massive silver bears gulped down cold water from a basin on the massive main floor. Dozens of camels were attended to by the Calica, making the fortress reek like a musty barn.

"Fresh air would do this dwarf good," Davin said. "I know underground better than men, but this stench is enough to make even me prefer the scorching heat, than sit here and smell these piles of shite much longer."

The soldiers in the room stirred as the Dune Matron ascended the stairs in the large room's corner. She was elegant, powerful, and graceful as she approached, all in the room bowing their heads to her as she approached.

Soren watched her as the bottom of her flowing dress kissed the floor. Scarletta had a certain sort of unique swagger. It was as if she were divine, loved by all, unkillable. She stopped just short of the three of them and gave a slight nod.

"Today is the day you make for Lynthyn. Are you ready?"

Soren, Blaje, and Davin nodded in agreement.

"The two bears are going with you, I presume?" she asked, turning her head to look over her shoulder at them. The faded black tattoos on her neck glistened on her dark skin from the sunlight that poured in through the many windows around the room. "They seem to have an attachment to you. A bond of sorts…"

"Well." Soren scratched his head, watching the bears walk over. Their immense silver-furred bodies drew all the attention from the room, gasps even. "From trying to kill me in Myngorn only weeks ago, I'll gladly take them wanting to protect us."

"They will draw all sorts of unwanted attention," Davin said. "We may have to have them keep a far distance, and stick to the trees, where there are some… and I don't know if they'll understand that request, anyway. Mihelik may have been their friend, and been able to talk to the beasts, but I think they're gonna walk with us whether we ask or not."

"I have an idea." The Dune Matron tapped her lips softly. "I know not if it will work, but my men are already working on something. I should be able to present you with an idea shortly."

"I'd appreciate that." Soren rolled his sleeves up. "We'll take all the help we can get. Blaje trusts you. So I trust you."

"I will lead you to the tunnel now," Scarletta said. "If you're ready."

"We are," Soren said. "We need to find Landran and figure out a way to get Seph out of the capital."

"Let's walk and talk." The Dune Matron turned and began walking toward the front gate. Two soldiers opened the massive gate, and blinding sunlight poured in, causing each of them to shield their eyes. The Dune Matron snapped her fingers, and soldiers pulled three camels their way. Sable meowed and licked her paws.

"What can you tell us about the tunnel?" Soren asked as they approached the gate. "You said it's been sealed and unused?"

"My men assured me it is sealed, and yes, unused in many, many years. It will lead you secretly into Lynthyn, out of the sight of the king's spies that lurk all along the border. You will emerge into Lynthyn, or rather just at the border between our lands, and you can make your way to Arkakus to find your old master. The road underground will be dark, and last for miles, so prepare yourselves for the journey into the Under Realm."

The words Under Realm sent a hard shiver through Soren's spine, rippling a tingle up into his scalp. He'd done everything imaginable to avoid going down there since the numbers of Black Fog and Shades multiplied, especially in the last decade.

The four of them walked through the gate, along with Sable, three camels, and the two bears. The Calica poured out after their lady.

They walked for a few hundred feet, reaching a sandy, rocky cliff, and the Dune Matron turned and took a path down the cliff. Soren was careful of his footing, as the morning breeze swirled grains of sand along the path. It was wide enough for the bears, but just barely. They walked down the steep path, just behind Sortistra.

It didn't take long for Soren to spot the area they were heading. Not because of a gate or grand entrance, but because of a single pillar protruding through the sand like an ancient finger breaking the sands, pointing up toward the heavens.

They all descended down the path, reaching the pillar, which was twice Soren's height. One of the bears stood, matching its height, pawing at it. The pillar was old, even older than the stone of Sortistra, Soren thought. Weathered through centuries of sandstorms—Soren thought the fortress may have been erected at the site, because of the pillar and underground tunnel.

The pack of Calica surrounded the pillar in a semi-circle, giving ample space between them and it. Sable walked straight to the pillar and clawed at its base. One bear snorted.

Scarletta Empressal nodded to two of the soldiers. Digging into the pocket at her hip, buried in her white linen dress, she pulled out a key.

Soren marveled at the way the early morning golden sunlight shimmered on the hard edges of the polished old key. She held it up for all to see. It looked old, but wasn't inlaid with jewels or remarkable in any way, other than it shimmered like glowing sunlight off the rolling tide's waves.

The Dune Matron walked forward, ten feet to the pillar's side. The pillar loomed over them like a shadowy beacon, a marker of a darker world, and a towering omen. She looked around her, twirling in circles, glaring down at her feet. She held the key out as if it would tell her which direction to walk in.

At her feet, to Soren's amazement, the sands shuddered. They shifted and vibrated, as if a massive worm crawled beneath. Scarletta approached the spot where the vibrations emanated. They grew harsher as she drew closer. She knelt, and the sands looked as if they were going to erupt.

She pressed the key down, and the shifting sands parted, revealing a single keyhole in the parted sands.

"Whoa..." Davin murmured, stroking his beard. "Old magic... these desert lands are filled with them."

"You have no idea," the Dune Matron whispered back, not taking her eyes off the keyhole as she slid the key in.

The key disappeared into the hole; the sand vibrated so intensely, Soren thought to run and grab the Dune Matron, carrying her away. Her arm shook as the key clicked, going all the way in. With a turn of the key, and another click, the sands suddenly stopped. There was no moment, no vibrating, only the sound of the breeze whipping by. But Soren thought he heard something else, something darker. Beneath them. It was almost a low whistle, or the sound of air filling the bellows of a great organ in an old church.

She stepped back, and two soldiers rushed in, both clearing the sand around the key, still protruding from its hole. They uncovered two round iron rings, and with great might, pulled up on them. The muscles in their arms bulged, and they clenched their teeth with great grunts as the two strong men pulled up on two mighty doors. They swung open, revealing a deep pit in the earth, a void of ancient darkness.

Stairs led the way down, and a stone floor led north. One direction. It only led into Lynthyn.

"Argh," Davin grumbled. "You sure about this, Soren?"

Soren gripped Firelight's handle tight. He nodded to his friend. "This is our path." He then glanced at Blaje, who nodded back. "We make for Lynthyn, and then Arkakus." He turned back to the Dune Matron and her people.

"There are ample torches, lanterns and fuel for the journey," Scarletta said. "May your path to your old mentor be true and may your swords and axes be sharp and ready for your battles ahead."

Soren nodded. "Let's go."

Blaje entered the tunnel first, walking all the way down the twenty-four steps and falling into shadow.

Soren put on the ring of the Twilight Veil, ready to disappear into the shadows. He felt the Shadowflame Heartstone dangling at his neck, ready for the magic within to spark alive when he needed it. The thought of becoming one with the darkness, truly, made the corner of his mouth curl.

Davin walked in next, no stranger to the underground. The Calica led the camels down, and Soren motioned for the two massive silver bears, who nervously walked down after the camels. The Calica soldiers walked past the bears nervously.

Soren was last.

"Close the doors behind me," he said. "Let none follow."

"May Shirava protect you," the Dune Matron said with a hand held above her head in his direction.

"You as well," he responded. "Protect your people. Before this war is over, there will be hardship and dark times. But brighter days are ahead."

The Dune Matron bowed her head. All the hundred Calica bowed to Soren as well.

"Lead us to victory, Soren Stormrose. That will be your greatest gift to this world, and your true redemption. Kill the king, save your niece, and bring peace to this world."

Soren nodded, went down the stairs, and watched the two doors swing closed behind him, casting a pure, unrelenting darkness upon them.

The Under Realm was their new path forward.

PART IV
WHAT EVIL LIES BENEATH

Chapter Sixteen

Stricken in darkness, devoid of all that gives light—the warmth of the golden sun—the Under Realm is a world all in its own.

Throughout history, many generations sought to capture the unknown. They dug with shovels and pickaxes, seeking fortune, adventure, or attempting to create a new venture for humanity. They created tunnels that connected cities, catacombs that spanned for miles, and some even attempted to create cities in the darker parts of the world.

Kings and queens had their escape tunnels dug and walled with stone. Those in search of treasure dug deep into the earth, praying for jewels and gold that would change their families' lives.

However... humanity was not created to live in darkness.

There are things that live and breathe in the deep parts of our world that were not meant to be stirred by the curiosity and greed of man.

There's a saying about the Under Realm that my grandfather told me, the author of this book, that I still remember as I write this.

-Heed the loving light of the golden sun. Beware the luring depths of the eternal shadow. Life grows like a deep-rooted tree under the warmth of our sun. Death draws life in with its killing claws of temptation, greed, and deceit. Beware the darkness of what lies beneath, and stay true to the world that was meant for man, not the shadow that threatens to devour it.

. . .

-Translated from the language of the Sundar. The Scriptures of the Ancients, Book IV, Chapter III.

The Under Realm, Zatan

Darkness swelled around Soren and the others like being cast off a great ship into midnight sea waters. There was no up, no down. Fingers and hands could not be seen before their eyes. Soren felt his fingers touch his face, but with the doors behind them closed, an eerie void trickled up from his toes to his stomach.

Soren feared the Under Realm. Ever since he was a child, his parents told him not to venture there. They knew his adventurous side. They knew his deep curiosity about their world, and as much as they encouraged him to find his calling, they told him strictly to stay away from dark caves and tempting crevasses.

A spark of steel hitting flint broke the silence, and Blaje was illuminated in an orange glow of fire as the torch in her hand engulfed in flame. She dug into the pack of one of the camels, pulling another free, handing it to Davin.

"You're welcome to one," Blaje said to Soren, but didn't pull a torch from the back for him, instead eyeing the jewel that hung around his neck.

"How does the Heartstone work?" Soren spun it in his fingers at the center of his chest.

"Should have plenty of time to practice it down here." Davin's hand inspected the smooth walls of the tunnel. "This is built long ago, as the Dune Matron said. These walls haven't seen life in years. This is a place of deep darkness... and lifeless."

"When in darkness," Blaje said, walking over and touching the Heartstone as both bears and Sable watched her. "Simply command the stone through your thoughts. A simple command will suffice. Why don't you try it out?"

Blaje was only inches from Soren, standing before him with her fingertips lightly touching his armor and soft shirt above it. In the flickering torchlight, she was exquisite. The curve of her lips, the gentleness, yet tenacity in her eyes, the angle of her cheekbones. She noticed him peering at her and gave a wink.

"Go ahead," she said, pointing down the tunnel, into the pitch darkness.

She dropped the Heartstone to his chest, and he strode off into the tunnel, alone.

Fifty strides down, and the black grew all around him. The walls were darker and his legs enveloped in shadow. One hundred paces down, and everything before him was cast into shadow.

He took a deep breath, narrowed his eyes, and said a single word in his mind... *See...*

A flash of light clouded his vision. It blinded him, and he took a wobbly step backward. His hand caught the wall beside him, reminding him which way was up.

He blinked hard, and as the white wall of light faded, a new world emerged.

The lines and cracks of the stone walls revealed themselves to him. He saw the dirt on the ground lying motionless, undisturbed by years of solitude. The long tunnel opened up to a passage that seemed to extend for miles and miles straight ahead, leading under the desert, eventually opening up to the capital kingdom of Lynthyn.

Amazing... absolutely amazing! With this, and the Twilight Veil, I'll be truly one with the shadows. Landran would be proud. I can finally be what I've always dreamed of—a true weapon of good in this world.

A smirk grew wide on his face.

Evil had better hide. I'm coming for you...

"Soren!" Davin shouted down the tunnel, letting the echo of his deep voice flow past Soren, reverberating off the walls. "We can't see ya. You all right? Did it work?"

Soren turned and walked back toward his friends. As soon as he emerged from the shadows back into the torchlight, each of their gazes snapped upon him. The two bears cocked their heads at his sudden reappearance, and Sable ran up to him as though he'd been gone for a week. Soren reached down and picked her up.

"It works," he said. "It works like a fucking charm."

"It's sacred to my people," Blaje said. "It's a high honor that it was gifted to you. It's a symbol that all of Zatan is behind you, and trust you."

Soren thought of all the failures in his life. All those people that he cared for, dying because of his faults.

"I will do my best," he said, a hint of sadness in his voice, though he tried his best to hide it.

"That will be enough," she said. "Now, shall we? We have many miles to go, and Seph and Landran await."

The pack began their journey into the darkness. Blaje and Soren walked at the lead, and Davin trailed at the rear. The two bears nearly filled the tunnel as they walked side by side, their monstrous bodies and shoulders scraping the walls as they followed Soren.

They walked for hours, deeper and deeper into the tunnel. It felt like a dream—a never-ending monotony of square stone —leading further into unyielding darkness. The thought caused Soren's stomach to tighten. His hand never left Firelight.

"What are you thinking about?" Blaje asked as the side of her bare arm touched Soren's shoulder.

The question stirred Soren from a sleepless, dreary daze. "Nothing I suppose. Nothing except this feels like a dream, or a nightmare rather, being down here. In the deep, dark..."

"I admit there are places I'd rather be. Well, anywhere but here," she joked. The torch she carried was in her hand opposite Soren. The warm torchlight gave her face a kind of warmth that made Blaje feel safe. And Soren realized, the more he got to know the Desert Shadow, the more comfortable he became around her. Not only was she an overtly skilled soldier, she was kind, encouraging, and he trusted her.

"Can I tell you something?" His question caused her to turn to look at him with an upraised eyebrow. She nodded.

I want to tell her about my vision with Cirella, but I also don't. I want to keep it inside. Keep it for me. On second thought, I think I'll keep it. Cherish it. Bury it.

"Yes?" she asked, pressing him with a nudge of her elbow.

"I think we should name Mihelik's bears. Better than calling them the big one, and the bigger one," he said, forcing a laugh.

She snorted. "The bears? I don't know. Sure." She looked away from him, glaring at the stone wall as they continued down the underground path. "Ask Davin. I'm sure he'd enjoy that sort of thing."

Soren didn't respond, not knowing what to say.

They walked side by side for another twenty minutes before Blaje broke the silence again.

"I was thinking, Soren... going into Arkakus, to find your old mentor... this path will take us further from Seph. I think this is the right path, but I feel we should talk about it further. I feel your... unease."

Soren scratched his arm.

"I feel," she began. "Weeks ago, you would have flung yourself full force at the enemy to free her."

He growled deep within. The thought of Seph all alone in the capital caused a heat in his chest to grow, emanating like a furnace. Only spilled blood helped calm that kind of fury in him.

She delicately place her hand on his shoulder. "I want to reassure you that I believe this is the right path. With how much foresight Landran had about the dagger of Vellice and the Demons of Dusk, he must have more knowledge that could aid us in our battle. We must find him. We must find him before the king does."

That was something Soren hadn't thought about, and suddenly, he felt himself torn in two.

Seph needs me. She desperately needs me. I'm her only family. But now... Landran might need me. He left me through his faked death, but he also gave me this weapon which has saved my life many times, and led me closer and closer to my revenge, and fighting off the evil that plagues our world.

"I never thought of it like that," he muttered. "Landran never needed my help before. He was always the strongest, the bravest, the most fearless and deadly man I ever knew. I never thought he may need help... from anyone..."

"We need his insight," Blaje said. "Landran Dranne was— is—revered by all the kingdoms for his prowess and reputation. He could be a powerful ally in our war against the king and the Demons of Dusk."

"You're right," Soren said, pinching the top of his nose, knowing the logic was sound, but knowing Seph was in grave trouble tore him apart at his core.

"I want you to understand clearly the battle we face." Blaje's voice grew direct and stern. "Seph is on her own for now, and you need to come to terms with that, Soren. She's a strong woman, and a powerful Ayl. You can't protect her forever from a world that hunts her. Even if you wished to storm Celestra or take it through the shadows, it would surely be a suicide mission. You could never get in and get her out in that city. Perhaps any other city, but not that one."

Soren knew she was right. Celestra was a fortress full of hundreds of thousands of people loyal to the king, hundreds of Synths in various stages of training, and all manner of trained killers, not the least of which were the Drakoons, and the Knight Wolf himself.

"You need to trust in Seph. She's a Whistlewillow." Blaje looked down at the floor as she said that. She cleared her throat after. "We may not be able to get her out, so we're going to have to trust, and pray to the goddess, that she finds a way out."

Soren rubbed his cheeks with his hand in front of his mouth. The thought of Seph finding a way out of the most fortified city in the realm was... bitter. It was possible, he thought. But she's the most coveted wielder in all of Aladran. The king would never let her go. Alcarond wouldn't ever let her go.

"I just don't—" Soren sighed.

"Trust in Lady Drake and the Dune Matron," Blaje interrupted. "You're not the only pawn in this war. There are many, many other players, and many of them are far more... conniving and planning than you. What they lack in skill with a sword or dagger, they more than make up for in subterfuge, secrecy, and surprise."

He couldn't help but smile at the thought. The way she said that really struck a chord with Soren.

"This is true," he said, looking up at the ceiling and breathing in and out through his nostrils.

"Trust in Lady Drake. Her spy in the capital is promising in many rights. For Seph, for Kaile, for the war."

Kaile, Soren thought, as his hands clenched into fists.

"Easy," Blaje said. "There may come a time when we are confronted with the archmage's apprentice again, and when that time comes, there may be a conversation to be had, before blades are drawn and magic is cast."

"Murder before magic," Soren said. "It's as simple as that. You let a wielder speak. That may be the last breath you draw."

"Fair." She put her hand gently on his forearm. "But there are many forces at play now. Alcarond is far more powerful than any other Synth, and the allure of his power is something you and I cannot fathom. Kaile is young, impressionable, passionate, and naïve. I'm not asking you to spare his life, but simply I hope you can hear him out in some respect. He will pay for his treason, but it may not have to be with his life."

"Why are you saying this?" Soren raised an eyebrow. "Are you asking me to spare the life of the one who took Persephone from me? To be tortured? She could be dead for all we know now."

"War makes for strange friends," Blaje said in an icy tone, far colder than Soren expected. "We are at a serious disadvantage when it comes to the Ellydian. There are only a handful of Syncrons and Synths that may be capable of attaining Lyrian power. Kaile is one of those, and what a weapon he would be on our side, should we discover some other truth to what happened back there on the top of Golbizarath."

Soren swallowed his rage. He knew she was right.

"Who do you think are the others? Who could take Alcarond's place as archmage when he falls?" he asked.

"Well... definitely not Glasse." She laughed darkly, licking her teeth. "Seph, of course. But Zertaan, Sophia, possibly Lady Sargonenth. Others I do not know of. It is still unclear if some in the capital, such as the Archpriest Solemn wield or not. His power may be his wisdom, but it is unclear his full potential as an enemy. The king keeps him as his closest advisor for a reason, and that reason may still be shrouded and hidden to us."

"It has always been a mystery why the king would take in a foreign advisor like he did." Soren scratched his stubbly chin. "He seemed to arrive right as Celestra was flooded seven years ago when Lake Rivengale flooded. He came from Eldra with his soldiers and never went back."

Chapter Seventeen

Soren and the others trudged deeper and deeper into the Under Realm. The darkness was complete, absolute, and held a deep feeling of emptiness.

While they walked, the camels and bears in tow, Soren felt the strength leave him. His muscles ached, his eyelids felt like anvils, and his stomach twisted into tight knots.

As much as the words of the Dune Matron and Blaje made his mind know for certain that racing to the capital wasn't his best option, his heart screamed for him to do the opposite.

One foot in front of the other, he told himself. *Just keep moving forward. Don't dwell. The past is what it is. The future is what's unwritten... and it's worth fighting for.*

Blaje had gone up ahead as Soren slowed, eventually falling to Davin's side. Davin in the torchlight looked like the glowing statue in a tomb of a perfect dwarven warrior. Stout, chiseled, brawny, and with a magnificent beard that made him look legendary.

Soren glanced at his friend, in what turned from awe to remorse.

Davin was an outcast from his homeland, summoned by his friend Mihelik Starshadow to help Soren.

I know the feeling far too well of losing your home. I hope that he's able to return someday. To see his kin, to smell the smell of his old-caves and underground cities, to wrap his family in his arms once again…

"What's going on in that sleep-deprived head again?" Davin asked, snapping Soren back to their reality.

"Nothing," he said.

"Bull shite," the dwarf muttered. "There's always something dark brewin' in that noggin o' yours. Spill it."

"Nothing. I know we are on the right path. Our allies are growing. We need to figure out our lack of the Ellydian, and quickly. But other than that, I'm enjoying the peace down here." Soren glanced back at the two silver bears, shoulder to shoulder, nearly filling the tunnel. "I am curious what to do about them, though."

Davin turned all the way around, walking backward with his short legs. "They do stand out in a bleak desert, don't they? Even in the wilds of Lynthyn, we are going to stand out like, well, torchlight in this darkness."

"They need names." Soren watched as Davin's face lit up at the thought, spinning back, walking straight behind Blaje and the camels.

"Names, eh?" The dwarf clapped a hand on his hard thigh. "Did you have anything in mind yet?"

Soren shook his head. "Blaje said it should be you."

Sable sat upon one of the camels, licking her paw, but stopped and looked down at Davin. She leaped down and then jumped up his chest, perching on his shoulder.

"Well, it's a male and female. The big one is the boy, and the other the girl," Davin said.

He squinted as he thought, the wrinkles at the corners of his eyes deepening.

Soren smiled at the joy and thoughtfulness Davin was putting into it.

"I've got it!" Davin shouted, his echo filling the hall, rushing down past Blaje. She halted and turned, waiting for them to catch up to her.

"And?" Soren pressed.

"Well," Davin said, puffing out his chest as Sable purred. "I was thinking of naming them after the archmage. He was their friend, after all, and I think he'd appreciate it."

Blaje folded her arms and shifted her weight to one hip. "You're not going to name them arch and mage, right?"

"No! But close! I wasn't thinking of Mihelik either. Too blunt, too obvious. But his last name…"

"Starshadow," Soren muttered.

"Shadow, the big one," Davin said. "So something like Moonshadow?"

"And Star, the smaller," Blaje said, her mouth curving to a smile. "So Sunstar?"

Davin nodded. Soren as well.

"Very well," Soren said. "Sunstar and Moonshadow, the two silver bears of the great, ancient Myngorn Forest, at our side in this battle. If only we could figure out a way to not make them reveal us to all with eyes."

"They will have to travel at a distance," Blaje said. "That's the only way."

"Who's gonna be the one to tell them that?" Davin laughed. "I don't speak bear. Do you?"

"Growl," Blaje said, pawing at Davin's face. Sable leaped to her arm and balanced her way up to her shoulder.

"Very funny," Davin said with a forced burst of a laugh.

They walked for another hour, further into the tunnel. The walls were unchanging, and it was a never-ending path that felt as if they were walking through a familiar memory. It felt as if it was a dream that seemed to last for eternity.

But it didn't last for eternity. It would have an end, Soren knew, and once they reached that end, then they'd be one step closer to finding Landran, and getting more tools for their battle against the king.

Behind, Star and Shadow slowed, growling low. It caused each of them to halt. Soren turned and watched as the coarse fur on the backs of the hides stiffened.

He slid Firelight free. Davin hefted his ax, and Blaje pulled her shamshir sword from its scabbard. Sable hissed, her fangs flashing in the torchlight. Soren walked up to the lead, glaring out into the darkness.

"What do you see?" Davin asked, remaining at the rear by the bears, whose growls seemed to shake the walls and ground beneath them.

Soren squinted, ready to use the Heartstone if need be. He heard nothing, sensed nothing, and saw nothing but deep black ahead. He strode forward, Blaje accompanying him. Her torchlight lit the tunnel ahead as they walked, and after only twenty steps, it was revealed what the two bears were upset about.

To their right, gaping in the wall, was a massive hole in the tunnel. Soren and Blaje walked up to it, both with weapons in hand, eyeing the great break in the tunnel nervously, ready to fight whatever may emerge from the bore deep into the earth.

Blaje held the torch up to the hole as the others caught up. Davin peered down the new tunnel, dug with a mix of smooth rock and rock marred with sharp claw marks.

"That ain't good," Davin murmured.

"No. No, it's not," Soren said, kneeling, touching the smooth rock wall, sniffing his finger after. "Black Fog. Black Fog and Shades made this."

"How recently?" Davin asked.

"Not very," Soren guessed. "The scent is very faint. Could be years ago. Perhaps they bored into this by accident."

"Accident or not…" Davin stroked his beard with a twitch in his eye. "We need to get the hell outta here before something bad comes up out of that hole."

Soren stood gazing down the hole. "Not yet."

Blaje and Davin both snapped their gazes at him in surprise.

"Soren?" Blaje asked softly, and with a curious tone. "What are you thinking?"

"This is a once-in-a-lifetime opportunity to see their world."

Davin grabbed Soren's arm, turning him to face the dwarf. "It's official. You've actually gone completely insane and suicidal. Absolutely not!"

"Soren?" Blaje pressed, requiring an explanation.

"I'm going down there. You move on ahead. I'll catch up."

"You can't be serious." Blaje slammed her fist into his arm. "Come. We can't lose you to a lair full of Demons of Dusk. You must be out of your mind."

"I have the Twilight Veil, Firelight, and now the Shadowflame Heartstone. They won't even know I'm there. I'll be one with the shadow, move with no sound, and see as clear as daylight. I'm going to be all right. Trust me. But I have to see this. I have to know…"

Davin gave a humph and folded his arms over his barrel chest. "I don't think there's any talking him outta this. When he gets that look in his eye, good luck talking him outta anything."

"You're a fool, Soren Stormrose," Blaje said, leaning in and kissing him on the cheek.

Soren's stomach fluttered and his heart beat hard. He felt his face flush.

"Be quick about it then," she said, pulling away, her lips half-puckered. "And catch up soon. Don't lead any of those monsters after us. Remember, you may have those relics, but we don't."

"I understand. I'll be quick about it."

"Soren and his damned mysteries he has to solve." Davin laughed. "They'll be the end of us someday."

Sable meowed, standing at the edge of the hole in the wall, staring down into the abyss. She hissed, scampering away behind Davin.

"Yes. I need to know. I need to see with my own eyes where they come from, where they sleep, if they do, and maybe find a vulnerability. I can still see that liquid light within the Black Fog. There's so much we don't know about them. Sure, we have our own war to wage still. But if we don't defeat them, then all our victories are for nothing. We need to find a way to rid ourselves of them, once and for all."

"The dragon helped," Davin said. Soren expected him to give a laugh, but his statement was as serious as any the dwarf had given.

"Agreed," Soren said. "And I expect that dragon will help, but perhaps of its own accord."

Soren took the ring from his pocket of the Twilight Veil, sliding it onto his finger, locking it into position near the jeweled bracelet that activated its magic. He took a step into the new tunnel.

"Good luck," Davin said.

"May the goddess watch over you," Blaje said.

Soren nodded to both. "Go."

Blaje and Davin turned and continued their journey through the man-made tunnel. The bears both looked at Soren with cocked heads and curious gazes.

"Go on," Soren said. "I'll catch up. I'll be fine. Go."

Shadow snorted, but turned to follow Blaje. Star did the same. Sable was the last to leave, sitting there, licking her paws, glaring at Soren.

"Go." Soren waved her on, and she sprung to life and ran down after the others. Soren faced down into the pure darkness. *See*, he thought, and the Heartstone on his chest warmed.

He drew a deep breath in. *Here goes nothing.*

He walked into the tunnel, his boots moving silently down the stone. The walls of the cave blazed to life in a pearly white glow. The cave steepened as more claw marks marred the smooth stone. Deep down, the tunnel was still black as midnight, with even the Heartstone not able to reveal darkness at far distances.

Soren went deeper into the earth, Firelight held tightly in his grasp.

We're going to finally find out what your world is like. You know ours so well, and it's time to return the favor. We need to level the field, and I want to know exactly what you're up to during the day, you little bastards…

Chapter Eighteen

❧

Celestra
The Illuvitrus Sanctum Tower

KAILE NUMBLY PICKED at his fingernails as he gazed wearily out the high tower window. Night was creeping in. A brisk wind whistled through the cracked window. But Kaile didn't feel a chill. He didn't feel the icy air hit his wet eyeballs. He licked the roof of his mouth as he watched the thin clouds glide past the moon, glowing brighter with every minute.

Below, Celestra still bustled. The city of lights glowed like it was swarmed with fireflies, glowing like a beacon in the dark lands of Aladran at night. Beyond the city walls, before the legs of the mountains, he watched the Black Fog emerge, scouring the plains and hills for fresh victims, those foolish or unfortunate enough to be shelterless.

Kaile remembered the fight Soren had with the Black Fog in Grayhaven, and wondered how safe those people below truly were.

Do they know about what happened? Do they know about Glasse using strange, dark magic to call the Black Fog into the city? Or did the king order his Synths to not speak of it?

After all, Glasse was a highly regarded wielder for the king. But then again... so am I.

All his thoughts were just distractions to Seph. Guilt was consuming him, threatening to take his humanity; already taking his innocence. His dreams were plagued with her torture in the Tower of the Judicature. He felt his fingers wet, and looking down, saw blood smeared all down the side of his hand, a nasty cut where he tore his nail off too deeply. He wiped the blood off on his pant leg; careless.

A clock tower in the city chimed, marking nine o' clock, stirring Kaile out of his daze. He was late for his lesson, and Alcarond would be irritated by his tardiness.

"What's he gonna do? Kill me?" Kaile muttered to himself. He stood facing the window, pushing the stained glass open, feeling the rush of icy air on his face. He stepped forward so the toes of his boots touched the wall. He glared out at Rivengale Lake, glorious in every right and sparkling with moon and starlight. He bent forward, letting his shoulders move out of the windowsill. He looked down the over hundred feet, thinking about a gull flying through the clouds, a bee buzzing through the trees, and a bat scuttling between rooftops.

He looked down at the hundreds of people below. He thought about their lives. Each of those people had their own dreams, hopes, and nightmares. He swallowed hard. The heels of his boots lifted from the floor as he angled out the window, gazing down, thinking about flying like a bird.

A hard knock came from the door.

Kaile lost his balance at the sound and gripped the windowsill tightly. He pulled himself in and shut the window behind him, latching it.

"Who is it?" Kaile walked to the door. With no response,

he opened it inward. Before him stood the Shadow Sorceress, with her wooden staff glittering with the raw gold and emeralds embedded in it. Her long black hair wove down her chest and back. She wore a tunic of red, the color she usually chose. Her hood was over her head, darkening her face as her deep brown eyes stared hard into him. "Sophia…"

"Kaile," she said flatly, even cold.

"What are you doing here?" Kaile walked over, grabbing his staff from his bedside. He fumbled it in his hand, smearing it with fresh blood. He saw her glance at the blood, but she said nothing about it.

"I'll be sitting in on your lesson," she said, her voice firm.

Kaile ran over to her. "I'm ready."

He went to leave, but standing right in front of the doorway, Sophia didn't budge. Instead, she narrowed her eyes, glaring at him. His eye twitched, and he itched his cheek.

"Everything OK?" he muttered.

"You've changed," she said, lifting a hand and pressing it to his cheek. All the breath in his lungs turned stagnant, and he suddenly couldn't breathe. Not from magic, but from her.

He reminded himself that the woman standing before him, Sophia Allathine, was the one who drove Mihelik and Alcarond apart. Breaking their friendship like a dagger in the heart. It would never be mended after they both fell for her, and Kaile couldn't deny her beauty. It was world renowned. She and Zertaan were perhaps the most powerful Synths in all Celestra, Kaile knew, besides the archmage himself, of course.

His stomach fluttered at her touch. "I feel like I've changed," he breathed. "But I don't know if I like it."

She examined his face, his expression, running her hand through his wild hair. Her hand arched down his cheek and to his chin. "I see you, Kaile Thorne. I see you."

He stumbled backward, catching himself with his staff.

"Now, come. We mustn't keep your master waiting. He gets

impatient when he has to wait, and impatience makes him angry."

Kaile followed her as she walked up the Illuvitrus Sanctum silently. Him following her as her tunic's tails slid gracefully along the ground. They made their way up to the archmage's quarters together, and once at the door, she stepped aside. Kaile went and knocked.

"Come," a voice called from the other side. Kaile popped the lock, and they both entered. She closed the door behind them.

They walked into the room, its high vaulted ceiling nearly shrouded in night. The many windows to the immense room sparkled in a mix of starlight from the outside and reflected candlelight within.

Alcarond sat at his desk, brooding over stacks of old tomes and scrolls. He snorted as they approached. A pipe smoldered at the side of the mahogany table. A subtle stench of expensive liquor hung over him and his desk.

"Sorry I'm late, master," Kaile said, with his head bowed. But Alcarond didn't answer, and Kaile looked up to see Alcarond stroking his beard, glaring down.

Kaile cleared his throat. "I'm ready for my lesson."

Alcarond seemed to snap back to life, sitting up and grabbing his pipe as he glared at Kaile, a mix of what seemed like disappoint and determination in his eyes.

Alcarond motioned for them to sit. They both sat in the chairs opposite him.

"I asked Sophia to join us, so that we may gain her wisdom to help guide you, Kaile."

"Guide me, sir?"

"Yes." Alcarond puffed his pipe. He grabbed the bottle and poured himself a glass of the amber liquor, pouring one for Sophia, sliding it to her, but not one for Kaile.

She sipped and crossed her legs under her tunic, her back straight and her attention focused on them.

"Golbizarath," Alcarond said, leaning back in his chair. "That was a great test for you. Your biggest yet. How do you feel you fared?"

Kaile tried hard to calm his nerves. He swallowed, but tried to hide it by dipping his chin to his chest. He knew he needed to be honest. Or at least as honest as he could be, just like when the king asked him questions.

"I think my magic was sound. I used the notes I've been practicing, and held them pitch-perfect as far as I could tell. My spells were true, attaching themselves to the notes near perfectly, and the power of the spells was enough for what I attempted."

Alcarond puffed as he watched Kaile explain himself. His expression was stern, and deep in thought, and Kaile then truly wished he could read his thoughts, and not have navigated the probably testing words that would come from the archmage's lips.

"I did as you made me do," Kaile said. "I admit, I did try to fight your power over me, but I gave in, because I was powerless over Zertaan's Alluvi Omnipitus you placed on me."

Alcarond nodded in approval. "You know, then..."

"I know *now*," Kaile said. "The Godkeeper Rune. The same mark she put on Soren when the Wolf cut the scars in his face. It's in me. Binding me to you, forever."

"Nearly forever," Sophia corrected. "It will fade if you live long enough, apprentice."

Kaile nodded. "If..."

"Yes, if," Sophia added.

"May I ask, master Alcarond, why and when did you place the Godkeeper Rune on me?"

"As a safeguard," the archmage replied without a thought. "For a moment such as that. If you decided to run off and attempt to disobey me, and disobey your king. It appears I was right to do so."

Kaile didn't refute the statement, and intentionally kept his anger deep within. He wanted to clench his fists, to spit, to curse, but instead he played with his hair. "And when? And how?"

Alcarond laughed unexpectedly. "You don't know? Or you don't remember?" He glanced at Sophia.

Sophia leaned forward, taking Kaile's hand from his hair. "The day you arrived in Celestra. After your long trek from Ikarus. The ritual you went through. It was in there. You should have felt something. It's an... abrupt... sensation, having the rune placed on you."

Kaile's memory of that day flooded into focus, and he then remembered Zertaan performing a ritual on him while standing before the king. He didn't know what it was, and remembered asking, but he didn't remember the answer he was given. Indeed, he felt washed out and slept for days after.

How could I not know? I guess I was younger, naïve... but... those bastards. They played me all along. I was like a digger bomb, just waiting to explode. And I did, on the people I cared about most.

"So don't go running off again," Sophia said coldly. "For there won't be a conversation like this again."

Kaile remembered his view from his high window only minutes ago. The thought of flying free consumed him, but brought with it a deep sorrow, knowing he could not do what he wanted most... to go far, far away from everything. From the war, from his captors. He wanted to rescue Seph from her prison and take her to Eldra, or Mythren, Davin's continent, or even Garrehad to the south. Or one of the forgotten worlds far out into the sea.

But... he couldn't deny the pull *power* had on him. He could wait. He could wait for years until Alcarond's passing. He could ascend to the role of archmage. A nobody boy from

Ikarus, becoming the most powerful Syncron in all of Aladran. He thought about all the good he could do in the world if he passed the Black Sacrament and laid waste to the Demons of Dusk.

But there was always… the king.

Kaile gritted his teeth, and the anger welled within him at the thought of the flames that tore through Erhil, killing all those people. He thought about Seph down in the dungeons below.

Alcarond and Sophia both watched Kaile's emotions intently. Alcarond puffing on his pipe and Sophia sipping her drink.

Behind, Kaile heard the door open. There was no knock, but a quiet shuffle in the room. They were big strides from long legs, with her shoes clapping softly on the floor.

He turned. His anger doubled at the sight.

Pale skin covered in black and red tattoos, devilish eyes, long blond hair, and bloody fingers.

"Zertaan," Alcarond said, blowing out a great plume of smoke. "What brings you here at this hour? We're having a lesson."

Zertaan placed both her hands on the back of Kaile's chair. Looking over, he saw the dried blood on and under her long fingernails, knowing it wasn't her own. He felt the beads of sweat form on his brow, and his heart pounded hard in his chest, all the way up to his throat. His vision tunneled, knowing this was the woman who forced the rune on him that made him betray his friends.

"Just stopping in to give an update," she said. Kaile couldn't see her face above him, but Alcarond seemed to notice her gaze on his table, and poured her a drink of the liquor, pushing along the tabletop towards her. She leaned over to grab it, her long arms reaching far. Her black robes draped over him, making his skin crawl. The side of her breast skimmed Kaile's cheek. She grabbed the drink, stood back up straight, and swirled it in one hand. "Persephone is doing well in her Re-Enlightment. I expect she will break completely, and we can retrain her completely. She will become a fine Syncron sorceress for the king."

"How much longer do you expect?" Sophia asked, switching legs and crossing the other one under her red dress.

"Perhaps a month." Zertaan took a slow sip.

"A month?" Sophia asked. "That seems excessive, Zertaan."

"It takes what time it takes," Zertaan said, placing her hand on Kaile's shoulder and squeezing. He shirked out of her grip.

All in the room noticed, and a deep silence grew.

Alcarond broke it after a few moments. "As long as she isn't permanently harmed. She must make it through the Re-Enlightment whole. That is the king's will."

"She will." Zertaan bowed her head.

"What if she doesn't?" Kaile asked, mustering all his courage and turning to finally look up at her torturer.

"Some don't make it through the process," she said with a bitter expression. "You know that. I'm doing everything I can to make it as smooth of a transition as possible. So I can make no promises. If the young Syncron resists, and ultimately dies, then that is what Shirava wants, and the young Whistlewillow will go to her."

Kaile had an inner battle unlike many he could remember. He wanted to stand and strike a note, casting a spell to kill the evil bitch behind him, but logic screamed for him to do the opposite. *Wait! Think! Patience! Now is not the time. If you strike now, you'll surely die, and Seph will have no chance. Wait… breathe…*

"I'm doing my best," Zertaan said, clapping his shoulder. "The process should be done in under a month's time. Then we will know for certain if the young Syncron will bend and bow, or will face another fate…"

"Thank you Zertaan," Alcarond said. "Will that be all?"

"Yes, archmage." She slammed back her drink, bowed and left back the way she came.

Kaile's gaze was down on his lap. Full of rage and hatred. At her, and at himself. He felt a hand on top of his, startling him. He looked up and Sophia held his hand. She was leaning toward him. Her beauty was breathtaking, as Kaile even caught a longing look by the archmage at her.

"We know you have feelings for Seph," she said. "But try to remember, feelings cloud judgement. It breaks friendships and makes men do crazy things."

Alcarond looked away and out the window, puffing his pipe silently.

"Steel yourself, young Syncron," Sophia said. "Your destiny is bright. Stay true to the path, and find what you are looking for in your dreams. You will find great success, knowledge, and power in your future, but only if you keep your mind right."

Chapter Nineteen

There was a long pause in the archmage's chambers. A deep silence that fell like an invisible shroud all around them. Kaile heard the tiny heartbeat of flickering candlelight all around them. The whistling winter winds howled hollowly outside the tower's walls. And his own fingers scratching his pant leg filled Kaile's ears as his thoughts swished around like a murky cocktail in his mind.

So much had happened since his escape from his master on the battlefield at Erhil, and Kaile gazed down at his lap in shame and worry. He knew he needed to bury those feelings, at least while he was in the presence of those who knew him best. He was back home, in the company of the enemy. Or those who were *more* the enemy.

He felt he was straddling two worlds. One foot in each. One the side of the rebellion—those who fought for freedom and a brighter world—and the other foot placed in the deep-rooted absolute monarchy. The king thought he was keeping balance in the world, or at least trying to restore his twisted view of their world. But Kaile had seen the world from the other side—the misery, the oppression, the fear—and he couldn't unsee or un-feel what that was like.

Alcarond cleared his throat, shattering the silence like a mirror falling and splintering on hard stone.

"I wanted to talk to you about another subject," the archmage said, tapping out his pipe and stuffing fresh tobacco leaves in. Sophia crossed her legs again and sat back in her chair, her long hair falling behind it.

"Yes?" Kaile said, sitting up with his shoulders square, still hunched slightly but trying to break the habit.

"You had a meeting with the king. How did that go?" Alcarond and Sophia both waited eagerly for his answer, Alcarond sitting back with his dark eyes upon him, and Sophia was silent as death.

"He... he wanted to know about the Silver Sparrows," Kaile said.

"I'm aware." Alcarond put his pipe on the table, light wisps rising from it to the high, vaulted ceiling above. He folded his arms in his expensive shimmering robes. "He told me when he asked to see you. What did you tell him? Tell us."

Kaile coughed into his hand. "I told him who their leader was." Kaile saw they both were anticipating his answer. "Soren. I told him Soren was their new leader. Mihelik was a soldier for them, but he was old, and his passing has definitely clenched his role as their general."

Alcarond tapped his fingers on his forearm, gazing at Sophia, almost waiting for her reaction.

"You don't believe me?"

Sophia took a sip of her drink. "Soren was just a vagabond months ago. He hid under his false name, Smythe. He hid himself so he could live a wandering, meaningless life. And now he's the leader of the most powerful gang that attempts to overthrow our king and plunge our land into chaos? He's good with a sword, but when was the last time that disgraced knight won a battle? He may be a symbol, but when it comes to *winning*, he's lost his edge."

Kaile blurted, "He defeated the Black Fog! No one had ever done that before him, and maybe never will."

Alcarond's mouth curled in a hidden smirk.

"You saw this?" Sophia asked, swirling her drink. "We heard of it, but witness testimony says all sorts of… contradictory things."

"I did. I was in battle with the dark Synth Glasse, but I saw it, yes."

Alcarond shifted in his seat, clearly uncomfortable with Kaile's description of the fallen wielder Edward Glasse.

"I'm right," Kaile said. "He was a Synth. In every definition of the word—he was one—even if you were friends or comrades. He called the Black Fog into Grayhaven. He had the ability to somehow beckon the beast, and he was also the one who tried to have Soren killed by planting a coin on him that was a lure for the fog. Glasse had some dark ability to manipulate, or communicate, with the Demons of Dusk."

Alcarond and Sophia exchanged worried glances.

"Your words are true," Alcarond finally said. "As much as it pains me. Shirava cursed him in the end for his treachery when he attempted the Black Sacrament, failing, and returning his Ellydian to the lands."

Alcarond set his pipe down, leaned over his desk, and steepled his fingers. A deep curiosity shimmered within him. Kaile knew the look. The colors of the archmage's eyes deepened, his voice hollowed, and his entire demeanor shifted. The Demons of Dusk had become his life's mission. Eradication was the only cure for Aladran, and Alcarond aimed to be the one to do exactly that.

"Tell me more about the battle with Soren and the Black Fog," the archmage said. "The carnage left behind from the battle will be spoken about for generations. With the fog was a

THE DARK SYNTHS

tapestry of fear unlike anything the people of that old city had seen in their whole lives. Tell me."

"Soren fought like a ghost," Kaile said, his words laced with a pure awe of admiration and respect. "He fought like an untouchable wraith that was as fearless as the night. With his Vellice dagger, he cut into the beast's tendrils. I've never seen anything so courageous, foolish, and heroic in all my life."

Alcarond shifted, meanwhile, never taking his gaze off of Kaile as he spoke.

"Within the tendrils," Kaile continued, "Soren told us later that while they burned, wrapped him with tremendous strength, and lacerated every part of his body, he cut deeper and deeper and deeper, knowing that his only chance was to get in close with Firelight, and cause as much damage to the body as he could. But what he saw within caused Soren to pause."

"Go on." Alcarond loomed, leaning in, feeding off every word of the story.

"What Soren found most shocking about the creature, which was the biggest Black Fog any of us had ever seen, was light."

"Light?" Alcarond said involuntarily, gripping the table. "What do you mean, light?"

"A murky, yet vibrant, pure silvery light," Kaile said, almost as if not believing the words himself, as he told the archmage and the Shadow Sorceress. "A liquid within, a pool that turns men to Shades. No organs, no bone, no muscle, just a sack of liquid like starlight."

Alcarond sat back in his chair, eyeing Kaile as if searching for lies interwoven in his retelling. But when he seemed certain his apprentice spoke the truth, he spun his chair away, facing the windows filled with deep night and dark clouds beyond. "Light?"

"That's quite a remarkable discovery," Sophia said. "That

would mean these creatures are unlike an animal in our world. They truly are not from this world. They are created from something darker. Perhaps the dark magic the Scriptures of the Ancients foretold of in their final volumes."

"I've read the scriptures," Alcarond said. "Before my master burned them. They spoke naught of such dark creatures or the creation of them. If Glasse did truly have the ability to summon them into the city, then there's something else at work here in this battle. Somehow Glasse gained access to knowledge that is beyond the Scriptures of the Ancients."

"Master?" Kaile breathed, wishing to hear more as Alcarond's face darkened as if taken by a swirling storm within his mind.

"I've missed something in my research," Alcarond said, stroking his strong chin, still facing away from them. "I've been staring at the lock when I should have been searching for the key. There's someone or something hidden in the shadows of this war. There's something darker and more sinister than I imagined."

Kaile had a thought, but it was one, even if he wanted to say it aloud, he wouldn't dare utter within Celestra...

The king. The king was the one who had unbridled access to all the wealth of knowledge of the old world and the Ellydian. Perhaps he knew more than he led onto with Alcarond, or even Mihelik. If someone knew about the dark magic alluded to in the oldest tomes of Aladran, it would be him.

"I have carcasses, you know..." Alcarond said, causing Kaile to cock his head.

"Carcasses, my master?"

"Shades," the archmage said. "From Soren's battle with the three of them on the snowy hills of Cascadia. He fought and killed three. All three were brought here for inspection. There was no light within them. Only innards like that of, what I could best compare to that of a great cat. A panther or the like.

Extremely thick bones, almost as if mutated. Muscles far denser than even that of a lion's, and organs that were deep in color, not red but a grayish-black. There was no light, no magic, only flesh and blood and bone."

"I know he was true in what he said he saw," Kaile said.

"I'm not saying he lied," Alcarond said. "Soren Stormrose is many things, but when it comes to whether or not I believe him... Soren wouldn't lie about a thing like that."

"And now..." Sophia added, "a dragon has come to Aladran. It is the only other weapon that's effective against the Demons of Dusk. It slaughtered hundreds of Shades at the site of Golbizarath after your acquisition of Persephone. Dragonfire and Vellice steel can kill them."

Alcarond popped his knuckles. "But we know naught how effective dragonfire is upon the Black Fog..."

Kaile imagined the spectacle of a dragon battling the Black Fog Soren fought in Grayhaven, and his leg bounced at the thought.

Alcarond turned and raised a brow at seemingly hearing Kaile's boot heel bouncing on the floorboards. "King Amón has sent ships for Garrehad." His words were meant for Kaile, and he licked his teeth, waiting to see how he responded.

"But... sending ships and men to the southern continent won't necessarily help acquire more Vellice weapons..." Kaile scratched his hair. "The king's armor and his sword Storm Dragon were gifts of old from Vellice, Master Kenji Ammorant. He died decades ago, and they were gifts in exchange with King Amón's father, King Râggahr."

"Your memory is sound and astute, my apprentice," the archmage said. "There was an exchange of gifts. The king's armor and Storm Dragon were given to the king in exchange for a slaughter of Kenji's enemies. A feud of thousands of years was smote by the king and his forces."

"But..." Sophia added, grabbing her drink and staring

deep into its contents. "There was no sword battle, no long-lasting war, or surprise attack. Plague was what King Râggahr used. Not a single soldier of Aladran or Master Kenji's people suffered or died. It was an absolute slaughter, and an extinction of a people."

Kaile's teeth gritted, and he felt his face twisting at the thought.

More children dead... more innocents. The wrath of kings. And for what? Weapons? Power? It makes no sense...

"Regardless of the past," Alcarond said. "King Amón wishes to acquire an armory's worth of the Vellice blades."

"He's mad," Kaile muttered beneath his breath.

It was loud enough, however, to warrant intense glares from both Alcarond and the Shadow Sorceress.

"Watch your tongue, boy," Sophia hissed.

Alcarond's eyes darkened. "You know not who has ears within these walls. Ease your words, son."

"What I meant, was... uh..."

"The king is wise," Sophia said, shifting the tone in the room. "He sent his best soldiers, merchants, and a small envoy of Syncrons. The Syncrons alone should be enough to do what needs to be done, and the soldiers will protect their bodies, their voices, and their notes."

"The Drakoons?" Kaile asked without realizing it. He held a secret terror of the dark knights of Eldra. He would most certainly enjoy none of those faceless men lurking in his home city.

"They remain here." Alcarond began loading more tobacco into his pipe and pouring a fresh glass. "The archpriest has insisted they are to stay to protect the king. That is their sole mission. They remain in the capital."

I wish they would've taken that monster Zertaan with them...

"With any luck we will have more weapons for the war

against the Demons of Dusk..." Alcarond puffed away, looking up at the ceiling. "Dragonfire..."

"Dragonfire?" Kaile muttered, suddenly realizing why his master said the word. "You plan to figure out what it is about dragonfire that can wound them?"

Alcarond nodded, blowing a plume of smoke into the air. It swirled in the candlelight above like a delicate, beautiful spell.

"Blades and magic can't kill them, but dragonfire somehow can..."

"Could we..." Kaile swallowed hard. "Create dragonfire?"

"It seems not." Alcarond brushed his hair behind his ears. "But it may not be impossible. Mutating fire into dragonfire, however, may be possible. But it will take no lack of time and research. And all for something that may be impossible in the end."

"It would be worth a try," Kaile said. "But how could we know what's on the inside of a dragon that causes the fire in the first place?"

Alcarond's gaze shifted to a scroll at the edge of the table. It lay unbridled and loose. Kaile leaned over and grabbed it. He unrolled it and expected to see some of the old language, Sarin or Durgin, but to his surprise, it was in the common tongue, and freshly scribed.

"This isn't from the Sundar, or the Polonians," Kaile said, feeling his eyes grow wide as he read. "It's the dissection of a dragon. This says from before the Great Divine Flood."

Alcarond nodded. "It was translated and written from an original, in the king's private collection. I just received it this morning."

"This is..." Kaile said, his fingers trembling as he read. "Amazing. Absolutely incredible."

"It may be possible," Alcarond said. "As improbable as it may seem."

"There's a trigger mechanism in the throat that sparks the gas from within," Kaile said. "Astonishing."

Alcarond nodded, glancing over at Sophia, then her glass. He reached over and poured her another.

Kaile laid the scroll back on the table, loosely unwinding as he placed it down.

Kaile itched his nose. "There's so much going on in the world right now. I hardly recognize it. I feel like we're fighting more wars than we can count: the Demons of Dusk, the Silver Sparrows, the Chimaera, the dragon… it seems to never end."

"The king will win the war." Alcarond's voice grew icy cold. "He will win all the wars. And we are going to help make sure of that."

Kaile swallowed hard at the thought of his friends back out there in the desert. All alone, infinitely outmatched against the king's legions and horde of Synths.

"What concerns you?" Sophia asked. "This should excite you. You're about to become a great Syncron lord in one of the greatest wars in the history of Aladran. This will set your name among the greatest Syncrons the world has ever seen. You, Kaile Thorne, will become a Lyrian, and you will help defeat the Demons of Dusk and the enemy rebellion once and for all. And you're not even twenty years of age."

His age being said aloud made him remember Seph down there all alone. And he remembered Zertaan walking in—surely intentionally—with her fingers still stained with Seph's blood.

Alcarond raised an eyebrow at him, but said nothing. He only puffed away at his pipe with the huge windows behind him filled with shadowy clouds skirting across the starlit sky.

Sophia rubbed her hands, glaring at Kaile. She then steepled her fingers and nodded with pursed lips. "What concerns you now, apprentice?"

Kaile sighed deeply, cupping his head in his hands and

hunching over, staring down at his boots. The turmoil inside him was about to break him. The walls of his sturdy, strong exterior were crumbling. All the lies, all the regret, all the shame…

He felt the other two were uneasy, but silent, ready for an answer.

Kaile grunted, gritting his teeth. The pain in his heart was too great. He needed to do something—anything—to help her.

He sat up, his eyes closed, and his fists clenched. He forced himself to breathe and uncurl his fingers. The tears in his eyes wanted to erupt, but he choked them down. His eyes opened, glaring up at the high, vaulted cone ceiling. A deep breath calmed him, and he looked squarely into Alcarond's dark gaze.

"Let me talk to her. Let me see Persephone. I can talk sense into her. I can speed up the Re-Enlightment so she doesn't endure pain she doesn't need to go through. I can help the king. Please, Alcarond. Let me go talk to her…"

A great unease filled the room, as if a dragon blew in a thick smoke from its lungs, making it hard for Kaile to breathe.

"Master?" Kaile pressed. "I'll do good. I'll help turn her to our side and see the light. I can help. I promise."

Alcarond leaned forward. Putting his elbows on the table, Kaile sat back instinctively. "Kaile…"

"I know, I know… you say I like her or love her or whatever… but I just want to help the king, and I don't want her to die down there."

"Kaile," Sophia interrupted, putting her hand gently on his forearm. "You know Persephone Whistlewillow's past."

Kaile nodded.

"Her family was killed in the burning of Tourmielle. The Chimaera was rampant, and her entire family was among the victims of the plague and the king's last resort. Do you think you can talk her into serving him? The man who commanded her hometown burned? Do you think Soren

Stormrose could be turned to follow the king... from a conversation?"

Kaile's eyes finally watered. He couldn't hold them back anymore, and the teardrops fell.

"Pain is the key to breaking her hatred," Sophia said. "That's the only way. She must be broken. Mind, body, and spirit."

"I'm sorry, my apprentice," Alcarond said. "You cannot see her. I know you care for her. I see the pain you feel." He reached out, and in a rare moment of compassion, grabbed Kaile's other forearm and squeezed. "There's nothing you can do for your friend. I'm afraid... she is at the mercy of Zertaan."

The mercy of Zertaan... there's no mercy there. She may as well be at the mercy of the devil Nazaroth himself...

Kaile bent over and sobbed into his hands. His body convulsed, his heart ached like it was going to wither and die, and he felt all hope was lost. He worried Seph was going to die all alone down there at the hands of that evil monster. And there was nothing he could do about it...

Chapter Twenty

The hours blended like shifting sands, interweaving, meshing together until time was a fleeting afterthought. All that endured, all that grounded Seph, was pain...

Thick, stagnant darkness hung heavy in the air. A single candle flickered its dying last breaths on the table beside her. The taste of the rusty rag in her mouth had numbed her mouth so much that there was no taste left. On her side, she lay with her hands bound behind her, and her ankles bound to the bed frame. Her vision was a blurry mess of daydreams and what she knew were hallucinations.

Soren would appear, freeing her of her bindings, helping her to her feet and sneaking her away through the dark underbelly of the city until Seph was free of her torture. She dreamed of casting a spell powerful enough to burn Zertaan's flesh and muscle straight off the bone, leaving only a crumbled pile of skeletal remains.

The dreams of rescue and escape were constant and crippling. There was no one coming into the lion's den to save her. No one was going to save her from the pain that threatened to consume and kill Seph. Even Kaile, the one who betrayed her more than any, was somewhere out there. But he'd turned. He'd returned to the Synths, so he was gone forever.

And she knew if she ever saw him again, she'd kill him for what he'd done.

Then, there was only the pain and the last breaths of the candle before her, dancing with a melancholy, dreamy movement of bobbing and swaying. The pain in her wrists, shoulders, and ankles were causing her to lose her grip on reality. She knew her body and mind couldn't endure much more. Even her soul was diminishing; a vague spot of light fading fast from deep within.

The fight in her was weak.

The drive to live was dying, as more and more she thought of the release of death, and what it must be like to feel *nothing*.

For she knew if she survived the Re-Enlightment, they were going to make damn sure she didn't have any fight in her left. Nothing buried down in secret. They were going to *break* her. Break everything about her.

"S—Soren," she muttered in her waking dream. "Where… where are you?"

The shuffle of armored footsteps clattered outside the door. She jolted, biting down on the rusty rag and snapping back awake.

A key slid into the door from the other side, and the two soldiers entered in the middle of a full conversation.

"You didn't…" one said, moving to untie her ankles from the bed.

"I did. Tits as big as me hands," the other said. "I'll never forget 'em. Nothing like what I got back at home. Pretty little mouth to boot," the other said, grabbing Seph's arms, ready to hoist her up out of bed.

"Too bad this one's got no meat on her bones," the first said, finishing untying her ankles.

"Aye," the other said. "No meat, and dirty as sin."

"Maybe Zertaan would let us bathe her…"

They both gazed at her with dark glares. "Maybe. She may not have handfuls for us, but she's young at least."

They sat her up, both looking down at her with looks that made Seph's stomach turn and made it feel like spiders were crawling up beneath her skin.

"What do you think there, dirty thing?" one said to her, rubbing her cheek with the back of his finger. "A few minutes to help out a couple of lonely, hard-working men?"

He toyed with the gag in her mouth, and she prayed to Shirava for him to remove it.

"Hey," the other said, slapping his hand away. "What're you doin'? You're a damned fool, and your pecker is gonna get us killed. She's a Synth. You forget that? You take that out and she's gonna send us flying up into the ceiling. We'd be crushed upside down, you moron!"

The first let go of her gag, scratching his head in embarrassment. Instead, his hand roamed down to Seph's neck, his scratchy, weathered skin causing the small amount of food in her stomach to lurch up. His hand went down to her stomach, groping her through her shirt, and then to her waist.

With a swift movement, she folded her knee up into her chest and shot her heel forward, slamming it into the man's groin with all the strength she could muster. Which must have been enough, because the soldier recoiled down with a twisted face and squinted eye. He fell onto his rear and rolled onto his side, groaning. "Fucking bitch!"

The other looked down at her with confusion, his fingers splayed and his eyebrows raised. She shot up, shoving her head into his nose. The sharp crack erupted from his face, and she was quick to her feet, running for the open door.

Seph ran with quick steps, both ankles still bound with iron braces and leather straps tied between them. She ran. She ran as fast as her feet could take her. Her wrists were still bound behind her, and her pace was erratic and more of a skip than a sprint. Seph huffed labored, rough breaths through her nose as she made for an exit. There had to be one.

All she knew about the Tower of the Judicature was the path from her cell to the Abiron and back. The soldiers had never taken her to any other parts of the dungeons, but she knew there had to be a way out. But behind her, the heavy footsteps ran quickly to wrap their awful fingers around her again. She panted as she ran, inspecting the dark, twisting, seemingly endless tunnels beneath the tower.

There's got to be a way out… there's got to be…

She ran frantically, heading down new tunnels, some dark, some torch lit.

Finally, she took a turn that led to a door. It wasn't a door like a cell door. There were no bars filling the open space at eye level. It was a simple wooden door painted white. She ran to it, hearing the soldiers behind scrambling to find her.

She neared the door, turning her back to it to wrap her hands around the handle, praying to Shirava it was unlocked. But as she twisted the knob, she felt it twist easier than natural. She moved away from the door, to see it open inward. Behind the door was the familiar face she'd wished to never see again.

The red eyes, the light skin covered in black and red tattoos, and the flowing golden hair.

"What are you doing out here, my plaything?" Zertaan hissed with a wide smile that dropped to a terrible scowl. "Are you trying to leave before we finish our fun? What a terrible thing you're doing. Naughty, naughty." Her eyes narrowed and her sharp teeth flashed.

Seph turned to run, shuffling her feet, but just down the hall the two soldiers came into view, both panting hard, and both their eyes shooting open wide at the sight of the Synth behind Seph.

"How'd this little thing get past you?" Zertaan glared at the blood on the nose of the soldier and scoffed. "Men... always distracted by their urges. Take her to the Abiron, and secure her tightly. We don't want my toy getting loose again..."

The two soldiers swarmed Seph, who fought and shook, screaming behind her gag. They dragged her roughly back to the Abiron, through the elaborate door, and to the chair where they bound her and smirked as if proud of themselves.

One leaned down and whispered into her ear. "You don't deserve to get fucked by me. You deserve to lie in the mud with the dogs and the rats." He spit in her hair, licking his teeth before adjusting his gauntlets and leaving the room, leaving the door cracked.

I can't do this again. I can't go through more torture from Zertaan. I don't think I can take anymore... I—I should give in, but I can't. I just can't. The king killed my mother and father. I can't bow to him.

Stay strong, Seph. You'll die before you bow. At least in death there's no more pain...

Zertaan walked into the room like a demon, shutting the immense door behind her. Seph could feel the eagerness dripping off her like melting ice. Her fingers were still stained with blood from their last session, and for the life of her, Seph couldn't remember when that was. A few hours? A day? More?

Zertaan didn't look at Seph, walking to the table with all her favorite tools instead. She took a strong pull off a bottle of spirits, letting out a soothing sigh after.

The Synth put her drink down and walked over to Seph, gazing down upon her like a wicked, ravenous serpent. Her eyes flickered the color of the setting sun, her pale skin glowed in the candlelight and her long fingers pressed into Seph's cheeks, causing her to recoil in fear.

A knock came at the door, and just before Zertaan went to answer it, she pulled Seph's gag free, letting it fall down to her chest. Seph coughed a shrill cough and smacked her dry tongue against the roof of her mouth. Seph could barely speak. Her mouth was so parched, and she let out another deep cough.

By the time Seph lifted her head, she saw Zertaan closing the door again, now with a pitcher and an empty glass in her hand. She walked over and put the glass on the table beside Seph, then poured the glass full, letting it fill and splash over the sides.

The sound of the water lapping into a pool in the cup made Seph lick her dry, cracked lips. Her gaze beamed at the clear, cool water, wanting nothing more than to shove it down her throat, licking up every drop off the table.

"You've been such a naughty little thing," Zertaan said, holding the pitcher before Seph. "Naughty little girls get punished. That's the only way they'll learn their lessons."

"P—Please," Seph moaned. "Please... water..."

"You want water, you say?" Zertaan leaned down so their noses touched. The foul, rank odor of Zertaan's breath made Seph's stomach lurch. "You want water?"

Zertaan stood straight up, towering over Seph, lifted the pitcher, and upended it, sending its contents into Seph's hair.

Seph licked the droplets she could, letting out deep moans.

Zertaan lifted her hand and sent a hard smack across Seph's cheek. Seph's world fogged and her vision blurred. The heat in her cheek ripped through her body, causing her to fight her bindings and scream like a wild woman.

Zertaan then smacked the full glass of water with the back of her hand, sending its cool contents flying across the room. The glass hit the wall behind Seph and shattered.

Seph began to cry, unable to hold back her tears any longer. "P—Please... I want to go home... I want to go back to Soren..."

"You want to go back to your uncle?" Zertaan knelt before

Seph with a false look of sadness on her face and in her voice. "You want to go back to the man who failed you over and over and over? Why? For love? Because he's your only family? Well... guess what... *I'm* your family now. You *are* home. The sooner you realize that, the sooner this can all end. We will take care of you and make you more powerful than you could imagine. But you have to trust me. Can you do that? Can you trust me?"

Seph's cracked lips separated, ready to speak. Zertaan leaned in, nearly licking her lips at the thought of Seph groveling.

But instead of words, Seph sent all the moisture in her mouth straight between Zertaan's eyes. The spit dribbled down her nose as Zertaan's red eyes flashed red in anger.

Zertaan stood back up straight and tall again, her long blond hair streaming down her back nearly to the backs of her knees. She rubbed her knuckles.

"That's fine," the dark Synth said, reaching back and taking another swill of her strong drink. "I wouldn't have let you off easy, even if you had begged for mercy and pleaded to let me into the king's grace." A demeanor sparked in Zertaan like Seph hadn't seen. It was a wicked determination, a challenge in a new sense. She was invigorated. She felt alive, and Seph shook in terror.

"This is going to be a long night naughty girl, and by the end of it, I'll have you begging... like the dog you are..."

That night, Seph wished for death many, many times. She screamed the goddess's name; she begged for Soren to come save her, and one time she even screamed Kaile's name. It wasn't in a vindictive sense. In her most vulnerable moments, and as the pain erupted in her, she yelled for Kaile to help her. In that moment, when the knife twisted into her shoulder blade, she wanted Kaile to burst into the room, and strike down the evil woman who was far beyond the evil of a Shade or a Black Fog. Zertaan was a true demon in every right, and Seph begged for the sweet release of death.

There are few in the world who knew the kind of pain and anguish Seph experienced that night in the depths of the capital. In the end, she never buckled. She never said she'd serve the king. She never said she'd obey Zertaan, which caused the Synth to double her efforts, employing all sorts of horror from her tools on the table.

By the time Zertaan had finished her work, a pool of blood grew dark beneath Seph. Zertaan left the Abiron without a word, only wiping her bloody hands on a towel on the table. She left whence she came, like a terrifying storm blowing out the door.

Seph was left slumped in the chair, her head hanging over the headrest, her body motionless. Blood dripped down her forehead, both shoulders, from a long gash in her stomach, from holes in her thighs, and from another fingernail broken off. Instead of water in her mouth, irony blood oozed from her gums where Zertaan had poked needles into them.

The world faded in and out of darkness, and Seph felt her life force depleting rapidly. The warm light of the afterlife pulled at her, and she was eager to give in. The pain was too great, and her options were too few. Give in, or die, with infinite amounts of excruciating pain in between. There was no winning this battle with Zertaan of Arkakus.

It was bow or die, and Seph was ready for death's embrace. Ever since she'd left Guillead and followed Soren out into the wintery plains, her life had meaning. It had adventure; it had purpose. She knew what it felt like to fight for something worth fighting for. She knew what family felt like. She finally remembered what it felt like to be loved.

It's all right. This can be the end. I've had a good enough life.

There's so much more I wanted. I wanted to take a lover. I wanted to have a child someday. I wanted to have a home and a family of my own. But not in this world. This world has told me there's no place for me in it.

I can die. I give myself permission.

Go to the afterlife and watch the rest from the Halls of Everice.

It's all right, Persephone. It's time…

Seph faded in and out of consciousness in the chair, waiting for death's cold embrace.

Finally, what she thought was death finally came. But, it didn't come in the way of deep, infinite darkness, or the cold grasp of icy fingers on her soul, instead… it came in the tune of a C note.

The note rang clear from the hallway, beyond the door, and Seph finally felt her tense muscles and weary bones and joints relax. The note was pure, crisp, bright, and with a slight tinge of melancholy.

This is it. Finally, the pain is disappearing, and I can go into the unknown…

The feeling of soothing aches and broken skin repairing itself warmed her spirit. The C note was the most beautiful thing she'd ever heard, like a babbling brook in the middle of the desert, or a double rainbow cascading over the barren volcanic wasteland.

The pain left her body, just enough for her to lift her head and put her chin to her chest.

"Thank you, Shirava… bless you…"

And her world faded to darkness.

Chapter Twenty-One

The Under Realm, somewhere beneath the deserts of Zatan

THIS MAY BE SUICIDE, Soren thought. *But what's life without a little... dramatic risk?*

"You can't die yet," he muttered to himself in the complete and overwhelming darkness. "Not until you find Landran, rescue Seph, and send that fucking king one thousand yards beneath me, buried with no tomb."

His hand gripped the slick stone, finding finger holds in the thick claw marks left from Shades... however, many years ago, this tunnel was created.

The world around glowed in a ghostly white, causing a milky fuzz around the tunnel's surfaces, guiding him down further and further into oblivion.

"Yes, this is definitely suicide. If I didn't have the Heartstone, I'd need a torch." He laughed. "Imagine that... an idiot wandering underground with a torch."

But I have to know. I must know. I have to know what their world is beneath our feet. We may gain an advantage. Do they sleep? Do they rest? Are they slow? Vulnerable? He clenched his jaw. *I have to know.*

A hundred yards in, he guessed, there was a fork. Two tunnels, both identical, leading further down into the Under Realm.

Soren thought.

He sniffed the dank air, but found no difference between the two, and wondered how many more splits there were beneath the surface. Did it grow to a vast network of tunnels like a honeycomb? He had no clue.

He scratched his stubbly chin. Then he sat on the stone, unlaced and removed his boot, and then his sock. From the sock, he plucked the end of a thread, eyeing it.

"Seems thick enough," he said as he put his boot back on his bare foot. He stood, inspecting the ground. Inserting the end of the piece of thread into a claw mark, he scooped up a rock and wedged it in, pinning the thread and nodding with approval. "Right it is then."

He started down the right tunnel, delicately letting the thread of the sock unravel.

Soren went down another fifty yards until another split. He took the left this time, tugging gently at the end of the thread behind him pinned on the ground. It seemed sturdy enough, so he continued his descent down into the darkness. Another twenty yards, another fork, and he took the right. The sock in his hands was disappearing fast, and he knew he wouldn't get much further. So he took his other sock off and tied one thread to another, going deeper and deeper underground.

Soren had spent most of his life avoiding the Under Realm. He didn't need Landran to teach him that. The plains of dusk meant most certain death, and the Under Realm was certainly doom.

But this time was different. His senses were alive. The

sounds of the Under Realm were a melody of thick emptiness, distant drops of echoing water, and that last eerie void. It was the kind of void where the sounds of the chirping birds and buzzing insects fade to nothing in the deep forest, while the hidden predator inches forward, closer and closer to its next meal, licking its lips and readying its sharp teeth.

Soren knew he was the prey, not the predator down there. He may kill a Shade or two if he was lucky. But this was their home, and remembering the army of Shades that surrounded them back in the desert of Zatan, he knew their numbers were seemingly endless.

There were two more forks before he reached what appeared to be... the end.

His toes were at the precipice of a great drop. It was deep enough that the Shadowflame Heartstone couldn't breach the darkness.

"Damn. I must've taken a wrong turn." He cursed his bad luck, not finding a way to go deeper. He went back up, picking the thread back up and wrapping it around the sock in his hand. His bare feet squeaked in his boots, though the ring and bracelet of the Twilight Veil hid those sounds while he was shrouded in darkness.

Taking a different route down, he went through more forks, realizing this was more than just a single passageway created by the Demons of Dusk. He thought, *If I were them, then I'd do the same. No one entrance and exit. If I could dig, I'd want ways to escape, hide, move around an enemy. And if I were in their numbers, then I'd want to have the network of tunnels for my soldiers to move around in. If this was my world, my men and I would be unstoppable from invaders.*

The thread was running out, leaving only a heel of the sock remaining, and he began searching his body for more thread. His leather and steel armor was over a shirt, which he could use if he had to, but anyone who'd worn armor without something underneath knew it was far from comfortable with the pinching and chaffing it caused.

Luckily, though, he seemed to catch a break. Nearly at the end of the two socks, a turn into a corridor opened up the world again to him, but this time… with a way down.

Upon the cliff he stood, a path led down to the right. The chasm was vast and no far walls were visible. He could shout out, waiting for the echo so he could guess how far down or out the cave went. But obviously, that wasn't an option.

With the Twilight Veil hiding his footsteps, and the Heartstone revealing his path, Soren felt for the first time in his life like a true assassin. He knew how to kill, and had killed countless in his life. All bad, he hoped, and believed. But with the weapons he'd been gifted—those two relics, and the Vellice dagger Firelight—he truly was as deadly as any that ever lived, and he wondered if any in history had had the combination of tools to kill like he had then.

He guessed not. If only he could wield the Ellydian, then he thought he might truly be unstoppable. But he was born with no magic, and acquiring it later in life was impossible. But even without magic, he knew his enemies were in a whole new kind of danger.

Even with them all in his possession, getting in, killing his foes in the capital, and spiriting Seph to safety alone was impossible. There were all manner of dangers that Celestra held that the rest of Aladran feared. Whether it be the unstoppable force of the Synths in the king's command, or the Drakoons, the archmage, the vast army and cavalry stationed there, or the network of spies; Soren knew that attack would require no lack of strategy and cunning. And he hoped that Lady Drake's spy could give him valuable insight on how to get Seph out of there.

But again, that would take patience—something Soren had

been lacking ever since his niece followed him out of her hiding hole in Guillead.

A darkness spread in Soren like the plague then. Any light-heartedness flickered away like the dying breath of a candle. The confidence he held from the relics he wore washed away like a receding tide. His eyes narrowed, his stature hardened, and his grip on Firelight clenched tight.

He slunk down into the darkness. Into the unknown. The Heartstone only revealed the walls of the cave to his side, the path beneath him, and the ledge behind, which quickly faded into darkness again. Thirty feet is what he guessed the Shadowflame Heartstone let him see, and that would have to be enough. It had to...

But there was something down there. He could sense it. Like the thumping of a slow-beating heart. He felt it. His pace slowed as he went down. The final thread left his fingers, falling delicately onto the stone path down.

Soren stopped and knelt, feeling the ground with his bare palm. He waited. Closing his eyes, he felt out for what was out there, what was with him in the darkness. And then he felt it.

It was unmistakable. Movement.

It wasn't quick and rapid like moving, scuttling Shades. It wasn't sharp and rhythmic like the centipede-like legs of the Black Fog. It was low and grinding, like stone lungs breathing.

There's something down here.

The path down suddenly straightened and opened up to a wide ledge. He looked behind to mark the defining rocks of the path that led back up to the string, and his way back to sunlight.

Then, he approached the end of the ledge, and as he did, something unexpected made his breath catch. Beyond the ledge, deep down in the Under Realm... there was a light.

Dim, with a green hue, and soft like sea fog, it glowed down into the depths beyond the ledge. Soren scooted onto his chest and belly, reminding him of the time Bael and he were hunted by the Black Fog in the forest, that later turned out to be after them because of the cursed coin the Synth Glasse had gotten into Bael's coin pouch.

As he pulled himself closer to the edge, the sounds below grew, filling his ears with the familiar sounds he was listening for earlier.

"Shades," he whispered to himself. "Lots of them…"

He peeked over the edge, letting the green glow fill his vision below.

A hundred feet below him was a huge cavern unlike anything he'd ever seen. He swallowed hard, inspecting the moving floor below.

Black Fog sat like statues. Hundreds of them. They rested motionlessly in the gloom, dimly lit by the green light that glowed from a cavern beneath Soren, hiding the source of the light. Between the Black Fog, the cave floor was a moving seabed of bodies. Shades, countless numbers of them, filling the room from wall to wall to wall.

There must be over ten thousand of the bastards… It's an army. A hidden army beneath our feet as we walk without a care in the world, not knowing the death that lurks beneath our feet.

The ground trembled as tiny pebbles beside his hands bounced. The earth shook, and just as Soren began to back away, a terrible noise filled the cavern. It was thunderous, like a mountain breaking in half, or a volcano erupting with terrible carnage following.

All his instinct told him to run, to hide, to live, to fight another day. No Black Fog made that sound he knew. It was something else, something far larger, and even more terrifying…

But he didn't run away. Instead, he pulled himself further over the cliff, looking straight down as the green light grew. The Shades scattered away from the moving light, and the

Black Fog shifted, buzzing like mad insects at first, then moving in a smooth sort of unison to the far wall, as the light intensified to an unworldly shade of green unlike any grass or moss Soren had ever seen.

And then... the source of the light revealed itself.

Soren's eyes widened, and he glared down with a furious curiosity, unable to avert his gaze at what emerged beneath him.

Huge wings of black with veins of green like jade streaking through obsidian...

Thick, enormous arms and legs with thick claws carried the monster forward.

It towered over the Black Fog like a great peak looking down upon foothills.

The beast roared again. Soren clapped his hands over his ears to dilute the echoing roar that filled the cavern, surely all the way back to his friends.

The Shades scattered into tunnels, but the Black Fog held their ground as each of them peered up at the black monster brimming with green light within its wings, the great curled horns on its head, and the streaks that flowed down its long horned tail.

Soren gasped. "By the goddess... A... A dragon..."

He couldn't believe his eyes or the words that left his lips.

"A dragon of the Under Realm. The Demons of Dusk are subservient to this monster. I have to tell the others. The world needs to know about this new, hidden foe..."

The dragon below spun, its long, green-horned neck turning back, showing the beast's head. As wide as a Black Fog is long, with eight eyes of evil, devilish green. The dragon had teeth longer than a Shade from tip to tip. They were gnarled and yellow, with a long tongue like that of an asp. It growled so deeply Soren felt it deep within the rocks below him.

He knew he had what he needed, and need not lurk longer in that hell.

Soren took one last look at the monster. It was the most terrible thing he could have imagined. The thing of nightmares, the thing of legend to destroy worlds, and the one thing Firelight had no chance against.

The dragon filled the cavern below, moving its head high, revealing its stature as its head rose halfway up the cavern. Its maw opened wide, and Soren saw the green fire brimming within the back of its mouth, the flames curling out of its throat like leeches. It let out one last roar, shaking the entire earth around him.

The thought that it may have sensed Soren somehow was enough to get him moving. He scooted back, getting to his feet, and running back up the path, hoping to Shirava that the Twilight Veil hid his footsteps from the beast and the Demons of Dusk.

He grabbed the thread and ran back to whence he came. Minutes later, he reached the man-made tunnel and sighed with relief.

"This changes everything," he said to himself, catching his breath. "Vellice steel won't solve this war. Dragons are about to escalate this war to one that will be told about for centuries. I've got to find Landran. I've got to figure out how to kill that dragon. For it seems... the world depends on it..."

His legs moved, and he ran down the tunnel.

He ran as fast as his legs could carry him.

This new revelation had to reach Lady Drake, the Dune Matron, and Lady Sargonanth. Soren even realized the king would have to know about this. Even his sworn enemy would have to prepare for the fight that could break the world itself.

PART V
KINGS AND MONSTERS

Chapter Twenty-Two

❧❦❧

Kings and their conquests.
 Pride, leadership, and eventual death comes to all kings. In all kings' minds, their work and rule is just and true. No king believes their power and decisions to be wrong. But a king must decide. The head of the lion points its way forward, through every meal, through every slaughter, through every carcass left behind, filling its stomach more and more. The lion grows in size and strength with each meal, causing its hunger to return—more ravenous and ferocious.

Kings, in their wisdom, must wield power. And there is one power that rises above all else... The Ellydian.

The royal lines of Aladran have always sought to contain this power for their own, causing many wars and deaths in their wake. Through the crown, wielders of the Ellydian gain access to the oldest knowledge of the connection of all things.

When the crown and the wielders of the Ellydian go to war with one another, there never ceases to be a lack of blood, horror, and torment in its wake.

The wielder must decide, then. To kneel and be protected from the hunt, and learn the oldest ways of our kind? Or, go out and be wild, but become a heretic, a loner, and be free.

. . .

-*Translated from the language of the Sundar. The Scriptures of the Ancients, Book II, Chapter XI.*

CELESTRA.

EARLY MORNING SUNLIGHT sparkled in the dust that wafted lazily through Kaile's room. He winced as the woman behind him washed the long gashes on his back. Shirtless, he shivered as the cold liquid seeped into the scars left by the vicious bear attack on him in the desert.

"Ah, fuck," he grimaced, gritting his teeth as the medicine bubbled on the long scabs across his back.

"Almost done," the old woman said. "Just need to re-bandage it and you're all set."

"Thank you," he said after collecting himself with a deep breath.

The old woman finished wrapping his back in fresh white linens and made her way out of his room.

It was early morning, just after daybreak, and coffee and breakfast were fresh on his mind as his stomach gurgled. He threw on a fresh shirt, dug his feet into his boots, grabbed his staff and went to the door, eager to fill his cravings. His mind had been so fraught over Seph, he'd barely eaten since his forced return to the capital, and his knobby ribcage told him it was time to replenish what he'd lost.

He grabbed the doorknob, but just as he turned it, a knock came from the other side. Opening the door, he saw a child in white and red robes. He must've been no older than eight, but had something on his mind as he eagerly waited for Kaile to greet him.

"Hi," Kaile said, opening the door wide.

"You are summoned to the Great Hall at noon for a proclamation by the king."

Kaile nodded, knowing that was all that could be done.

The child bowed and ran back off, surely to the next person on his list.

"Noon," Kaile muttered to himself, but then sighed. "It never ends here. One thing after another. What is he going to do now?"

***

HOURS LATER, as the sunlight had faded to a dreary, overcast sky—with thick fog filling the streets below like a massive anthill cut lengthwise and lay flat on its side—Kaile made his way down the Illuvitrus Sanctum Tower.

Down the winding tower with hundreds of stone steps, many worries flooded Kaile's mind. The king hadn't held a meeting in the Grand Hall since Kaile had returned, and Kaile chewed his fingernails in anxious worry.

Not only was he holding a meeting, but he summoned me. The one who fled with his enemy. I'm a traitor in every right, in every aspect, except for the fact that Alcarond had a backup plan for me. That's the only reason I'm still alive; because my treachery to my friends ended up being greater than mine to the king.

Kaile's shoulders slumped as he walked down, chewing his ragged nails, thinking only of Seph.

I'd give anything to go back and change what I did. But I didn't know they had the Godkeeper Rune placed in me as a backup plan. Shit. How did I not know? I'm so foolish... who am I kidding... I could never be the archmage. I'm too stupid... I'm a loser...

Kaile made his way out of the tower and into the streets of Celestra. His wild reddish hair made him stand out like a rose in a snowstorm to the people of the city. Many glares trailed him as he walked through the fog-filled cobbled streets. His fingers raised his hood over his head as he slumped, making his way toward the Grand Hall of Vael Vallora Keep, the king's fortress at the center of Celestra.

As he approached, the high walls of the keep spread out wide, encircling what looked like another city hidden behind the royal gate. Kaile stopped, marveling up at the entrance to Vael Vallora, with an immense wall of golden light towering above him. It looked like a portal to another world, shimmering magical golden light decorated with weaving patterns of lighter shades of gold. Ornate by every accord, the magical gate was impenetrable by every standard. Forged by the Ellydian, and only opened by the Ellydian, a crystal clear A note rang out constantly from beyond the gate.

Kaile remembered the first time he saw the gate. He thought it was the most wonderful and awe-inspiring thing he'd ever seen in his life. But then, it looked like a barred door to an eternal, inescapable prison.

The front guards noticed him and waved him over, immediately recognizing him. They led him through a side door beside the huge golden gate, and he walked into the keep, heading straight for the Tower of the King. Passing hundreds of soldiers, and a few gloomy, terrifying Drakoons keeping watch before the Tower of the King, Kaile's brow wetted from sweat, even in the wintry cold.

He entered the enormous tower gate, staff in hand, ready to face whatever lay inside. It was a stark reminder that he was back in the king's service; his servant, his weapon, his slave...

Kaile choked up, smelling the fresh-baked breads and roasted meats within, thinking only of Seph surely starved and beaten below his feet. But he swallowed his sadness again. There would be plenty of time to cry later, he thought. But he needed to be strong. He needed to put on a face. Because he knew he'd be no good to Seph dead. He could still help her.

Somehow, some way, he'd save her... even though he had no idea how.

Kaile entered the Grand Hall, lit by hundreds of candles, glowing torches, and two burning pyres before the steps that led to the king's throne. There was no king. The empty, huge iron throne sat atop the ten stairs, carpeted with plush red. The throne's jewel at its top sparkled magnificently, letting the light of the burning fires reflect off its brilliance in a sheen of all colors.

Beside the empty throne sat the archpriest, Solemn Roane, his head hidden by his hand as he peered down at his lap. He looked deep in thought, but Kaile wondered if there was something else going on with the man who looked far too young to be in his position. At the other side of the iron throne sat Alcarond, stroking his chin as he looked out at the hundreds of people filling the room.

As Kaile walked down the carpet, he marveled at the rows of men and women to his right.

It's... it's all the wielders of the Ellydian. All of them.

Zertaan and Sophia were standing at the front of the rows. Zertaan and Sophia couldn't be more of a contrast, Kaile thought. Zertaan—a ghostly white, with her skin covered in faded tattoos, and her thin, tall frame wrapped in black robes with extremely long, straight hair flowing down. Sophia wore shimmering red robes that glowed like ruby in torchlight. Her wavy black hair and tan skin made her a beauty by any standard, but Kaile knew the truth about the cunning, powerful sorceress. She was conniving, highly intelligent, and ruthless. Outstanding traits if she's on your side, not so much if not...

Behind them were the Synths of the king. Over a hundred Synths in every shade of ornate material and cloth for their cloaks and tunics. They came from all over Aladran. From every corner, every small village, every vast capital city, and from all walks of life. But they all had two things in common:

they were born with the gift of the Ellydian, and they knelt and swore fealty to the king.

Kaile knew those colorful robes were for ceremony only. Only the most powerful Synths in the world would dress in bright colors like that while out in the plains and other cities. While Zertaan was as recognizable as an orange in a sea of apples, most other wielders weren't powerful enough to invite surprise attacks when resting or sleeping. Alcarond, on the other hand, the sole Lyre in the world, could wear whatever color he damn well wanted. It wasn't an invitation to be attacked; it was a threat to stay away. Something not unlike a colorful green and yellow venomous snake, coiled in a tree, ready to strike its next victim.

"All rise for his majesty," a court attendant called out. "His grace, King Malera Amón."

All rose that weren't already standing, as a rear door opened, and the king walked out. It was the same door the king had entered from when he called Kaile in privately. Kaile walked off the red carpet and stood beside Sophia, stepping back to avoid Zertaan's red-eyed gaze at him.

The king wore silky white robes with gold trim, flowing down his muscular body like a finely carved marble statue. The Vellice sword Storm Dragon was sheathed at his hip, which he had to move slightly to sit. As he sat on his throne, he stroked his black beard, his deep blue eyes scanning the room. The Drakoons stood behind and in front of his throne. Soulless weapons ready to erase from existence any threat to his majesty.

With a wave of his hand, the room sat.

Below the white jewel of the throne, the king's six-spindled crown sparkled.

"My people..." The king's voice was deep and filled the room with a sort of divine presence. "We are at war. I asked for no war, but here we are, at the precipice of two. One that inches its way to our doorstep, threatening our way of life, and the other, roams beneath our feet, waiting for the shade of night to kill our fathers, our brothers, our children…"

Archpriest Roane finally perked up from his deep thoughts at the mention of the Demons of Dusk.

"But we have discovered a weakness in the Demons of Dusk," the king said. "Not only has the steel of Vellice proven to kill the beasts, but a dragon has arrived in Aladran. Its fire scorched and destroyed hundreds of Shades at the site of our archmage's battle against our human foe. Luckily, Alcarond, with the help of his planted apprentice, killed the treasonous former Archmage Mihelik Starshadow, and brought back with him the last of the line of Whistlewillows. But it was not without sacrifice…"

Alcarond stood and pulled his sleeves up, revealing the painful scars on his forearms from Mihelik's spell.

"And sacrifice will be needed to win these wars, and restore peace to our world." The king paused, eyeing the crowd of hundreds, seemingly reading every single person in the room. His icy gaze hit Kaile but for a second, and that was all it took to send a freezing chill down his neck to his stomach. Kaile felt the tight scars on his back from the bear's claws at the sight of Alcarond's injuries.

"But we will not sit idly by." The king gave a devilish smirk. "We are about to go on the offensive on both fronts."

The enormous doors to the Grand Hall squealed open on their hinges, and every person in the room turned to see who was entering. Many hushed gasps sounded around the room as the hulking Knight Wolf strode with gigantic steps toward the king.

The king stood. "We will not sit and watch the Black Fog and Shades kill without repaying their evil ways. The Vellice blades will be used to slaughter those bastards, even if it takes a hundred years. We will cut each and every one of them down until the night plains are safe for humanity once again. I would rather see the plains burn than to watch another night go by with only those monsters skulking about, waiting to feed on the innocence of my people."

The Knight Wolf stopped just before the stairs, all the Drakoons' bloodshot gazes heavy upon the enormous man. William Wolf unsheathed his massive sword, the Ember Edge and held it before him, before twirling it upside down, sticking its infinitely sharp tip into the carpet and kneeling. "I am ready to hunt," the Knight Wolf said.

Kaile swallowed hard, ready for the terrifying man to be anywhere other than in the same city as he.

"Then take what you need, my most heralded knight, and begin your hunt. Bring me the bodies of those you destroy. Meanwhile, Archmage Alcarond Riberia and the Shadow Sorceress Sophia Allathine will remain here, discovering a weapon capable of ridding our world of their dark evil, once and for all."

The Knight Wolf stood, bowed, turned and walked with huge strides back out of the Grand Hall. His cape of deep red and shimmering gold trailed behind him as he swept out of the room. Kaile felt his body relax once the enormous man was gone.

"Now." The king shifted in his throne, placing his hands on the armrests and leaning forward. "As for the rebellion... Archpriest Roane..."

The archpriest rose from his seat at the king's side. His demeanor was calm and collected, like a man who didn't have a care in the world other than his pure vision for what it was meant to be.

His long ivory robes flowed down his slender figure. His granite-colored eyes glared heavily into the room, as his wavy auburn hair danced at the sides of his face, tickling his collarbone. His tall five-peaked biretta shown like a snow-capped peak of a great mountain. He cleared his throat softly before speaking.

"Our king has asked me to address the depth of the treason we are facing in our great nation. The kingdom of Zatan, a land rich with culture, respect, and strength, has declared war upon not only our kingdom, but our way of life. Shirava watches down on us with a divine blessing that cannot be diminished, cannot bleed, and cannot die. Through her golden light we will defeat our foes, end this nonsensical, unethical, unwarranted rebellion. And we will usher in a new world full of wonderful, inspiring, pure light. We will create a tomorrow that will outshine any great span of history. We will create the new greatest age our world has ever known. We will inspire generations to continue on the path we define right now. Bless you, bless our king, and all praise the great Shirava."

"Praise Shirava," those in the room proclaimed. All but the Drakoons. Kaile always thought it weird the Drakoons never spoke, even to praise the goddess their lord Roane held in the highest regard and worship.

The archpriest bowed and sat.

"Bring my children in," the king proclaimed.

Instantly the rear door opened again, and a school's worth of children poured out. Nearly forty children, ages fourteen and down stood on the red carpet before him. The babes and toddlers were carried by the king's wives and nurses.

Sophia leaned over and whispered into Kaile's ear. "He didn't want them here for the talk of the Demons of Dusk. That may frighten the children."

"Not the war, though," Kaile whispered back. "He wants them to see his strength."

She nodded. Kaile caught Zertaan listening in on their conversation.

"The Silver Sparrows sickness has spread." The king stood and his voice carried strong through the Grand Hall. "The

Calica Clan and Lady Sargonenth have proclaimed war upon the crown. They have said they would rather die than bow to their one true king." The king turned his attention to Kaile, which caused the apprentice to swallow hard and shove his hands into his robe's pockets. "The archmage's apprentice has assured me that with my former archmage's passing, that leadership of the Silver Sparrows has transferred to Soren Stormrose. He is joined by Davin Mosser, a dwarf of Mythren, and Blaje Severaas, the Desert Shadow of the Calica."

The king stepped forward, forcing his strong shoulders back and staring up at the ceiling. "Three. Three against an entire army of my soldiers." His gaze dropped to the rows of Synths behind Kaile. "My soldiers and my fine Syncrons. The wielders of the greatest power our world has ever known. We will not let this rebellion advance, spreading its lies and heresy through my realm. I won't let them. Not my kingdom, not my lands, not my world."

He turned and nodded at Alcarond before sitting again. Once sat, he waved his children to be taken away, which they were quickly ushered back out whence they came.

Kaile snicked inside at the charade.

He only wants his children to see him as strong and commanding. But he doesn't want them to know the truth. It's not only about a rebellion. It's about him losing control. The king is secretly seething with rage. He's losing control even though he remains collected.

A darkness crept into Kaile like jumping into an ice-cold lake. Kaile quickly realized the darkness that could consume Aladran if the king unleashed his ultimate wrath upon the world. Fire would devour and consume. War would know every corner of Aladran, and Soren and the others would be overrun…

Kaile swallowed down his fear, presenting himself as a sturdy apprentice to the archmage, destined to become the most powerful of all the Synths behind him.

As Alcarond stood, the feeling in the room changed.

The king was the one who all knelt to and swore fealty to. They were forced into subservience. The king was the ruler of the free world, but Alcarond...

As Alcarond stood before the king at the top of the carpeted stairs, glaring down at the hundreds in the Grand Hall, a sort of deep reverence and admiration filled the air. The king may be their ruler, but in a sense, Alcarond was their protector, their guardian, the most powerful person in all of Aladran—and he was their chosen king, for lack of a better term.

The Synths behind Kaile all stood at attention, nearly breathless, eagerly awaiting their leader's words and commands. Each was as eager to serve the archmage as they were their king.

"The Silver Sparrows have taken a foothold in the desert lands of Zatan," Alcarond said, his finger tapping on Diamond Dust. "A dragon has returned to Aladran. These are not losses. These are opportunities. The Silver Sparrows, although their lies spread far and wide, are at a certain, devastating lack of strength compared to that of the king. They hold few wielders of the Ellydian, and those they do, don't hold a shaving of the wealth of knowledge each of you possess, my Syncrons. They had two powerful Ayls, who are both with us again. Kaile Thorne, my apprentice, did a tremendous job of infiltrating their ranks at my command, gaining us a wealth of knowledge into the operations of their leadership. And we have Persephone Whistlewillow going through Re-Enlightenment. She will become one of you."

Alcarond turned and walked sideways across the platform, his oceanic blue robes glimmering in the light of the burning pyres. A ray of sunlight beamed down through a break in the clouds, shining through the many windows up the high walls of the Grand Hall, and reflected off him like Shirava herself cast him in her majesty.

"Soren Stormrose has killed Shades, defeated a Black Fog and drove it from Grayhaven. He killed a bounty hunter of the king, and continues his journey through our lands, inspiring others to his useless and false cause. Soren still wields the Vellice blade he dubbed Firelight. It was a mistake letting him keep it, but a mistake I realized too late as Persephone secretly sent the blade back to him with an A spell I did not detect in the winds. It's a mistake I intend to remedy."

Alcarond stopped and turned back, walking back toward his seat. The archpriest had a curious look in his gray eyes as he watched the archmage, as if he himself wasn't sure what Alcarond was about to say.

Alcarond stopped before his chair. "With all his prowess for his fighting abilities, and legendary wrath; Soren Stormrose has a critical weakness. His rage blinds him. He advances through the desert toward his next destination, and although the king's spies are unable to locate him currently, he will reappear, and when he does—we will be waiting for him. Soren has no Synths with him. Zatan has few Synths remaining. That is his true weakness. For all his skill with a blade—against the Ellydian—he is all but already defeated."

The king spoke. "Archmage Alcarond, have you selected your force to hunt down and kill the rebel?"

Alcarond bowed.

Kaile felt his stomach in his throat. He didn't know what to expect, but he agreed Soren was helpless against the Ellydian.

"I have selected three Syncrons to hunt down Soren Stormrose, and quash this rebellion once and for all," Alcarond proclaimed. "Please step forward before your king, Albertus Sterren, Claudine Prest, and Myranda Cloutter."

Three Synths broke their rows and stepped forward into

the center of the Grand Hall. One man and two women, all in colorful robes with tall staffs in their hands.

Alcarond struck the bottom of Diamond Dust to the ground, leaving a hollow echo through the room. "You three have been selected to hunt down and kill the leader of the Silver Sparrows. It is a great honor, and you have been chosen for your aptitude and dedication of and for the Ellydian. You three Ayls will destroy the Silver Sparrows. You will kill Soren and his allies and end this madness."

Kaile shifted uneasily. He knew the three Synths Alcarond had picked. He'd trained with them for years. He knew they were three of Celestra's finest and knew Soren wouldn't have a chance against them. Perhaps one. Soren may silence one, but all three? The three Synths were versed in battle and coordinated attacks. They would guard against any method Soren might employ to silence their notes, but he would fail. Kaile knew in the depths of his soul that Soren couldn't defend against them.

The beam of sunlight faded, and the overcast gloom returned to their world.

"We will find a way to defeat the Demons of Dusk," Alcarond said. "I swear it, if it's the last thing I do. And you three will end this rebellion."

The three all bowed low.

The king smirked, nodding his head in approval. He then stood.

"All rise for his grace, the king," the attendant proclaimed.

The Drakoons shifted in unison, a brilliant movement that caused many in the room, including Kaile, to flinch. They led their king out of the room, and many in the room stirred, heading for the main doors. Alcarond and Solemn exchanged words. They were both stern looking and serious.

"Are you surprised he didn't pick you, or me, or Zertaan?" Sophia asked.

Kaile shook his head. "I know why. Zertaan is with Seph. You are going to try to determine and recreate the secret of dragonfire, and he won't send me because…"

"Because why?" Sophia pressed, with Zertaan turning and fully facing the two of them.

"Because he's training me to be his true apprentice. He wants me to take up his role as archmage someday. He's molding me. I see it, and I accept it."

Sophia nodded. "The Ellydian is strong in you. And it grows. You must embrace it, Kaile Thorne, for someday you will perform the Black Sacrament, and you will succeed. You will change this world, but you need not confront Soren to do so."

Zertaan's face twisted at the mention of Kaile and the Black Sacrament. She spun and walked off into the Grand Hall, heading for the front doors. Kaile's heart sank at the thought of her storming down into the Abiron and taking out her frustrations on Seph.

"Patience," Sophia said. "Patience Kaile. Everything will be right, but for now you need to step back and focus on your studies and your gifts. You will be a force in this world, but right now, you must take the time to focus inward. The world can wait…"

Chapter Twenty-Three

After the king's proclamation in the Grand Hall—essentially claiming his kingdom was going to open war, and not just a manhunt for Soren—Kaile's legs wobbled.

His mind fogged, his arms felt full of lead, and cold sweat beaded on his brow. He did his best to calm himself as he walked out of the throne room, hiding his foggy gaze beneath his hair. He raced down the hall, faster than a walk, but slower than a sprint. Bursting into the privy, he ran to the stall, vomit erupting from his stomach into the latrine.

The knots in his stomach twisted and tightened. Sweat poured down his brow, dripping off his eyebrows, stinging his eyes as he retched. He retched until there was nothing left to come up. He slunk onto the floor, his knees on the cold stone floor.

Tears flowed down his cheeks. But they weren't from sadness. The vomit forced them down his face, but the dark turmoil within him was more than just sadness. It was a deeper, longer lasting sensation. It was something that reminded him starkly... of Soren.

The need for redemption.

The need for revenge.

The urge to take back what he lost, and prove to himself—and the world—that he was better than his lowest point.

"Soren... what have I done?"

Kaile's head fell back against the latrine wall, staring up at the ceiling with emptiness filling his soul. "What have I done?"

Seph is going to die down there, or they're going to break her completely. She won't be the same woman I know and care for.

Soren won't stand a chance against those three wielders. Even with Davin and Blaje... there's no defense against the Ellydian.

He wanted to believe there was a chance, but Kaile knew the power of those three: Claudine, Myranda, and Albertus. They were hardened sorcerers. They'd trained their entire lives for battle. They knew exactly how to take down a team of non-wielders, and they'd probably barely break a sweat. A simple A note could be enough to break Soren's bones.

A man's throat cleared elsewhere in the privy, and Kaile rose to his feet, wiping his mouth with one sleeve and his tears and sweat with another. Kaile opened the door behind him and exited the latrine. A soldier stood at a washbasin, giving him a curious glare with one eyebrow raised.

"Bad turkey, I fear," Kaile murmured, rushing out of the privy and back out into the hall.

Droves poured out of the Grand Hall, and Kaile ducked into a corner, pretending to be working something through in his mind, running his fingers in patterns along the stone-walled corner.

Once most of the citizens and Synths had gone, Kaile steadied himself. He had a meeting with Alcarond in his quarters at dusk again.

How can I fix this? What can I do to tell Soren what's coming?

Even if he had one wielder from Zatan, they'd be no match for fully trained Synths of the king. Their knowledge and training is far superior to what the Silver Sparrows have. And with Mihelik dead... it's only Lady Drake and Lady Sargonenth that are true Syncrons. The lower Dors of the realm wouldn't stand a chance against these three coming for them.

You need to do something. You have to do something! Think! Think!

"Everything in order, apprentice?" A familiar voice came from just behind him.

Kaile swallowed hard, turning quickly and brushing his hair back to reveal his face, and show he had nothing to hide.

It was a face Kaile didn't expect and was possibly the last one he wanted to see at that moment.

Kaile bowed. "Archpriest Roane..."

"Rise, my son," Solemn said in a voice as elegant and regal as Kaile had ever heard.

"Yes, yes, everything is in order," Kaile said. "Just working through some of my studies." He swallowed, rubbing his chin in an attempt to hide it. "Hard to concentrate with all these people around."

"Agreed," the archpriest said with a slight smile.

Kaile was so taken aback by the sight of the archpriest he'd failed to notice the two Drakoons behind him, a dozen paces behind, both with their icy gazes fixed on Kaile like magnets to metal, or an eagle's to a scampering mouse.

"Why don't we take a walk," Archpriest Roane said, waving for Kaile to follow. "Nice day to walk the gardens."

Kaile looked out past the vast ceiling of Vael Vallora Keep, out into the great sky full of sweeping towers and magical lights filling the deeply overcast sky.

"Nice gloomy day," Kaile said, itching his thigh. "Anything alive in the gardens?"

Archpriest Roane chuckled, his fair skin, wavy brown hair, and slender smile showing a warmth Kaile found... unsettling. "Death is not without its beauty too, apprentice of Alcarond, the powerful. It only takes a different eye to fully appreciate."

They walked away from the Grand Hall of Vael Vallora

and around the corner to the King's Gardens. As they made their way toward the gardens, Kaile looked over his shoulder to, sure enough, see the two Drakoons following. Both in their sleek black armor with their curved swords sleeping in their sheathes. Kaile then looked above to see the colossal Tower of the King stretching so high into the sky that its peak disappeared into the gloom.

The archpriest's words about the beauty of death stuck with Kaile, rolling around his head like a handful of marbles, clattering against each other as he struggled to understand the depths of what he possibly meant—beyond the words.

"You know…" Archpriest Roane said as Kaile felt his hand grip around Kaile's bicep, causing Kaile to gasp. "The king and the archmage have grand plans for you. But it may surprise you to hear that I, too, have high hopes for your ascension."

"I take that as an honor, archpriest," Kaile said, feeling Solemn's fingers digging into his arm as they walked.

"Destiny is a powerful, yet fickle thing." Kaile gazed curiously at the archpriest, a man seemingly speaking in half-riddles. His ivory robes trailed behind, his five-peaked biretta making him feel like a sort of divine demigod. "Your destiny, Kaile Thorne of Krakoa, Ikarus, is vivid in our minds, but could be so easily quashed and erased from our grand plans should some ill fate befall you."

"Ill fate, your highness?"

"A primary reason you were not sent out to defeat Soren Stormrose and his rebellion."

"You think I wouldn't be able to defeat a traitor like that? One without the Ellydian?" Kaile asked, surprised at Solemn's words, and also trying to hide his inner turmoil.

"No, no, young apprentice," the archpriest said. "I'm quite certain you'd easily kill them, even on your own. But even the most seasoned Lyre could fall with the slice of a sharp dagger to the throat in his sleep, or a sword tip through the chest and into the heart."

Kaile nodded, knowing the statement to be true. "War has no lack of ways to die. Does it?"

"It does not," the archpriest said as they entered the King's Gardens.

The gardens were a myriad of walkways woven through ancient garden beds of stone, dry intricate fountains and elaborate statues as pristinely kept as the day they were carved.

Kaile had spent much of his days walking through the gardens, contemplating his lessons, his studies, and working to perfect his craft. But that was normally during the springtime, when all manner of shades of flowers and plants flourished in the warm sunlight. Then, their dead, wintery-brown remains withered and rotted.

Solemn breathed in deeply as they walked down a long pathway, patchy grass growing in between the flat stones laid into the ground. "Beautiful, isn't it? It reminds me of back home."

"Back in Eldra?" Kaile asked, for some reason noticing the golden crosier staff the archpriest walked with for seemingly the first time. Foreign black and silver diamonds wove up it in waves. Kaile thought it must be priceless. There was surely nothing else like it in all of Aladran.

The archpriest nodded. "My home in Vattica. The capital of Eldra. I truly hope you get to see those gardens with your own eyes someday. All different species and genuses of flora that would make your mind whirl. A beauty unimaginable. Breathtaking in every aspect. Indescribable in books, un-replicable in paintings, and their utter beauty disastrously underwhelming by my own failing words."

"Yes, I hope to see it someday," Kaile said. The archpriest released his grip on Kaile's arm.

"You are primed to become the most powerful Syncron in

all the world," the archpriest said, causing Kaile to itch his cheek. Solemn suddenly grabbed Kaile by the collar and pulled Kaile to face him. His strength was far more intense than Kaile would've guessed for a man as slender as he. Kaile's eyes widened as he was left staring fully into the archpriest, whose expression darkened and the corners of his mouth curled down. "Do you understand what that means?"

"I—I—" Kaile stammered. "I'm going to become the archmage someday. I'll fight for the king."

"It's more than that, you child." Solemn's words twisted to a condescending, gravelly tone. "Do you understand the weight of carrying such a power? You will be no less than a god to those who grow your food, and can't take their eyes off you when you walk down any road in all the world."

Kaile nodded, unsure what to say.

"The archmage's duty is to train you to become the most fearsome man in all of Aladran, but the challenge of molding you into the man you must become. I feel he will falter in that effort."

Kaile gulped, still staring squarely into the archpriest's granite eyes.

"If you allow me, I will guide you to become that man. You will not only wield the power of the stars and skies, but you'll have the wisdom to not only know when you use your gift, but when not to. The power of the mind is the missing piece to your gift. You may be able to turn water to fire, but you must know how to best serve this world. Because it's going to need you, and you must rise to that challenge."

Kaile nodded. "I aim to."

"Your generation faces the greatest threats since the time of the Great Divine Flood. And when history is written, it will remember you for what you are. Mediocrity is the gospel of those archmages that came before you. The only ones that are truly remembered by normal man are the first great Syncron, Jeziah, and Mihelik Starshadow. Even, I fear, Alcarond's name will fall into the list of those with no redeeming qualities. Unless your master deciphers a way to defeat the Demons of Dusk—his rightful obsession—then his name will blend into the history books and fade with the page it was written on."

Kaile had never really given much thought to Alcarond's legacy in the grand scheme of time. His gaze finally averted Solemn's, and the archpriest released his collar.

I've always idolized my master. I've never considered how he compared to the archmages of the past. I always assumed he was one of the greatest. But now that I think about it, how will his legacy compare to Mihelik's? Even with Mihelik burning the Scriptures of the Ancients, his power and magic were legendary.

"Someday," the archpriest said in a stern tone. "Alcarond's obsession will consume him, and he will confront the Demons of Dusk... and if he fails, he will fade into the afterlife, his tale will be scribed in history, and then you, Kaile Thorne, will lead the Syncrons of the king. Will you be ready when that time comes? You will bear the great burden of commanding the greatest force this world has ever known."

"Except the dragons," Kaile said, causing the archpriest's brow to furrow. He didn't acknowledge Kaile's statement.

"You will perform the Black Sacrament, and you will pass the test."

Kaile took in a deep breath, looking up into the sky thick with clouds. "Yes, I will."

"There's a test you must pass before that time comes though," the archpriest said, with the slightest hint of pleasure in his voice. "You know of what I speak..."

Seph... he's going to mention my feelings for her... I can tell... that's all anyone seems to care about with me anymore...

"The Whistlewillow's future is hers," Kaile forced out of

his mouth without a hint of a weakness or a crack. "And mine is mine." Kaile began walking through the gardens again, but he could almost feel the gears grinding in the archpriest's thoughts.

"That's good to hear," Solemn said. "I admit that I… was concerned you formed feelings for the girl. And we all know how Mihelik and Alcarond's feelings for Sophia ended up…"

Kaile nodded. "I remember."

"Neither got what they wanted," Solemn said with a certain pleasure on his tongue. "And it could be argued they both lost because of their feelings."

"So, your lesson to me now is to ignore feelings and focus on my studies and my future…"

The archpriest's palm smacked Kaile hard in the cheek, raking his face and causing Kaile's head to jerk to the side.

"Don't play stupid with me, boy." The archpriest's words were full of anger, and as Kaile turned to look back up at him, he saw his pale cheeks were flushed and a mean glower hit his face. "You need to become a man. You need to start acting like one. Grow up, stop playing these political games here, and be who you were meant to be. Don't squander your power. Use it! Don't get lost in your books in your master's chambers. Unleash your power so the world sees what you truly are. You're destined to be the mightiest human in this beautiful world. It's time to stop acting like a lost child. Decide! Decide what your destiny will be and embrace it with both fists! Time is the gift that diminishes us all. Don't waste. Don't want. Now is the time. Now is the time to take what is yours. Fretting over the fate of a girl who will do nothing to serve you, but take from you, is the same as waiting to become what you were meant to be. Don't wait, master apprentice. Become."

The archpriest didn't wait for an answer. Instead, he spun and walked back towards his Drakoons, both shifting their positions in unison, walking behind Archpriest Roane as he strode back toward the castle.

Kaile was left with a stinging cheek, and a barrage of jumbled thoughts bumbling around.

He's at least half right. I need to decide. I need to focus. I only have one life… and I need to use it…

Chapter Twenty-Four

The Under Realm, Zatan.

BURSTING THROUGH THE TUNNEL, Soren sprinted forth to return to his friends. The musty tunnel had a different kind of feel to it then. As he ran, the tunnel didn't feel like the safe road the Dune Matron had proclaimed it to be. Instead, it reminded Soren starkly of the Under Realm.

It felt as if only the insane and those who wanted a sure death would travel through such a place. It was a mistake to travel down into it. It was a terrible, terrible mistake.

Over his shoulder, he gazed back down the tunnel behind; the Heartstone blazing the dark walls to life in an ivory haze. No Shades seemed to creep through the darkness, and he praised the goddess that his relics worked well enough to shield him from their predatory senses.

What was a dragon doing in the Under Realm? How in the fuck did it get down there without anyone seeing? Someone would have seen a green-

glowing Shadow Dragon flying all the way in from Eldra or one of the other continents.

How long has it been down there? But more importantly... how much longer does it plan to stay down there?

Up ahead, as Soren panted, he saw the beginning of a warm glow far down.

He dared not holler, so he continued with his haste to return to his friends, which he quickly did.

Davin spun with his double-sided ax, leading the way. Blaje slid her shamshir curved blade out of its sheath with a subtle, yet sharp ring of the perfect steel. They both quickly lowered their weapons at the sight of their scarred friend.

Sable darted between Davin's legs and rubbed against Soren's boot. The two bears—Moonshadow, the larger male bear, and Sunstar, the smaller female one—both watched Soren curiously as he heaved heavy breaths.

"Soren," Davin said, with his ax hanging in one muscular arm. "What did you find? And what in the goddess's name was that sound from below? I thought the whole tunnel was gonna come crumbling down on our heads."

Blaje sheathed her weapon and walked to Soren's side, placing her palm on the side of his arm. "What did you find?"

"A nest." Soren drew in deep breaths. "So many of them. And there was another... something far worse than Black Fog. I think it may be a clue to why they are here..."

"Well, what is it, man?" Davin pressed. "Spit it out..."

Soren shut his eyes hard, not wanting to manifest what new evil was lurking in the depths under their feet, making the night war even more insurmountable to win.

"A true monster. Unlike any we've ever read about in books and tales. It was an enormous winged dragon. Smoke smoldered from it, and a vile green glow lit the webbing of its wings and the spikes on its back."

"Another dragon?" Blaje gasped, withdrawing her hand to

cover her mouth. "Underground? In the Under Realm? We've... we've got to let the Calica know... we've got to let Lady Sargonenth know."

Davin spat. "Why? What good is that gonna do them? If they can't kill a bloody Shade, how in the goddess's green fuck are they gonna be able to stop a damned evil dragon?"

Blaje's face twisted at the thought, and Moonshadow growled low.

"We need to leave this place," Soren said, regaining his composure, with his hand on Firelight's grip. "Immediately."

The others nodded, and they ran.

The further they got away from the break in the tunnel's walls, the better, Soren knew.

Worry about the new revelation plagued Soren as they ran. Things just never seemed to get better. They always, always just seemed to get worse.

Kill a Synth, and an invincible Shadow Dragon pops up in its place. Fuck...

They continued to run through the dark tunnel, their torches lighting their way forward. The flames flickered as they ran, their warm glow bobbing as they ran. The bears huffed as their huge paws pounded softly on the stone floor. Sable sat upon Sunstar.

Davin grumbled to himself as they ran, cursing inaudibly as they ran. Soren caught bits and pieces.

"Fucking dragons... why did I choose to come to Aladran... Aladran of all the lands I coulda chose... fucking damned dragons..."

After hours of making their way through the seemingly never-ending darkness, a small peek of light glowed from a thin line ahead. The air felt cooler, crisper, fresher...

The torchlight revealed before them a large angled door of metal, and Soren grinned. *Finally... we can get out of the underground...* They'd arrived at the end.

Soren quickly went to the latch between the two doors. Blaje went to his aid.

He unlatched the strong iron mechanism at their center. Their old, unmoved hinges squealed like swine at the slaughter. Soren looked nervously over his shoulder as the latch finally popped, and he and Blaje set their shoulders to the heavy door. They both pressed hard upwards with all their strength, but there was something on the other side that was impossibly heavy. They both groaned as Davin laughed.

Soren and Blaje both stopped and looked with annoyed gazes. Blaje shrugged as Davin laughed with his hands on his girthy midsection.

"Out of the way, you two." He laughed, stroking his beard.

"You're gonna do it? Or you gonna give us a hand?" Soren asked, with his hands out wide.

"Always thinking with your muscles, instead of your brain." Davin laughed, moving to the side of the tunnel, pointing to the two silver bears.

Soren clapped his forehead. Blaje smirked and stepped aside as Moonshadow and Sunstar both walked past the camels. The two monstrous bears barely fit beneath the two iron doors, but as they both pressed up with their front paws, a light flooded the tunnel like nothing Soren had ever seen.

The blinding light caused them all to shudder backward, but the feeling of the pure sunlight filled Soren with a sort of hope and protection that was impossible to replicate. The two bears swung the doors open high, and then toppled them outward, both falling to the ground on their backs with a deep-rooted thud.

The bears walked out onto the landscape, with the others quickly following. Soren's eyes adjusted, and his mouth flattened, with a humph rumbling in his throat.

"Well, ain't that a sight for sore eyes?" Davin said with a pleasant sigh.

While sand drifted at their feet with a cool breeze washing through, before them towered high rising mountains of stone. A welcome sight in every sense. The desert was behind them then, and white clouds meandered by the huge peaks. An incredibly blue sky flooded the world above them, and trees protruded through the earth, revealing a deep, old forest before them.

Davin dropped to a knee and felt the ground. Sand blew in circles over the rocky ground, blades of dead winter grass dancing in waves before them, leading into the forest.

A calm washed over Soren as he gazed into the forest—always a welcome sight, since the Demons of Dusk had become such an overwhelming threat. He was so taken by the sight, entranced in its magnificence, it took Blaje's tug on his sleeve to get him to spin back, seeing what she meant for him to see.

The two doors were opened upon a hill rising upward, and at the top of the hill was a ring of tents. From those tents, men came down the hill.

Soren rushed to draw Firelight instinctually, but Blaje forced his hand back. Soren didn't recognize the near dozen men, but he knew from their dark skin and loose-fitting tan and white clothing that they were men of Zatan.

Blaje spoke in their language, Sarin, to the men. It was thick and throaty, but Soren caught bits of it. He didn't think Blaje directly knew the men, but they were certainly of the Calica. He assumed they were from the northern part of the kingdom, so perhaps she'd never met them because of that.

After a brief conversation between Blaje and one of the men, his face half wrapped in a shawl, he nodded and walked back to the tents.

"What did he say?" Soren asked.

"He's got gifts from the Dune Matron." Blaje rubbed her hands, and didn't smile, but Soren could feel her excitement.

There was an unsaid connection between them. It was as if a string had been tied between them, binding them with an invisible radiance.

"She did promise us something to help in our quest," Davin said. "I hope it's something good..." He rubbed his hands as they walked up the hill, following the men of the Calica.

The men welcomed them with handshakes and smiles. Soren felt good just being out of the Under Realm in one piece. The men offered them food and drink. Soren and his friends welcomed it. A couple of the men hurled meat down to the bears, surely wary of the two completely out of place creatures in the desert.

Blaje and the lead man continued their conversation in Sarin, while Davin chomped away at a leg of smoked meat. Sable nibbled at a bowl of chopped chicken by his side. Soren ate meat slowly, listening in on Blaje's conversation.

She said something to the man, and Soren understood she was asking if he spoke the common tongue. The man cleared his throat harshly, and holding up his fingers in a pinching motion, said, "A little bit."

Soren and Davin both perked up, eager to hear what the man would say. The other men of the Calica stood around, not eating, but listening, and many of them glared at Soren with a sort of... admiration. There was hope in their weary eyes, a sparkle where perhaps there was none before. Their kingdom had waged war, and Soren was the leader of that movement against the king. The king's burning of innocent villages in the name of battling the Chimaera had moved into open war.

"What news of the Dune Matron?" Blaje asked, waving for the man to address Soren and Davin.

"The Dune Matron gives you blessing on your path to find... old master." His broken language was heavy with his desert accent, but Soren nodded in appreciation.

"Thank you, and thank her," Soren said. "Her gift, the Shadowflame Heartstone, has already proven its worth."

The man raised an eyebrow.

"I have information for the Dune Matron," Soren snorted, unsure how useful the information would be, as there was nothing to do about it, but he said it anyway. *The world has to know about this new evil, even if it only causes despair.* "There's... another dragon... it's beneath the desert. I found it in a cavern dug by the Demons of Dusk into the tunnel beneath us. Do not attempt to use the tunnel again. It's unsafe. And a huge cavern rests beneath it. There are thousands of Shades and Black Fog infesting it."

"A... dragon?" the man muttered with great interest, stroking his chin with eyes wide. The other men around looked confused, surely reading the man's expression but not understanding his words.

Blaje cleared up the confusion by saying the Sarin word, "Dargüsh." She pointed down, under the sand and dirt.

The men muttered between themselves, repeating the word with many gasps and some with sweat beading on their brows.

"What dragon?" the leader asked. "From where? How?"

"I don't know," Soren said, rustling the sand by his boot with his finger. "But it's here. And if that thing comes out of the Under Realm. We are in for a lot of trouble. The only thing that could fight that is the dragon from Eldra, Sarrannax. No Vellice blades are going to cut that monster down."

The man nodded. "I will tell the Dune Matron."

"Thank you." Soren glanced at Blaje, who scratched her thigh, unsure what to do about such a revelation.

"Now," the man said. "You cannot stay here. Too many eyes. Too many spies. I have gifts."

Davin's expression changed as he set the cleaned bone down on a plate and leaned in toward the man.

"First," the man said, turning and motioning to another behind him. "Horses."

Soren gave a great sigh of relief.

"Thank you," Blaje said with a bow.

"Camels bad for grasslands," the man said. "Fine horses the Dune Matron sent."

"Thank you, and send her our thanks." Soren bowed his head as well.

"Also," the man said, reaching into his pocket. Soren glared eagerly at what was so small that could fit into his pocket.

"The bears," the man said, pulling out something in his hand, with thin leather straps falling out of it. "Can't hide with them. Too dangerous."

Soren raised an eyebrow, not wanting to send the bears away. They were too great an asset for what attacks were sure to spring up. Gideon Shaw wasn't the only bounty hunter for the king…

The man opened his hand, and Davin sprang up from his seat. "By the Halls of Voschung!"

The Calica man held out his hand for Davin, three leather straps hanging from sparkling jewels, glistening a lush violet in the desert sun's rays.

"Drixen stone!" Davin shouted excitedly. "You mean to disguise the bears! That's fuckin' genius! How did you find such stones out here?"

"More treasure for you. To help." The man rose and handed the pendants to Davin. Three Drixen stones were cut into exquisite teardrop shapes, just like the one hanging around Soren's neck.

"Pixiestone," Soren said with a smile. "Rare and cut to replicate the ones Seph and Kaile have. What an idea."

"Will it work with such huge animals?" Blaje asked.

Davin nodded. "It should. We use the ability on animals in

Mythren, although it's rarely needed. We don't often take silverback bears to war."

Soren laughed. "First time for everything. Especially in these days."

Davin bowed. "Thank you and thank the lady. What a precious gift. We thank you."

The man bowed his head. "You must go. You have far to travel, and eyes always watching…"

"There's one for you," Davin said to Blaje, handing her the pendant.

She took it.

"Think carefully about how you want to appear," the dwarf said. "You only get one choice."

"I remember," she said seriously. But they all knew the joke about Davin being stuck with his female form, and Soren desperately still wanted to know what bet he lost…

"Let's get moving." Soren stood. All the Calica men's gazes were fixed on him, his dagger, the Twilight Veil relic, the Shadowflame Heartstone, and the Drixen pendant. Soren couldn't deny they felt good on him. He was far from invincible—his reputation completely embellished—and for all his failures that marred his soul, the relics felt good. They felt really, really good.

Chapter Twenty-Five

They rushed back down the hill, each of them knowing that the silver hides of the bears made them stand out like a huge dark, hairy mole at the tip of a nose. Even the men of the Calica followed, wanting to witness the magical transformation with their very eyes.

Soren stopped, though, causing all the men behind him to pause. A thought crept up in him, something always at the forefront of his mind.

"Seph..." he said, facing the man who spoke his language, but motioning around for them all. "Persephone. Is there any word from the capital?"

The men looked at one another, seemingly not understanding. The one who spoke his language did recognize the name, letting out a sigh, understanding the gravity of the situation.

"No word of your niece," he said. "I'm sorry."

"If you get word," Soren said forcefully. "If you or the Dune Matron or Lady Sargonenth, hear anything. Anything! You send word to me immediately. Understood?" Soren caught himself pointing angrily at the men, but caught himself and withdrew his hand. "Please..."

The man nodded. "I understand."

"C'mon, Soren," Davin said. "We've got to get moving. No telling what's out in the trees, mountains, and plains."

"With the horses," Blaje said, first one to the bottom of the hill, below the still open iron doors, "we will ride for the Lyones Mountains, and ride along the foothills, camping for tonight. We will find the Driftmire River by sun fall tomorrow. And then we enter into the king's lands... Lynthyn."

"Davin," Soren said. "Get these spells up and let's be on our way."

Davin nodded, handing one of the Drixen necklaces to Blaje, and then walking over to the bears, who both had hesitant movements. They moved their heads away from him, both growling. Davin put his hand up onto Sunstar's head first, stroking the coarse silver fur, finally causing her to lower her head. He put the necklace around her neck. It was a perfect fit. "Dune Matron knows what she's doin' all right." He stepped back from Sunstar and went to the bigger, meaner bear—Moonshadow. The male bear growled, flashing its huge yellow teeth. Sable appeared out of nowhere between Davin's legs and jumped up Moonshadow's front arm, up the shoulder, and walked on his back, purring.

Moonshadow lowered his head, easing his growls.

Davin placed the necklace over his head. The silver fur pinned it perfectly in place. Stepping back, Davin rubbed his palms together, then pulled his own necklace out from under his shirt. He closed his eyes, holding the Eldrite Stone—rarer than diamonds, and sacred to his people, close to his chest.

His lips moved, whispering soft words none of them recognized. A soft, dark blue glow emanated out between his fingers, turning to a pale white magical hue.

A humming cast out from Davin's Eldrite Stone, causing the Drixen stones to hum back. Soren and the Calica watched in amazement as the silver fur of the great bears shrunk.

Moonshadow's fur turning to a deep, short black fur, and Sunstar's turning to a brilliant full-moon white. Their bodies shrank to nearly a fourth their original size. Where huge snouts were, were replaced by long, slender muzzles. The coarse fur on the backs of their necks transformed into gorgeous manes of flowing hair. Their enormous, clawed paws turned to hooves built for running trails, mountains, and plains.

They both neighed, Sable purring softly upon the black horse Moonshadow. The cat didn't even seem to notice the transformation.

Many of the Calica's jaws dropped at the rare magical gift of Mythren.

Then, all gazes shot at Blaje. She held the Drixen stone clutched in her hands as her skin tone lightened, and her long dreads shrank from her belly up to her collarbone. Her dark eyes beamed a vibrant green, her skin turned a deep tan like tree bark, and her hair unknotted and flowed to a soft, thin blond.

"Nice hair." Soren laughed. "Blond?"

"I'll only get one chance to change, so may as well go all the way," she responded with a wink.

"I liked you better the other way." Soren slapped his leg.

She walked up to him, completely changed in appearance, but he could still tell she was in there by the way she looked at him. Blaje ran her finger from his temple to the tip of his chin. "Good."

A shiver shot all the way from Soren's toes to the tip of his head, sending all of the hairs on his neck stiff.

God, what a woman. I've never met a woman quite like her... She may be the best thing sent my way in years, or she may be the death of me... I suppose I'll find out. But keep it together, Soren. The mission is paramount. Your feelings can wait...

"What do you want to be called?" Davin asked her,

nodding, admiring his handiwork, even though she was the one who chose her appearance.

"Ginger," she said, folding her arms, seemingly proud.

"Ginger?" Soren covered his mouth as he chuckled. "This disguise spell is really getting out of hand."

"Your name is Victor." She laughed back. "How is that better?"

"It's far better!" Soren shoved her shoulder playfully.

"Vic is in no way better than Ginger…" she said with a deep scorn, shoving him back. She looked up at the Calica, who seemed quite confused by it all.

The lead Calica man seemed to agree with her, though, pointing her way and nodding quickly.

"That doesn't count," Soren said with a grin. "He's scared of you. Of course, he's going to say whatever you want him to."

She grinned back. "Well, what does that say about you? That they're more frightened of a woman than the man who's supposed to save the world."

"I suppose that means we're a good team," Soren said.

Blaje walked into him, nearly pressing her body against his. Her sweet breath he felt on his lips. Her smell ravaged his nostrils, and his brain tingled at her near touch. "I agree, Soren Stormrose. I think we make a fantastic team."

All air seemed to be sucked out of the desert as the two stood staring deep into each other's eyes. Soren was stuck, as if pulled into them with a powerful spell. The Calica stood breathlessly, watching. The bears, now horses, both watched as the world seemed to slow its rotation, so that even time could watch two of the deadliest figures in all Aladran embrace.

Soren leaned in; his lips eager to press against hers.

"All right, all right," Davin shouted. "Enough of the gooey nonsense. Let's get moving before you two strip down naked before all of us, making us wish we were going home instead of to war with the two of ya."

Blaje winked and ran her finger down the length of Soren's arm again, causing spiking chills to run through his body.

She drives me wild. I've never met anyone like her. I loved Cirella. I loved Cirella more than anything in the world. But there's something different about Blaje—something dangerous, something darker, something hardened—

She's the Desert Shadow. Fierce by every account, as deadly as the Chimaera, and as fucking beautiful as a sunset over the never-ending plains.

Yup… She's going to be the death of me all right…

"Ready?" Davin asked with a groan, and inspecting the packs secured to the other horses they'd been given. "Or do you two need a room and a bed?"

Soren cleared his throat, feeling his cheeks heat.

"Ready," Blaje said, mounting a horse with a fluid swoop of a leg over the saddle. Sable followed, running up the horse's side and standing right in front of the saddle, meowing at Blaje. Blaje sighed. "Why always me?" Sable meowed again, turning and shoving her tail up above her. "Mount up. We ride for the mountains."

Soren gave a quick look at the bags packed on the horses, and was thoroughly impressed. *We will have supplies and food for weeks with this.*

Soren mounted his steed, with the two bears taking off ahead, surely to make sure the path was clear. The ivory and ebony horses ran as smoothly as any steed Soren had ever seen.

Soren smiled at the sight. "We may not have the Ellydian yet, but we sure do have a force to be reckoned with."

"Aye, brother." Davin, with a glow of the pendant around his neck, transformed into the ravishing woman known as Bonnie Rifkin. Thick, lush hair, curvy hips and long legs, she easily mounted the magnificent horse. "Any bounty hunters are gonna have quite a surprise when they come to collect the bounty on our heads. Surely it's got to be well over a million torrens now."

"Five million," the lead Calica man said with an obvious smile. "For the three of you. Soren is three million alone."

"You hear that, lass?" Davin shouted. "You and me are worth a million each!"

Blaje didn't bat an eye. Instead, she flicked the reins and rode after the bears, pulling the extra horse behind, who hefted the bulk of the extra supplies.

Soren kicked his heels into his horse, missing Ursa, wondering what became of his best friend. He turned in the saddle and looked back at the men of the Calica. "Remember. Any word from the capital about Seph, you tell me immediately. Wherever I am. You find me, you hear?"

The lead man bowed.

Respect. Such a sign of the people of Zatan. I will truly miss these lands, as unbearable as the winter tundra is. Their people are at least honorable and somewhat predictable.

The other men of the Calica bowed. Soren returned one, lowering his chin to his chest.

"Here we go," Davin said, flicking the reins and groaning. "Don't be thinking you're worth three o' me, Soren. I'm just as dangerous as you. More so, even. You haven't seen nothing yet."

"I'm sure, my friend," Soren said with a grin. "I'm absolutely sure of it."

They rode that night, with each stride of their horses, a little bit more sand turning to dry grass beneath their hooves. The Lyones Mountain range growing more immense with each step. The range that created the border between Zatan and Londindam would be their safety from the demons of the night. Lynthyn was only a day away, beyond the Driftmire

River. Arkakus, wasteland in its own right, lay a few days' ride from there.

Everything seemed to be set for them to find Landran Dranne, should Soren prove right in his prediction of where his old master chose to spend his last years.

While they rode for the mountains, Soren remembered the time when Soren was Seph's age, and his master told him about his plan for his final years.

"There's a place in the dark recesses of Arkakus," Landran told Soren all those years ago. "A place where no one will find me, and I can have peace. You see… I don't want to die stuck in a bed in Cascadia. I want to go where there's new things to discover, new air to breathe, and more mystery to keep my brain busy."

Soren remembered listening to the words, not understanding why such a great man would choose such a miserable place to end his days. But Soren, after all he'd been through, had a new understanding of his wishes.

Solitude, intrigue, change.

I get it now.

"There's a place in Arkakus, beautiful in its dismay and hardship," Landran said, smoking a pipe by the fire, his wise eyes glimmering a vivid golden red hue from the firelight. His weathered, wrinkled skin had known many battles, and his hair had grayed far beyond its time. Possibly from war, possibly from Soren's antics. "A place where the light of the erupting Mount Carraxion reflects off a clear water lake, unaffected by the ash and harsh metallic odor there. It's a cover with a lake shaped like a giant paw print from an ancient creature time forgot about. A tree is rooted in its center, an enormous tree unlike the others of Arkakus. From it, white petaled flowers bloom in the springtime. The nectar of those pedals is said to cure any poison. If you're brave enough to get there…"

Chapter Twenty-Six

That night, Soren and the others sat in a ring around a warm fire, its smoke weaving through the tree branches above, reminding Soren of simpler times. There was a heightened sense of security as their disguises hid their identities, packs were full of supplies for the long journey, and the horses lay asleep.

Moonshadow was the only animal awake. With his black hair on his coat sleek like oil as the scant moonlight glistened on it. The dark horse was vigilant, staring with its golden eyes down the foothills and out to the desert that slowly transformed into plains.

Davin smoked a pipe, deep in thought, his belly full of crunchy bread with creamy butter and smoked meat. Blaje twiddled her straight hair with her fingers as she glared into the fire. Soren sat in a half trance with Sable sleeping between his crossed legs. Sleep had eluded him two nights, and the weariness was growing in him like a spider spinning fresh, murky webs in his mind. His eyelids felt heavy like iron, and his arms and legs felt like lead cast on his bones.

"Well, I'm done for the night." Davin sat fully up, wiping

the crumbs off his stomach and out of his beard. "We've got another long one tomorrow, eh? You two get some shuteye, too. Ya hear? Soren?"

Soren just nodded as Davin turned over with his back to the fire, pulling the covers over him tightly. Within minutes, the dwarf was slumbering soundly, only his faint snores stirring the blissful night air occasionally.

"There's something I'd like to ask you," Soren said, taking a bottle of wine from beside him and uncorking it. "If that's all right."

Blaje's gaze rose from the fire to him. Her eyes and appearance were different, changed from the power of Davin's Eldrite Stone to their Drixen, or Pixiestones. But Soren saw her in there still. Blaje was still behind the new shade of her eyes, and the lighter tones of her skin.

"All those nights back in the desert, back in Taverras," Soren said, taking a sip of wine after. "What was it that Lady Sargonenth whispered to you? I still want to know. There shouldn't be secrets like that between us. At least, I don't think so. Not after what we've been through, and what we face ahead together..."

She waved for the bottle, and he leaned forward, handing it to her. Blaje took a deep drink. "That goes both ways, Soren."

"What do you mean?"

"I'll tell you. But I want to know something in return," she said, handing the bottle back.

The one thing Soren thought she may ask about was Cirella. He began to tell Blaje about the vision he had back in the Ash Grove. And he didn't necessarily want to tell Blaje, well... because he had growing feelings for Blaje, and didn't think his old feelings of his old love needed to add any complication to what was a great mutual respect between them. Respect... with a hint of lustful desire.

"You know what I want to know," Blaje said. "I can see it in your eyes. You're already thinking about it. I'll tell you what the lady told me, if you tell me what you were going to tell me about what happened in the Ash Grove."

He sighed, taking another drink. "Seems fair. How about you start, though?"

She nodded, taking the bottle back. Sable stirred in Soren's lap from all the movement, stretching out wide and yawning, showing her sharp teeth and fangs.

"When we were leaving Taverras," Blaje said, sitting upright with her legs crossed, "the lady talked to me about you."

"Me?"

She nodded, taking another deep drink. "It was a warning."

Soren didn't reply, only waiting for more information. A deep curiosity welled inside of him. He didn't know if the lady didn't like him, or had an apprehension about his methods.

Blaje leaned forward with a sort of grim smirk at the corner of her mouth.

"So?" Soren pressed.

"You're not going to like it. Are you sure you want to hear?"

"Then why are you smirking?" He itched his stubbly cheek.

"Because sometimes it seems like you like a little bit of pain." When she said that, Soren wanted to throw out a scathing rebuttal, but deep down, he thought she might be right. He wanted to tell her about the pain he'd experienced, and the hope that no one had to go through what he did. But... he couldn't deny, some of the most alive he ever felt... was in deadly battle. His instincts heightened beyond what he could imagine. While defending what he felt just, he felt a sense of pride, worth, and purpose. It was the rest of the time he felt out of place, worthless, and cast out.

"Go on," he said.

"Lady Sargonenth warned me about your attachment to Persephone."

"Warned?" Soren shouted. "About my niece? About my only attachment left to this world?"

Blaje cocked an eyebrow and took another sip. Her look said everything her lack of words did.

Soren calmed his rushed breathing.

"She said you were going to play an important role in the new world we are all hoping for. A better, brighter world. But... your true weakness, as well as your greatest strength, lies with her. And you know what, Soren... she was right. Wasn't she?"

Soren swallowed down his pride, feeling the pang in his chest tighten. "What did she warn you about?"

Blaje sighed hard, giving in to a softer, calmer, less snarky side. She reached over and put her hand on his knee. "That you need to be shown that this isn't all about Seph. It isn't all about family. There's an entire world that needs you. Your insight, your determination, your thirst for vengeance. We need it all. It can't all come down to one person. If Seph dies... the fight needs to go on. I'm sorry to have to say it out loud, Soren, but deep down, I think you know what I say is the truth."

Soren gritted his teeth. The thought of Seph dying was too great a loss to bear. It made him want to ride at full speed for the capital, rush through the front gate, and kill every last person who tried to keep him and Seph apart.

"Lady Sargonenth wished I would try to help you keep your focus on the war, and should something happen to Seph, to help guide you."

"Guide me?" Soren felt his brow furrow, petting Sable as she purred.

"I think she sensed our connection," Blaje said in a soft, delicate voice. "She's always had a knack for that kind of insight."

Connection? Soren didn't respond. He felt it. He felt it like a brick to the head. He knew it was there. It was the first real attachment to a woman he'd felt in a very, very long time. Sure, there was Alicen, and a few others. But those relationships were intensified by his turmoil, his loneliness, and his lack of human touch in the wilds. Often, there was also money involved.

After a long moment, he finally let out a deep breath. "You're right. And you were right not to tell me this until now. You're right about it all. I don't know what I'll do if Seph doesn't make it. I really don't know what I'll do."

Blaje stood, walked to his side, and sat beside him, both gazing into the fire. She rested her head on his shoulder.

"I know the feeling all too well. Remember," she said, "I've lost loved ones too. I lost my mother, my father, and I lost my first love."

"Lady Sargonenth's son?"

Blaje nodded. "A noble can't marry a woman of the Calica. We're just outlaws to them, or at least we were, until this war…"

"I'm sorry," Soren said. "The lady forced you apart, and then he passed at Katamon Outpost…"

"I never really got to say goodbye," she said, glaring into the fire, her hair tickling Soren's neck. "Even after all those years. I wished we got a true goodbye, a fair way to wrap up all of our feelings. Destiny wouldn't let us be together, but I always hoped…" She wiped a tear from the corner of her eye. "Never mind. That doesn't matter anymore…"

Soren, listening to Blaje's deep regret, was reminded of his own anguish over the years, since Cirella's death at the hands of the king, the Knight Wolf, Zertaan, and whoever else was there when Tourmielle burned.

"I got my goodbye." The words left his lips like a secret,

finally escaping its confinement deep in his soul. "I finally got it. I have peace."

Blaje's head perked up and looked at him. "What?"

"Cirella," Soren said, still gazing into the crackling, whipping, dancing fire. "I got my goodbye. I feel a sense of closure, like I never did before. It feels... incredible."

"What do you mean? You got to say goodbye?" Blaje turned completely to face him.

"In the Ash Grove... I saw her... Cirella."

"Soren..." Blaje muttered, her eyes wide and her breathing hastened. "You..."

A guttural growl sounded beyond the fire, deep and troubling.

"Soren..." Blaje muttered again, but as the horse's growl intensified, and Moonshadow got upright, his amber eyes scanning the high cliffs behind them, both Soren and Blaje stood, hands on the grips of their weapons. The other horses got up and stirred, including the ivory-maned Sunstar.

Soren's eyes narrowed as he scanned the cliffs above. Moonshadow, still in horse form, growled and trudged slowly to Soren's side, glaring up. Black Fog and Shades were never a worry up in the mountains, so Soren was never used to worrying about them, until now... until the Black Fog was called into Greyhaven, or the Shade that was in that tower in the desert.

Soren kicked Davin. "Get up, we're not alone."

Davin groaned and was quickly up, ax in hand.

"What is it?" the dwarf whispered.

"Not sure, but something is out there." Soren unsheathed Firelight. It glistened a rippling blood red under the starlight.

Blaje held out her thin, curved shamshir blade as Sunstar went to her side. Sable leaped up onto one horse, hissing up at the tall rocks above them.

"What's there?" Davin asked. "I can't see nothin'."

"What is it, Moonshadow?" Soren stroked the horse.

A figure rose from the tall rock above them. The rock cliff was fifteen feet, and the shadowy figure rose at least eight feet above it. Shrouded in darkness, it had coarse hair all over its body, including its long, sturdy arms that reached down past its knees. A club rested in one of its mighty hands, clicking against the rock as it glowered down at them. A wild, thick hair frazzled out from its head, as two reddened eyes watched Soren with a sickening, predatory gaze.

"Troll," Soren muttered.

"Trolls?" Blaje said with a seething curiosity. "Trolls don't come this far into the desert."

"They do if we killed some back in Londindam," Davin said. "In my homeland, trolls will hunt long distances if they're attacked. They're one of the few races that know of revenge. Their thick skulls are at least capable of that. Though they seem stupid enough to attack us…"

A pair of shadowy figures emerged. One on either side of the taller troll in the middle. One hefted an ax, and one a greatsword crafted by human hands. What would take a strong man two hands to wield, the troll easily gripped it in one.

"These are mean ones, eh?" Davin said with a wide grin. "Good. I've been getting bored of running and hiding."

Blaje snapped into a fighting pose; legs apart, sword behind, ready to dart in with a flurry of attacks.

Soren took a wide stance as well, gazing up at the monstrous trolls silhouetted against the starry sky. Beyond them, a tree branch snapped. But no small twig. It was as if a tree itself was smashed under a gigantic weight.

"C'mon, you bastards," Davin roared. "Don't make me climb. My ax is thirsty!"

The lead troll leaped down with a simple step forward, crashing into the ground before them with a thud that shuddered the mountain beneath their feet.

The other two followed, each landing on sturdy legs with low grunts. Their red, beady, veiny eyes glowered hatefully at Soren. The three trolls grumbled to Soren in a language he didn't understand. It came from the back of the trolls' rancid mouths and rolled out with long words.

"Your kind attacked me in the cave in Londindam," Soren said, waving Firelight for each of them to see. The campfire's reflection cast from the Vellice blade onto their faces. But something around the neck of the tallest troll caught his immediate attention.

Lit in the campfire's light, a necklace of skulls hung on its muscly chest. They were no animal skulls, though—they were human.

Soren clutched Firelight tightly. "You see the necklace?"

Blaje scowled. "I see it."

"These aren't cave trolls," Soren said. "This is a hunting pack."

Davin grinned widely. "Good. I've been hankering for a good kill. Something to take the edge off, losing against the archmage. I'm gonna enjoy this..."

Soren's eyes narrowed, and his heart pumped hot blood up into his shoulders and down his arms. A deep, haunting anger consumed him at the thought of Alcarond taking Seph. "Me too..."

Chapter Twenty-Seven

The three huge trolls towered over them in the fire's light that lit their hideous expressions. The leader, standing well over eight feet tall, with arms as long as Soren was tall, roared. Human skulls dangled from his necklace as his yellow teeth flashed, and his rank breath reeked of rotten, decomposing flesh.

Davin rushed forth, wielding his ax, swinging in a massive arc at the lead troll, who stepped back with his long legs, shoving his heavy clubhead into the ground. Davin's dwarven ax collided with the sturdy club, its fine edge sticking into the club, marring it with another scar. The troll snickered, its muscly shoulders protruding as it laughed.

"They didn't attack from behind or in secret," Soren said as the troll with the greatsword lunged at him. Soren deflected the massive human-crafted blade away with a smooth swipe of Firelight. "They came for a fight. They want to test us, toy with us."

"They don't know what they're in for," Blaje said, ducking beneath the other troll's ax head. Blaje's movement was perfect.

Every pose, every gesture, every single movement was exquisite. The Desert Shadow spun and swiped with her shamshir blade at the troll's shins. The blade cut across smoothly, drawing blood, but doing little damage to the thick bones of the beast. The troll roared, and Soren quickly realized it was a female by the shorted canines, and smaller nose and jaw.

"If it's a fight they want," Soren said. "Then it's a fight they're gonna fucking get." He shot forth with a flurry of Firelight, slashing at the air before the huge troll. Its frayed hair and necklace of skulls bounced as the giant troll stumbled back. The flurry was as much to attack as to overwhelm Soren's foe.

The horses neighed behind, too scared to run down the foothills out into the plains, but also too startled by the trolls. They gazed all around, trying to find what to do or where to go. The two horses that didn't think to flee were the two golden-eyed bears, still in disguise, glaring at the trolls with deep, stalking gazes.

Blaje unleashed a fierce storm of attacks upon the ax-wielding troll, whose movements were slow compared to that of the assassin of the Calica. Soren was driven back by the third troll's greatsword, swooping in huge arcs at him. Soren easily evaded with a couple of quick movements, as much scanning the troll's abilities—and limitations—as dodging the deadly attacks.

Davin fought fiercely against the eight-foot troll. Davin was still in disguise, much taller and quicker than his normal, stocky form, and he used it to his advantage, swinging his ax high, colliding off the troll's scant metal armor and thick, bristly hide.

As the fight erupted around them, turning the mountainous campfire scene into an embroiled battle, Soren felt the heat growing inside of him. As the steel flashed in the fire's light, and the trolls heaved merciless, powerful attacks meant to destroy bones and kill, Soren's vision sharpened.

The animal inside him was coming out. Soren watched his friends fight and defend, and it only reminded him of how many friends and family he'd lost over the years. His arms felt like they were made of iron, and a brimstone forge burned in his gut, fueling his burning hatred.

The two bears remained back; watching, waiting…

Soren sent another flurry of attacks at the troll with the greatsword, and in the middle of the attack, he glimpsed something in the troll's eyes that screamed into Soren. It was fear. The troll had the first look of fear in his eyes Soren saw, and a curl came to the corner of Soren's mouth.

He attacked faster, his vision focusing into the fine details of every swipe, every parry, every thrust.

A thrust landed, digging Firelight's tip into the troll's dense hamstring. The troll didn't cry out, but scowled deep, holding Soren's hand in place, lowering its gaze to him, and gritting its yellow, chipped teeth.

"You are one ugly son of a bitch," Soren said through his teeth, fighting to pull his hand free. But the troll's strength was far too much for Soren. With a great tug, Soren felt the troll pick him up by the wrist. Soren struggled to break free as he kicked at the troll's massive chest. The troll pointed the greatsword's tip at him, ready to pierce straight through Soren's armor and into his stomach.

A flash of shadow shot between them. It was so fast even Soren didn't have time to catch what the shadow was. It reminded him of a sleek, deadly panther in the throes of a dark jungle in the midnight hours, but he caught the familiar fragrance of lavender oil.

Blaje…

Soren felt himself fall. Above him, half of the troll's arm fell after him. Blood spattered down like rain as Soren's boots hit the rocky ground. The troll's hairy arm, severed at the elbow, fell to the ground as the troll roared a nasty growl.

Blaje landed on the other side of the arm. Her sword was cast in fresh blood.

She didn't even glance at Soren. She darted behind the troll, leaping onto its distracted back, her sword ready to do more damage.

Soren only marveled at her for a moment. Her wild hair snapping behind her like a squid's tentacles flowing behind in deep water. The killer instinct was vivid in her dark eyes, like two obsidian marbles snapped to her prey like magnets. Every movement she made was deliberate, precise, and tactical. It was like a dance, a dance one learns over decades of practice and perfection.

The troll Blaje had been fighting lumbered forward with its ax ready to swing down onto Blaje's back, hard enough to cut through her and into the one-armed troll.

But Soren had other plans.

With quick steps, he shot between them, Firelight leading the way. As the troll hefted the huge ax over its head, ready to send it cutting down through Blaje, Soren stabbed mercilessly into the troll's stomach.

Blood spattered over the blade as he cut deep, the smell of irony blood and entrails filling his nostrils. The instinct to kill was fully alive in him, like a freshly sparked digger bomb, and he was ready to explode.

You won't hurt my friends. Not here, not now, not ever!

The attack wasn't enough to kill, but it was enough to drive the troll back. It staggered back to the rock cliff behind it, clutching its stomach as blood poured out and intestines dangled beneath.

"You want her? You're going to have to go through me," Soren growled as Blaje leaped down from the one-armed troll, and Davin joined their ranks. They heaved labored breaths, ready for another attack.

But something was off.

Something still wasn't right, and another break of a branch sounded above them, high on the cliff still.

The trolls shouted in their tongue, thick with long, harsh words.

And then a shadow loomed over the cliff, far taller and wider than the lead troll. The new foe was huge, easily over twelve feet tall, and nearly as wide.

"Oh my," Davin gasped, his eyelids drawn back at the sight of the gigantic monster above.

It lifted an immense tree trunk of a leg and jumped down off the cliff, landing with a thud that shook the rocks at their feet like an earthquake. Its beady, black eyes focused on Soren with pure hate.

"An ogre," Blaje growled. "They brought a damned ogre with them."

Its wide head and beady eyes moved slowly. Its huge mouth, full of sharp and cracked teeth, was agape as it glared at Soren. Wet, long black hair slicked down its round, yet muscular face. The trolls stepped away from the monstrous ogre, looming over the entire campsite area. The horses neighed and fought to break free. They were tied down by their reins to a pair of nearby trees. But they looked as if they'd rather run off in terror down into the plains, taking their chances with the Shades.

The ogre took a lumbering step toward Soren as the trolls spoke in their language. Soren couldn't recognize the words, but he noticed the shift in their tones. They had fresh hope, and a nasty cockiness with the appearance of the new foe.

The ogre wore ragged clothes that stretched tightly over its immense body, probably weighing over a ton, Soren thought. In its fist was a spiked club, with jagged, broken bits of iron protruding from the hardwood. Hardly a man alive could even pick up the hefty club, the weight of a full-grown adult, but the ogre wielded it as easily as if it were a twig.

"Where did such a monster come from?" Blaje asked, taking long strides back.

"Not from here," Soren grumbled, holding his ground. Like the elemental manans, and the dragon that flew in from Eldra, this ogre was not of Aladran. "It most likely came from the south, or to the lands west of Arkakus. This monster is not welcome in our world. So I will *remove* it."

The trolls crashed back into a maddening attack, ax, greatsword, and club swinging in vast arcs as they led the attack.

The ogre roared, hulking over them with gigantic muscles rippling in its broad shoulders and arms. The ogre moved forward, and the battle erupted all around them.

Steel clashed with hardwood and steel as Soren and the others were forced on the defensive, overpowered and outnumbered. All the while, the ogre's gaze was fixed upon Soren, its dark eyes drifting between Soren's feet and the flashing of Firelight's unusual steel.

As Soren fought off the offensive of the powerful trolls, the ogre ran in with its huge, spiked club, swinging in such a powerful arc that the air seemed to get sucked from the area. It whooshed above Soren thickly, as if it collided with the air itself.

Soren ducked and rolled away, watching as Davin and Blaje knocked the immensely powerful trolls' attacks away.

"Davin," Soren shouted, dodging the ogre's attacks, which were much quicker than they should be for such a huge foe. "The spell, drop the spell!"

Davin cocked an eyebrow, but quickly realized what Soren meant. With a flash of dull light from underneath Davin's shirt, the appearances of the three of them then faded and shifted.

Davin was then a bearded, hard-forged dwarf, Blaje was reverted back to her striking self, and Soren's scars returned to his face.

More importantly, and what Soren had asked for, two of the horses transformed, doubling and tripling in size to the two silver-furred, golden-eyed, terrifying bears. The smaller Sunstar roared as she ran at the trolls. The three trolls, wide-eyed at the sudden appearance of such ferocious predators, froze, taking in the shift in the battle.

Sunstar barreled into the lead troll, knocking the eight-foot monster off his feet and onto his back, the bear ravaging him as his bony arms fought off the vicious attack. The other two trolls staggered back, paralyzed in confusion and what could be construed as fear.

Moonshadow ran on all fours toward Soren and the towering ogre he was embattled with. The ogre didn't recoil like the trolls though. Instead, a hint of a smirk curled up on its gigantic mouth. A breath escaped between its cracked, yellow teeth, and Soren's nostrils filled with sulfuric, rotten breath.

Moonshadow collided with the ogre in a blow that sent out a shockwave that burst through Soren's chest. It woke him from his curious fascination with the new battle. He burst forth. "Attack!"

The scene exploded into a bitter fight. Steel flashed, and a violent eruption of claws, teeth, and fur had entered the mountaintop. Soren, unleashing punishing attacks with Firelight upon the ogre with Moonshadow, tried to keep a vigilant eye on his friends as the fight grew to an ungodly, bloody battle.

Firelight slashed and stabbed at the ogre's unnaturally thick hide. The Vellice dagger cut deep, doing what few man-made blades could. The ogre roared, swinging its spiked club in unruly swipes, knocking off the mountain's rocky face, or whooshing above in monstrous arcs.

Moonshadow tore at the ogre with savage attacks, biting at

the ogre's neck, drawing dark blood onto its massive chest. The silver bear clawed ferociously at the monster, who tried to shove the bear off with its immense, gnarled hand.

The others battled the three trolls, with Sunstar leading the charge.

Everything seemed like the tide had turned with the joining of Mihelik's bears of the Myngorn. The battle had seemed to shift, even without the power of the Ellydian, and Soren found himself in his element. His blade moved with deliberate accuracy, moving like a third arm he'd always had.

However, the attacking foes weren't going to go down easily, and even with the two bears evening the fight, the lead troll with the necklace of human skulls barked fresh orders. The ogre's ears twitched, understanding the dark foe's language. With a flurry of maddening attacks, forced sheerly with its brute force, swung its club at Soren, and shoved off Moonshadow with its free hand.

Soren was caught off guard by the speed of the blows, falling onto his back. Staring up at the ugly ogre, fifteen feet tall and as wide as a house, the ogre raised its club high over its head. It was ready to barrel down onto Soren, squashing him like an overripe melon.

"Soren!" Davin shouted from the other side of the rocky outcrop. As the club came crashing down, Soren knew Firelight couldn't help him, and the club was raining down with a speed he knew he couldn't evade. He swallowed hard and his mind raced.

Move, Soren, move! Oh, fuck… this isn't good…

Chapter Twenty-Eight

Swift and furious, the mad ogre's club rained down on Soren. The muscles in Soren's legs tensed, pushing against the rock beneath him with all his might. He tried to leap out of the way of the massive, spiked club, but the ogre's strength was too great.

I'm not going to make it...

The club came speeding down on him.

In a flash of streaking light—and with a force into Soren's side strong enough, he thought his ribs may break—Soren was knocked to the ground, the smell of lavender oil filling his nostrils.

The club came crashing down. The impact was so immense that the rock beneath it broke and cracked. The club's spikes went flying like metal nails zipping through the air.

Blaje lay atop Soren. A mix of pleasure and annoyance filled her face as she looked down at Soren, their noses nearly touching.

"Didn't your master Landran teach you to move your

feet?" A serious, bitter tone laced her words. "Get up, you fool. Fight!"

Blaje and Soren were back up on their feet quickly, as the ogre brought his huge club up over his head, ready to squash them both.

Beyond, the silver bears surrounded the three trolls with Davin. The trolls easily towered over the bears and dwarf, and suddenly Soren wasn't so sure of victory. The trolls and ogre's attack wasn't quite a surprise, but they were powerful foes. Far larger and more fearsome than any old ragtag pack of trolls.

No, these hunters were skilled, packed with animalistic strength and speed. And the ogre needed to die, Soren knew. It was far too deadly a creature for Soren to let live and kill whoever it wished.

He had to form a plan...

"We've got to end this," Soren growled to Blaje, Firelight flashing in his hand. Blaje's hair whipped over her shoulder as she held her shamshir curved blade out, both of them spreading apart, trapping the ogre on both sides. Its massive head snapped back and forth at them. It whirled its club in a great arc, missing both of them. Soren and Blaje lashed out with quick swipes, drawing blood from the great monster, but slowing it little.

"Sure, would be nice to have Kaile here with us right now," Blaje said through clenched teeth. "He could lift the ogre up into the sky and drop him into a broken mess."

Soren felt a rising heat build in his chest at the sound of Kaile's name. It was the kind of heat that brought out the animal in Soren. The predator returned, and his senses sparked alive.

The ogre turned to Blaje for but a moment, but that was all Soren needed. He sprinted to the ogre in quick strides. His boot found the ogre's thigh, and he leaped up the beast, grabbing a fold of thick skin on the back of the ogre's neck. Firelight rose high above it, and before it could even reach up for Soren, he drove Firelight straight down into the back of the ogre's neck.

A ferocious roar left the ogre's giant mouth. It fought and spun, trying desperately to reach Soren, perched upon its back like a spider injecting its venom into a much larger bug. Its club flailed, causing Soren to duck his head and tuck close to the ogre's body. He unleashed a ruthless assault of stabbing cuts into the ogre.

Blood pooled and soaked the back of the ogre's body. The roars erupted from the monster's maw in the most terrifying way. Should anyone in the hills and mountains hear such a horrifying cry, they'd surely run as fast as they could in the opposite direction. Firelight was covered in thick, fiery blood, as were Soren's hands and forearms.

He stabbed mercilessly, but the ogre's cries didn't relent. The hideous ogre, in a throe of desperation, flung his huge hand back, nearly gripping Soren's head, but Soren jumped down from the beast. As Soren leaped back, Blaje shot in.

The ogre's attention was upon him, and Blaje took the opportunity. Her blade slashed through the air with the kind of precision that took decades of training. Soren watched with a pride that he rarely knew in his life. He'd known many soldiers and warriors, but none moved the way she did.

Her blade was a part of her. She moved like a renowned song. All the notes hit the perfect pitches right where they needed to be. They flowed and strung together with delicate precision. As she wove her song, blood spilled from the ogre's midsection, coating her blade and stoking the fire within her.

As the ogre turned to fight Blaje, Soren joined, leaping up again on the ogre, this time fully mounting its shoulders. Out of the corner of his eyes he saw the trolls frantically trying to make their way to Soren, to stop his and Blaje's ruthless assault, but the bears and Davin pushed them back with a vicious scramble of flashing fur, steel, and claws.

Soren took his chance and plunged Firelight down with such force onto the ogre's head that it split its thick-boned skull. Soren squeezed the blood-soaked dagger's grip as tightly as he could. The ogre let out a hollow groan as the Vellice-steel blade pierced its brain. Soren twisted the dagger for good measure and jumped down, joining Blaje.

The ogre staggered, feeling the top of its head, blood staining its huge fingers as it did so. The rest of the battle slowed as all watched the towering ogre stagger and sway, dropping its massive club to the rocks with a clink. In a flash of steel, Blaje sent her sword swiping across the ogre's throat. It gasped and gurgled as it tried to draw in a breath. Blood poured down the ogre's great, heaving chest as it fell to a knee finally. Sunstar and Moonshadow's instinct kicked in and they turned away from the trolls, running to the ogre and unleashing a brutal onslaught of teeth and claws, tearing flesh from bone.

As the two silver bears consumed the ogre's body until it lay in a motionless, broken pile, Soren turned his attention back to the trolls. Blaje rejoined him. They strode towards the three hunters.

"You two finally done with that one?" Davin grunted, ax firmly in hand. "I've been busy fighting three over here…"

Soren, Blaje, and Davin squared off against the three trolls as the bears followed, leaving the ogre's corpse behind.

The trolls, creatures known for their strength, seemed to have a sense of something deep in their expressions. Their eyes darted, their roars turned to moans and their language hastened between each other.

They turned and climbed up the rock face behind them quickly. Soren was impressed with their speed for such animals, but knew they were accustomed to the rocky, darker parts of the world.

"We should go after them," Blaje said. "They'll return, next time with something worse, possibly."

As they considered chasing the trolls, finding a way up the sheer cliff to follow, the two bears burst past them, part of their silver fur then soaked with crimson blood. Sunstar and Moonshadow ascended the cliff behind the trolls as if it were no more than a curb on a cobblestone street.

"Let the bears show them no mercy," Davin huffed, letting his ax dangle loosely at his side.

"Should we join?" Soren asked.

"Did you see what they did to that ogre?" Davin said with a sinister satisfaction, a wicked curl of his lips turning to a wide smile. "I think I'm gonna enjoy our new companions, even if they don't wield the Ellydian."

Soren nodded. "Agreed. They are welcome. And I fear whoever stands in our way will meet similar fates to this pack."

Blaje wiped her sword clean and sheathed it. "Come, let us wind down. I doubt we need to fear any more from those trolls this night."

Over the next half hour, Soren calmed the horses. Davin fell surprisingly back to sleep, snoring loudly. Blaje sat by the fire, warming herself as she stared into the flames. The fire's light caused a fuzzy amber glow to envelop her, and as Soren finally joined her, she gave him a curious glance. She nodded, but bit her lip and cocked her head slightly. It was somewhere between a "good job" and "we could've done better."

"Yes, I know," Soren said. "I should've sensed them sooner. I should've been quicker to respond after the bears sensed them…"

"I don't care about that," Blaje said, crossing her legs as she sat upon the log. Her boot pointed at Soren as she glared at him. "Your senses will never be better than the new companions that ride with us. I want to continue our conversation before we were attacked."

Soren's mind whirled back to their conversation before the attack, and then snapped back to the present. He didn't want to continue his talk about what he saw in the Ash Grove, but he'd made a deal, and she'd divulged her conversation with Lady Sargonenth to him...

"Where did we leave off?" he asked, grabbing a bottle of wine and taking a sip.

"In the Ash Grove." Blaje leaned in, her voice just barely over a whisper. "Tell me about it."

Soren glared into the fire. It hissed, popped, and crackled. He placed another log on. Fresh sparks flew from its bark as it sparked alive. Soren sighed deeply, thinking of the vision of Cirella's face back there before they entered the tower of Golbizarath.

"I saw her. I think it was more than a hallucination or vision. I think it was her. I felt her spirit there. She was alive, but not alive. We had a full conversation, and I got my goodbye… I finally got my goodbye…"

He took another sip and cocked his head to wait to see her reaction. Her chin rose, and she glared up at the wintry night sky and the endless blanket of sparkling stars in the sky. She took a deep breath, letting the air freeze her exhale into a great plume. She reached out for the bottle, and Soren handed it to her. After a deep gulp, she wiped her lips clean and stared deeply into Soren.

"You don't believe me," Soren said. "I don't blame you. I can't explain it. But I thought I'd tell you. I didn't want to before…"

"Why?" she asked simply, but forcefully.

He knew the answer, but didn't want to say it aloud. *Because I have complicated feelings for you, and I don't want to talk about the love that I lost.*

"You should have told me," Blaje said with a serious, yet kind, expression. Her eyes softened, and she scratched her thigh.

"I know. I'm sorry."

"I do believe you," she said. "The Ash Grove has an old memory. It may be dead, but that old wood has a vivid history. It was worshiped by the Sundar. It was an oasis once, remember…"

Soren held his knees and glared into the fire as the log was engulfed in whipping fresh flames. He remembered Cirella's face as if it were more than a dream, and he smiled widely at the memory.

"Soren…" Blaje stood, walked over, and sat by his side, sitting on the same log as he and placing her hand into his unexpectedly. He raised an eyebrow.

"What?" Soren asked, unsure why what he told her made her approach him so.

She took a deep breath. "Seeing a vision like that in the Ash Grove has far more implications than you realize. That was a divine oasis, sacred to the Sundar centuries ago. Even thousands of years ago. Before the Great Divine Flood even. For you to have a conversation with an important person like that, there, well… it's…"

"What?"

"For you to have a connection strong enough to reconnect with your lost love in the Ash Grove… Soren… I think that means you have the blood of the ancients in you…"

"Blood of the ancients?" Soren asked with wide eyes and his fingers spread on his knee. She squeezed his other hand and leaned in.

"Soren… I think you are one of the Sundar. An ancestor of the old world. The Sundar were thought to be gone forever. But I think their blood lives on in you. You, Soren, have the blood of the ancients in you…"

Soren looked at her with a puzzled expression, his mind whirling and many visions in his head of Cirella, his parents, grandparents, and his past.

"What does that mean?" Soren asked. "I mean to you... what would that mean?"

"No one could have survived this long with that blood. The Polonians hunted them to extinction just before the Great Divine Flood. Your blood couldn't have survived unless it was a deep secret. You, Soren, are all that's left of the old world. You carry a gift."

"I'm a Sundar?" Soren muttered, as much to himself as her.

"Yes, and I fear that will have implications that ripple throughout Aladran if it's true. You, Soren Stormrose, are among the most legendary and wise people the world has ever known."

PART VI
DEATH SENTENCE

Chapter Twenty-Nine

❧❧❧

The fall of my people, the Sundar.

This is just as much a personal entry as a historical one.

And I write this with a broken heart, tears in my eyes, and an emptiness that is impossible to describe. I sit here, alone. Perhaps as alone as anyone has ever been. Living on the mountain in my seclusion, I watch the flood water rest like a new ocean, a sea of total destruction.

What was once the most beautiful world imaginable, something from an ancient fairy tale written by a master poet, is now wiped away from history, memory, and existence.

I am truly alone. My people are beneath those waves. The Sundar, and I assume the Polonians, are gone. Aladran has been wiped away from history. And through the greatest tragedy the world has ever known... My question screams of importance, but in the current state of the world, it is also meaningless.

Why?

Why did these waters come?

Those left in our world will be left to tell the tale. If there are people left to read history. I am leaving soon. I will search for survivors. I will find any left of my people and help how I can. My seclusion was to further life, to understand the way of the world, and understand the Ellydian so that we may use it for great good.

But now my people need basic help, not philosophy.

I hope that those that survive forget about the centuries-old fighting between our people and Polonians. We are the same. We are different, but we are the same. We are the same children of God. We share this world, and can, together, create a new one.

God, why have you cursed us? What did we do to deserve this reckoning?

If history is to be remembered, I've been calling this the Great Divine Flood to myself. And I believe this is a defining moment that will separate ages. The flood has changed everything.

Now… with great despair and sadness, I say… it is time for a new world.

-TRANSLATED *from the language of the Sundar. The Scriptures of the Ancients, Book V, Chapter III.*

CELESTRA

The winds shifted during the night, bringing with them a new, crisp chill. A layer of ice blanketed the city, causing a bright sheen as the sun peeked up over the horizon. The biting winds were harsh, causing Kaile's eyes to water as he looked down at the ancient city transformed to a brilliant shade of white.

Winter still had a firm grip upon Aladran, and Kaile looked out the window of his room. Windows cracked open wide, the fire danced and suffocated as the icy winds rushed in and filled the room. His gaze was fixed upon the front city gate, three riders on horseback riding out. Their mission was too important for the king; no ice storm would delay their mission.

Three Synths to kill Soren. Three. One would do it, but three, to make damn well sure Soren and his Vellice blade didn't have a chance.

Kaile stood like a statue, watching them ride out past the front gate and turn west, riding out into the vast hills and plains. His hair whipped hard in the winds, lashing his cheek and neck, but he didn't flinch. He didn't budge. Like a statue, he stood—his mind whirling—and he felt as if he'd already lost.

Everything he fought for, everything he believed in, and those he loved most; he'd betrayed. He swallowed hard, watching the three riders disappear into the white washed storm. His eyelashes froze, his eyes watered from both the icy breath of the storm, and the storm raging within him.

There was nothing he could do for Soren then. He was alone in his tower, locked in like a hostage. Kaile didn't know what he was going to do. The talk with the archpriest in the gardens still left him with an awful taste in his mouth. Alcarond only wanted to focus on their mission, and continue Kaile's training to become strong for the king and the capital.

Kaile blinked and looked down at the city. He watched as the empty streets remained a pure, vivid white. Not a shoe print marred the perfect tapestry cast upon the great city.

All these people thinking their king is just and true. And all the while, he causes so much suffering in this world. All the power King Amón wields, and all the armies, the Synths. I just don't know how the Silver Sparrows could even imagine toppling such a powerful monarch.

It all just seems so foolish now. So many are going to suffer and die.

Just then, something else caught his eye. It was movement at the front gate. A caravan of horses and wagons was assembled, and riding out into the storm as well. At their lead was an unmistakable, massive steed. Atop it was an enormous man with blond locks and a flowing red cape. A great sword crafted in Vellice swung at his hip.

"The Knight Wolf is heading out. He's going to kill Shades..." Kaile breathed. He hoped it was Shades he was after, as the king commanded him, and not Soren.

Kaile wondered what was in the wagon, and why he wouldn't just take a couple of soldiers with him. After all, William Wolf was the only one with a Vellice blade capable of causing harm to the Demons of Dusk. Any others with him would be incapable of causing damage, and would likely be torn to pieces themselves. Or if eaten by a Black Fog... transformed to Shades themselves.

Hours later, Kaile sat at the long table in Alcarond's study. Hot food sat on platters. A stew sat in a lidded pot, fresh rolls lay under a kitchen towel, and figs sat beside them with honey and butter too. Kaile didn't eat though, his stomach gurgled and growled, and his intestines felt tied in knots.

Alcarond and Sophia ate, with two more of the king's Synths seated, munching away. The Synths were two elder wielders, surely feeling quite accomplished and proud to be at the archmage's table, figuring out a way to kill the night creatures that plagued Aladran.

Freshly scribed copies of the dissection of the dragon before the Great Divine Flood were given to each of them at the table. The work had begun. Alcarond puffed his pipe and ate a roll as he sat back at the table, his legs crossed, and the images and description of the dissection in his other hand.

Sophia gazed out the high windows of the archmage's tower. Surely the images from the dissection were fresh in her mind. The other two Synths read the notes, writing their own notes to the side.

"Where's your mind?" Alcarond asked, causing Kaile to jolt.

"Here, sir. I'm focused."

Alcarond snorted with a malicious laugh. "We've worked together a long time, apprentice. Your mind is not on your work. Fix it. We all need to dive into our research. The world depends on it."

"Yes sir." Kaile grabbed the pages and began going over them. Well, he appeared to be going over them. He studied the illustrations of the inside organ structure of an old dragon that died before the catastrophic floods, and before the modern Age of Enlightenment. He saw the huge lungs that were said to breathe our common air, but there was a third lung with a mysterious gas. That was the secret. The gas was dragonfire.

One of the elderly Synths rubbed his beard. "Does the igniter at the back of the mouth and top of the throat contribute to the dragonfire? Or the gas the only secret?"

Alcarond stroked his chin. Sophia continued staring out the windows at the biting storm.

Kaile spoke, trying to prove he wasn't completely distracted by Seph and Soren's misery. "I believe the gas is the secret. It's too bad they didn't have the knowledge to decipher what kind of chemical was in the third lung. One of the common flammable gases doesn't burn hot enough to scorch down to the bone in seconds like we know dragonfire does."

Alcarond nodded, smoking his pipe, agreeing with Kaile, or at least taking his comment in.

"It could be a common gas, but more concentrated?" one elder Synth asked. "Or a combination of them?"

Alcarond puffed away, deep in thought, sitting back in his chair, glaring out blankly into space.

"I don't think so," Sophia said. "The structure of the third lung differs from the other two. The way the lining has smaller pockets signals to me they were designed to hold in a different type of air. Something that isn't breathed, but produced in the body. I believe the secret is there. Not only in the third lung, but throughout the system of the rest of the body. The secret is there, in the rest of the body. We need to look at the arteries and veins that lead to the third lung."

Alcarond nodded, and Kaile felt intimidated by the wisdom of those around him. He was far younger than them and kicked himself for not thinking of that. But he admitted to himself that this was not normal work for him. Normally, before the burning of Tourmielle, he was a focused student. An eagerness to learn and grow had always been a gift that was deeply embedded in him. But since then… his focus was elsewhere. It wasn't hyper fixated on books and spells; it was shifted outward to a larger scope.

"Agreed," Alcarond said. "We will all dig into the composition of the rest of the body and find what causes the buildup of the gas in the third lung. That's where we'll find our answer. Once we find the gas and can replicate it, then we will test our theory."

"This is wildly exciting," one Synth said. He eyed Alcarond, waiting for the archmage to share in his excitement, who didn't return it the way the Synth had hoped.

"Excitement will come through the epiphany," Alcarond responded. "We will celebrate when a Black Fog burns, not now."

The Synth swallowed and returned to gazing down at the sheets in his hands.

Just then, a horn blew out in the city. One horn turned to two, which soon turned many. The bells chimed and each of them raced to the windows, looking down upon the ice-capped city. But their attention was focused incorrectly. As thousands poured out into the streets, all of them in a mass confusion… the unworldly roar from the sky answered every single citizen's question immediately.

Gazing up toward the heavens, the magnificent beast came into view. Monstrous wings cascading with waves of grays and blacks cut through the clouds. An enormous body, seemingly as big as a mountain from maw to tail, shot through the air like nothing Kaile had ever seen. His jaw dropped at the sight. Its ancient gray body tore through the clouds like a ship through crashing waves. Its enormous head cast trails of smoke out of the corners of its mouth as it flew. Its vast wings flapped in the rushing winds; tattered, thick, and powerful.

"It's… magnificent," Alcarond muttered.

Kaile tore his gaze from the dragon above and looked at the archmage. Kaile had never seen his master like that before. There was a twinkle in the archmage's eyes, full of wonder and delight. It was as if they had decoded the secret of dragonfire right then and there.

"What's it doing here?" one Synth asked, his voice trembling.

"Hopefully just flying past," the other answered.

"It's learning this world," Alcarond said. "This may be its new home. It's studying us like we are studying him. He's the new alpha predator. He's claiming his territory."

Kaile knew Alcarond was right. No human would stand a chance against such a monster. Even William Wolf would surely fall against the dragon, a thought that quite pleased Kaile, as he'd always imagined the legendary knight as invincible. Even to Kaile's hero—Soren.

"The answer is somewhere in there," Sophia said, watching the dragon fly over while writing notes on the paper in her hands. "Somewhere in Sarrannax is the key to saving our world from the Demons of Dusk."

"We'll find it," Kaile said. "We have to…"

Chapter Thirty

Another dream...
It's just another dream...
Seph told herself it wasn't real. The terrors when she closed her eyes at night were almost worse than the torture Zertaan put her through.

The world whirled in deep mists—as black as coal, smelling like rancid sulfur, and permeating every pore of her skin.

She couldn't move. She was trapped in a swirling maelstrom of despair. Deep cuts slid through her arms and legs, shouts erupted from the high rising funnel that caused her hair to whip her cheeks and neck.

"You're nothing!" one shouted.

"You'll always be alone!" another yelled in the storm.

"Nobody loves you!" a woman's voice shrieked.

Seph dropped to her knees, sobbing. "It's not real. It's just a dream. It's not real..."

The dark mists crept inward, threatening to devour her. Seph clutched her ears with clenched fists, swaying her head from side to side, muttering to herself that she'd wake and it would all be over.

But then, the storm and the shouting ceased. Cautiously, she opened her eyes... the storm was gone. Only a deep emptiness surrounded her. She felt as alone as she ever had. There was nothing but her and the loneliness. Except... there was something there. She couldn't see it, but she felt it. Like an icy finger hovering just above the back of her neck, causing the hairs there to stiffen straight.

She spun, and what she saw caused her to audibly gasp.

"Soren!"

He stood above her, a deep look of concern in his eyes as he held a hand out for her.

Seph desperately tried to grab his hand, but her arms felt filled with hardened lead.

Something was wrong, though. Something was terribly wrong.

There are no scars on his face... She tried to shout, to scream, but nothing emerged from her open mouth except a whisper of her words.

Soren's eyes darkened slowly, and the scars began to etch their way down his face. They glowed an ethereal gold as they cut down through his eyebrow, over his eye and down his cheek. The gold faded and was replaced by streaks of blood dripping down from the open wounds.

"It's all right..." he said. "I'm coming... Hold on, my Persephone... I'm..."

His dark eyes popped open wide, and his mouth gaped. From behind, a sword plunged through his chest.

Seph tried to scream, tried to stand, tried to cast, but nothing happened. She was glued to her kneeling position.

The sword was coated in his blood as Soren gripped the blade with both hands. But it was no ordinary sword. As Soren gripped the sword, all his fingers were sliced, cut completely through by the rippling waves of steel of the Vellice-crafted blade.

His fingers fell to the floor with dull thuds; like wine corks plopping to the ground.

"He's not coming," a foul voice from behind muttered. "No one is coming for you."

Soren's eyes rolled back, and he fell forward. Seph tried to catch him, but her hands were stuck, moving impossibly slowly as hard as she fought. He fell to the floor, onto his face.

Standing before her then, looming over Soren's dead body, like the god of the Nine Hells, Nazaroth, was a dark, murderous bastard. It was no god. But it was just as evil as the dark God.

A sinister smile crept up along the king's face as he towered over her; his Vellice blade Storm Dragon coated in blood. A dark tunic covered his Vellice armor as he grinned.

"No one is coming. You're going to die down here, you fatherless brat. You're alone. And you're all mine…"

Behind King Amón, a heat built that caused Seph to recoil. It was so intense she was finally able to raise her arms, if only to shield her face. The waves of heat radiated from behind the king like a new sun emerging. Hot enough to burn the world.

She peeked through her fingers to see a blinding inferno raging behind the king, who stood unscathed by the flames. His laugh blistered to an echoing storm, raging like a fire-filled tornado as Seph screamed.

※

Seph lurched up from her bed.

Bound, her restraints kept her tied to the mattress. Her chest heaved labored breaths as she gasped for air through her dry nostrils. The rusty cloth that gagged her kept her screams muffled. Cold sweat poured down her brow as she cried.

Keys jingled from outside her door as the latch popped.

Seph fought to break free of her bindings. She couldn't

handle more torture. She was breaking. Her soul, mind, and body were all on the brink of giving up. Her spirit was all she had left. The pain was too great. She needed to escape.

Seph knew she was going to die down in the bowels of the Tower of the Judicature. If she didn't get out of there soon, she was certain she'd die. Either by the hand of Zertaan's fucked up, sadistic means, or by her body finally breaking and giving up—she knew she'd never leave this place again.

Two men entered the room, and Seph could immediately smell the strong alcohol on their breaths.

"Up," one said, grabbing her bare feet in his firm hands. The other grabbed her wrists as they both untied her binding to the bed frame. Tying them to themselves instead. One sat her up forcefully. He then wiped the tears from her face as she scowled at him, unable to curse the way she dreamed she could.

"Don't worry, sweetheart," he stroked her cheek with the back of his hand. He belched unexpectedly, causing her stomach to revolt, thinking she might vomit. "It's only going to hurt for a little bit."

They gripped her arms hard and lifted her from the bed. She fought to break free, but there was no fighting the two. Seph was normally thin, but she'd become borderline emaciated in her time down in the depths of the Judicature, and in the Abiron. Her strength was fleeting, leaving her with her crippled spirit.

The two men led her down the hall to the Abiron, her feet dragging upon the floor as she struggled to stay conscious. She tried to tell herself that, too, was a dream. But she knew it was real, and the terror in her body shot through in waves.

They led her to the room, and bound her to the chair, leaving her alone with only the chair, table, and Zertaan's vast collection of "tools."

Crisp, freezing air clung to Seph's sweat. As Seph shivered

from cold and terror, the hairs on her arms and feet stiffened to a point of breaking. Time passed, but Seph couldn't read time like she used to. It could have been ten minutes or an hour... but eventually the door cracked open, and Seph fought violently to break free.

Zertaan entered the room without a word, shutting the door behind her.

Seph cried, fought, raged, and screamed.

Zertaan didn't even bat an eye at her. Instead, Zertaan, with her back to her, lowered her robe, revealing her long golden hair and back covered with tattoos. She cracked her knuckles and went to the table, eyeing the tools.

"Please... please... don't hurt me anymore... please..." Snot dribbled down Seph's nose and over her lips. Spit hung from her chin, and her face streaked with fresh tears. "Please... please... I can't take anymore... I'm going to die if you don't stop. I can feel it. I can feel my body breaking..."

Zertaan grabbed a short blade, a one-inch curved razor at the top of a wooden handle; one of her favorites... The blade glistened in candlelight as she inspected it. Seph shuddered in terror at the blade, and her head slunk as she sobbed.

Zertaan strode before her, bare from the waist up, and she took an uncharacteristically long breath, a sort of sigh that Seph hadn't heard. Seph sniffled and looked up.

The Synth of Arkakus stroked Seph's cheek. "My sweet, sweet little lamb... you are young and full of life. You can take more. You've just never been tested through pain like this. You grew up sheltered like a princess with your last name shielding you from the real world. But this..." She held up the short blade between them, spinning it slowly as it flickered in amber light. "This is meant to show you the depths of your strength and resolve."

Seph sobbed again. "Please... no more... I can't take anymore..."

"You can, and you will…"

As Zertaan said that, Seph raged, fighting her bindings, gritting her teeth, and crying for help.

"Persephone…" Zertaan said, standing up straight and watching her struggle against her bindings, "you may feel like you have nothing left to give. You may feel that your body is failing, but let me assure you… it's not. You have so much more to give than you realize…"

"I can't," Seph huffed. "I can't take anymore…"

Zertaan laughed, but her tone darkened quickly after. "I've been doing this a long time. Trust me when I say… you've got a long way to go before you fully give up. I'll take you to the edge, but I won't push you off."

Seph sobbed, muttering to herself in a daze. Her head swirled and fear gripped her like a set of huge jaws squeezing her body like a vice.

"I spoke with the king." Zertaan had a nasty smile across her face.

Seph looked up at her, her hair soaked from cold sweat.

Zertaan smiled widely. "He asked about your progress."

A flurry of emotions sparked through Seph, causing her mind to race and a tiny sliver of hope to sprout up like a spring rose, but it quickly got squashed like a muddy boot trampling the flower.

"I told him you had a long way to go to Re-Enlightment." Zertaan knelt before Seph, glaring deeply into her with the Synth's red eyes fixed on her like a snake's. "You're mine, Persephone Whistlewillow. It could be months before you even see sunlight again. You and I are going to become quite close down here. I told him the blood in your Whistlewillow veins will take much to break you and make you fully submit to him."

"No…" Seph screamed as she fought. "No! No! No! Soren! Kaile! Help! Help me, please!"

Zertaan gave a long sniff, as if smelling Seph's terror and desperation.

"No one is coming to save you," Zertaan said, running the side of the blade down Seph's bare arm, sliding down the sweat easily. "There is nothing but you, me, and pain. The power you carry inside of you is far too great a force to take chances with letting free. We can't have you using it against us, can we? Even with the king's newfound abilities, we can't chance that you'll turn. You need to be completely and utterly broken, and then… you can ascend to the rank of Lyre Master. You will be free to become as powerful as I and Archmage Alcarond."

Newfound abilities? What is she speaking of? Does the king possess more than his armies, Synths, and madmen? I need to tell Soren about this. I need to get free…

"The world is changing," Zertaan said. "I'd be a fool to not admit that. I can feel it. The world and Aladran taste differently. Things will be different. I know not how, but I can see it. A new world is forming. The Chimaera is breaking it from the inside while the Demons of Dusk encroach from the outside. The rebellion is just another chink in the king's armor. He's going to need you for the war to come, so let's not waste time, shall we? We have much work to do to prepare you for the war. Sitting here crying and squabbling will get us nowhere. Now… where should we start?"

Hours passed of unimaginable pain for Seph. Her voice broke from blood-curdling screams of anguish and agony. Her heart beat so fast and so hard she thought it was going to explode many times, even hoping it would so all the pain would finally end.

But, Zertaan a master of her craft, always seemed to stop just as Seph felt as if she may fall into the abyss of pain or death.

No one came to rescue Seph, again.

It was just her and Zertaan, behind the closed door of the Abiron, beneath the bowels of the capital. No Ellydian, no magic, no hope.

But, at the end of all the torture, and after Zertaan put her clothes back on and left, a single note rang in the middle of the night. Seph, in her utter misery, didn't know if it was a dream or not. But the note rang out subtly from the other side of the Abiron door, and Seph's body warmed. It warmed just enough that she drifted into a deep, dark slumber.

"I'm ready to die. Please... let this be the end..." she muttered before drifting off into darkness.

Chapter Thirty-One

Kaile stood in the snow, snowflakes floating down the gray sky. He looked up as the snowflakes landed on his cheeks and eyelashes, causing him to blink them away as they melted on his warm skin. He stood before the Tower of Judicature—a monumental tower nearly as old as Celestra itself. Once a prison, it was reformed into a tower to hold trials, seek truth, and hold those who broke the law.

Only months ago, Kaile revered the tower and what it stood for. But now it seemed only a prison—a prison to torment and torture the one he cared about more than anything.

Kaile was temporarily barred from entrance, so he knew going to the front gate was out of the question. He'd be denied entry and the king and Alcarond would be told of his attempt. There were no back entrances he knew about, and no windows large enough to even crawl through. Not only was it impossible to break out of, it was always impenetrable.

Double-walled foundations of hard stone, thin windows that rose the hundred feet to its roofed cone peak, and filled

THE DARK SYNTHS

with guards and soldiers, the Tower of the Judicature was a fortress in its own right.

Kaile tussled his hair, unsure why he was even there. After their meeting about dragonfire had ended, his mind raced while his feet took him to the tower. He marveled at the old, gray circular walls as if pleading with them. He gave them his respect, hoping that Shirava would grant him some sort of grace, some sort of forgiveness, some sort of mercy.

Seph was down there. Right then, she was at the complete mercy of Zertaan and the king. Re-Enlightment had always had an aura of darkness when spoken about by those that wielded the Ellydian. But those that were Re-Enlightened, although obedient, were changed.

The Re-Enlightened had a part of them missing. They were human, but lacked certain qualities that made them—different. They were dark, lacking empathy, hope, and had an especially acute taste for violence. It was all by design, and in the ranks of the Synths of the capital, they were a dark breed. All three of the Synths sent by the king and Alcarond after Soren were Re-Enlightened. That was how trustworthy they were after their torture. Even let out into the plains, the king *knew* they would obey him. Their obedience was so certain that he trusted those three with taking out his most hated enemy, and the one who left the scar on the king's face from Firelight's edge; Soren.

"What am I doing here?" Kaile murmured as he turned his back to the tower. "I shouldn't even be seen here..."

Facing away from the tower, he turned to gaze back at it again. There was a pull that beckoned for him from within the tower. Like a powerful spell, he felt connected to the tower. Like there was a piece of string connecting the two, it wound itself onto a spool within, pulling him in like a vortex pool in his hometown waters of Ikarus.

He, again, wandered toward the great tower, but then a

familiar voice jerked him back to reality, severing the string that pulled him. Like a pair of shears snipping the line in two, the voice had a gravity that made Kaile feel as though he'd been discovered doing something wrong.

Kaile spun to see Alcarond standing like a broad-shouldered statue behind him. His blue robes were speckled with black and gold trim, and his wise eyes glared down at Kaile with a curious intensity.

"Why are you here?" the archmage repeated, beckoning an answer.

Kaile was so caught between worlds, he didn't know how to respond. Below ground was Seph, who he desperately wanted to save, and before him was his master, the one destined to help Kaile become a powerful Syncron. Kaile felt as if his soul was being torn to shreds.

"Archmage... I..." Kaile murmured, gazing around feverishly, trying to find the words to hide his attachment to Seph.

"Come," Alcarond said. "Let us find a more... appropriate place to have a talk."

Kaile felt the color flush from his face, and his mouth instantly dried. As Alcarond turned, Kaile followed, his head low, and his reddish-brown hair falling before his eyes.

The archmage led them just half a road down to a shop with a small round table seated before windows that gave a breathtaking view of the Tower of the Judicature. Alcarond motioned for Kaile to sit, which he did. Alcarond sat after, waving for a woman behind the short counter. She came over. Her hands shook at the sight of the archmage. She cleared her throat to speak.

Alcarond lay a calming hand on her jittering hands. She let out a calming gasp. "We'd like two teas, please."

"M... milk or honey?" she managed to get out.

He nodded. She went back off to behind her counter,

disappearing behind the short counter, most likely just hiding to regain her composure, Kaile thought.

"I—I'm sorry, master, I…" Kaile began, but Alcarond hushed him with a wave of his hand, glaring out at the tower.

The girl brought over two teas and lay the milk and honey between them.

Alcarond poured both into his herbal-scented tea, swirling it with a tiny spoon. For a moment, Kaile was reminded of the fact that Alcarond walked around the capital city without a security detail. No one else high ranking did so. It was a reminder of his power and the fear he struck in people.

"I had feelings in this city for a woman, too," Alcarond said, very unlike him, talking about his emotions, and not the Ellydian or Kaile's training. "Perhaps I forget that training you to become what you were meant to be, isn't all about magic and war at hand."

Kaile sipped his tea. The warm cup felt wonderful in his freezing hands, and it instantly calmed him as it hit his lips and warmed him from the inside.

"I didn't mean to come down here after our meeting. I apologize, master. I should focus on the task before us."

Alcarond's mouth flattened, and he shut his eyelids hard.

"When are you going to start telling me the truth again?" Alcarond asked in an agitated, yet compassionate tone. "We used to be so close, you and I. When did we drift apart?"

Kaile knew their connection was severed when he saw the king and the Knight Wolf incinerate the town of Erhil. But he knew Alcarond well enough to know he was alluding to something before that.

Alcarond leaned toward the window and looked up to the gray, cloudy sky. "A dragon flies the skies of Aladran again. I never thought I'd live to see the day…"

"It was breathtaking," Kaile said. "In the best and worst ways, I mean."

"Agreed," Alcarond said, swirling his tea. He pulled out his pipe and tobacco pouch. He loaded the pipe and held the pipe out for Kaile. Kaile struck an A note with his staff and fire sparked his finger. He dipped his finger to Alcarond's pipe as the archmage inhaled. It was something of a parlor trick they used to do. But he'd stopped doing it years ago, and it made Kaile remember the years he'd spent with Alcarond.

"The world is changing fast," Alcarond said, puffing his pipe, folding one leg over the other under his deep sea-blue robes. "We need to unify if we are to survive what's coming."

Kaile nodded, but knew he was hiding too much of himself to comply fully.

"I know you are preoccupied with worry for your friends—Seph and Soren." Kaile swallowed hard as Alcarond said that. "I know you love Seph, and you want to help your childhood hero, Soren."

"I don't know how to shut out my feelings," Kaile said, momentarily giving into the truth. He was so utterly tired of hiding in plain sight, he gave up for a fleeting moment. "They're all I think about. I can't stand the pain that Seph must be going through down there. And if she lives, she won't be the same. And it's all because of me. It's all my fault."

Alcarond reached across the table and lay his hand on Kaile's shoulder, squeezing it firmly.

"I understand. I've been there too, son. I've been there too."

Kaile sighed. "All due respect, sir—I don't think you have."

"Why do you say that?" Alcarond said, leaning back, puffing his pipe and waiting for a response. "Are your feelings for them so much greater than the feelings others have? Is your love more powerful than all the other love in the world?"

Kaile had never thought of that. He was so trapped in his feelings of guilt; he *forgot* about the rest of the world. He knew there was a great lesson to be had in that sentiment.

"As you know, I too, had my heart broken, my most important connection lost forever, and a new enemy made. My world crumbled."

Kaile knew he was referring to the love he had for Sophia, and his relationship with his master, Mihelik Starshadow, broken to the point where they fought, and Alcarond used the Wraithfire spell on Mihelik, permanently blinding him.

"But you didn't betray her..." Kaile was careful about the tone of his voice. He didn't want to push his master, but he was trying to be as honest as he could without crossing boundaries. "I betrayed them, master. I betrayed them in a way they could never forgive. And now Archmage Mihelik is dead... because of me..."

"Don't confuse things," Alcarond said. "Mihelik turned traitor. He burned the Scriptures of the Ancients. All that priceless knowledge lost forever. He deserved his fate and lived well beyond his years."

"You, master, you betrayed me. You used me. And now I have to live with the consequences of decisions I had no control over. I think about it night and day. I have terrible nightmares and even think about doing terrible things... I don't know how to live with myself. I feel like I'm an empty vessel meandering through this world, just waiting for death to take me, so that I can pay my penance."

"Don't talk like that, Kaile. You're strong. You need to remember that."

"I'm weak, sir." Kaile's head dropped with a deep sigh, thinking of Seph's face blowing in the winter winds, her smile on camelback, her laugh, her intoxicating smell.

"Kaile, listen to me, and listen good. Look at me." Alcarond's voice was commanding, like a father to his son who just lost an important competition. Kaile looked up at him. Alcarond put his pipe down and squared his shoulders, looking deep back at Kaile. "You are stronger than you feel at the present. You, Kaile Thorne, born of nothing, set the sea ablaze. That is a far rarer gift than you may still realize. Turning saltwater to flame is difficult for even the most powerful Syncrons. And you turned the surrounding sea aflame in your anguish. You are destined to become something great. Your future is so bright, I believe, that statues will be made of you in the towers of Celestra for ages. One day, you will pass the Black Sacrament, you will become a legendary Lyre Syncron, and you will help me save this world."

Kaile felt pride in those words, but not nearly enough to brush off the deep scars of guilt on his heart.

"But why did you do that to me, then? If you want me to trust you, then why did you and Zertaan put the Godkeeper Rune on me without telling me?" Kaile clutched the sides of his head in his fist and shook. "I feel like I'm going insane sometimes. You tricked me. You deceived me for years, and in the end, you used me."

"To be fair, and you may not want to hear this, but they are our enemies. The Silver Sparrows are trying to overthrow not only the king, but our way of life. They want to dismantle what we've built here. The order of Syncrons that protect this realm are vital to our survival."

"But..." Kaile said, trying to form his words carefully. "What if what is right, isn't what we've built and what the king is, but somewhere in between?"

"Be careful, my apprentice," Alcarond's voice grew grim. "This discussion is bordering on treasonous, and ears are everywhere in this city."

"I'm just trying to say..." Kaile leaned in to whisper. "What if what happened in Tourmielle and Erhil wasn't to burn away the Chimaera? What if it was all done for another purpose? And the people are starting to see that?"

Alcarond did something then that Kaile didn't expect. It was a rare sight to see the archmage nervous. But a rare twitch in Alcarond's eye hinted the archmage knew something, but wouldn't dare say it aloud.

"He is our king," Alcarond finally said, after a deep throat clearing, tapping the ash out of his pipe and nervously stuffing more tobacco in. "That's all there is."

He knows... he knows what the king did was wrong. Even if he can't say it, or admit it to himself. He knows! I can feel it! There's still humanity left in him... at least I deeply hope there is...

"Yes." Kaile nodded. "He's our king."

"Remember that, my apprentice. You will go far in this life, but we all would do well to remember that."

Kaile nodded, drinking his tea with a brief satisfaction.

"These wars will change our world in unseen ways," Alcarond said, peering out the window at the Tower of the Judicature, and Kaile wondered specifically what he thought would come from the wars. "The dragon, Soren leading the Sparrows, the defeat of Glasse, and the Black Fog entering Grayhaven. These are all leading to something bigger. But I cannot see what. You and Persephone have significant roles to play as well. The capital needs you both. I need more Lyrian Syncrons at my side. Perhaps it's selfish of me to want to keep the line of Whistlewillows going, even though they deserve to die off for their treason. But even myself as a boy looked up to their family legacy, like you looked up to Soren and his sword battles as a child."

Kaile sighed, unsure of what to say.

"Our part in these wars is coming," Alcarond said, muttering the words, almost as if to himself as he gazed out the window. "We are being invaded, Kaile. I know you care about Seph and Soren, but you have to forget about that momentarily. The Demons of Dusk are coming. Their numbers grow every passing night, and they're growing more brazen. They will soon enter the cities. They're going to kill absolutely everyone and everything. There's not going to be a future soon. No one to care about, no one to love. All human emotions will become extinct, and I fear they will spread even to the other continents. It's a pure evil that has stricken our lands. An evil that we must purge—together. I'm so close to figuring it out, Kaile. I just need more time. Help me. Help me figure out a way to defeat them. This is our war, and if we can't figure out a way to win, then nobody will."

Kaile scratched his elbow, not fully willing or able to commit. Seph was too important to him. But he knew that Alcarond's logic was sound. If they didn't find a way to save the world from the Black Fog and Shades, then they would be overwhelmed, and even the Syncrons of Celestra would be helpless to defend the millions of souls that called Aladran home. Only Vellice steel and dragonfire had proven useful in killing the monsters that plagued their lands. "I'll try."

"That's enough. We must try. Now, let us get back to work. There's so much to do, and so little time… So, so, little time…"

Chapter Thirty-Two

Soren rode atop the horse's back, the smell of fresh, grassy dew tickling his nose hairs. A stark contrast to the sandy morning desert smells, Soren admired the plains before him, as if it was a sort of homecoming. It was a bitter, yet welcoming feeling.

The early morning sun broke the horizon with a fiery red glow. Clouds streaked through the sky like sharp claws raking the sky itself. Rows of all shades of reds and oranges filled the eastern sky as the red sun revealed itself more and more with each passing second. A cool wind whipped through, causing a hint of a reminder of spring—subtle, yet wonderful.

This was the Aladran Soren knew. Before him and his friends sprawled out the gorgeous lands of Aladran, in this case, more specifically Lynthyn, the capital of Aladran. Rolling hills grew to the great Lyones Mountain range behind them, and before them were hundreds of miles of stunning plains.

The tunnel had taken them underground under some of the most surveilled areas of the border, where the Driftmire separated the capital kingdom from the desert one, Zatan. They were then in the king's lands. The spell of disguise had been reactivated. Even Sunstar and Moonshadow, after returning from their hunt with the ogre, were transformed to two unsaddled, wild horses. Moonshadow a deep midnight, and Sunstar a brilliant, milky white.

With the safety of the morning rays, Soren, Davin, and Blaje had ridden out of the foothills and into the plains, filled with a thin blanket of crunchy snow and tall dead grass. Sable purred in Soren's lap as he scanned the area for any forms of life. Since the arrival of the Demons of Dusk, and especially within the last decade, few animals roamed the plains. Most deer and mammals had been slaughtered, needlessly killed in the name of killing. Their remains were left to rot, or picked clean by buzzards when the sun rose and daylight washed its protecting aura over the lands.

As they rode into the plains, Moonshadow and Sunstar trotting at their sides, the sun rose, dimming the breathtaking reds and oranges, transforming them to a heavenly gold and clear, vibrant blue. The snow on the ground sparkled a dazzling white at the right angle, and a breath of warmth wafted through, again reminding Soren of spring. He thought if the clouds thinned, then they may feel a warm sun that day, causing much of the faint snow to melt.

But Soren didn't drop his guard at the welcoming landscape. There was trouble in every direction. To the northeast lay Celestra, still hundreds of miles off. The kingdom of Arkakus was northwest, the same distance away. To even get to Celestra, one would have to pass through the Whitestone Mountains, the most heavily patrolled and watched range in all of Aladran. To reach Arkakus, and hopefully Soren's master Landran, they'd have to pass through the Gloomdrake Mountains.

As they rode through the plains, heading northwest toward Arkakus, Soren's head swam with a mash of troubling thoughts. At the forefront was always Seph. His eye twitched about thoughts of her, mixed with his lack of sleep, which had evaded him greatly as of late. He hoped that wouldn't backfire when he needed his focus and strength most. But he couldn't not worry about her, and that worry was beginning to consume him.

He told himself that she was strong. Seph had learned the Ellydian on her own in the orphanage. Not only that, but she'd succeeded in rising to the rank of Ayl, worthy of praise from any who wielded the Ellydian.

He muttered to himself, "She'll make it. She has to. She has to survive. She will. She's got her mother's blood in her veins. She will..."

Blaje seemed to hear his muttering, gave him a worried glance as she rode beside him.

The other thing that filled his thoughts was what Blaje had said to him—that she thought he had Sundar blood in him. He didn't know what that meant for him, and wondered if it meant anything... but the ability to speak with the dead in the Ashgrove surely meant... something.

Landran would know... aside from Archmage Mihelik, Landran Dranne was the wisest man Soren ever knew. *Landran will know... he's got answers that will aid us in our fight. I just... I just can't believe he's still alive after all these years... and he sent me Firelight for our war.* Soren laughed. *He always was good at surprises, and always with the dramatic flair for impact.*

He will join us! He will join us in our fight.

Landran was Soren's master, and even better with a sword and dagger. He'd be a true asset in their fight against the king and their enemies. After getting Landran on their side, all they'd need was Syncrons to join their side. For without magic, there would be no chance of success. The king knew that without Mihelik, Seph, and Kaile, Soren was at a devastating disadvantage—a disadvantage Soren knew would spell certain doom unless they rectified that—and soon.

Gazing out at the plains, lit in a golden veil of the blossoming sunrise, Soren leaped down from his horse. Davin and Blaje both watched curiously. Soren rubbed his glove into the ice and dirt, lifting the ice to his nose and breathing in deeply.

"These are the enemy's lands," he said grimly as he wiped the dark ice from his gloves. "We need to be on extra guard from here on out."

"As if the desert weren't tricky enough," Davin groaned.

"This is our path," Soren said. "We ride at a steady pace for Arkakus." Soren got back up on his horse. Sable meowed angrily, missing the warmth of his lap. She snuggled back in as he sat in the saddle.

Soren dug his heels into his horse and they were off.

They rode down a hill into a valley, across a stream, and found a ridgeline to the northwest they rode into. They hoped the ridgeline may lead to foothills they could camp in during the night. For hours they rode, until the warmth of the day faded, stars returned to the sky, and they made camp.

Nestled into foothills, which transformed to a compact mountain range, Soren finally got his boots off and warmed his feet by the fire. The bears wandered up toward the mountains, either searching for meat or checking for the enemy. *Perhaps both*, Soren thought.

Davin gazed up at the stars, his disguise still masking his bearded face, into that of a tall woman with long locks. He lay on his back, arms folded behind his head, and his stomach gave a great growl. Blaje snickered. "What I wouldn't give for a frothy ale right about now…"

Soren fiddled with a dried blade of grass and agreed.

"Your people did a fine job with supplies," the dwarf said to Blaje, "but they forgot all the libations I require for an enjoyable journey."

"Oh, did they?" Blaje asked with a raised eyebrow. "Or perhaps they thought it best not to weigh a horse down with the gallons of booze you'd drink in the first couple of days back on the road?"

"Gallons…" he laughed, but then scratched his chin, realizing she may be right.

They ate a quick meal of dried meat, sharp cheese, and dried fruit.

Soren's gaze fogged as he glared into the fire. He dearly hoped sleep would find him that night, and fought away the intrusive thoughts that crept in like spiders inching their way toward prey just caught in their web.

"Soren," Blaje said. She was leaning with her hands on the ground behind her. The golden hue of the fire glistened on her tan skin, illuminating her emerald eyes like they were lit in a magical radiance. The long blond locks of her disguise reached the blanket beneath her, and her expression was dark and serious.

"Yes?" Soren replied, snapping out of a deep daze.

"I'd like to ask you some questions about your past," she said, sitting up straight and crossing her legs.

Davin perked up too, who was lying on his side, watching the fire.

Soren nodded.

"The Sundar were thought dead," Blaje said. "But somehow their blood flows in your veins. I want to understand how that is possible."

"What do you want to know?"

She cleared her throat. "Tell me about your parents… your family… so that we can get some insight into how that is possible…"

Soren sighed, itching his thigh and looking up at the stars. "My parents were Annabelle and Clive Stormrose. Both born in Cascadia, and both died when I was ten. My mother's parents were born in Lynthyn, but left and moved to Cascadia just before she was born. My father's parents were from around here, in a town called Shambly. They also moved to Cascadia. My mother and father met in Tourmielle and fell in love. They had me and a brother who died stillborn."

"Did they ever speak about the Sundar?" Blaje asked, rubbing her brow. "Do you ever have any reason to believe they had that blood in their veins?"

"No, not that I can remember. They didn't wield the Ellydian. My father was okay with a sword, but he was a baker. I did, however, show somewhat natural skill with a sword. Hence why Landran chose me."

"Tell me about that, Soren," Blaje said. She sat up straight at full attention, eager for his following words.

"Well, I was told when I was around six, Landran picked me. I was just a lad, and Landran came into town atop a mighty warhorse. The whole town was in a roar about such a famed swordsman coming to our small corner of the world."

"He came just to train you?" Blaje asked, her eyes narrowed as if a spark had lit her blossoming curiosity.

"I—I believe so…"

"He must've known," Blaje said in as much a statement as a question.

"I—I don't believe so," Soren said. "He never said anything like that. But he did mention the Sundar. He was quite the scholar and the swordsman. Landran taught me nearly as much about history as he did about fighting. He believed the secret to defeating the Demons of Dusk was buried somewhere in the past. He taught me about the old wars, the floods, and the long-lost races. He even told me about the dragons that roamed the skies far before our time here."

Davin slapped the hard ground with his palm. "I'd put one thousand torrens down that he knew you had Sundar blood. How else could he have thought to come and train you, and live in your small town?"

"My parents just told me I was special," Soren said. "As

surely all parents do. And I was just a boy. I thought I just had a knack for fighting." His hand instinctively went to Firelight's grip, unsheathing the dagger.

He held it between him and the fire. Under the veil of stars, the Vellice blade glowed in rippling waves of red light. It was a red hue like blood sheen under moonlight.

Davin tapped his finger on his knee. "How did your parents pass?"

"A flood took them," Soren said. His voice was hollow and took him back to a dark time in his life he didn't want to remember. "I was too young and weak to save them. They were swept away. I watched them get washed away as Landran held me back, saving my life."

"A flood? That's terrible, Soren," Blaje said, reaching out and touching his hand with a loving squeeze.

"It was a long time ago. I came to terms with it. I couldn't save them, but I doubled down on my efforts to train and become strong so that I could save more people."

Blaje pulled her hand back and fiddled with her hair. "Landran must've known. Why else would he travel to Tourmielle just for you? And remain there? He should've been leading armies, training hordes of soldiers, but instead, he stayed with a child to train him."

"He was more than a master. He was my friend."

Davin groaned, deep in thought. "So, if ya can talk to the dead, what else could ya do if you're Sundar?"

Davin and Soren both shot glances at Blaje, expecting and hoping for an answer from her.

"The Sundar are long gone. Mostly it's whispers of the past that remain. But their connection to the deceased was remembered. That skill was lost with them, as their ability to connect with loved ones in the most sacred places in the desert was an invaluable tool in understanding the past and learning from it." Blaje scratched her head. "I do not know what else they could do differently than us. I only know many gossips. Lady Sargonenth and the Dune Matron should know about this. They have old texts in their possession that may help shed light on this. But I do feel Landran will know more than he led you to believe."

Soren cracked his knuckles. "Then let's make haste for Arkakus, and pray that he's there, and still alive. He may be the only swordsman in this world that could best me in a sword fight."

"Forget not the king," Blaje said grimly. "You may get past the Drakoons, but the king's skill with a sword is renowned, nearly as much as yours."

"I'll kill the bastard," Soren responded quickly, and with no lack of grit. "I'll sever his head free of his shoulders and cast it off the highest peak of his castle."

"Will your revenge be complete, then? Will you be able to let that part of you rest after?" Blaje's words were clear, but the softness in them showed a genuine care.

"There's an animal in me," Soren said. "It's a part of me now. I don't know if it's ever going to go away. But killing the ones who wronged me and took everything I ever loved… that's going to help. That much I promise you, and I promise myself. Because I don't know if I can live with myself if I can't right the wrongs I've done. I let them all down, and for that I have to atone… atone with their blood."

Sunstar and Moonshadow let out deep growls then, causing Soren, Blaje, and Davin to shift in their seats. The white and black horses gazed up at the sky to the east, growling low and deep.

Soren and the others looked up to the night sky but saw nothing but a dark, pinpricked starry sky. The horses continued to growl, and Sable leaped up, jumping up onto a log just on the other side of Soren. She watched the sky too, silently.

Sunstar got up from her rest and gazed up at the midnight sky. Soren and the others stood as well.

"What is it? Anyone see anything?" Davin asked.

"Nothing," Soren said, straining his weary eyes, peering hard at the eastern sky.

Moonshadow got up, going to Sunstar's side.

"I believe I see something," Blaje said. "It's flying, and it's huge."

Soren swallowed hard, knowing something large flying in the sky toward them was more than a pack of trolls hunting them down. "Search for somewhere to hide."

Davin kicked the fire out with his boots, spreading the embers out and tossing rocks onto them.

Blaje ran and took the horses, leading them into a thicket of thin trees. Soren unsheathed Firelight, her blade glowing a shimmering blood red.

Glaring up at the sky, though, as the two bears in horse form growled low, Soren watched as the flying object tore through the sky. It soared with astonishing speed, growing from a speck near the horizon to a dark form enormous, terrifying and awe inspiring.

Davin's mouth gaped. "It's… enormous…"

From maw to tail, the dragon ripped through the dark sky, high above, its monstrous wings spread like ship's sails.

"Sarrannax," Soren breathed. "It's even bigger than I remember."

Silhouetted against the night sky, the dragon from Eldra resembled a god. Like a magnificent divine being tearing through the sky like a sharp knife through a stream. A flicker of light kissed the tip of his toothy maw. *Dragonfire*, Soren thought. The one other thing that can kill the Black Fog and Shades.

The dragon Sarrannax flew high above them, not slowing as it reached the hills Soren and the others rested upon. It cast a brief, dark shadow down upon them as it passed overhead, continuing its flight northwest.

"Where do you think it's going?" Davin asked, hiding the hint of shakiness in his voice.

"Anywhere but here, I hope," Soren said. "And hopefully it's helping rid the world of what plagues it."

"Soren," Blaje muttered. "I can't help but think about what you saw in the Under Realm…"

Soren scratched his cheek. "You're thinking about the Shadow Dragon I saw down there. You're thinking if Sarrannax could defeat the new foe?"

Blaje nodded.

"I do not know," Soren said. "I hope the Eldra dragon could kill such a monstrosity. But all I know for certain is… I wouldn't want to be anywhere near such a fight."

Davin cleared his throat. "Agreed."

Chapter Thirty-Three

❦

After a long night of toiling over notes, ideas, and running into no shortage of dead ends, Kaile retired to his room, promptly falling into a deep, exhausted sleep. Dragonfire filled his dreams. The structure of it, the heat, the destruction... Kaile fell back into his studies, and it aided him to a full night's rest. That was until...

A loud series of knocks came from the other side of Kaile's door, jolting him awake. He ran to the door, still in his underwear. Wiping the sleep from his eyes, he opened the door, unsure what such an abrupt, and early, knock was for. As he opened the door, lit in the rays of the early morning sun that sparkled through the tall windows, was a man in formal wear —a velvet, golden vest over stark black silks. He was stout, round in the face, and pursed his lips regally.

"His Excellence expects your attendance at noon this day." The short man's chin lifted as high as he could muster.

Kaile looked down at him and nodded. "Very well."

The king's attendant shifted his stance, spinning away from the door with a pleased smile.

Kaile, closing the door slowly, sliding it closed with a click, turned and walked over to his window, peering down into the city.

"The king? Again? With me?" It was all too much to guess what he wanted. There were too many moving pieces in the world. Kaile didn't know what to think. Perhaps he would try again to slyly and subtly convince the king to take mercy on Seph.

"Yes, that's what I'll do. It's worth a shot. I can't leave her down there all alone."

Yesterday was a welcome distraction, but I can't live with myself with her down there like that. Alcarond is wrong. She's worth fighting for. I can't let her become one of the Re-Enlightened. I just can't!

He slammed his fist against the windowpane. "I can't let her suffer any longer. I've got to try again..."

THE SUN HUNG high in the sky above Vael Vallora Keep, and the Tower of the King as Kaile entered. He passed through the magical cascading golden gate that protected the keep, a solid, clear A note ringing from multiple sources beyond the veil.

Kaile entered the Grand Hall, but when he entered the king's throne room, he stood at the entrance, scratching his head, trying to figure out why it was only him in the hall.

"It appears it's just you and me," a voice came from behind Kaile in the shadows. He instantly knew the familiar voice and turned to face his master.

"Alcarond," Kaile said, "do you know what this is about?"

The archmage shook his head. "Come, let us find out."

Alcarond and Kaile walked deeper into the Grand Hall, both standing between the pyres, unlit but smelling of spent fire. Kaile shoved his hands behind his back to keep his fidgeting hands hidden.

Alcarond stood beside him, his flowing blue cloak decorated with stitching of the sea and stars, flowing and sharp waves at the edges and bottom, and delicate, soft stars sewn throughout. A crescent moon was the size of his head on the middle back of the tunic's cape.

It didn't take long for the commotion to come from beyond the throne, and Kaile heard the unlatching of a door. From behind, the Drakoons came first, cast in their sleek black armor that shimmered in the warm afternoon light that poured in through the stacks of windows all around the room.

Then, after four Drakoons, the king and the archpriest stepped out, and began walking up the stairs to the throne. The king didn't even glance at Kaile or his master, but Archpriest Solemn Roane gave each of them a hard gaze before following the king up the stairs.

The king sat, his powerful body covered with an ivory gown of some of the finest material Kaile had ever seen. A sash crossed his chest and flowed down to his ankles. His shimmering, six-spindled crown sparkling majestically in the bright rays. His dark hair flowed down his shoulders, his mouth flattened, and his black beard didn't budge. The king had an angry glower as he glared out the windows.

The archpriest stood beside him, draped in ivory and gold, and wore his five-peaked biretta. He hefted his golden crosier at his side, embedded with black and silver diamonds that wound up it in waves. Solemn sighed, looking down at the floor.

The Drakoons glared straight into Kaile, as if wanting to cut him down with their curved blades.

Kaile fidgeted harder behind his back and felt the beads of sweat forming at his hairline.

"Your highness," Alcarond said, with a low bow.

Kaile was so fraught in his thoughts, he didn't bow until Alcarond turned his head and ushered for Kaile to follow his lead, which Kaile did with a bow of his own.

"My archmage," King Amón said in a strong, stern tone. "And his apprentice."

"My king," Alcarond said, bowing his head.

"My king," Kaile repeated with a similar bow.

"After much thought," the king said, finally releasing his gaze from the windows and sending it down at the two of them. "I have come to a decision, and deemed it important enough to tell you directly, before I send my royal decree out into the public."

"I appreciate that, my king," Alcarond said. "What is it you wish to decree?"

King Amón leaned forward on his throne, a heavy groan leaving his lips and a twisted expression crossed his face. He snorted, and Kaile instantly wanted to turn into a wet puddle on the floor. A deep anger welled in the king, which Kaile had seen many times, but never directly at him.

"I have a deep disappoint in the two of you, and I've been unsure what to do about it over the last few days. Alcarond…"

Alcarond stood at attention with his shoulders back, ready to listen to whatever the king had to say.

"You failed to get the Vellice dagger from Soren Stormrose. He still evades my grasp, and he still has the dagger he calls Firelight in his possession. I sent you with specific instructions to retrieve Kaile, Persephone Whistlewillow, and the dagger."

Alcarond lowered his gaze. "My apologies, my liege. I didn't expect Persephone to be able to send it back to him with a spell. I assumed she was weakened by the fight. It is a mistake I shall not make again."

"And you, Kaile Thorne…"

Kaile looked up at the king, fuming with veins protruding from his neck and brow. The archpriest had a sinister expression that resembled a mix between anger and elation. Kaile wished he could wash away into the floor and disappear forever from the kingdom.

"...You fled a battle and joined with the enemy."

"Your liege..." Alcarond protested, taking a step forward. All of the Drakoons shifted immediately, shooting between Alcarond and the king. Each of them stood in fighting stances with feet spread and swords ready to draw.

"You may have let him go..." King Amón raised his fist, slamming it down on to the throne before standing. "But your apprentice was under the impression he did it of his own accord. He fled my service to fight for... *them*..."

Kaile moved his lips to speak, but Alcarond hushed him with a squeeze of his forearm.

"My king, Kaile, was instrumental in learning much from the inner workings of the Silver Sparrows... he..."

"Silence!" The king staggered forward, Storm Dragon firmly fixed in the scabbard on his hip.

Alcarond forced his lips shut.

The archpriest looked as pleased as Kaile had ever seen him.

"My old Archpriest Mihelik betrayed me and burned sacred scriptures. My new archmage failed in securing one of the few Vellice blades in my lands, and his apprentice deserted his post at my side for the enemy. What am I to do about all of this?"

Alcarond sighed, letting his arms fall loosely to his sides. "We will redeem ourselves by providing you with the greatest army of Syncrons the world has ever known, so that you may defeat your enemy. Also, we will develop a weapon that will help eradicate the Demons of Dusk from our world completely." He bowed his head.

"I do not disagree. I desire those things very much. That is why I am not punishing either of you directly."

"My king?" Alcarond asked with a raised eyebrow.

The king sat, snorting his frustration out. He raised his arm, pointing at the archpriest. Archpriest Roane pulled out a scroll from his pocket. He unrolled it, holding it before him, and cleared his throat.

Archpriest Roane eyed the scroll, and he read, "By royal decree, on the day of the twentieth of Januar, the heretic Persephone Whistlewillow will be executed for her crimes against the crown."

Kaile's heart pounded like a drum being stricken by a mace. He clutched his chest and wanted to lunge forward, casting out a note and killing all in the room.

The archpriest continued, with a sly smirk out of the corner of his mouth. "Persephone Whistlewillow, the last of the Whistlewillow name, will be purged of her sins by fire. Her soul will be cleansed and returned to the Halls of Everice, where the great goddess Shirava will guide her soul to be with her ancestors."

"No!" Kaile shouted, his fists clenched tightly at his sides. He dropped to his knees screaming, "No! No! You can't…"

"That is the will of our king." Archpriest Roane gently rolled the scroll back and placed it in his pocket.

Tears streaked down Kaile's face as he gritted his teeth and felt the sweat building between his fingers and palms. His heart raced, and he felt the pressure build in his arteries. A heat shot down from his head to his toes and everywhere between. His world was crumbling, and he felt he had nothing left to live for.

Kaile shot to his feet, a stern finger pointed at the archpriest. "You can't do this. She doesn't deserve to die! She's a good person! She's got a whole life to live, and she's already been through so much. You can't do this to her!"

Alcarond grabbed Kaile by the shoulders from behind. "Slow down. Calm yourself," he whispered into Kaile's ear, calming Kaile slightly.

"My liege," Alcarond said. "Persephone will be a powerful ally. She's a Whistlewillow. We'll need her. Give Zertaan and me a chance to guide her to the path."

The king gave a surprising grin at Kaile, a toothy smile underneath his dark beard. The smile caused Kaile's blood to heat to a level he thought all he could do was cast a spell out into the room, killing all of them.

King Amón's grin snapped shut, and a mean glower fixed upon Kaile. "You, you who left my ranks on the battlefield for the enemy. You who conspired against me willingly, and you who still spew lies to your king, ask that I spare the life of a traitor who would usurp my throne?"

Kaile choked down his rebuttal about spewing lies.

"You want me to believe that Soren Stormrose leads the Silver Sparrows? A swordsman who hasn't won a fight that mattered in decades? You want me to believe that you had nearly zero insight into the enemy while you were with them for weeks? You conspired against me, fought my men, and truly believed you were fighting in a war against me!" He slammed his fists onto the throne and stood, pulling Storm Dragon free with a shrill ring of steel that filled the room. "I should kill you right here, right now, for your treason. I should burn you to ashes for betraying me."

The only thing Kaile could think to say was, "Then do it. Kill me, and spare her. I'm the one who should be punished. Not her."

"This is your punishment," the king said. "She will die as a reminder to you of what your path is. You will continue to work in my servitude. You will find me a way to destroy the rebellion and the Silver Sparrows. One day you may even succeed Alcarond in becoming my archmage. But now, you are to be locked in your room until the time comes when your Seph is burned alive."

The king's eyes flared alive with a bewildering, infuriating light. His normally deep blue eyes glowed a dim golden light, like flames trickling out of his menacing gaze.

"Please don't do this," Kaile sobbed into his sleeve. "Take me. Don't hurt her. She doesn't deserve any more pain."

Archpriest Roane spoke, "Your reaction proves the king's decree correct. Your attachment to the girl is a weakness that needs to be severed, cut like a fishing line to a great fish that would pull you under the dark waves of treachery."

Alcarond's jaw clenched, rubbing Kaile's shoulders as he sobbed. "We need the girl. She's helping to topple our enemies. My king, I beg of you, spare the girl so that I may use her. She will be a powerful ally. She may even become a Lyrian Syncron one day. That's an opportunity we can't pass up…"

"Alcarond Riberia, my archmage," the king said in a heated voice, the light of fire still reflecting in his eyes. "You have been a loyal servant, and a powerful archmage. Don't lose my trust by defying what must be done. You've been loyal to me. Don't let this little Whistlewillow bitch send you down a path you can't recover from. The Whistlewillow bloodline will end. And when her soul burns in cleansing flame, then we can move the Song of the Ellydian forward in a new, guiding light."

"No," Kaile murmured. "You can't do this. Please don't do this."

Archpriest Roane folded his arms, his wide-cuffed sleeves hanging low. His golden crosier still clutched in one of his hands. "She's going to die as a reminder to you, Kaile Thorne. This is your last chance to serve. If you fail in your duty to your king, then others you care for will get hurt until you learn your role."

"Others? What others?" Kaile muttered as he looked up, his face streaked with tears and his hair messy, stuck to his brow from sweat.

The king glared down at Kaile, his mouth twisted and his nose scrunched in anger. "You have a brother in Ikarus still. If you want to see him again, then you'll do your duty, and forget all about your sinful ways."

The heat in Kaile rose to what felt like his blood was going to boil, and his heart would burst. He readied to strike his staff, sending out a note that would cause all in the room to die in one fell explosion, but Alcarond grabbed him by the wrists. Kaile was so deep in anger and hatred, he hadn't noticed that the Drakoons had all pulled their curved swords free and were in wide stances, ready to cut him down in a second.

"Calm yourself," the archmage whispered. "This is not the time or the place. You'll die, and she will still die too. Breathe. Calm yourself."

Kaile choked on his tears and sobbed into his hands, dropping his staff to the cold stone floor.

"Take him," the king said. "Return him to his room and take his staff. That's where he will wait until the traitor is sent to the afterlife, and we may move forward past all this."

The king stood. He and the archpriest left the throne room as two soldiers grabbed Kaile by the arms, while another picked his staff up from the floor.

"Don't fight," Alcarond said to Kaile as they carried him out of the room. As they led him all the way back to their tower and to his room, Kaile sobbed. He felt as if his life was ending, and a new torture was beginning.

Chapter Thirty-Four

The door to Kaile's room flung open from one of the soldier's boots, and both of them hurled Kaile into the room. He fell hard onto the floor on his side, the injuries on his back throbbing as it knocked against the hardwood. The soldiers grumbled and closed the door behind him, locking it from the other side.

Kaile rushed to the door, desperately trying to open it, but his hand didn't fit around the knob the same way it used to. He quickly realized it was a new lock and latch. And there was a keyhole… from the inside.

"No, no, no," Kaile shouted as he rocked his head side to side, clutching his temples as if he was going mad. "This can't be happening. I did everything right. I played their game. They can't do this. The king can't do this!"

Five days… five days! I need to get out of here. I need to get into the Judicature and get Seph out.

But how? They'd know to be watching for me. And I can't get out of this fucking room!

"This isn't happening… this isn't…"

A knock came at the door, and Kaile ran over. "Help, help! Open the door!"

"Kaile..." Alcarond's voice was somber, with an exasperated tone. Kaile heard the archmage's deep sigh from the other side. "I'm... I'm sorry..."

"You're sorry?" Kaile pounded on the door with his fists. His face streaked with tears and he huffed uncontrollably. His vision blurred and his mind only thought of Seph. "You're not sorry. You tricked me and you brought us here... you brought *her* here!"

"I—I didn't think the king would do this... I'm so sorry, Kaile... I'm sorry for a lot of things... but I'm truly sorry for this..."

"No, you're not." Kaile felt his face twist in disgust. "This is all because of you. I can't do this anymore. I can't..."

"Kaile. You need to hold on. I know what you're going through. I've lost ones I love before as well. You'll get through this. Stay strong. Think of our work. Think of the good we can do for this world."

Kaile drew in a deep breath. "This world isn't worth it. So much pain. So much misery. So much hurt. There's no fixing that. Soren's the only one who could fight the evil of this world, and he's got three Synths after him as we speak."

Alcarond didn't respond, but Kaile heard him breathe out deeply through his nostrils.

"Just go away," Kaile said, putting his back to the door and sliding down to sit. He wiped his tears away as the futility washed over him. He lost all strength in his shoulders and arms as he put his head back to the door and cried.

"You'll get through this, Kaile. It'll be tough, but you'll get through it."

"I'm never going to trust you again," Kaile sobbed. "Why did you do this to me? What did I do to deserve this punishment? She's had a horrible life filled with pain, and she has such a gift to the world, and the king is going to rob the world of that? Why? Because of spite? Because of hatred or jealousy for her family name? I hate him..."

Alcarond sighed, and Kaile could tell he was kneeling at the other side of the door. "This life is hard. We all experience significant loss. This is yours. I don't ask that you don't go through your feelings, but remember the bright future we can help to create. You can do it in her name. You can help me save this world so that her death isn't in vain."

"You don't know anything about how I feel..."

"You're right," the archmage said. "I don't know exactly what you're going through right now. But I'm here for you... I'll always be here for you. You're more than an apprentice to me, Kaile. You're like a son. And a father never wants his son to hurt like this."

"I have a father," Kaile said, wiping angry tears away. "And I hate him."

Alcarond didn't respond.

"Just go away..."

Kaile heard Alcarond stand. "You're going to get through this, my apprentice. I promise you will. It will be hard, and you'll feel like giving up, but stay strong. Think about the good you can do. One day you'll become the archmage, and you can use your gift to change this world for the better so that no one else has to go through the pain you're going through now. But until then, just stay strong. The world needs you. I... I'm sorry..." The archmage then sighed deeply, and Kaile heard his footsteps as he went off into the tower, returning to his quarters.

Kaile leaped to his feet, rushed to the window, and opened it wide.

The biting, icy air rushed into his face, taking his breath away. The wind glazed his eyes over. It was crisp as it went down into his lungs, and his hair whipped madly at his neck.

He leaned out the window, gazing down at the city streets below.

He thought about flying. Kaile wished he was a bird that could spread his wings and glide down through the air, escaping his new cell, and escaping the misery of his broken life. Not since he'd moved to the capital had he felt so low, so lost, so empty. The shame was eating him like a wild bear, tearing out his heart and stomach.

On his tiptoes, he glared out the window, as unnatural winds rushed out from the winter sky into his room. His fingers gripped the windowpanes as he bent at the waist, looking straight down. Tears choked him, his world spun in disarray, and he felt all hope had left him.

"They can't kill Seph. They can't..."

His bare feet left the floorboards and moved up to the windowsill. He crouched like a tiger, eyeing the world below. The thousands of people that roamed the streets below, living their simple lives—finding food for their families—and trying to just make it to tomorrow. He envied them. He yearned for their anonymity. Kaile wanted to disappear from his life. He wanted to escape his torment, his shame, and his fear.

"I'm so sorry, Seph. I thought I could save you... I thought I was strong enough. But I'm not. I'm weak. I'm alone, and I'm so, so tired..."

Kaile stood. He stood tall on the windowsill, his entire body feeling the icy winds. The winds were so strong; it was as if a force was pushing him back in his room. But he fought it with tears streaming down his cheeks and his mouth quivering. He arched his back and stood tall, his fingertips the only things holding him back.

Kaile wanted to fly. Kaile wanted the pain to end.

He wanted a new life, one not so torn to shreds. He was completely at the mercy of the king. King Amón won.

Alcarond won. The archpriest, the Knight Wolf, Sophia, Zertaan... they all won.

Soren was going to die. Davin and Blaje too. The Silver Sparrows were going to get crushed under the might of the capital, and the Demons of Dusk were coming for them all. There was no fight left in him, and as Kaile stood, hanging out the tower window, he felt it was time...

"I'm sorry, Joseph," Kaile cried, his stomach twisted in knots. "I'm sorry I couldn't be the brother you needed me to be. I'm not special. I'm no hero. I couldn't save you... I couldn't save anybody. Even with this power I carry, I fear I've made the world a worse place. So much pain... so much misery... I feel like I've died on the inside."

His fingers loosened their grips, sliding slowly as he hung further and further out the window, the world below beckoning him to spread his wings and fly.

"I'm sorry Seph..." He choked on his words as the wintry winds bit his tears. "I'm so, so sorry... but I'll see you soon. May Shirava bless us and show us the way to the Halls of Everice together... May our souls find each other in the afterlife. May our pain end, and peace find us..."

His fingertips slid out the window. Kaile felt the freeing embrace of the bone-chilling winds as he prepared himself for the pain to go away, forever. He closed his eyes, holding Seph and Joseph's faces clearly in his mind.

The winds whipped through his hair, savoring the last enjoyment of the world as his fingers loosened their grips.

"One last flight..." he muttered as his fingers released the window frame. "One final, pure journey..."

A shuddering knock came from the room, and Kaile's eyes shot open, as if awakened abruptly from a dream. His fingers released the windowsill, and he fell. His feet slid from the windowsill, his body instantly tensing at the feeling of falling from the high tower window. In an instant, with a great deal of instinct, he quickly spun his body as he fell—his arms turning and clutching at the windowsill—his feet dangling high above the snowy, hard ground.

Kaile held on for dear life, his full weight pulling him down, and his arms clutching the windowsill as if it was his only salvation. His feet fought to climb up, continually slipping and sliding back down. Kaile fought to climb back into the window, but the icy stones of the tower proved more difficult than a springtime climb would have been.

His gaze went to his door in the room, where he assumed the knock had come from, and he wondered who was on the other side of the door. To his amazement, instead of another knock, a letter slid under the door into his room...

He hung out the window, eyeing the envelope. Confused, he stared at the letter, and to his amazement, a metal object slid in after it. It skidded across the floor, glinting in the hazy light that filled the room. It shimmered like moonshine on the floor.

A key... it's a key!

Kaile swallowed hard, mustering all his strength, pulling himself up with all his might. His feet caught enough footholds to hoist himself up, and he pulled himself back into the room, falling onto his side, heaving deep breaths. Crawling on his elbows and knees, he made it to the key, grabbing it and feeling the cold steel in his hands. He wiped his tears away, grabbing the envelope.

He broke the seal, an unmarked smudge of wax. On his knees, he pulled the letter from the envelope and his eyes widened as he read the words.

'Kaile, this key opens the door to your room. Another key awaits you outside the Tower of the Judicature. Look to the rose bush with a statue of a girl watering a plant. This is your one chance to save her. It must be tonight. Stick to the alleyways. Wait for the cue. You'll know it when it happens. Shirava watch over you.'

Kaile read it twice, three times, picking up the key and marveling at it.

His demeanor darkened, and he felt an overwhelming sense of purpose and hope again.

No signature…

He scratched his chin. "Thank you, whoever you are."

He stood, key in hand, went and grabbed a necklace of tuning forks from his desk. While the desk drawer was open, he stopped and stared at a small dagger in the door—he grabbed that too before going to his closet and putting on his oldest, dingiest, gray cloak.

"I'm coming, Seph. Hold on just a little longer. I'm coming!"

Chapter Thirty-Five

The nightmares got worse. Whether awake or asleep, Seph's reality was pain. She was afraid to close her eyes and drift off to sleep, for the worry of terror her dreams would be. But sleep was inescapable. She faced unrelenting insomnia when she needed sleep most, and fell off to dark dreams after her body and mind were overloaded with atrocious malice.

She awoke in the Abiron, her body shivering and her hair soaked in cold sweat. Her hands were bound behind her, and her bare feet were tied flat against the freezing floor. Her palms and feet were wet with slick sweat, and her vision fogged as she awoke.

Seph let out a guttural moan as pain rushed up her entire body, erupting in a cutting headache that made her wince. Her head throbbed as the heat from her forehead pulsed. Gazing down at her body and torn clothing, she saw the scars and scabs caused by her captor.

Zertaan must've gotten too drunk to tell the guards to take me back to my room... But she admitted to herself that waking up, sitting up and bound was still better than the awful cloth they bound her mouth with.

Twisting her wrists, she tested for any give or play in the knots, but found none. The rope was tight and secure, digging into the cuts there, sending searing pain up her arms, up her neck and causing an eruption of pain in the form of a pounding headache.

She smacked her dry, cracked lips, desperate for something to wet her throat. Seph didn't shout, though. Being alone and without the devil was a sort of respite, even with the floor stained with her blood.

"Is this a dream?" she muttered, her voice raspy and harsh. She hardly recognized her own voice. Under her arms, she felt her ribs like a washboard under her skin with little fat protecting them. "Am I awake, or am I dead?"

Footsteps came down the hall. They were long strides with sharp-sounding heels that Seph immediately recognized. Her body tensed hard, her eyes popped open wide, and she let out an uncontrolled gasp.

Zertaan entered the room. Seph could smell the stale booze on her breath. Zertaan's red eyes were hazy, her long blond hair was disheveled like Seph had never seen it. Seph had no idea what time of day it was—even if it was closer to noon or midnight—and she'd never seen the woman of the White Asp of Arkakus look so… unkempt.

She entered with a different aura than normal. Zertaan didn't disrobe and go to the table full of her wicked, sharp instruments. Instead, she stood before Seph, a sort of… sadness flushed on her angular face.

Seph glared at her with a puzzling hatred, unsure of what to make of the terrible Aeol before her.

Zertaan, wearing a black dress with thin straps at the shoulders, crossed her tattooed arms and swayed to lean on one hip.

THE DARK SYNTHS

Her mouth twisted, almost as if she didn't know what words to use.

"Get on with it," Seph growled, her voice scratchy and utterly parched.

Zertaan laughed. Seph was caught off guard by the strangely... genuine laugh. It wasn't shrill or forced. It was real. That terrified Seph more than she expected.

What's going on? For some reason, I'm more scared of her words than her cutting or burning my skin...

"I bring news," Zertaan said, gazing down at her prey as she swayed, arms folded still.

Seph didn't respond, but waited with bated breath, forcing herself to not shake from the terror of what followed. Her immediate fear was that Zertaan had come to tell her that her uncle Soren had been killed. But that was not the case.

"The king has made a decree... about you..."

Seph, again, didn't respond, but was instantly relieved Zertaan made no mention of Soren, which she almost certainly would, to hurt Seph even more.

"I don't know exactly how to say this... but," Zertaan unfolded her arms and sighed. She reached over and put her fingers against a candle that burned, wax pooling over the holder and onto the table. Her crimson eyes fixed on the flame.

"Out with it," Seph finally said. "Tell me what you fucking came here for..."

Zertaan's gaze snapped at her like a hungry asp in the midnight jungle. She took a great breath.

"Our time together is at an end." Zertaan almost sounded sad.

Seph raised an eyebrow, unsure how to take the statement. "And...?"

With a swift movement of her arm, Zertaan smacked the candle holder across the room, the flame quickly extinguishing and a familiar anger spilling out of Zertaan. She fumed like a mother wolf defending her den.

"He can't take this from me…" Zertaan whispered to herself, but Seph heard it as clear as crisp spring water.

Seph waited, bound and powerless, waiting for the Synth to calm enough to finish.

Zertaan went to her table of tools and grabbed both ends of it, hovering over it, her long, silky blond hair flowing all the way down her back. She eyed her prized tools as if she was saying goodbye to them for the last time.

"He's taking you for himself," Zertaan finally uttered.

"What's that mean?" Seph asked forcefully.

Zertaan spun, fuming. Her eyes blazed with anger. "He's ending our time together. I could've turned you. I could've broken you. And you… Persephone Whistlewillow, would have been my prized accomplishment. A walking medal of my achievements. Having broken you, and set you free as a Re-Enlightened Syncron, I may have had the strength to pass the Black Sacrament." She slammed her fist onto the table, but Seph didn't flinch.

"Sounds like you failed."

Seph's words caused a fire to roar inside Zertaan. She lurched forward, wrapping her wretched fingers around Seph's throat and squeezing.

"I did not fail." Her words twisted and seethed with hatred and disgust. "He has deemed you too dangerous to turn."

"I *am* too dangerous to turn," Seph gasped as Zertaan's long, strong fingers squeezed.

"I could've broken you," Zertaan hissed, her face inches from Seph's.

"You never would've broken me. I'm a Whistlewillow. The blood in my veins is too strong for you to break. I'd die before I turned."

Zertaan then smiled a toothy grin with her sharp yellow

teeth glistening wet in the candlelight. "Then you're in luck, you little bitch... you're going to get exactly what you want..."

The thought of death was a welcome one for Seph over many days of torture she'd endured, but when finally confronted with imminent death, Seph was frightened. Though she wouldn't show it and give Zertaan the satisfaction.

Zertaan twisted her fingers, turning Seph's head to the side, scanning it as if admiring her work, or giving a semblance of a goodbye.

"We still have time together." Zertaan's gaze was empty, devoid of expression, and with a chilling tone to her voice. "I may not be able to turn you, or kill you, but we can sure have some good times to savor, before the king purges your soul... in fire..."

Seph glared at the candlelight as her head was held to the side, her neck at the brink of snapping. Zertaan released her, with Seph's weakness showing as her chin fell to her chest as she heaved breaths, gasping.

At first, Seph feared the flames. She remembered the shrieks and blood-curdling cries for help of those who burned in Tourmielle and Erhil. *At least I'll go as my family did. Perhaps they'll be waiting for me in the Halls of Everice. And we can finally be together again...*

"So..." the Synth of the White Asp of Arkakus said with a hiss. "What should we do first? What are your favorites?" She went to the table of tools and lifted a short-bladed knife, waiting for Seph's reaction. "No?" She put it down and picked up a pair of iron pliers. "This one? No?" She placed it back on the table with a thud. "Oh, I know..." Zertaan picked up an iron rod with a wooden handle, holding the iron tip up to the torchlight behind her.

Seph tried hard to not show any reaction, but her body betrayed her, and she winced at the sight of the iron beginning to smoke. Her body convulsed, a stark reminder of the last time Zertaan had used the hot iron on her. Seph still had the deep scab on her side and many scabs and scars on her thigh.

"Yes…" Zertaan hissed. "This is the one…"

Seph wanted to shout. She wanted to scream and fight, but she couldn't deny her body was drained of all strength. And what was left, she'd need to survive her next round of torture. She'd had nearly no food, barely enough water, and her body ached terribly from all of it.

Zertaan lifted the iron rod from the torchlight. It glowed a dull red hue as it smoked. The Synth waved it between them, showing it off like a prized toy as the smoke rose to the ceiling.

The Synth eyed Seph, and her body, running the hot iron over her skin causing Seph to grit her teeth.

Footsteps came from the hallway. Seph noticed them right away, but Zertaan didn't seem to notice, as her gaze was fixed like a viper upon Seph's stomach.

But the footsteps grew louder, eventually coming to the door of the Abiron. Seph couldn't see who was outside the room, but by the man's voice, she knew it to be one of the guards.

"Syncron Zertaan…" he said, his words were rushed as if he'd run all the way to the Abiron from wherever he'd come.

"What is it?" Zertaan never took her eyes off Seph.

"Your presence is requested immediately…"

Zertaan snapped to him, her devilish red eyes beaming at him, and Seph heard an audible gulp from the man. "What? Not now."

"It's from Archmage Alcarond. He says it's urgent. You are needed in his study immediately."

Zertaan clenched her teeth and seethed. "The archmage?" she murmured. After a long moment, she hissed, "Fine…"

The guard waited beyond the doorway as a sense of momentary relief washed over Seph. But that sentiment didn't last long, as a searing heat ripped into Seph's side, and the awful smell of burning skin and hair overwhelmed her nostrils. Seph let out a guttural, terrible shriek as the pain overwhelmed her entire body.

Zertaan jabbed the scalding hot tip of the iron straight through Seph's skin, poking into the side of her stomach with a pain that Seph thought might kill her.

The Synth yanked the rod out of Seph, letting it fall to the cold stone floor, clanging and hissing as it fell into the moisture. Seph reeled in pain. The pain tore through her with an anguish that made her feel as if all her skin was blazing in flames. She screamed until her voice broke and then she cried. She cried out Soren's name, causing Zertaan to return a satisfactory grin.

"Don't die, little one… not yet…" Zertaan left the room, following the guard back out of the prison.

Seph sobbed, muttering Soren's name. The pain dulled as Seph fell into a spiraling darkness. All hope had faded. There was no more fight in her. It was over. She'd lost, and soon death would be hers.

She'd welcome it when the time came, she thought. Anything was better than this pain and the overwhelming helplessness she was in. There was no way to survive the misery that shrouded her. It was an orchestrated evil, and her Ellydian was useless…

Soon… it would all be over, and then she could rest. No pain. No torture. No Zertaan. But there would be plenty of regret. There were so many things to do. There were so many people she could help. There was Soren, Davin, Blaje, and even Sable… her friends, her true family… she'd die without being able to say goodbye.

She whimpered one last time.

Again, though, something grew in the darkness. A sound. A warm, vibrant, ringing sound that emanated from the hallway like a dream.

Seph thought she might be dreaming, but the cool, calming feeling on her side where Zertaan had stabbed her relaxed her entire body. Seph knew she was awake and knew the sound was a note from a tuning fork. It was a bright D note, cascading from the hallway like a heavenly waterfall. It rang in sharp, angelic waves, as the pain in Seph's side alleviated.

Then another sound entered the room. It was something Seph didn't expect and startled her. It was a metallic ringing as something skidded across the dark floor. A glimmer of candle-light caught the small metal object as it slid across the floor, stopping to a halt just by her feet.

Seph's eyes widened.

Sharp, short, and curved… a… a knife…

Between her feet, resting in a pool of dried blood, was a small, curved knife with a three-inch blade, jutting out from a perpendicular handle, meant to be held so that the blade stuck out from between the middle fingers of a clenched fist.

Seph scooted the blade in with her feet, hiding it beneath them.

No tears streamed down. No blanket of sorrow enveloped her. Instead… a fire raged from deep within her, and a wicked smile carved up on her face.

Thank you… whoever you are, my mystery savior. Thank you…

PART VII
THE DARK SYNTHS

Chapter Thirty-Six

❦

I have only seen rebellion once in my many years, and while necessary, there was no lack of suffering brought with it. For those that wield the most power, are oft susceptible to the most devilish and fiendish forms of corruption.

Mind you, none that cause pain and suffering do so lightly. Each person believes their path to be true, their vision clear, and their actions justified. In each story, every villain is their own hero. But in the eyes of the old gods or the goddess, good and evil must fight occasionally so that peace may prosper.

The rebellion of the Sundar cost countless lives. Both sides—the Sundar and the Polonians suffered greatly—and in the end, neither side won. Wastelands were left littered with the fallen, their bones picked clean by vultures and insects.

Peace is not achieved solely with peace.

War does not always breed more war.

The sword and the staff are symbols of both, and for good reason.

-TRANSLATED *from the language of the Sundar. The Scriptures of the Ancients, Book III, Chapter XVI.*

. . .

As the key slid into the lock, and with a turn the latch popped open, a surge of excitement shot down Kaile's body like leaping naked into an ice-cold lake. The thrill rippled through him like the breath of a new life.

Everything had changed.

Hope, though. From the crippling, crushing weight of despair, he'd been saved. Hope had returned to him like a freshly sharpened sword in his hand, or a newly crafted staff, eager to fight his way to what he wanted more than anything else… to save Seph.

Kaile didn't know who Lady Drake's spy was, but assumed it was them that left the key. "Thank you," he muttered as he opened the door, gazing out into the torch-lit stairway.

Night had finally fallen, as the letter instructed him to wait. He clicked a tuning fork against the outer door handle, and a dull, yet clean E note reverberated quietly from it. He readied a handful of spells in his mind, one for defense, and many for offense, should the need arise.

As he stepped outside his room, everything was different. Leaving the room, he openly defied the king's order, and therefore was—once again—an outlaw, and part of the rebellion. He was a part of the Silver Sparrows.

Like a hunting panther, he made his way all the way down to the base of the Tower of the Archmage—the Illuvitrus Sanctum. As he cracked a back door open, the night air rushed in, taking his breath away as he inhaled deeply through his nostrils. He smelled the burning wood stoves, the rank smell of old booze, and a meaty stew simmering nearby.

Hood over his head, he tucked his hair into his shirt, hiding his distinct hair from whoever may be out. There were no soldiers at the door, which Kaile thought odd, but didn't question it and counted it as a blessing. Seph and the Tower of the Judicature were his destination.

He huddled in the shadows, walking casually into the nearest alley. His tall stature may reveal his identity, so he slouched as his arm grazed the alley wall to his side.

Kaile thought about the letter that had been delivered with the key. *The rose bushes with the statue of the girl watering flowers...* The statue didn't immediately jump into his memory, as there were many old statues that decorated the square outside of the tower. The letter told him to wait until the cue. He didn't know what the cue was, but the key worked, so the cue must work too. *It must!*

Kaile made his way to the tower. The thought of saving Seph was so overwhelming, and thrilling, that he'd forgotten a very important aspect to saving her... Zertaan...

Kaile had known Zertaan as long as he'd been in the capital. She was as feared as any Synth in the king's service, and was as close to a Lyre as any, without actually being one. She had mastered all manner of crippling, violent spells, and was far above Kaile's talents. Even he had no shame in admitting that to himself. She was older, came from a powerful family with seemingly unlimited resources, and was heralded by the king and given access to some of the most powerful secrets of the Ellydian.

If they were to fight, Zertaan would most likely be the victor, and his quest to save his friend would be over.

But... if Kaile could somehow get Seph out of the Abiron, and get a tuning fork into her hand, then together... they may be able to...

A thunderous boom tore into the northern part of the city then, and Kaile felt the blast of the explosion shudder in his chest. He turned a corner and looked north, a terrible hazy light glowed high above the building. Embers tore into the air, and screams rose from the fiery area.

"Was that the cue?" he muttered to himself, rubbing his chin.

Another explosion blasted to the northeast. It was blocks away from the first, more flames rising high into the sky.

"That's definitely the cue." His legs felt fresh life, and he ran. He didn't need the shadows any longer.

Another explosion roared as hundreds of people flooded into the streets. They were slow and confused, and Kaile's long legs ran at speed. Soldiers poured out of their posts, just as confused as the civilians.

Bell towers chimed throughout the city, and a great horn blew from the direction of the Vael Vallora Keep. The alarms and the chaos didn't impede Kaile's progress forward—it only hastened it! He sprinted as fast as his long legs could carry him.

"Apprentice," a forceful man's voice shouted from behind. "You can't be out here… you can't…"

As Kaile spun to see who had shouted, a sudden groan caught his ear. A soldier with wide eyes and a crooked, shocked expression gripped his chest. A bloody sword cut through from his back. The soldier gripped the sharp blade with his bare hands, further bloodying the blade. Another man holding the sword behind gritted his teeth. Yanking the sword free, the soldier dropped to the ground, bleeding out.

The man looked hardened and eager for more blood by the frenzied look in his eyes. "Kaile Thorne," the man said in a low, growling tone. Kaile was shocked at the mention of his name. He struck a tuning fork. A crisp C note rang out.

The murderous man's eyes popped open wide, and he threw his bloody sword to the ground. His hands raised, Kaile paused, yet readied to hurtle the Inferous spell at the man.

"I come to aid you," the man said, slowly reaching behind him.

"Don't!" Kaile shouted. "Stand still, don't move!"

"Lady Drake sent me," the man half-whispered. "The Silver Sparrows... this is our time. We go on the offensive!"

"The Silver Sparrows? Here? Now?"

The man showed his palms to Kaile before slowly reaching back again. He moved a satchel at his back forward, reaching in, and slowly drawing out a short staff of wood.

Kaile's eyes widened, and he nearly drooled at the sight.

The man tossed Kaile the staff. Holding it between them so Kaile could eye the man while inspecting the staff, Kaile saw one dazzling jewel at the two-foot wooden staff's crest. A single green emerald the size of an apricot was embedded in the knobby staff.

Simple, light, effective... yes... this will do fine!

"Thank you," Kaile said. "What other information do you have for me?"

"You don't need information," the man said, kneeling and grabbing his sword. "It's time to fight. You have your mission, and we have ours. Save the girl. She's the key! Save the girl. Go!"

Kaile was off, sprinting at full speed again through the chaos of Celestra.

He rushed through the chaos of the mired confusion of the citizens of the city. Guards struggled to maintain order while trying to figure out themselves what the explosions were. As Kaile ran, he saw many of the citizens wielded weapons, often hidden under clothing.

Kaile couldn't believe what was happening. It was as if he were still stuck in a dream. Not only did he have a chance to save Seph, but the Silver Sparrows were causing an all-out assault on the kingdom of Aladran.

The balls, Kaile thought. *What could Lady Drake be doing causing a rebellion at night? I'd guess she was causing a distraction for me, but the man back there seemed intent on a mission of their own. I've got to find out what that is... but first...*

He leaped over a wagon cart; he dove around a pair of men fighting with sharp swords; all the while a solid C note rang clear, humming from deep within the staff in his hand.

"Hold on, Seph... I'm coming..."

The Tower of the Judicature came into view, its lofty peaks visible between the buildings as he drew closer and closer. Skirmishes filled the frenzied chaos. Soldiers fought against unknown assailants in the frigid night air. Kaile rooted the Sparrows on, feeling the adrenaline pumping hard in his chest, arms, and legs.

His legs carried him on, spurred and fueled by the image of Seph's face as he ran. It had been a long time since he'd felt that fire burning like a furnace within. He'd done terrible things, but this was his one chance.

Even if it meant his life, he'd try. He'd try for her. She was worth it.

He ran into the courtyard before the tower. Another explosion blasted to the north, hurtling fiery planks and other materials into the air. A woman near him shrieked at the explosion; a baby cried loudly in her arms. Two other children huddled into her.

Kaile watched briefly. His heartstrings tugged. But he knew he couldn't save the city. He had to save Seph.

"Go inside and lock your doors," Kaile said to the woman. "The fighting will be over in the morning." The woman nodded at him; her eyes filled with tears. "Go!"

The woman took her kids into a nearby dwelling, and Kaile scanned the courtyard for the rose bush and the statue. He ran from garden to garden, seeing many dead, thorny rose bushes, but not finding the statue. After eight different gardens with rose bushes, not finding what he was looking for, he gazed all around, his hands on top of his head as he grew frustrated.

But there, down the road, he caught the sight of a small statue tangled in dead vines, surrounded by more of the bushes. He ran to it, and as he drew closer, a brilliant smile sparked on his face. A girl in a dress, bent at the waist, watering the ground with a bucket in her tiny hand. And where the water would have splashed out of the bucket onto the ground, a key protruded from the frozen ground.

His hand dove into the thorns, cutting his forearm, but he felt no pain. His stiff fingers gripped the key handle and yanked it from the ground. He held it up to see it lit in the reflection of torchlight from a nearby home.

This is it!

He ran straight to the tower, not caring who saw him then. His hood flapped to his back as he ran, and as he approached, he saw the door was unguarded.

They'd either retreated inside to protect their own, or ran off to join the battle. Sounds of clanking swords, shouting men, and terrible shrieks of war filled the city.

Kaile found the keyhole, slid the skeleton key in, turned it, and with the most beautiful sound he could have imagined, the lock popped open!

"I'm coming, Seph. Hold on. I'm coming…"

Chapter Thirty-Seven

The drip, drip, drip of the hallway outside of the Abiron was like a heartbeat that soothed Seph's ears. It kept her awake enough to keep her senses alert, but yet also caused her eyelids to grow heavy, and made the weariness in her aching body call her to slumber.

She sat in the chair in the darkness of the Abiron, the one place in the world where the Ellydian was powerless, even with the strongest and brightest of notes. A single candle gasped its last breaths as Seph's chin slumped to her chest. She wheezed breaths as a slight mist escaped her nostrils in the chilly air. Her arms behind her were bound; her wrists chaffed from the scabs underneath the rope tied at her wrists. Her ankles swelled as the rope cut into the soft skin there.

Seph felt washed out, depleted, and ached for even the awful, scratchy mattress the guards took her to.

But as she drifted in and out of consciousness, something echoed in the distance. She raised her eyelids with no lack of effort. A moan left her lips as she lifted her chin to watch the doorway in the scant candlelight.

Footsteps.

Seph did not know how much time had passed since she'd been stabbed in the side. It could be an hour or a day. She was so confused and at the edge of hallucinating; she didn't know if the footsteps were real or not. Seph wondered if she was in a dream, but the gnawing pain at her wrists, ankles, and the terrible throbbing in her side where she'd been stabbed screamed to her to wake up.

Someone is coming. This isn't a dream. Wake up, Seph. Force yourself awake.

The footsteps sounded different. Not heavy and dragging like the usual guards, and not light taps like that of Zertaan. They were more rushed. Sloppy even. The revelation caused Seph to wake up instantly, her instinct slapping her into the cold reality of where she was and the danger she was in.

A muffled explosion tore into the city above her.

What was that? What is happening in the city?

The footsteps grew louder as they approached. They were different, yet familiar.

It's definitely one pair of feet, and it's getting close, faster.

There was a sudden stumble, just outside the door, and Seph straightened in her chair at the sound. Terror clogged Seph's throat, lurching up from her stomach and gripping her in fear. Whoever was outside the door had fallen, and was staggered on the ground, silent.

Seph wanted to speak, but her throat caught, and the pain in her body subsided as her adrenaline pumped in her arteries. Her heart pounded like a thumping drum, and her limbs and neck heated.

"Hello?" she finally managed to squeeze out of her throat.

She heard whoever was outside the door stagger back up.

A hand gripped the outside latch of the door to the Abiron, and Seph heard whoever was out there stand.

The faint candlelight finally suffocated, and the room was plunged into darkness.

No. Not now. "Hello? Who's there?"

Seph prayed to the goddess it was Soren, or someone to rescue her from her misery and torture.

A sudden familiar smell wafted into Seph's nostrils, and a horrid fear gripped her again.

A voice responded to Seph in the darkness. Familiar enough to know she was in danger—terrible danger.

The sound of flint and steel striking on the back table sent a terror up from the tips of Seph's toes, sizzling up her skin, to her neck and the peak of her head.

A candle glowed from the strike as the figure before her held up the tinder to the candlewick.

The figure before Seph caused all hope to fade, and her heart raced, beating wildly in her chest.

"Hello, young Whistlewillow," the red-eyed Synth said with a shaky, excited breath.

Seph glared at Zertaan, uncertain of what was different about her, but then Seph realized the familiar scent was that of the distinct booze heavy on her breath. As Zertaan lit another few candles on the table, Seph saw the knees of Zertaan's dress were scuffed and had a faded pink of trickling blood seeping through.

Zertaan collapsed into the seat, spinning one of her favorite tools as she slouched. She laughed to herself—a shrill, insane laugh.

"What's funny?" Seph said, irritation and hate thick on her breath.

Zertaan lifted the tool, a sharp metal pike six inches long. She stabbed it into the table aggressively, and turned it, digging its tip in deep.

"Everything. All of it."

Seph twisted in her seat. "What are you talking about? What's going on up there in the city?"

"Sparrows," Zertaan hissed.

Sparrows? The Silver Sparrows? Hope welled in Seph instantly, a glowing bright force forcing the shadows within her at bay.

Zertaan scowled at Seph. Her face darkened, and her eyes beamed a deep crimson in the candlelight. "Don't get your hopes up, you fool. They're not here for you. They're heading for the capital."

That did indeed diminish the hope that briefly sprung up in her. *They're going after the capital? The king? Is Soren here? Is he here to finish what he started?*

Zertaan stood, cocked to one side, leaning on the chair. A sinister, predatorial, insane smile crossed her pale face. Her sharp teeth glistened a faded yellow, and the animal inside awakened.

Seph's body tensed in terror. She'd seen that expression before, but not like that. There was something different about Zertaan, more than just the drunken stupor she appeared to be in.

"What did the archmage say?" Seph forced herself to say, partly to distract the dark Synth, and partly to understand what in the Nine Hells was going on.

"It doesn't matter," Zertaan sighed. "None of it matters. All that matters is you. You and me. Right here. Together… one last time…"

One last time? Oh, no… she's… she's going to kill me before the king can. She won't share me. In her eyes, I'm hers and hers alone.

Seph didn't respond, but couldn't help but glare at the Synth with pure hatred.

"That's it," Zertaan hissed. "I want it all from you. One night to devour every emotion you can give me. You see, Persephone… our bond is a sort of… once-in-a-lifetime one…"

Seph felt ill at the thought. Her stomach turned and her blood heated.

Zertaan left the pike sticking up from the table as she staggered forward.

"Our souls are connected. Don't you feel it? In this room, in this aura, what we've been through… all of that bonds us. Everything we've shared together has brought us to this moment. Two souls, both bound to the sacred Ellydian, and the connection of all things, also bound together in pain. It's a beautiful, impossible to describe thing."

"What did the archmage say?" Seph lurched forward in her bindings, trying to force an answer from the distracted demon.

A single burst of laughter escaped Zertaan's lips. It was a futile, frustrated laugh. "He said our time is over, and I've got a new mission."

A brief relief washed over Seph, but it quickly faded, as Zertaan was standing right in front of Seph, with violence thick on her breath.

Zertaan reached down and caressed Seph's cheek before cradling her chin in her fingers, angling Seph's face up to look at her. Zertaan leaned in close, the rank booze on her breath overwhelming. The hairs on the back of Seph's neck straightened and an icky feeling crawled under her skin.

"You see… I love you." Zertaan brushed Seph's lips with her thumb. "And you love me, whether or not you realize it. We… two of the most powerful Syncrons in all the world, get to share one last night together. And I'm going to make it so… so special for us. I can't let them take you from me. You're my prize. I've been waiting my whole life for someone like you. You're the key, don't you see?"

Another explosion rocked the city overhead, and dust fell from the ceiling onto them, and onto the floor. But Zertaan didn't flinch. Her heated gaze was fixed upon Seph, and Seph returned it with a hateful scowl.

"They can't take you. I won't let them. The king wants you to burn. But he doesn't understand... *us*. Our souls are connected in a way he doesn't understand. You're mine. You belong to me. And I'm the only one who can save that connection. Because if you burn, I will grieve our loss."

Zertaan rubbed Seph's lips as Seph scowled and drew her lips in.

"We have no connection. You're insane. You're insane and Soren is gonna kill you! Somehow, someday, he'll get you. Even if you kill me, you're going to die knowing you couldn't pass the Black Sacrament, and that you're a failure. You're a phony, a liar, and a fake. You don't deserve the Ellydian. That's the reason you'll never be the archmage. The king and Alcarond don't like you, and they don't trust you. I could see it from the moment I saw them with you. You're nothing to them. You're just a toy in their game. You mean nothing to anyone, and when you die, history will so easily forget such a forgettable Synth."

Zertaan squeezed Seph's cheeks hard, covering Seph's face as Zertaan seethed in anger. She huffed deep breaths through clenched teeth.

"I'm going to enjoy seeing that light die in your eyes," Zertaan growled. "I'm going to carry that gift with me forever, knowing I was the one to snuff out the line of Whistlewillows forever. And good fucking riddance!"

Another explosion rocked the city above, and from behind, Seph suddenly swung her arm, swinging it in a round arc, a sharp glint of metal protruding from her hand. Zertaan's eyes widened, and she tried to move back, but she wasn't quick enough, and Seph sent the short dagger plunging into the side of Zertaan's neck.

Blood spattered onto Zertaan's pale flesh as Seph felt the dagger sink all the way into the skin, muscles, and tendons.

Zertaan was more shocked than anything. The confusion in

her eyes and the mystery of how Seph got the blade while securely tied meant only one thing…

"How?" Zertaan gasped, clutching Seph's hand, and the blade clasped within. "Who?"

Zertaan's powerful grip yanked the blade out, still holding Seph's hand tight. Her other hand shot forward and her strong fingers wrapped around Seph's throat. Seph choked instantly, starved of air. Her own hand went up and attempted to wrestle the Synth's hand off her throat, but to no avail.

Seph couldn't get Zertaan's grip off her throat or release her other hand. So Seph fought. She fought off the panic setting in, and the bleariness in her vision. She fought to stand, all her limbs loose from her secretly cut bindings. She rose. Zertaan may have her overpowered by her towering stature and more mature muscles and bones, but Seph had an animal in her.

She'd seen it in Soren many times.

The bloodlust in his eyes.

The blood dripping from his hands after a vengeful kill.

The wrath of the goddess oozing off him.

Seph stood, and Zertaan's blood-red eyes widened.

Unable to breathe, Seph forced the words out, "You have no power over me… not anymore…"

Hooking her leg around the long-legged Synth, Seph pressed all her weight forward onto Zertaan's body, toppling her over and landing on top of her with a grueling thud. A powerful gust of breath shot from Zertaan's mouth as they both crashed onto the cold stone floor.

Cocking her head back, Seph sent her forehead down hard onto Zertaan's nose, hearing the crack and immediately seeing the blood where the break happened. Zertaan momentarily loosened her grip on Seph's throat, and Seph drew in a deep inhale, filling her starved lungs. She brought her head back again, but Zertaan gathered her wits quickly and moved the dagger between their two raging gazes.

"You little bitch," Zertaan hissed, her breath raspy and wheezy, not able to breathe from her blood-clogged nostrils.

"How's it feel?" Seph growled through her clenched teeth, eyeing the blood pour out of the cut in her neck. "You're not so powerful after all, are ya? You need women tied up to have control over them. You're just a weak little sheep in wolf's clothing, aren't you? A fake. You're no Syncron, you're a weak little Synth any one of those Dors in the city could easily take. Face it, your legacy is done."

"Nothing is done," Zertaan steamed, her face twisted in hatred, blood pouring from her nose.

With an incredible burst of strength, Zertaan yanked Seph's wrist crooked. The knife twisted, pointing back at Seph, the blood-coated tip eager to plunge into her eye.

Seph put her other hand on top of Zertaan's, and the fight for the dagger heated. As Seph straddled Zertaan's hips, Zertaan forced the blade upward with all her might, forcing blood to gush from her shattered nose and out of the wound on her neck. A fierce demonic darkness took her red eyes. Her sharp teeth reddened with blood, and a surreal, primal strength erupted through her arms.

The dagger shot upward, slicing up toward Seph's head. Seph cocked her head to the side, but it wasn't quick enough. The dagger's sharp edge cut along her cheek, up the side of her face, and cut straight through her ear. A sharp pain tore through her as she winced in agony.

The cold air stung the fresh wound, and in her haze, Seph neglected to notice Zertaan had released her grip of the dagger, and the Synth's fist went knuckles first into Seph's cheek. Seph lost all focus, and Zertaan took her opportunity. The Synth brought a knee up and shoved her boot into Seph's chest, kicking her off with the power of a mule.

Seph flew back, landing on her back, the dagger flying out of both their grasps. The wind burst from Seph's lungs as she landed, a searing pain pounding on the side of her head. But the sight of Zertaan crawling to the door sent an urgency like lightning through Seph.

Getting to her feet, Seph leaped forward. The dagger lay by the doorway, still as a death. Zertaan crawled, her fingers coated in fresh blood. Seph landed at her legs, hugging them tightly, while Zertaan tried to kick her off, crawling toward the blade, and toward the door that would lead to the power of the Ellydian.

Zertaan kicked and Seph fought to keep hold. Seph's fist drove into Zertaan's stomach hard twice, causing the Synth to halt just enough for Seph to crawl on top of her again. Seph sent her fists pounding into Zertaan's already battered and broken nose. Blood poured out as Seph's knuckles drove in harder with a fury that reminded her of her worst times in Mormond Orphanage.

"You'll never hurt me again!" Seph's arms fought off Zertaan's longer limbs, trying to find breaks in her defenses to hurt the Synth. "You'll never hurt anyone ever again!"

A fire burned deep within Seph, like a burning forge powered by deep bellows, rushing hot air up and sending an inferno up through Seph's entire body. All the pain she'd endured, all the agony, all the loss, and all the treachery was gone. It was just blood, anger, and pain that remained.

Finding an opening, Seph sent her small fist square into Zertaan's nose again, feeling it break even more. Zertaan unleashed a bone-chilling scream of pain that caused a warmth in Seph's heart and spirit.

The strength in Zertaan's arms and hands briefly faded as her focus waned. Her eyes rolled back, and Seph crawled off of her, digging her fingernails into the floor, crawling for the door and the dagger that lay between the doorframe.

She was almost there, just another couple of feet... just another couple of pulls...

A grip like a vice gripped Seph's ankle.

"We're not done here yet..." Zertaan said with a deep hiss in her voice, sounding more like a serpent than a human.

Zertaan pulled her back with tremendous strength, pulling herself forward at the same time. Seph clawed desperately at the cracks in the floor, eager for the dagger, or the hallway where she could use her magic.

Fight, fight just a little more. Get the dagger, send it into the bitch's heart!

They both fought viciously. They clawed with breaking nails; they pounded at each other with bloodied fists. Hair pulled and yanked, shrieks of pain filled the room, and a brutal, savage fight enveloped the two on the floor. Both crawling, both desperate, both at the brink of collapse.

Zertaan, in a moment of clarity and brutality, sent her fingers raking against the side of Seph's face, yanking her dangling ear clean off. Seph screamed as the pain erupted throughout her entire body. The Synth took the moment, shoving Seph off her, and crawling to the dagger.

Seph's mind reeled in grueling agony. The air bit at the open wound on the side of her head, and she cupped the gash with her hand. But panic instantly set in as she saw Zertaan crawl to the dagger, clasping it in her hand. She scooted onto her back and elbows, holding the dagger out at Seph. Propped up on an elbow, the Synth's pale albino face was completely covered in blood, dripping down onto her chest and stomach.

She laughed a dark, unworldly laugh.

"You thought you could beat me? You thought you could best me? After killing you, I will become a great Lyrian Syncron who will change this world forever. And you... you'll be burned to ash, forgotten by time, and mourned by none..."

"You're wrong," Seph growled, stuck in place, worried if

she moved. Then Zertaan would scoot out the door, and the battle would be instantly over with the sound of any tune. "People care about me... that's far more than I can say about you. You're a plague on this world. And when you're gone, the world will be a far better place."

"I guess you'll never know..." Zertaan scooted back slowly.

I can't let her reach the door. Something... think of something...

But there was only one real choice... and Seph knew it was risky. But it was all there was left.

Seph got her feet under her in a swift motion and dashed with a great leap toward the Synth. The dagger gleamed between them as Seph hurtled through the air. Zertaan's eyes widened as she crawled back, grasping the doorframe with one hand.

Seph landed hard on the Synth, trying to brush the dagger and her arm away, but Zertaan fought her attempt, shoving the dagger up into Seph's side. It drove deep into the open wound there. Seph's hands caught Zertaan by the wrist, trying to prevent further injury.

The amount of pain Seph was in surpassed all the torture she'd endured at the hands of the wicked Synth. But this time was different. She wasn't bound; she was on top of the sorceress, and a primal energy roared through every vein, muscle, and bone.

A staggering adrenaline rushed through her, pulling Zertaan's arm back, and the dagger with it. Zertaan pulled with all her might on the doorframe, pulling both of them closer to the hallway.

All she'd need was to get her mouth out into the hallway and it's over. I can't let her. I can't! Soren needs me. And I need him...

Zertaan pulled, her mouth inches from the hallway, and an evil smile crept up on her blood-stained lips.

"You're not going anywhere," Seph growled. But Zertaan was too strong. The evil that poured out of every pore in her body overpowered Seph, and she pulled both of them hard through the doorframe. Seph gasped in fear as Zertaan's mouth was lit in the hallway's torchlight.

The Synth opened her mouth, and the beginning of a note rang out. Seph's skin began sizzling as the spell erupted in the room. The heat that enveloped Seph was like nothing she'd ever felt. She was burning from the inside out. Time had run out. The Synth had won.

But Seph wasn't dead yet.

At the brink of succumbing to the pain, Seph used every bit of strength she had left, yanking the dagger free from the Synth's hand. Zertaan burst the note from her mouth to a full ring. The searing pain in Seph's skin erupted as she turned the dagger over in her fists, slamming its sharp point straight down. Zertaan put her arms up to stop the blow, but Seph sent it crashing down with incredible force like she'd never known.

The dagger cut down into Zertaan's open mouth, knocking teeth out, cutting into the back of her mouth and up into her head. The note was replaced by a deathly gurgling. Zertaan's hands fought to pull the dagger free, but Seph put all her weight onto the dagger's handle, holding it down.

Seph's shaky breath was inches from Zertaan's mouth. Zertaan struggled to breathe; gasping, wheezing, suffocating on her own blood.

"The Nine Hells beckons," Seph said, heaving breaths, the fire under her skin fading. "Another devil returning to where they belong."

The disbelief in Zertaan's eyes was the most beautiful sight Seph had ever seen. The Synth tried to speak, but the damage was too great, and as she died, a single final exhale rose from her mouth.

"May you rot eternal," Seph said, sitting up, her chest heaving, her hands shaking and her body completely exhausted.

She rose with wobbly knees. Blood covered every part of her body as she stood. Her blood mixed with that of her fallen foe's.

"It's over…"

But Seph's relief was far too soon as she heard footsteps rushing down the hallway. They came from both ends, and they were many. The clanking of metal told her it was soldiers. At least four of them. Their shouts came from both sides, but in Seph's utter exhaustion, she couldn't make out what the words were.

She stumbled into the hallway, opened her mouth, trying to make out a note.

It needs to be an easy one. An A. Use an A note. Don't risk it. You have nothing left, but you're going to have to find something. Think of Soren. Think of Davin. Think of Blaje…

The A note that left her hoarse voice was muffled, intermittent, and broken.

The soldiers rushed at her with sharp swords, eager to cut her down. They had hate in their eyes at the sight of the king's dead Synth at her feet.

They shouted with their swords eager to cut into her.

The note wasn't there. She had no staff to concentrate the note, and her Ellydian was gone. There was nothing to grasp onto. Her lungs were failing her, and terror gripped her. Seph knelt and pulled the small bloody dagger from Zertaan's mouth, holding it up as the dozen soldiers rushed at her, ready to kill.

But then something happened, something Seph didn't expect. A beautiful tone filled the air like a break in a feverish hurricane. It was like spring rain, or a shimmering rainbow after a day's long deluge.

It was a note. A gorgeous, pure C note. It was the most blissful thing Seph had ever heard in her life.

A blue haze filled the tunnel. Sparkling white snowflakes

shimmered within the dark hallway as the soldiers slowed their advance. Seph held out the bloody dagger, ready to defend herself.

The soldier's faces twisted in horror as they slowed to a crawl, and a deep, thick plume of vapor bellowed out of Seph's mouth as she watched. One final breath left the lips of the lead soldier as he froze in place, the skin on his face and neck a soft, deadly blue.

The C note rang curiously through the air, as crisp and pure as fresh mountain spring water. Seph considered using that note to cast her own spell, and she readied herself to try. But after the days or weeks of torture, she knew she was at the very brink of exhaustion and collapse. Her knees buckled, her head throbbed, and every joint in her body screamed in pain.

A pair of footsteps ran down the hallway, weaving through the statuesque bodies of soldiers—their blue eyeballs were frozen solid and no more breaths left their icy lungs. The soldiers were all dead, standing like terrible monuments while the single pair of footsteps encroached.

Seph held out the dagger, her vision blurry and her voice hoarse. "Don't come any closer! I'm leaving this place…" She choked the words out as tears streamed down her cheeks. "Don't try to stop me. I'll kill you like I did her…"

The footsteps got louder and quicker at the sound of her voice, and from behind the dead soldiers a familiar face shone under a hood, strands of reddish-brown hair weaving out like a bird's nest.

Kaile's mouth fell agape at the sight of her. He stopped short of her, her hand shaking as she held out the knife, her free hand covering her mouth as she looked up at him.

"Seph… you're hurt…" His voice trembled as he let the note fade into the chill air.

"Stay… stay back." Seph waved the dagger between them as Kaile took weary, yet eager, steps forward. He lowered his staff and let the note trail off to nothing. "Stay back…" She could barely get the words out. The pain was too great to bear. The sight of her former friend, and biggest betrayer, was unbearable. She dropped to her knees, and Kaile rushed in, grabbing her to aid in her fall.

He took the dagger from her weak fingers and let it fall to the stone floor.

"Seph, by Shirava, you're alive. You're alive!" He cradled her in his arms. "You're hurt…" He grabbed the dagger and cut a piece of his sleeve off, pressing it to the side of her face. He covered the wound where her ear had been as she grimaced in pain. Next, he cut a long strip of clothing from Zertaan's tunic, pushing it into the wound in Seph's side, and wrapping another long cloth around her midsection to hold it tight.

She glared at him as if she were in a dream, but while trying to grip the reality she faced, her mouth flattened, then her teeth showed as a blistering anger lit in her. She slapped Kaile across the face as hard as she could. He took it; his head cocked to the side. She did it again, this time harder. Then her lips quivered and more tears streamed down her face.

Seph's vision blurred as her eyelids were hard to keep open. They felt weighted, and the tears stung her eyes.

"It's all right," Kaile said. "You did it…" Kaile whispered. "You killed her. I knew you could… I knew you'd survive."

"Don't touch me," Seph muttered. "Don't touch me… you traitor… All I endured… it was because of you…"

"I know…" Kaile said, finishing tying the bandage around her waist. "I deserve everything you want to give me for that. But first, we need to get you out of here. More will come, and the Silver Sparrows are leading an insurrection in the streets above. It's our chance to get away. But we've got to get you to your feet, and get you out of here."

"I—I'm not going anywhere with you... you betrayed me, Kaile. You betrayed Soren."

"I did. Hopefully, I'll be able to prove myself to you again... someday..."

"I—I hate you," Seph cried into his shoulder. "I hate you..."

The words cut into Kaile like a hot spear tip through the heart, plunging through his breastbone like a hammer.

"You're alive," he said. "That's enough for me. I plan to keep you that way. I'm going to find a way to get you back to your uncle. Just hold on, Seph."

"Soren..." Seph muttered at the edge of consciousness.

Kaile put her arm over his neck and lifted her. She groaned deeply as he hoisted her up. "C'mon Seph. We've got to go... now..." As he picked her up, he looked down at Zertaan's body, her face completely flat and her nose shattered. She was covered in dark blood, with all light gone from her devilish eyes.

"I—I'm not going anywhere with you..." she mumbled, her head falling limp over his shoulder and her eyes shutting. "Traitor... traitor..."

"Seph," Kaile said in amazement, eyeing the fallen Synth at their feet. "Do you know what this means?"

Seph muttered something he couldn't understand.

"Zertaan is dead. The curse is broken. It's been lifted."

"What?" Seph asked, her eyes opening, drawing in a deep breath as if awakening from a long, deep sleep.

"The curse... Soren's curse she placed on him. The Alluvi Omnipitus, Godkeeper Rune that the Knight Wolf had Zertaan place on Soren when he cut the scars into his face... it's gone. It's gone forever!"

Seph choked as she smiled, staring up into Kaile's eyes. "It is? Did I do it?"

"You did it, girl. You did it."

She smiled wide, but after a long look at him, her eyes wetted again and her lips quivered. "You betrayed me, Kaile. You betrayed everyone. Why? Why did you do that? I was left all alone in that room with her... she did... terrible things." She sobbed, and Kaile began to cry. The tears dripped down his cheeks and fell off the tip of his chin.

"I'm so sorry, Seph. I'll make it up to you somehow. I'll show you that you can trust me..."

"I—I don't know if I can..." Seph cried.

"I understand, but we've got to get you out of here first. That's the first step..."

"Kaile..."

"Yes, Seph?"

"Thank... thank you..."

Kaile grinned widely while the tears still streaked down his cheeks.

"Soren's curse is lifted? We need to tell him..." Seph said, half awake.

"Yes... his curse..." Kaile's jaw dropped at a revelation. "Soren's curse is broken... and... so is *mine*..."

Seph pulled her eyes open, pushing past the sleep that fought desperately to drag her in. "Yours?"

"Alcarond and Zertaan placed the Godkeeper Rune on me in secret, when I was just a boy who started training. He put it on me so that I wouldn't know he'd have a secret control over me if he ever needed it. That's what he did to me at Golbizarath. He used the curse to control me." He wiped tears from his face. "You broke my curse too, Seph. I'm finally, truly free."

She smiled, raised her arm, and brushed his tears away with her blood-soaked thumb.

"I knew you wouldn't betray me. I knew there had to be a reason."

Kaile lost it, sobbing hard as she glared up at him with a familiar look of trust, and love.

"I knew you'd come save me," she breathed. "I knew it."

"I'm here, Seph, and I'm never leaving your side."

An explosion rocked the city above them, sending dust and debris falling from the ceiling. One soldier toppled over, landing with a solid, icy thud.

Kaile hoisted her up again. "Now, c'mon. We've got to get out of here…"

Chapter Thirty-Eight

"You've lost a lot of blood." Kaile had Seph's arm over his shoulder, making their way out of the Tower of the Judicature. They wove through the frozen bodies of the soldiers, captured in a spell of Bone Frost. Eventually, the ice inside them would melt and they'd tumble dead to the ground.

Seph moaned as they walked through the tunnel. "Soren…"

"I'm going to get you back to him." Kaile gulped, carrying most of her weight. "I don't know how… but I'm going to get you to him…"

Finally, they left the cells, wound around a corner, and got to the staircase that led up into the streets of Celestra. Through her foggy vision, Seph's eyes widened slightly, as every part beyond the prison door was new to her. She breathed the fresh, crisp air—smelling partly of burnt wood and smoldering fire—from the explosions that tore through the city.

"Where… where will we go?" Seph asked, a sudden strength returning to her legs. She gripped the cloth on the side of her head, not wanting to know the full extent of the damage. They needed to get out of the city. That was the most important thing.

Kaile swallowed hard. "West. With hoods up. I wish we had our disguises still." But he looked at the staff in his hand and his distinct hair flowing out from his collar. "We'll go quickly. But not too... blend in, we must. Blend in with the chaos. We should be able to make it." He dug into his pocket and fished out the ring of tuning forks. Pausing at the front door to the tower, he pulled one fork off the ring and handed it to Seph. "An A. The easiest one. For if you need your magic."

She took it with trembling fingers and clasped it in her hand.

"Now... let's go. This isn't going to get any better. The city is going to be crawling with soldiers, guards, possibly even the Synths and the Drakoons."

"I'm ready," Seph said, trying to reassure herself as much as she was to him. She indeed had lost a lot of blood, and every second she was fighting off the sleep that clawed desperately at her. It deeply wanted to embrace her as she shoved it off.

Kaile carefully pressed the door open. Immediately, the shouting to the north filled the air. There were more than explosions rocking the capital—there was fighting and confusion. The war had begun. It was more than Soren versus the world. The Silver Sparrows had launched an attack, and Kaile wondered what it was the man who gave him the staff alluded to. He said they were there for something... and Kaile hoped to find out what that was...

"Took you long enough," a voice said from the other side of the door, causing Kaile to nearly fall back down the stairs. His sturdy grip on the door tightened. Seph struck the A note on the door frame, the clear note ringing out sharply. "Whoa, whoa, whoa."

A familiar face emerged from the other side of the door

with both his hands raised. Lean, tall, balding with blond graying hair, and a welcome, yellow-toothed smile; the view of the man was a welcome sight.

"Einrick!" Kaile gasped. "What... what are you doing here?"

"Showing you a way out... again... come, come. We don't have time."

Kaile and Seph left the Tower of the Judicature and followed Einrick around the tower and to the alley on its side.

"We've a path to traverse out of the city, and have horses at the ready," Einrick said. "But as soon as they discover you two are missing, you will become the king's top priority in getting back."

"Let's make haste," Kaile said.

As they walked, Seph's pace quickened, and the sight of the secret Silver Sparrow Einrick, who'd helped them plan the attack in Grayhaven against the Synth Edward Glasse, and find a way out of the city afterward, had proven his worth, and was a sight for sore eyes.

"You're gravely injured," Einrick said, gazing at Seph's blood-soaked rag against her head and the swelling red mess under the bandage on her side.

"I'll—I'll be fine," she said, trying to mask her pain and fatigue.

"We will get you healed up once we're out of this city," Einrick said. "But there's no time to waste. Follow me."

They didn't make it two strides before Einrick seemed to change his mind, and stopped, spinning to face Seph. "Tell me... the Synth of the White Asp of Arkakus... is she?"

Seph's demeanor darkened, remembering the brutal, bloody fight. "Dead."

A wide grin crossed Einrick's face. "Good. Very good. This will shift the tide. Soren must be told his curse is lifted. The Knight Wolf is at last vulnerable to Soren's blade."

THE DARK SYNTHS

"We need to tell him," Kaile said.

"I'll send ravens once we are safer." Einrick glared back at the high rising towers behind them. The Tower of the King, the Illuvitrus Sanctum, the Lūminine Grand Cathedral. "Good riddance."

They moved through the alleys of Celestra, hiding in the midnight shadows as best they could. Soldiers moved sporadically through the streets, shouting and barking orders. Mostly they moved north, toward the Tower of the King. But while the soldiers were occupied, many eyes watched the three of them move through the alleys. Gazes from windows, from surrounding roads, and even from the alleyways themselves watched them.

With haste, they moved. Seph's head throbbed and the gaping wound in her side constantly sent a crippling wave of pain into her entire body. "Just a little further," she whispered to herself. But Kaile, who was still helping her walk, heard.

"Almost there, Seph. Hang on. We'll soon be out of this miserable place. Thank Shirava. And thank Lady Drake…"

"Don't thank them just yet," Einrick said. "We won't be safe for quite a while…"

"Soren…" Seph's voice suddenly cleared. "What news of my uncle?"

"Later," Einrick said. "We need to get out of the—"

"Tell me! Is he alive?"

Einrick looked at Kaile. "Ask him," Einrick said.

Seph's gaze took in Kaile, and he gulped. "He's alive. But he has no Syncrons with him. The king sent out a pack of Re-Enlightened to find him. Three Synths. Very dangerous ones."

"We need to get to him," Seph said, removing her arm from around Kaile's neck.

"He's nearly half a world away," Einrick interrupted. "They're heading for Arkakus. His master is supposedly still alive, and Soren believes he's there."

"Arkakus?" Seph muttered. "Well then, we make for there."

"Agreed," Kaile said.

"C'mon then," Einrick said. "Less talking, more moving."

They made their way through the capital, evading all unwanted gazes, hoping—praying—for their luck to continue. They walked for what felt like miles. Every part of Seph's body shuddered in crippling pain. Every part of her wanted to collapse, but the freedom that enveloped her gave her the strength to push through. She had to fight. The war wasn't over… it had just begun.

"Einrick," Kaile said with shaky breath, winter vapor capturing his words. "The spy… Lady Drake's spy… who is it? Who gave me the key?"

"And slid the dagger to me?" Seph added. "Whoever it was healed me during some nights after Zertaan left. I feel I have much to thank that person for."

Einrick's mouth flattened, and he paused, leaning against an alleyway stone wall. "I know not who helped you. I was contacted by Lady Drake days ago after I got out of the madness of Grayhaven, and she told me to travel here. She said to wait for a raven here. It came this evening. It told me to wait at the Tower of the Judicature for the two of you. Or perhaps one, depending on how things turned out in the Abiron. If I had to guess, though, I would say it was one of the guards, or an attendant to the king who had access to both towers."

"But you said they healed you?" Kaile asked, eyeing her injuries.

"A note filled the hallway some nights. I should've died many times. But I didn't. I woke with cuts closed, bleeding stopped, internal damage mended."

"So it was a Synth?" Kaile rubbed his chin. "It must have been. All the Synths of the king would have access to both towers. There are hundreds of them. There's no knowing who it could've been."

"Do you think..." Seph said with a raised eyebrow. "Do you think it could have been the archmage?"

"Alcarond?" Kaile murmured, scratching his temple instead. "I—I don't know. He did have a conversation with me recently that was about you... it was more... *sympathetic* than normal, I guess I'd say..."

"If Alcarond was the spy for the Silver Sparrows," Einrick said with a wry smirk, "then he would be a great ally in the war."

"Undoubtably so," Kaile said, brushing his hair back behind both ears, hefting the staff secretly half-hidden in his sleeve. "If Lady Drake was in league with the most powerful Syncron in the world, then we may have a chance..."

"That's a big 'if.'" Seph shrugged.

"Come," Einrick said, "we are not safe here..."

They continued through the city, leaving the fighting near the Tower of the King far behind. The city calmed the further away they got. Glowing lanterns dimly lit the streets as they stuck to the alleys, weaving through the many roads that led to the outskirts. Kaile mentioned he was happy they got to stay above ground that time, and not knee deep in sewer water like in Grayhaven.

"There," Einrick said after hours of walking. "There's our ride."

On the city outskirts, where the buildings shrunk and were spaced further apart, a trio of horses were stabled outside of a tavern. A newfound energy found them at the thought of getting up on saddles and heading as far away from the capital as possible.

They rushed to the horses, all prepped and ready.

But Seph noticed something about one of the steeds quickly that took her breath away. Midnight black, eyes like coal, yet a deep wisdom dwelled in them. A familiar glare back at Seph assured her she was correct in her assumption. She knew the horse well and embraced the magnificent steed with both arms around her muscular neck.

"I thought you might like that surprise," Einrick said with a snicker.

"It can't be…" Kaile gasped. "No way…"

"Ursa," Seph gushed through a tremendous smile. "Hi girl. It's been a long time…"

Ursa neighed, and Seph mounted the saddle with a deep groan. The pain had become unbearable. And once Seph mounted Soren's horse, she fell forward, curling up into her pain.

Einrick held the reins tight, eager to be off. "There's supplies not far from here, out in the forest beyond the city."

Kaile cocked an eyebrow, fiddling with his reins nervously. "We're… we're going to ride through the plains… now?"

"You want to stay here all night?" Einrick asked. Kaile shook his head, but understood completely.

"It's not far," Einrick said. "Maybe twenty minutes of hard riding, and we should be safe for the night."

"But… Seph's not…" Kaile began.

"I'm fine," Seph groaned, sitting up. "We've no time to waste." She whipped Ursa's reins hard, and the black steed was off with powerful strides.

Einrick followed her out of the city. Kaile swallowed hard, gazing out into the moonlight wintry plains, scanning for any sign of Black Fog… he didn't see any. He dug his heels in, flicked the reins and was off after his companions, out into the plains of Aladran, and out of the city that held them captive, away from their greatest foes, and towards their friends.

That night, they made their way safely to the forest. Einrick and Kaile helped bandage Seph's wounds. A deep puncture wound in her side, dozens of lacerations on her skin, burn marks scattered around, and a hole where her ear used to be.

That night, Seph fell into a deep, deep sleep, filled with dreams of flying through the summer blue sky. Her arms spread wide like a bird's wings. Her flowing black hair whipped at her chest, neck, and back. The smell of fresh green grass filled her nostrils. She felt free. She felt as free as she ever had in her life. And at the core of her being, she felt a tremendous determination.

A gravity had formed in her soul that anchored her to a specific purpose.

She had survived the most grueling experience of her life. She was the only person to ever survive the Re-Enlightment without succumbing to darkness and becoming one of the king's Synths. She'd defeated the one who had cursed both Soren and Kaile. She had proven that she was stronger than the king, and Zertaan had assumed she was.

She was the last Whistlewillow. She'd survive whatever the world threw at her. If she could survive that onslaught of torture, then she could survive anything.

And she assumed that included the Black Sacrament.

It was her time.

It was her mission.

I'm going to rise to my destiny.

I'm going to become a great Lyrian someday.

I'm going to bring about a new age of my bloodline.

And I'm going to help kill King Amón, and every last one of the bastards that follows him.

Hold on Soren, this time... I'm coming to you.

Chapter Thirty-Nine

Two days later.
Januar 17, 1293
Kingdom of Lynthyn.

THE HORSES SLOPPED through frigid puddles as the rains came down hard. A murky sun hid behind hazy clouds. Thick raindrops pattered onto Soren's tunic as his horse led their way along an old trail through the hilly plains of Lynthyn.

They were in the king's lands, and Soren's gaze scanned the horizon in all directions. But there were so many hills and woods in the area, he knew they were at a disadvantage if there were spies scanning the areas. However, the two silver bears' keen senses had proven to be invaluable. Their heightened awareness gave him respite as they made their way northwest, toward the volcanic lands of Arkakus. Landran Dranne was their destination, and Soren knew with all his heart that if his former master was indeed still alive, he'd be there. That was his master's promised hideaway for his later years.

Blackburn was the region Landran had told him he'd go to

spend his final years. Soren had never seen it, but Landran had spoken a few times about its isolation, and it's peculiar, distinct beauty.

Sharp volcanic rocks jutted from the earth, making Blackburn look more like a place one might find in lands among the stars, not in Aladran. Yet, if one knew where to look, hunting was good, fresh water was in abundance, and best of all— privacy and solitude. There were no soldiers, no Synths, no politics, and no wanderers.

There were those that lived in Arkakus, but they were mostly natives. The natives lived in the cities there, or hid while traveling. Their black cloaks made them blend to the rocks like moths to tree bark.

Davin didn't speak as they rode. His beard glistened in the hazy sunlight, dripping with rainwater. Blaje had Sable huddled under the clothing in her lap, which Blaje did her best to shield the dry area with her back.

Other than Landran and Seph, Soren's thoughts were glued to one terrible thought. His mind's eye was constantly reminding him of the beast that lay secretly with the hordes of the Demons of Dusk in the Under Realm. Referring to it simply as the Shadow Dragon, Soren knew there was nothing to do about the new enemy, only hoping that it remained hidden away until he had time to deal with the new threat.

Soren fretted at the possibility of the Shadow Dragon taking to the skies, burning everything asunder and everyone in its wake. He tried desperately to push the dark thoughts aside, focusing more on the tasks at hand. But he knew if that monster emerged from the ground, nothing would ever be the same. From whatever hell that beast was birthed, Soren hoped it remained hidden. For he felt the only forces in Aladran that had any hope of felling such a beast was Sarrannax, the elder dragon that had come from Eldra, or perhaps the army of Synths in the capital. But that was a tremendous gamble, as the

Ellydian had no effect on the Demons of Dusk, so he assumed that same nullifying effect applied to the Shadow Dragon.

The hours dragged on as they rode. The clouds darkened and deepened to an impenetrable gray. Rains poured throughout the day, without pause. Thunder boomed within the thick clouds—hiding the sky and stars beyond—yet flickering with powerful lightning within.

A forest appeared on the distant horizon, the Grimshaw Glade, one that Soren had rested in many times over the years. It would prove fine cover from the Black Fog and Shades that were rampant in Lynthyn. There was a spot that was Soren's favorite as a campsite. An overhanging rock protected from the elements, as well as held the warmth of a campfire well. It would be a perfect place to rest where they could dry their clothes and dry their sopping hair and skin.

There was plenty of time to reach Grimshaw Glade before the sun would drop. Weariness filled Soren's mind and body as the world fogged around them. A gloomy haze filled the world as they made their way along the narrow path. Dead blades of grass jutted from the dirt on both sides of the path, and the hills and valleys only deepened the further they got to the glade. Soren rode at the front, with Davin in his female form behind, and Blaje at the rear.

Moonshadow and Sunstar both rode off the path, each at a side, riding through the dead grass. Fifteen yards away on either side of Soren and his comrades, they were both in their disguises as horses with no riders. They too were sopping wet, and surely eager for sleep at a warm, dry camp.

Soren rubbed his eyes and yawned. He even thought he may sleep that night, and with the protection of the bears, he'd have no regret for not staying awake to watch for intruders or any unwanted attention. They were well on their way to Arkakus, where hopefully answers would lead to a way to win the war against the king and the Demons of Dusk. But until they reached the border between kingdoms, there was only the road.

Lightning crashed into a hill to the north, and thunder boomed violently. It shook the air with an electric tinge. Soren's horse neighed.

"Easy." Soren stroked her neck, eyeing the hills around. "Easy. We're almost there."

Beneath the dark clouds, the world darkened. The gloom and haze furthered the pull of drowsiness that gripped Soren. The Grimshade Glade was just up ahead. Another twenty minutes of riding or so and they'd be in the woods, with another twenty to the campsite. Soren yawned, and he heard Davin do the same.

"Stop it, Soren," the dwarf growled. "Save it for once we're there."

Lightning crashed in the northern sky, sizzling the air. Thunder clapped immediately after, surging throughout the plains with ferocious tremors.

Soren noticed something off, glancing at both sides of him, and seeing both bears paused in their tracks. Both of their horses heads' were fixed to the northwest, focused on the peak of a hill that glowed with a hint of sunlight.

He tugged back on the reins, watching the two horses stand silently like statues. And then something appeared from the gloom that made Soren's neck hairs stiffen, and a deep, horrifying worry deep in his core.

A clear hum of a note struck at the hill's peak, and Soren pulled Firelight free immediately. "Ride!" The word broke from his lips immediately, kicking his horse's sides and whipping the reins hard.

But his horse didn't budge. In fact, it was stuck midway in stride. The two bears growled deep, but hadn't moved in seconds.

Soren immediately knew they were in terrible, terrible trouble.

"Off the horses!" Blaje shouted. "We are under attack!"

Soren got down, Firelight fixed in his hand, ready to run.

Davin and Blaje both got down from their steeds, gathering together, side by side. Sable was at Blaje's feet, hissing at the hill.

Soren wanted to run, but knew the truth. There was no running from the predicament they were in. Whoever was casting the spell that bound the horses could easily bind them as well. But whoever was casting, had decided not to... at least not yet.

It didn't take long to figure out who was casting the spell, as three riders emerged at the hill's top. They were cloaked in shadow, all three with long staffs, and each draped in colorful cloaks. Lightning blasted through the sky behind them, dampening the clear ringing of the E note momentarily. The three stood stoically at the top of the hill, all staring down silently at Soren, Davin, and Blaje.

"What do we do?" Davin asked behind clenched teeth, his double-sided ax clutched in his muscly fingers.

"I fear there's not much we can do," Soren said. "Hope they get close enough and give us a chance to throw our weapons. With luck, we could instantly kill each of them. But at this distance, I fear we may be at the end of the road without Seph."

Blaje shifted uneasily at the prospect. "I can't die without a fight. That's not how I'm meant to go into the afterlife. It can't happen like this."

Soren huffed, "Agreed."

"Think, Soren, think..." Davin said. "There's got to be something."

"They're choosing to keep us free," Soren said. "For some reason, they haven't frozen us yet. Let's hope they keep that going, at least to give us one chance. For I fear that's all we'd get."

The E note seemed to come from a single source, perhaps the taller of the Synths at their center. And to Soren's dread, the other two Synths struck their staffs, and two more terrifying E notes rang out.

The three Synths, clad in shadow, began a slow descent down the hill on their horses.

Soren readied Firelight, eager for one shot to take out any of their approaching foes. But as the three rode down, Soren felt his body seize, frozen, and terror gripped him. He fought to break free of the spell that bound them, but he knew it was hopeless. Even if they were low level Dors from the capital, no man or woman could fight the Ellydian. As long as those notes rang out, Soren and the others had no hope of breaking the spell.

He watched helplessly as the three cloaked Synths road down, the E notes growing ever louder and clearer.

Soren and the others were stuck stiff by an extremely powerful spell. His body was locked tightly, as if frozen in a block of ice. Soren didn't fight it. He knew there was no use. If they were to live through this... he'd have to use his words.

The three Synths rode into their ranks, glaring down at Soren with hateful, insane glares.

These three don't have the same looks as normal wielders of the Ellydian... they're Re-Enlightened. There's no use in trying to talk to them. They've endured torture and have been brainwashed into the king's service... Shirava... if you're listening... help us... please...

One man and two women. All stoic with dark eyes and emotionless expressions. Emotionless... except their eyes. Their dark eyes were filled with a primal sort of insanity and cruelty. They were enjoying this. They were enjoying the hunt and finding and cornering their prey.

"King Amón sends his regards," the tall female said, rain

pattering on her head and shoulders. She had long red hair with streaks of silver. She was adorned by a cloak of sleek crimson with weaving gold decoration. "I am Claudine Prest, wielder for the crown. You should know the names of those that have finally bested you, Soren Stormrose."

Soren could've spoken, but waited. He wanted to let them have their moment. The pride of Synths was well known.

"You've been busy doing the devil's work," the other female said. Her dark-skinned head was shaved bald, with lavishing green robes and silver bracelets and earrings. "I am Myranda Cloutter, wielder for the crown. You deserve to know my name, Davin Mosser of Mythren."

"You're far from your desert," finally the man said. He wore deep violet robes with white decorations of flowers at its edges. He had tan skin and scraggly auburn hair. Missing an eye, one eye glared angrily at them, while the other half hung open, empty beneath its wrinkled eyelid. "Albertus Sterren. You should know my name, for I will send you to the afterlife, Desert Shadow…"

"You all… look different…" the tall, lean Claudine said with a wry, scornful smile. "But we know it's you under that magic that hides your faces. Why don't you reveal who you really are to us?"

Davin glanced at Soren. Soren nodded, and Davin released the grip of the spell of disguise. Davin shrunk to half the height of the tall woman he had been. The shades of Blaje's hair and skin darkened, and the tattoos lined her body from neck to toes. The scars appeared back on Soren's face, and the two silver bears grew to monstrous size, still stuck staring up at the hill the three Synths had ridden down from.

"Very good," Claudine said, riding her black steed all the way up to Soren, pointing her wooden staff at him. "There's the Scarred. The man most wanted by the crown, and the cause of so much pain in these lands."

Soren choked down any words. *Let them play their games first. I've got to find a way to get them to relax their magic for just a moment. I could get her right between the eyes. But I need a second.*

Then something occurred to him, staring straight into the tall Synth's eyes.

Their skin. The hairs on their arms and neck are limp. They're Dors. All three of them were Dorens.

Soren knew it was common practice for higher-level wielders to cast defensive spells when going into battle. But these three Synths hadn't. When an Aeol casts a defensive spell, it was subtle, but the hairs on their skin straightened like static—or fear. But there was none of that.

They're not able to cast within their own bodies, only externally. That would make killing them even easier... but I need a shot.

Claudine sat up straight in her saddle, looking down at the three of them. "You've come to the end of your journey, and it will be my absolute honor—and pleasure—to rid the world of the shadow that follows you. You, Soren Stormrose, die tonight."

Chapter Forty

A growing tension gripped the world all around them. The demeanors of the three Synths deepened as their grips twisted angrily on their staffs slick with rain. The hazy sky beyond the veil of gray clouds above darkened. The sun beyond the clouds was dipping further and further down into the horizon.

"Hold," Soren finally said, feeling the determination building within the three. They seemed fixated, drooling even, at the prospect of killing the one the king hated most in this world. "There are things you don't know. There's more to these wars than the king and Alcarond have told you. I ask you, give me time to explain what I've found. It will alter the course of these wars. The Demons of Dusk aren't exactly what they seem."

Claudine raised an eyebrow, scanning his body. She looked at the other two Synths, who both had minimal reactions, even any at all.

"Alcarond is the most knowledgeable in all Aladran of the Demons of Dusk," Claudine replied in a hollow, wise tone.

"He is the master of knowledge. We are the weapons of the king. We enact and deliver justice. We don't determine guilt or barter for freedom. We are soldiers, not judges."

"You don't know who you fight for," Blaje said, trying to control her temper. "The king is evil. He's killed so many innocent women and children in these lands. And you dare to call Soren evil?"

Albertus rode close to Blaje, holding his jeweled staff of bronze at her. "When the world is rid of you, your clan, and the Silver Sparrows, then there will be no need for his highness to purge through fire. The world will know peace again, and he will remain the one true hero of our time."

"Hero?" Davin spat. "He's no more a hero than a Black Fog. You're all blind in your ignorance and hate. You haven't seen the things we've seen."

Soren didn't agree with the anger in the dwarf's words, but he agreed completely with the words themselves.

"Let us free," Soren said softly. "And we can show you what we know. There's more to the Demons of Dusk than you know, and if we don't figure out how to defeat them, then there won't be a world left to fight for. They'll invade every village, town, and even the capital city. There will be nowhere else to go. It will be the end. The end of man. The end of woman. The end of everything."

The three Synths paused in thought, each letting Soren's words swirl around in their minds.

"We are not here to kill the Demons of Dusk." Claudine's voice was shrill, seething in malice, and dark enough to dampen Soren's hope to survive their hunters. "We came here... to kill you."

Claudine reached into her crimson cloak, sliding out a glimmering silver dagger from a hidden sheath. The dagger rang as its fine metal slid from the sheathe. She held it out before her, pointing it at Soren. The world still rang with the pure E note. It was a powerful note full of dread, filling Soren's ears with a melancholy, foreboding fear.

She held the dagger loosely between them, slowly spreading her fingers so that the dagger hung in midair. Soren gazed at it, gulping as it pointed between his eyes, hanging only feet away. The rains intensified as Soren's heart pounded like a thumping drum.

The two other Synths both brought sharp daggers out from their cloaks, holding them before Blaje and Davin. Both Synths released them, leaving the daggers hanging like the first.

"Soren Stormrose," Claudine said, rain beading on her cloak hood, dribbling down her face. Her face showed no emotion, and her red and silver hair wafted at her shoulders from a powerful gust of wind. "Blaje Severaas, and Davin Mosser; you all three have been sentenced to death by King Malera Amón, first of his name, and Lord of Aladran. Your bodies will receive no burial, no cleansing fire, or remembrance of any light. Your bodies will rot and decay where you stand, and history will remember you only for the traitors and murderers you are. May your souls rot in the Nine Hells, tortured by Nazaroth himself."

The three daggers began to move. As the E note grew in intensity, the air shuddered with the growing note that sounded like an orchestra of horns blowing the same, bitter note. The three daggers inched their way toward Soren and his friends. Soren noticed two more silver daggers creeping through the air, both gliding towards Sunstar and Moonshadow.

A primal rage tore through Soren. His ears heated, his arms and chest pumped with fiery blood, and beads of sweat dotted his brow. One dripped off his eyebrow onto his cheek with a plop. He narrowed his eyes and stared deeply into Claudine's.

Think, Soren, think! What the hell am I going to do to get out of this mess? What would Landran have me do? I can't let Blaje and Davin die. Not here, not like this...

"Soren?" Blaje said out of the corner of her mouth.

Soren gritted his teeth, thinking... desperately thinking...

Soren watched as the daggers both stopped as the tips of their blades touched Blaje's and Davin's throats. Soren felt the cold steel press against his own Adam's apple.

"Soren?" Blaje asked again, this time her eyes stricken with worry.

Soren thought as hard as he could. He tried with all his might to break free of the binding spell. But it was no use. He was overpowered by the powerful spell of the Synths. Moonshadow and Sunstar both let out deep whimpers that made Soren's heart pound in fury.

All Soren could think was, *Seph... where are you? Where are you when I need you most? I'm sorry I let you down again. I'm so, so sorry...*

Claudine, Albertus, and Myranda all had sinister, toothy snarls marring their faces. An insidious pleasure washed through them as the daggers began to dig. A trickle of blood dripped down Blaje's throat, pooling between her collarbones.

This can't be it. This can't. I haven't come this far just to have it all end by these three. Think, Soren, think. There's got to be a way.

At once, all three Synths began to chant. It was a mysterious, deep chant, full of words Soren didn't recognize. He thought it might be a language of the Under Realm or some cult in Eldra, but he'd never heard a wielder of the Ellydian utter such dark language.

Davin groaned as the dagger pierced deeper into his throat, blood dripping down as he fought.

The chant billowed in Soren's mind like organ pipes. The malicious E note danced with the dark, foreign words in his mind like a destructive tornado. The winds swirled in his mind, fueling his hatred to deepen. He watched as the daggers slowly dug into his friends. The silver bears growled in agony, mixed with light whimpers. Sable, too, was frozen at Blaje's feet, stuck in place like a figurine.

The words in their chant ignited something in Soren. It felt like a hidden string had been plucked, sending deep vibrations through his body like a hammer pounding an anvil in a fiery forge. Something inside him stirred. He felt changed. His hatred fueled that furnace within him. The hazy clouds turned from a muted gray to a vivid, specular red. The sky burned in flames, and suddenly he looked all around, his eyelids pulled open wide, his teeth unclenched and his jaw dropped.

"Am I... am I dead?" he muttered to himself. His boots dug into the deep sand as the fiery red and orange sky swirled in a magnificent storm, with him at its epicenter. The surrounding hills and mountains transformed into magical sand dunes as tall as the mountains of the Tibers.

He felt he may be dead, passing into the afterlife, but there was something pinning him to the world. The sands swirled at his feet, erupting high into the sky, a funnel of sand rushing around him. And then... everything stopped.

The sands returned to the ground. A deep lack of sound took the world—a silence that drowned out everything—causing him to hear his thumping heartbeat, and nothing else. The red sky darkened to a deep black, and the desert floor was no longer lined with sheets of sands, but corpses. Thousands of corpses. Soren strode out into the mess. Men and women's bodies lay all around him. Swords and spears protruded from their backs and bellies and chests.

The blood had dried long ago, and the crows picked at their motionless bodies.

"This... this was a massacre..."

But then Soren leaned in to inspect the bodies. Those in

armor seemed to adorn two different sigils. One bore the blazing sun with a red lion at its center, and the other a dragon with black wings over a haunting, full moon. He knew these sigils. The red lion for the Sundar and the black dragon for the Polonians.

"This... this was their battle... long ago..."

The deadened sky sparked alive then. An intense heat flashed and sizzled through the surrounding air. The sky brightened to a blinding light as the heat grew. The hairs on his arms singed, and that smell of burnt hair filled his nostrils. Strands of flame erupted from the sand at his feet. The flames licked high, engulfing the bodies of the fallen.

Soren tried to step back, stagger even, but his boots were stuck in the sand. He raised his arm over his eyes and shut them hard. The scorching heat swirled all around him, and he thought that if death had not already taken him, then it surely would then. It built to a heat so hot he thought he may have been thrown into the sun.

But then he felt a splash of something soon on his forearm. A trickle of water that bested the heat, falling down his arm and plopped into the sand below. A cool mist hit his face like fresh, biting spring water. He lowered his arms to see a new mountain on the far horizon. It sparkled with a white sheen as it lifted the horizon line. He looked down at his feet to see water pooling in the sands.

"That's no mountain..."

The flames hissed as they suffocated in the rising water. The corpses disappeared beneath the waves as the water rose above his knees. What he thought was a mountain, rose to a cascading wave that approached.

"This is it... this is the Great Divine Flood that changed our world." His arms hung strong at his sides as he puffed his chest out and inhaled deeply through his nose. The smell of burning, rotting flesh was replaced by a mossy morning spring dew.

The world vibrated as the enormous wave approached. The water at his feet pulled away back into the wave, and as it towered above him, ready to crash into him, he thought of one thing—Seph. His only living family, not even by blood, but bonded by a different kind of blood—love. She was still out there, and she needed his help.

Just as the wave was about to topple onto him, he lifted his arms out wide, raising his chin to glare up at the towering, powerful waves. He closed his eyes, smiled even, as the waves crashed down onto him. As they fell, the rest of the world drowned out. There was no light, no noise, not even the sound of the violent wave. He floated in the abyss. He existed in oblivion. He had become something different.

Soren opened his eyes.

The desert was gone. The water and fire had seemed like nothing more than a dream. Perhaps they were, but with his eyes opened anew, reality had shifted. Before him were the three Synths, his friends, the hills and valleys, and the twilight haze that swirled in the sky.

But there was something new. Something very, very different.

Before him, the three Synths stood wide-eyed, with a sort of insane, perplexing confusion. All three daggers that had been magically cutting their way into Soren and the others' throats dropped to the ground. Albertus beat the metal of his staff over and over, but to Soren's amazement, and to the Synth's horror—his staff produced no sound. The E note had completely faded away to nothing. Less than nothing. The world was completely void of all sound.

As Soren's excitement rose and his hatred faded, he at last noticed the air itself had changed. A soft blue aura surrounded them in a spectacular, magical dome. White wisps wafted through the blue dome, reminding Soren of what angels might sprinkle behind their wings as they flew in the Halls of Everice.

Soren looked over to see Davin trying to say Soren's name, but no words left his lips.

The three Synths struck their staffs madly, feverishly, desperately trying to produce even the faintest of notes. They tried to scream and yell, but not a single utterance left their wretched lips.

Their Ellydian is gone... they're powerless without sound...

Davin hefted his ax; Blaje held her shamshir blade out at the three. However, Soren took Firelight and sheathed it.

The three Synths, frantic in their dismay, and completely vulnerable, took their one shot and hopped on their horses sloppily. Davin went to run after them, but Soren stopped him with a firm grip on the dwarf's shoulder. Davin raised an eyebrow, and Sable hissed without sound at the Synths. Blaje sheathed her curved sword as Soren did. The Synths kicked madly at the horses' sides, making their way back up the hill to escape.

Soren folded his arms and watched as the two silver bears ran an incredible speed at the much slower Synths. The bears' strides were enormous, awe inspiring even. And as Moonshadow and Sunstar crashed into the Synths and their horses, a smirk crept up on Soren's face. The two bears mauled the dark sorcerers with a savagery known exclusively to nature. The predators had become the prey.

Sharp teeth tore into flesh. Blood soaked the dead grass beneath them. The Synths fought with utter futility, banging their staffs against the overwhelming beasts that crunched down on their puny bones. The two bears were so vicious in their attack, all three Synths were left with their heads separated from their bodies, their tunics torn, tattered and stained with fresh blood. Each of the Synths' horses, startled as they were, got up and ran off as the bears killed the king's Synths.

Once dead, Soren felt his body relax, and a strong inhale and exhale calmed the veil of blue magic that surrounded them. It shrank down, returning to a pinpoint spot at the center of Soren's eyes, disappearing into his skin, and he heard his own sigh as the world returned to normal.

Davin and Blaje were both left speechless. Soren himself was still gathering what had just happened, and what that meant moving forward. The two bears returned from the bloody mess, eyeing Soren as if he was a different person for them to behold. Both sniffed him with a newfound curiosity.

"It's okay," he said, petting both their gigantic heads. "It's me. I'm just different... changed, I suppose."

"What in the blazes was that?" Davin's face was as pale as a sheet and his mouth was left agape.

"I—I don't know..." Soren looked at Blaje for an answer.

But the Desert Shadow was stuck in bewilderment. "I—I have no clue. I've never heard of anything like that before. I..."

A shifting movement in the distance caught Soren's gaze, and the gravity of the moment returned to him. It returned to all of them.

"Fog!" Soren shouted, mounting his horse as quickly as his body could carry him. Davin and Blaje immediately felt the weight of the twilight that had arrived while the battle had ended. Soren kicked his horse and whipped the reins, narrowing his eyes at the forest up ahead. At a full sprint, it was still ten minutes away, he guessed—at the minimum.

They were off along the path, with the two bears running for the forest as fast as their massive legs could carry them. Soren knew he was the only one who could fight the Demons of Dusk, as Firelight had tasted the flesh of a Black Fog before, but every part of him wanted to avoid another fight with one of those monsters.

He glared over his shoulder, and to his horror, the Black

Fog was rushing after them at speeds far quicker than any animal he'd seen. Its centipede-like black glassy legs propelled the smoky monster forward. It was quickly catching up and would be on them within minutes. All around, Soren felt other figures joining the chase. Their horses' hooves clapped through puddles on the trail as they ran as quickly as they could.

Another Black Fog joined in the chase, running beside the huge one in pursuit. Shades from all directions were darting through the dead grass after them. They wove over hills and through deep valleys. Dozens of them were after Soren.

Soren's heart beat wildly in his chest. The adrenaline surged like wildfire within, and he urged his horse to run with all its might.

They approached the forest, halfway there, but looking back, the Black Fog were nearly upon them. The overwhelming horde of Shades was about to encircle them, trapping them and their progress toward the forest.

"Soren..." Blaje said, a worried tone was thick in her voice.

"Keep riding!" Soren shouted in the rain. "Whatever happens, keep going!"

We're not going to make it... But they can...

Soren jerked back on the reins, slowing the confused horse. It was so terrified, Soren felt his only option was to leap off, so he did, instantly hearing the shouts of his friends as they continued their ride with looks of horror on their faces.

"Soren! No!" Blaje shouted, but her words were cut short by a thunderclap overhead.

Soren unsheathed Firelight as her rippled layers of Vellice steel glowed red as scant starlight flittered through the patchy gray clouds. Soren widened his stance as the two Black Fog were joined by a third, hurtling toward him like monstrous waves about to crash into him.

As the horde of the Demons of Dusk took the bait, letting Blaje, Davin, Sable, and the bears make it safely to the woods,

Soren felt a great sigh of relief. *I may fall, but they've made it. That's what matters. As long as I saved them successfully one last time. That's enough… that has to be enough…*

The encroaching Black Fog didn't slow as they careened forward. The Shades ran with all their hollow eyes, glaring at him with primal, hungry gazes. They flashed their deadly teeth, ready to tear Soren limb from limb. They flashed their sharp claws as they tore the ground beneath them, lunging with huge strides at him.

Firelight flashed red as they approached, nearly upon him. And just as they were ready to barrel into him, something happened that took even Soren by surprise.

The sky darkened. In fact, the world darkened. An enormous shadow fell over that part of the world Soren stood upon. He felt a great gravity to the moment, as if the air had been sucked out of the lands, and a stillness made way for a great predator. And that great predator landed beside Soren with a force that cause the ground to shudder.

A heat radiated from its enormous maw that sizzled the hairs on Soren's hands. His wet hair whipped wildly at his neck as the dragon's wings flapped out wide.

"Sarrannax…" Soren said in awe, still sturdy in his defensive pose. He stood beside the dragon as it straightened its neck, focusing its attention on the three Black Fog. Each of them instantly halted their advance, pausing for a moment before revealing their holes for mouths at the top of their shadowy, worm-like bodies. They hissed a devilish hiss as their hundreds of small sharp teeth showed.

Sarrannax let out a roar from its huge maw that caused Soren to throw his hands up to cover his ears. The Shades stopped where they stood. Hundreds of them surrounded Soren and the dragon. Sarrannax let out another roar that sent a surge of heat through the air. The brimming dragonfire licked out the corners of the dragon's maw, smoke smoldering out from between its huge teeth.

The Demons of Dusk remember what the dragon did to them at Golbizarath. They're studying the dragon. They remember...

The Black Fog began to slowly creep backwards, their sharp legs carefully easing their immense bodies backward in fear, an emotion unknown to them until that moment, Soren thought.

Sarrannax stood up on its hind legs, towering over everything and everyone in the hills of Lynthyn. A ferocity enveloped the dragon that was unlike Soren had ever seen in his life. Indeed, the dragons had lived up to their reputations, and this one, as ancient and gigantic as it was, seemed to be the epitome of the danger of dragons.

The Shades turned and fled. It was a sight that made Soren's body tingle from tip to toe. An exhilaration overwhelmed him as he watched the Black Fog recede back into the plains, disappearing into the night like a bad dream.

Sarrannax fell back to all fours, and it grumbled deep within its enormous body. Its massive neck curled and its head lowered to Soren's side. Its gray scales encompassed an aged eye that glared deep at Soren. The red eye with streaks of heavenly yellows and golds held a dark slit of a pupil at its center. It was keenly interested in Soren, only four feet away.

Soren's nostrils filled with the scent of dragonfire, that same burning sulfuric smell he smelled when the same dragon incinerated hundreds of Shades that were about to kill all of them in the desert.

Firelight returned to her sheathe, and Soren took a slow step toward the dragon. He delicately placed his hand below the dragon's eye, feeling the hardened, legendary scales. He felt the raw power within the monstrous dragon, and Soren nodded in appreciation for such a creation of nature.

"I remember you," he breathed to the dragon. "I remember you."

Sarrannax glared back at Soren as Soren stroked the dragon's face.

"I think you remember me as well."

Sarrannax let out a low growl, something softer than Soren expected. It was what he was hoping for.

"I believe we may have similar quests, old dragon. You have saved my life twice now. And I intend to repay those debts."

The old gray, ancient dragon groaned again.

"You are godly in your might. Everyone and everything in this world knows to fear you. But there is one thing that dwells deep under the earth. There is something dark and terrifying that is yet to reveal itself to the world. And I fear that may be the one thing that threatens your rule. There is a Shadow Dragon living with the hordes of beasts that curse this world. I will help you defeat it if you join me in my war to free this world of the evil that haunts it."

Sarrannax gave Soren one last long glance before returning up on its hind legs, and with a great inhale, it let out a roar straight up into the sky that shook the air like a lightning strike. The roar echoed for miles, and Soren knew that every living creature, including the Demons of Dusk, heard that roar.

"That's it. Let them hear. Let them know. It's their turn to know fear now."

Soren unsheathed Firelight and sent it cutting through the air above him, letting out a hellish roar of his own as the rains crashed down, thunder boomed in the background, and the two of them let all of Aladran know—death and vengeance were coming. It was time for the king and the Demons of Dusk to know fear for the first time. The tide of war had shifted once more, and Soren was eager to kill all who stood in his way.

He would have his revenge. No matter how long it took, or how many of his enemies had to die.

"I'm going to rid this world of the Demons of Dusk once and for all. And I'm going to kill you, Amón. Mark my words. You will die by my blade, and you'll die knowing I was the one who ended your evil reign. This world will know peace one day, and I'll make you watch everything you built crumble before your eyes, and then... you can die."

The End.

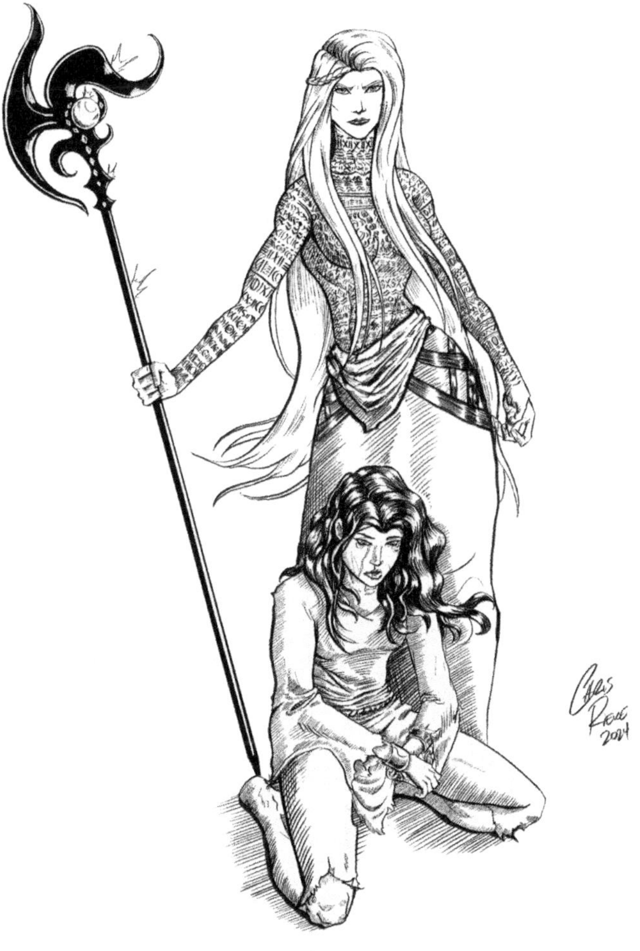

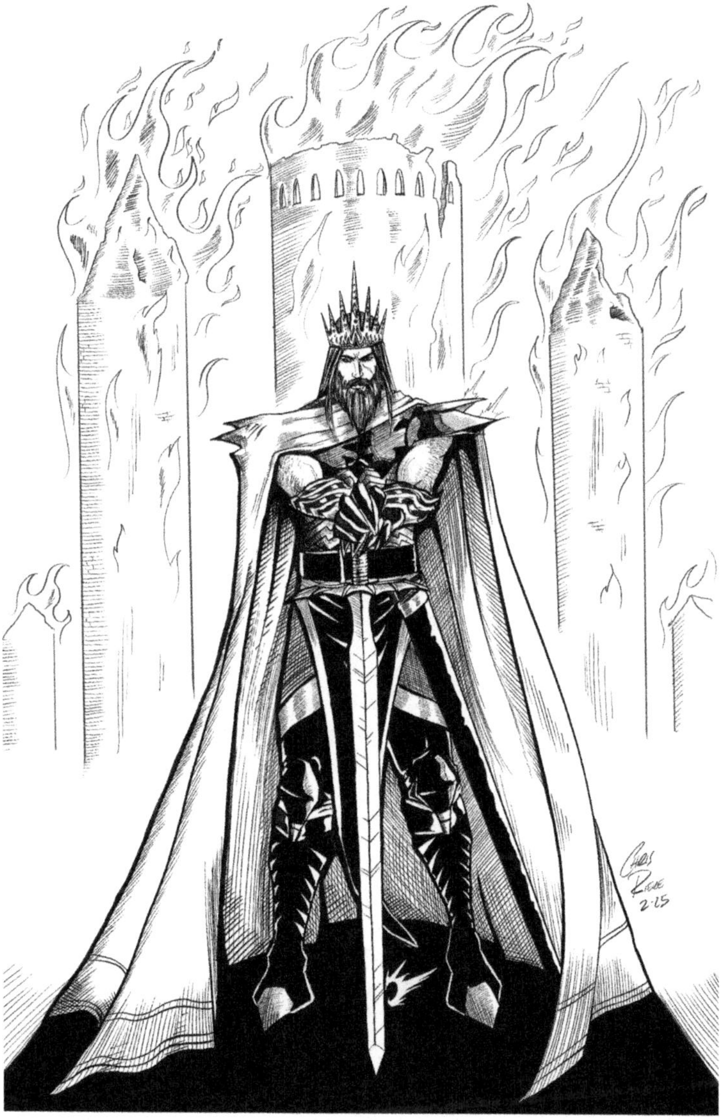

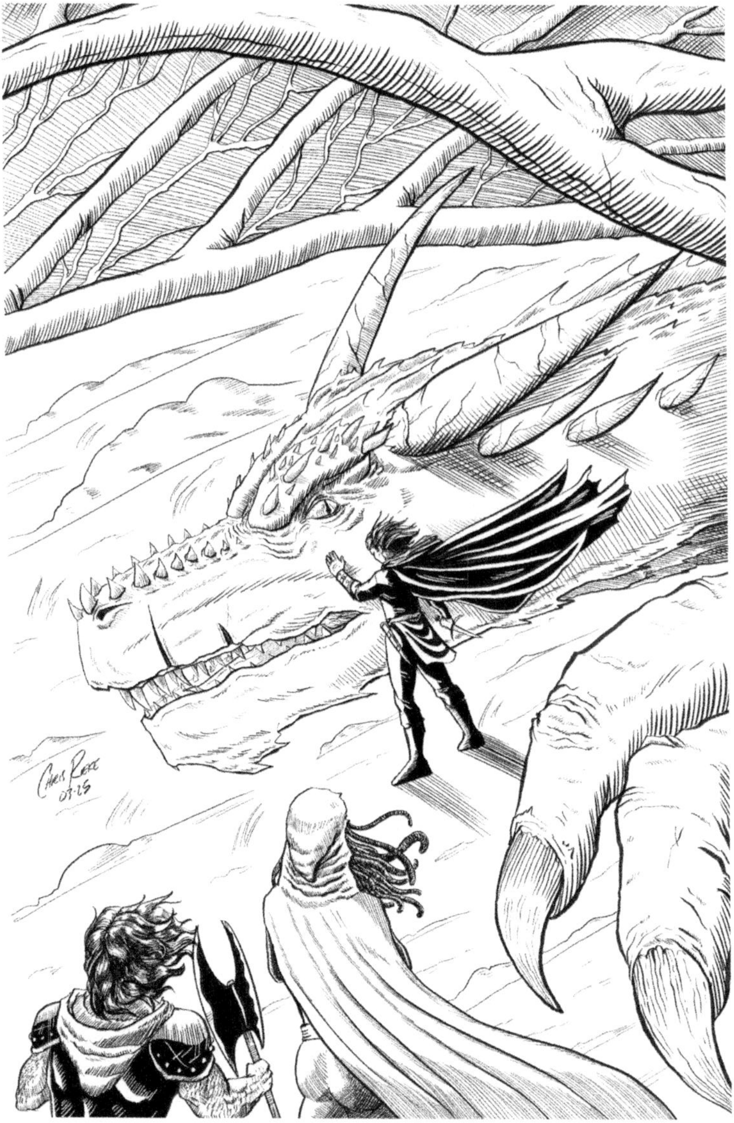

Pronunciation Guide

Aeol – A-ol
   Aladran – Ala-drawn
   Alcarond Riberia – Alka-Rond Rye-beer-ia
   Arkakus – Ar-kackus
   Arnesto Piphenette – Piffin-ette
   Arnor – Are-nore
   Ayl - Ail
   Bael - Bale
   Belzaar – Bell-zar
   Blaje Severaas – Blage Sever-os
   Cascadia – Cas-cad-ia
   Celestra - Selestra
   Cirella – Si-rella
   Davin Mosser – Davvin Mozer
   Dor - Door
   Doren – Dor-en
   Ellydian – Ellid-ien
   Erhil – Air-hill
   Everice – Ever-iss
   Garland Messemire –Mess-i-mere

PRONUNCIATION GUIDE

Golbizarath – Golbee-za-wrath
Guillead – Gil-ee-ad
Ikarus – Ick-arus
Katamon – Cot-a-mon
Larghos Sea – Lar-goes
Londindam – Londin-daam
Lynthyn – Lin-thin
Lyre - Leer
Lyrian – Leer-ien
Malera Amón – Mal-er-ra A-maan
Manan – Maw-nin
Mihelik – Mi-hay-lick
Myngorn Forest – Men-gorn
Roland Carvaise – Roland Car-Vase
Shirava - Sheerava
Siracco Tower – Seer-a-co
Solomn Roane – Solum Rone
Sortistra – Sort-ee-stra
Sundar – Sun-dar
Syncron – Sin-chron
Synth - Sinth
Taverras – Tav-er-ass
Tourmielle – Tour-me-el
Vellice - Vellis
Yancor Brothers – Yank-or
Zatan – Za-tan
Zefa – Zeffa
Zertaan – Zer-taan

Magic of the Ellydian

The Ellydian Magic System

Lyrian/ Lyre– Highest Level – Must successfully go through the Black Sacrament. Unknown power limits.

Aeol/ Ayl/Aeolian – Mid Level - Can manipulate their own bodies as well as outside objects.

Doren/ Dor/Dorien – Lowest Level - Can move/manipulate objects outside of their body.

Syncron – A wielder of the Ellydian who uses their magic for good.

Synth – A wielder of the Ellydian who uses their magic for evil.

Singular notes and tunes (Such as A) are the easiest to cast with. More complex variations (Such as G Minor or C Sharp Minor) cause much more powerful and different spells, but require more focus and training. The Lyres may use melodies of varying different notes to cast superior spells.

The sounds produced must remain constant for the spell to stay intact.

The Black Sacrament – A spell, that when cast, will either kill the wielder, or elevate them to the supreme level of Lyrian.

Author Notes

Well, here we are again—four books deep into *The Song of the Ellydian*. I gotta say, I'm pumped. This book was an absolute blast to write, tearing the characters apart—lol.

The first draft took five months to write, which is fairly normal for a 400-page book for me. I'd love to be faster, but it is what it is.

Soren. There were some new revelations about him that I wanted to explore in this book. He's suffered so much and lost so many battles lately, so I wanted to give him a few wins. Losing Seph and being separated from her is already so hard on him that giving him some new gadgets and powers seemed appropriate. And that dragon! Actually, *both* dragons! What's gonna happen with them?

I knew this would be a hard book for Seph. She really had to go through the meat grinder and come out the other end whole—or at least *mostly* whole. I wanted it to be dark, but not *too* dark, if that makes sense. She's just such a badass and such a thrill to write. She's got Soren's spite, fire, and anger in her, and it's coming out more and more, which is so fun.

Kaile went through his own kind of torture in this book.

AUTHOR NOTES

Being thrown back into the gauntlet of politics and the monsters that live in the capital, he really suffered—knowing that Seph was suffering *because* of him. I tried to put myself in his shoes—how trying it would be to be on the path to getting what he ultimately wants (power, respect, authority) but at the cost of the only people who've ever really appreciated him for who he is, not just for his power. That would be brutal. Seeing him come back to himself at the end of the book was a great payoff for me, and I hope it was for you, too.

Hitting the Big 2-0!!! So... this was my *20th* book. To say that wasn't a big goal of mine would be a lie. Even from the beginning, getting to 20 books was *the* big goal for me, and honestly, I never knew if I'd get there—because writing books is so fucking hard, lol.

But I *love* it. Creating worlds, characters, scenes, dialogue, and drama has always been a passion of mine. When I was a kid, the things I wanted to be when I grew up were a movie director, a comic book illustrator, a chef, and an author. I got three out of four, so who knows—if Hollywood calls someday, maybe I'll insist on directing my own movie, lol.

Either way, 20 books is something worth celebrating. To some people, it's a lot. To others—the big authors I admire—it's hardly any. But this is my journey, and I'm glad you're here with me on it.

I've got a couple of projects to hit hard and fast next, and then I'm jumping back into writing Book 5 as soon as I can. Because, like you, I can't wait to see what happens next.

Writing this book, I mostly listened to the band Hammock. It's chill, light on vocals, and just awesome to fire up at 7 in the morning to crank out words to.

Cheers,
    'Til next time.
    C.K.

About the Author

C.K. Rieke, though he constantly dreams of oceans and mountains, was born and lives in Kansas. Art and storytelling were his passions, beginning with "Where the Wild Things Are" and Shel Silverstein. That grew into a love of comic books and fantasy novels. He always dreamed of creating his own worlds through the brush and keyboard.

Throughout his college years, Rieke ventured into the realm of indie comics, illustrating and co-plotting stories that hinted at the epic narratives to come. But it wasn't until his early thirties, inspired by the works of fantasy luminaries, that he turned his hand to writing his own tales. The labor of love that was "The Road to Light," painstakingly crafted over two years, marked his debut into the literary world under the guidance of a revered editor.

Within the pages of his novels, Rieke spins tales of daring adventure and intricate character arcs that ensnare the heart. Yet, be warned, dear reader, for his pen is not without its blade—occasionally, beloved characters meet their untimely demise, prompting fans to pen letters of both torment and anguish.

C.K. Rieke is pronounced C.K. 'Ricky'.

Go to CKRieke.com and sign-up to join the Reader's Group for some free stuff and to get updated on new books!

www.CKRieke.com

Printed in Dunstable, United Kingdom